# The Lodestone Puzzle

**Dr. Zen Mystery, Volume 1**

Lynn Emery

Published by Lazy River Publishing, 2021.

# Chapter 1

Zen congratulated herself. Her social engineering skills, picked up from her days at the prison, had worked magic. Her best friend since college would be proud. Zen's father would stutter into a fit at the risk she was taking. Her mother would remind him Zen was always a source of trouble. Except this time, she wasn't pulling a prank or breaking curfew. She was trying to catch a serial killer. Alone. In Madrid. Without official sanction. The words "breach of global investigations treaty" kept popping into her head. Zen batted them away for the umpteenth time. She needed to stay focused.

She'd talked her way into the apartment building pretending to look at a flat. The electronic entry system dinged as she left the two-bedroom flat. The door whisked shut behind her. The manager would assume Zen was checking out the amenities. The high-rise had a gym, a large rooftop terrace which could be reserved for parties, and the high-tech laundry room in the basement. Instead, Zen took the elevator to the sixth floor, 603-A, to be exact. Where her target lived.

Zen smiled at a woman who brushed past while rummaging through a tote bag; she willed herself not to look over her shoulder. She needed to blend in as though she belonged. Not look like a burglar. Although technically... Zen arrived at apartment 603-A and casually inserted her electronic key. When the beeps sounded, she hissed out air. In reflex, Zen glanced at the woman, who now stood at the elevator.

The woman shrugged. "*El nuevo sistema, ¿eh? Mainténiendono tan seguros que nos vamos a casa a comer un poco.*" Then she laughed.

Zen gave her a self-conscious smile. The translator earpiece gave her the English version and in seconds provided the correct response in Spanish. "*Si, muy frustrante.*"

"Ah, Americana. Yes?" The woman turned fully toward Zen with a wider smile. "Don't worry. I'm not one of those angry with your country. I know it's not your fault."

"Whew, that's a relief. I'm visiting a relative." Zen flinched when the light turned to red on the door lock. Her ninety seconds to complete entry had elapsed. *Focus.*

"Him? Extraño. Lo siento. I didn't mean..." Again, the woman shrugged.

Zen's laugh was genuine at the woman's easy candor. They were the same age and Zen assumed she, too, had odd older relatives. "Uncle is eccentric. I haven't seen him in a while. But we try to keep in touch—the family, I mean."

"Hmm, I know he travels a lot. See him with his suitcase from time to time." The woman's eyes lit up with curiosity.

"My mother married his brother. Dad's an engineer," Zen said easily, spitting out the true parts of her story—her target's family history.

"Well, good luck with him. He certainly likes his privacy."

"I have a hotel room." Zen tensed up at her mistake. Her father's voice clanged in her head like a warning bell. She was talking too much. "I'm going to fix him a farewell American meal before I go."

The woman used her free hand to hold the elevator door a few more seconds. "Nice to have met you. Adiós."

The elevator door slid shut and Zen blew out air. She slipped the elastic silicone and urethane sleeve onto her forefinger. Navarro's fingerprint and bio markers were embedded on it. Then she used the key and pressed her finger to the glass square above the lock. Four green buttons flashed, a click sounded, and the door popped open a few inches. With one last look over her shoulder, Zen pushed her way in. She resisted the urge to call out. The man was in Tokyo. She'd confirmed it seven different ways from Sunday, to quote one of James Batiste's favorite archaic idioms. The image of her father calmed her, sharpened her senses. To business.

Zen performed a thorough search, careful not to leave traces. She detected several traps he'd set to alert him to any disturbance. She didn't touch the book, the glass paperweight on the desk, or any of the its drawers. Too obvious. She glanced at her watch. Twenty-five minutes had passed. She was pushing it. Her friend, a local police detective, could only distract the building manager for so long. The internal system would alert her that someone had entered apartment 603-A. But Zen counted on her "eccentric uncle's" secretiveness about his movements. He was too clever to leave such a trail; a witness who would know his movements. Most residents would notify the manager or building maintenance staff of being away from home. All apartment locks linked to an internal security system engaged at will by owners. That way staff would know instantly if someone entered while a resident was away. Zen double-checked the security panel. Just as she thought. He hadn't set it to send a signal to the main system. Still, she didn't have the luxury of time.

"Come on, come on. Think," Zen muttered aloud as she turned in a circle to scan the room. "You've got maybe ten minutes before the cameras turn back on."

One more rule she'd broken. Her friend Chloé, the network systems genius, had hacked his security cameras. He wouldn't get an alert or watch Zen search his apartment on his cell phone. Chloé had hacked his mobile IP as well. At least for a while. Zen imagined she heard the loud ticking of a clock inside her head, reminding her she had to get in and out. Then she spotted it. An extra hinge on the wide, wall-mounted television. Cautious, yet aware of the time pressure, Zen moved fast. She checked to make sure another alarm wasn't connected to it. None. She used the tiny signal detector, another gizmo provided by Chloé. No pops or buzzing. Using her sleeved finger, Zen pressed a lever. The thin, fifty-five-inch screen swung out at a light touch. A flat panel looked like more wall space at first glance. One faint line gave away the panel. Anyone searching would assume it contained the wireless router that transmitted signals to the television. Zen looked around and spotted the slim, dark-gray device on the bookshelf.

"Let's see what's behind door number two," Zen murmured. She pressed the panel and was rewarded with a swish as it opened. "Gotcha."

Her celebration had to be brief. She opened a box, again with the sleeve, to find twelve eight-by ten-inch brown envelopes. Dates and odd symbols had been written on each one. She removed them only to find more. The wall compartment was deeper than it looked. The stack shook Zen. More victims than even she had imagined. All of the envelopes contained a trophy. A locket. A single gold hoop earring. Along with those, articles about the murder of each woman. Zen's hands shook and her stomach turned as she took out a slender plastic round vial. She gasped at what must be inside. Rage replaced the nausea in her gut. Zen reached deep into the cavity to find an older envelope. With quick efficiency, she arranged the safe's contents in precise order she'd removed them. When he scanned anything Zen had touched, he'd find his own fingerprints. That would give her more time, but not here and now. Muffled sounds announced she had to move.

Zen looked at the small screen nearby. A couple walked past the external camera that gave a view outside the front door. Seconds later they shared a kiss and entered apartment 605-B down the hall. A quick survey of the apartment assured Zen it looked untouched. No doubt her paranoid target would still sense something was off. The man had an almost supernatural skill for escaping detection. The alarm on her smartwatch went off, a buzzing vibration against her wrist. She touched the screen and saw a text from Balduino, her local detective friend. *Saia*—Portuguese for "Get out."

Zen hurried out still wearing the skin like gloves that would leave no trace. She slipped them off as she went past the elevator. Fortunately, she didn't meet anyone as she scurried around a corner. She took the stairs and arrived in the lobby minutes later. Balduino gestured as he spoke to a tall woman with blond hair pulled into a thick ponytail. The property manager who had shown Zen the apartment, shorter with dark hair, looked relieved to see her.

"This is Señora Sophia Santos, my boss. She owns this building and several others," the manager said in a breathless voice.

"How do you do. Señor Navarro didn't mention a niece coming to visit," Mrs. Santos put in. Her suspicious gaze started at Zen's feet and traveled up to Zen's face. One dark eyebrow lifted.

"You know he's not that big on sharing," Zen said with a casual wave of one hand.

"It's true. He likes to keep to himself. Very particular," the building manager jumped in with a nervous twitter. She darted a look at her boss.

"Besides, I was in Portugal on business and decided to check on him. Mama hasn't heard from Uncle Peter in almost a year. Asked me to see if he was still in the land of the living." Zen laughed to indicate she didn't really take his non-communication that seriously.

"Hmm, I see," Señora Santos replied.

"Since I'm assigned to more clients in Europe, I thought to relocate. My company will pay for an apartment. Cheaper than flying me first class all the time." Zen tugged the front of her seven-hundred-dollar Norwegian wool coat.

Señora Santos recognized quality. Her chill thawed a bit. "Really?"

"Yes. Uncle seems to like this building since he's lived here so long. And we know how particular he is. My mother said, 'If anyone knows a good and secure building it's your uncle.' Though this might be too close for both our comfort. I value privacy, too." Zen darted a glance at Balduino, who flashed a handsome grin back.

With dark, wavy hair, Balduino turned heads everywhere he went. His smile would melt hearts—and underwear. At five feet eight, his dazzling charm and handsome face made up for extra inches in height.

"I can confirm the excellent standards of all Santos properties, si." Balduino stood close to Zen but didn't touch her.

"You own other buildings in the area? I love this neighborhood. So near the park. Plenty of shops and restaurants nearby." Zen made a show of peering through the glass doors. "You own a building in the Salamanca, yes? It drips history."

Any hesitation Señora Santos had was swept away. The mention of the swanky nearby barrio sealed the deal. Zen had the means to rent an even more expensive apartment. With Madrid vacancy rates above fifty percent, Zen knew dangling such a plum would distract the two women. Their sparkling eyes and bubbling descriptions confirmed it. For the next hour they looked at pictures of several properties. Leaving behind the property manager, Señora Santos walked them a few blocks to another building she owned. Balduino squeezed Zen's arm a few times as he suppressed a grin. On his cop salary, living in such sweet digs was way out of his reach. Finally, Zen glanced at her smartwatch.

"Absolutely breathtaking. And the views. What do you think? Vising me here would be lovely." Zen flashed a flirtatious smile at Balduino.

He chuckled and tugged a lock of her thick curls. Then he turned to Señora Santos. "I've been trying to convince her to move here since we met a year ago at a conference."

"You are a police officer as well?" Señora Santos looked at Zen with curiosity.

"I work for a private security corporation. We consult with law enforcement in several countries," Zen answered.

Señora Santos clucked her tongue and launched into a nationalistic speech. "Ah, such important work with so many bad things happening in the world. One of the prices of this whole open borders nonsense."

"I really have to go," Zen broke in after a moment. She tapped her Fossil smartwatch.

"Not that I'm against America, mind you. Expanding our markets keeps us from dependence on those arrogant English. After so many generations, they still don't realize their empire days are over. But enough politics. I must fly myself to another meeting." Señora Santos gave Zen a warm smile and handed her a card.

"Yes, I'll call you for sure. The two bedroom at Barquillo IV is perfect for me," Zen said as she took it. "I'll be in touch soon."

"Excelente! Adiós." Señora Santos waved and strode off.

Balduino faced Zen. "You're not looking for an apartment, are you?"

"I was, am. In a manner of speaking," Zen replied with a grin. She looped her arm through his and tugged him along until they walked a few steps.

"You're up to something."

"Let's go somewhere to chase away the chill."

Zen pulled on his strong arm until he moved with her again. She steered him into Sana Locura, a coffee and tea café she'd fallen in love with during her stay. They ordered two cups of café con leche and pastries. Zen unbuttoned her coat and let it fall over the back of her chair. The thick red sweater she wore kept her warm enough inside. She sipped coffee and sighed. She started to speak but stopped when Balduino held up a palm.

"I don't think I want to know," he said and drank from his cup as well. He continued to gaze at her over the rim. He looked away when he lowered it. "Have you left the great and powerful Department of Justice? Or whatever secret arm of it you actually work in."

"You do want to know. I'm trying to save lives," Zen said.

"*Veo.* This is the same thing you said the last time you got me in big trouble." Balduino wagged a forefinger at her. He broke off a piece of churro, dipped it in chocolate sauce, and chewed on it.

"Algiers was *your* fault. I told you my local contacts had it covered. Don't dwell on the past." Zen took the last half of his churro, drizzled chocolate over it and ate as well. "Almost as good as beignets back home."

"Almost? How dare you. No comparison." Balduino feigned patriotic outrage. Then his smile faded. "Truly, Zenobia."

"Oh-oh. I feel a lecture coming on," Zen quipped and savored more of the pastry.

"Dr. Batiste," Balduino said, his voice pitched low. He dropped the churro and wiped his hands on a napkin. "Are you here on official government business? I heard you'd left the Department of Justice. Which I didn't believe for one second. I need to know if an investigation is about to blow up between our countries."

Zen sighed. "We're going to be serious and dreary. Fine. I'm not an Interpol liaison now."

"You never were," Balduino cut in.

"I may have had one or two field duties," Zen said with a shrug. She drained her cup and signaled the waiter for more. "And you don't do undercover work anymore. Settled down with a wife and baby."

"You're investigating me, too?" He stroked his beard.

"When did you decide to grow it?" Zen reach across to touch the fine dark hairs on his chin. "Pilar must approve, I guess. Or maybe two o'clock baby feedings make it easier not to shave."

"Miguel is two years old."

"Wow. It's been that long." Zen studied his handsome face for a time and looked away.

"You ran back to the safety of Washington, DC," Balduino said.

"Don't be dramatic. Besides, you know I don't run." Zen pulled her hand back and accepted the fresh cup from the waiter.

Balduino tapped his fingers on the tabletop a few seconds. "You have a hotel room, eh?"

Two hours later they lay tangled in sheets, still breathless from the passion they shared. After a time, they exchanged small talk. Zen sniffed his chest, savoring the smell of his skin. Balduino. The one that got away. But if she was honest, he was the one she left behind. Not out of fear though. Much as she enjoyed being with him, Zen couldn't pull her then-fourteen-year-old daughter away from her school. And moving to Madrid without Astra was not an option, though Zen's ex would have been fine with it.

"Astra is already getting acceptance letters from top universities, even one in France," Balduino said.

Zen sat up to stare at him. "Are you taking part in the experiments?"

"I don't know what you're— Ouch." Balduino flinched and rubbed the spot on his bicep where Zen had punched him.

The field of cognitive enhancement for law enforcement continued to evolve. In the past three years she'd become an opponent of it as well. Which hadn't exactly pleased her superiors at the DOJ. Brain boosts, as most field staff called them, were all the rage.

"Haven't you read any of my papers? The long-term effects of those so-called improvements are unknown." Zen glared at him as though he were a disgraced student and she was the teacher.

"There are research studies that say otherwise. Stop looking at me like that." Balduino took one of the four pillows and hid his face.

"This isn't a joke, Nino."

He tucked the pillow behind his head, fluffed it and sat up. Then he pulled her naked body against his chest. "You still worry about me, huh? We could still be together."

Zen pushed free of his embrace. "You're unbelievable! You just got married, just had a kid—"

"He's almost three, and getting married seemed like a good idea at the time once you abandoned me. Pilar, eh. She's not thrilled at the long hours I work or that I don't talk about what I do. And if I'm honest, we're not happy. She's visiting her mother in Peniscola. A trial separation, I think. She hasn't mentioned coming back and I haven't asked."

"And then I'd have you on my hands? No thanks." Zen yanked the sheet up until her full breasts were covered. She slapped his hand when he tried to slid a hand under it.

Instead, he massaged her through the high-thread-count fabric. He sighed when her nipple hardened. "But you like my hands and my smile. And my tongue."

Zen melted when he ducked beneath the covers. The sensation of his smooth lips grazing her skin worked magic. For another thirty minutes she forgot what they'd been talking about, why she'd been irritated with him at all. Later, as they showered together and got dressed, Zen tried on the idea of considering them as a couple. He was right. They understood each other, could relax in a way she couldn't with another partner. But then there was the downside. A huge con that had contributed to the end of her marriage. What made them good operatives also led to clashes. Strong-willed, independent, and selectively ruthlessness. Those traits bled into the way they interacted.

They sat over dinner in a nearby restaurant. Zen had roasted chicken with potatoes. Balduino enjoyed tender filet mignon. Zen could almost imagine life in Spain with him. Astra would soon attend Rice University in Houston, or maybe Xavier in New Orleans. Or Spellman. The child couldn't make up her mind. Astra would love visiting Spain again. She'd have a chance to use her Spanish, travel to Portugal, and even Africa.

"I'm not your ex-husband. I don't take life too seriously," Balduino said without looking up from cutting into a section of steak. "And Astra likes me. She'd fall in love with her new little brother."

Zen laughed and shook her head. "Too much wine again."

"Hmm." He smiled and chewed. After washing down his food with wine, his expression turned serious. "About these lives you're saving..."

"Thanks for helping, but I won't tell you more. Let's just say it'll be worth the trouble if I take him down." Zen lost the light mood when the image of those envelopes flashed in her mind. Then she remembered the soft sobs of a grieving father at a morgue.

"A man. I see. And he lives in the apartment building we visited." Balduino nodded, chewed, and grew quiet.

Zen put down her wine glass and leaned forward. "I see those wheels turning. Don't, Nino. I've broken a few rules. If you get involved, I can't plausibly tell them I lied and used you."

"A few rules? My lovely Zen, you burned the entire book and dropped the ashes into the ocean you crossed to get here.

If he's that bad, then maybe I'll sign up for getting in trouble, too," Balduino replied in a hard voice.

"No need. I've taken care of it." Zen reached across the table and gripped his hand.

"A dangerous man in my city—"

"Trust me, Nino." Zen squinted at him. "Remember Chicago?"

Balduino gazed back at her for a few seconds. He lifted her hand and kissed it. Then he leaned back with a sigh after letting go. *"Que el Señor tenga misericordia de su alma."*

"He doesn't deserve God's mercy. Believe me," Zen said with a grimace. She inhaled and let out a slow breath to calm the wrath burning inside. "Let's not spoil our last few hours together. Tell me something bright and happy, like the sunshine on a summer day."

"Ah, summer in the south. I so look forward to it. At least I'm not in the frozen north anymore." Balduino gave an exaggerated shiver. "That was brutal. I might be able to swing finding us a home in Cosa del Sol."

"Anywhere in Malaga would be wonderful."

Zen gazed out through the glass at the busy boulevard. People bundled up against the cold March wind scurried by. But Madrid vanished in her mind. Instead, she pictured Moorish architecture, beaches, and blue seawater.

Balduino's deep voice broke into her musing. "Astra would love it. She'd become a true global traveler. More sophisticated than her teenage friends. Think how she'd enjoy impressing them on visits home."

"Astra," Zen murmured in response.

The thought of uprooting her daughter and the storm that would cause snapped her back to reality. Astra's current crush was headed to Texas Southern University, hence her keen interest in Houston colleges. That aside, Zen had her own reasons for sticking with the United States for now. Her career had fascinating possibilities. She smiled at the handsome face that had other women around them envying her.

"Oh, there's that look. What?" Balduino raised an eyebrow at her.

"You could join me in America. With your family influence and stellar professional achievements, a job at the Spanish embassy is a snap. We could take trips to Miami. You love it there. Maybe even get assigned to the Miami consulate." Zen tilted her head to one side and gazed at him.

"My son is so young. To be that far away..." Balduino sighed. "You have made your point, *feminista*."

"*La vida es complicada, eh?*" Zen lifted her wine glass.

"*Si.* I will miss you, us. *Salud.*" Balduino clinked his glass against hers.

ZEN WOKE TO A GENTLE touch on her arm. She gazed up at the flight attendant smiling at her. She'd dozed off, and no wonder. Up at four a.m. to catch her early-morning flight, her energy had finally flagged. The deep hum of the electric engine of the airplane had lulled her asleep.

"Coffee, tea, or juice?" the young man said.

"Apple juice for now, please. Coffee with breakfast," Zen replied with a smile back at him.

She rolled her shoulders to get out the kinks. The first-class seat next to her was blessedly empty. When the flight attendant returned, she accepted the short glass and murmured a thank you. Then she looked out the window. Electric commercial flight aircraft had become the norm forty years ago. The technology was perfected in 2044. Global air travel transformed into a faster, less polluting means of travel. Still, the expense limited the number of planes. Once again, the wealthy received the benefit of quiet comfort. Zen appreciated the cushy seat and the individual attention of first-class on a Tesla jet. Even if she felt a tinge of regret at being part of the have and have-nots divide.

"Breakfast is almost ready, madame. Here is your coffee. Two creams, no sugar. Yes?" The soft French accent of the attendant made it all sound gourmet.

"Perfect."

Zen breathed in the aroma of eggs and sausage. She settled against the seatback and sighed. Moments later a small plate with two fried eggs and toast arrived. Zen enjoyed her cup of African coffee blend from Côte d'Ivoire. She flipped open her slim iPad and set it on tray table of the empty seat beside her. At voice command, she opened the news app. Headlines from around the world scrolled by. Something about Spain caught her eye, but she had trouble calling it back up. Zen switched to swiping with a fingertip.

"Can't be. It's too soon," Zen murmured with a frown.

"Pardon?" The other flight attendant, a woman, paused next to Zen's row.

"I'm fine, thanks." Zen waved her way.

She went back to staring at the screen. Then she got smart and pulled up CNN's European website. She found the tab for Spain. The headline hit Zen like a gut punch.

"Local Police Officer In Critical Condition. Terrorist Attack Not Ruled Out."

SEVEN MONTHS LATER, Zen finally faced the consequences. She'd chafed at a boring assignment that amounted to no more than filing the reports of other analysts. Her boss took daily pleasure in the fact that she was buried in a windowless office as punishment. She spent her days sorting through streams of data on the server. She did research for agents with more interesting assignments. Worse still, she had to peer at page after page of the federal register. Zen had become an unwilling expert on the tedium of rulemaking that helped the wheels of government grind. Slowly.

But today was different. Three women and two men sat around the crescent-shaped table. Most of them wore studied impassive expressions. They would judge Zen's actions with impartiality. At least that was the official stance of the disciplinary committee. The committee members, all in her father's generation, weren't bureaucrats. All of them had years on the ground doing investigations, domestic and international. Zen's big brother had done a profile of each. Her father knew two of them personally from his days at the CIA, a fact that wasn't necessarily a plus. James Batiste had built an almost legendary career, but he'd had his share of critics as well.

"Dr. Zenobia Batiste. You have a master's degree in social work, with an emphasis on mental disorders. You completed a doctorate in forensic psychology at Kesler University." One of the women, Black with iron-gray hair, spoke first.

Bertice Illinois. Zen recognized her from press conferences held by the DOJ. The two other women, Susan Huynh[1] and the other a blonde from California, Taylor Kirkland, looked at Ms. Illinois with respect as she spoke. The two men studied Zen instead.

"I did a course in forensic sociology, actually," Zen interrupted in a mild tone.

"Kesler didn't offer a doctorate in that field. You lobbied relentlessly and had it added. Then became first to get one," Ms. Illinois continued. She seemed unbothered, though her female colleagues favored Zen with a frown.

"A double doctorate, actually, in forensic psychology and sociology. We live in an increasingly complex world, if that's possible after the last forty years. But now we're moving toward even more globalization. That means crime that crosses border warrants analysis, study. I—" Zen stopped when Ms. Illinois held up a hand.

"Yes, I've read the position paper you wrote to the university president. You're a persuasive young woman. Determined, almost unstoppable when you've decided on a path. Reminds me of your father, Dr. James Batiste. And your older brother." Ms. Illinois's dark eyebrows pulled together.

"That doesn't sound like a compliment," Zen mumbled.

---

1.      https://surnames.behindthename.com/name/huy11nh

"It is and it isn't," Ms. Illinois clipped. She stared at Zen for a few minutes, looked aside at the others, and then down at the slim screen in front of her.

"I did what I had to do. I couldn't watch the bodies pile up and do nothing." Zen's gaze swept around the table until she focused on Ms. Illinois again.

"Your immediate superior informed you that the target was being monitored. You didn't have proof of anything," a thin man with sandy hair spoke up. "We've had to work for over a year to clean up *your* mess."

"But I found solid evidence in the apartment where he actually lived. He owned two properties and—"

"We've read the file," the man broke in.

The CIA and her agency, a joint division of the NSA and DOJ, had Navarro under surveillance for almost a year, one of four suspects. Globalization had affected many things, including law enforcement. Intelligence agencies had been combined. The lines had blurred between national and international special agents. ISA, International Security Agency, dealt with those blurred lines.

Zen had studied the files until her eyes ached. Her instincts told her something didn't fit. Navarro seemed to vanish for days. He had to have another place to live. She'd used ISA resources to pick up the patterns that led to Navarro.

"He killed on US soil. I would have thought that meant something," Zen snapped.

"You take nationalism seriously?" The other man spoke for the first time. Gray hair surrounded a shiny bald spot. He had never looked up from his own slim computer screen. But his head snapped up when Zen slapped a palm on the table.

"I take murder and serial killers damn serious. Or maybe I'm the only one around here."

"We do," Ms. Illinois broke in before the man could speak. She shot a steel-hard look at him. He nodded and went back to studying his screen again.

"Then why are we here? Navarro is in custody. There won't be another victim, if the WCC doesn't screw it up," Zen said with a grimace.

The United Nations developed a criminal division of the World Court in 2055. It no longer only handled disputes between countries. An entire set of international criminal laws had naturally led to its creation. The World Criminal Court, or WCC, handled prosecutions of major offenses that crossed the old international boundaries. The downside was that politics and intrigue took root there, just like in other branches of criminal justice.

"Zenobia Chatelain Batiste, thirty-four years old. An academic phenom. Finished high school at fifteen. Undergrad by eighteen. By age twenty-two you had your first post-graduate degree. Interests include psychology, forensics, and astronomy." The bald man read parts of Zen's life in a dry tone.

"Not astronomy—space exploration to be precise. They weren't merely *interests*. I studied those subjects and a few more. I've published six articles in journals in the past two years," Zen replied. She almost smiled at the way his jaw muscle went tight.

"Thank you for the clarification," he replied. His blunt fingers moved over the silent keypad. "I'll have my people update your profile."

Anxiety formed like a knot in her midsection. He was letting her know that she had been shadowed. Clearly, her brother Elliot had missed something about this man. Clive Anderson, age fifty-six, white male. Married with two college-age kids. Anderson worked for the Secret Service. At least on paper. Federal law enforcement was a convoluted world at times. Which was one of the things that Zen loved about it. And what made her lose sleep on occasion. But today she wouldn't let his smooth dig get to her.

"You've studied me. I've studied you. Now that we've gotten that out of the way, let's do this. Tell me if I'm fired, demoted, going to jail even." Zen made a show of looking at the square screen of her smartwatch.

"Young lady," Ms. Illinois barked and stood, both fists on the table. The other committee members, including Anderson, cringed. She came around the table as she spoke. "You endangered three major international treaties, including the 2026 Global Criminal Investigations Accord. It took my father and a host of diplomats from over twenty countries ten years of negotiating to get it. You almost destroyed it in five months. A member of Spain's top intelligence community ended up in the ICU. All because you decided to become Ms. Captain America and deliver your own brand of justice. So, trust me—if we've got time to be here then so do *you*. Do we understand each other?"

Zen, determined to hold her own, suppressed a shudder at the force the woman exuded. In that moment Bertice

Illinois looked like her mother, times a hundred. The older woman's expression had a "Say one more smart remark; I dare you" message. Time to change tactics, Zen concluded.

"Yes, ma'am. I appreciate the gravity of my current situation. I took extraordinary steps to avoid any negative outcomes. But I promised Jennifer Pembroke's family I'd do everything in my power to catch her killer. When I realized her death was connected to at least one more in this country alone..." Zen blew out a sigh. "I counted fifteen envelopes in that hidden safe, ma'am. Not just names. They were human beings with people who loved them left behind. Wondering why and who."

"And because you didn't ask for official help, the envelopes disappeared in the time it took Spanish authorities to search for them," Ms. Kirkland said.

Zen jumped to her feet, her head suddenly pounding. "That can't be possible. I—"

"Luckily, Mr. Silva managed to hold onto the one you tried to mail," Ms. Illinois broke in. "Which only leaves circumstantial evidence now they're gone."

Zen gazed back at her for a few moments. An old saying her grandfather liked popped into her head. In for a penny, in for a pound. "Not gone. I took pictures of the contents."

Ms. Illinois blinked rapidly and took a step back. The two female committee members blurted out words of indignation. The man muttered, "Unbelievable." Clive Anderson rubbed his jaw as he studied Zen, ignoring the jabber of his outraged colleagues. While they debated, Zen used her phone to send an email.

"Tell us more," he said.

The Korean woman sprang to her feet. "Clive, Bertice! You can't really mean..." She sputtered as if at a loss for words.

"Sir, check your messages on the secure FTP server." Zen couldn't stop the smile that tugged her mouth up at one end.

# Chapter 2

James Batiste stared at Zen. His thick black eyebrows pulled together to form his most intimidating frown. Former intelligence subordinates knew it well. His students at the London School of Economics and Political Science would quake under its heat. Zen merely shrugged. As usual his fierce look melted away after a few seconds. He huffed in exasperation.

"Girl, what were you thinking? I taught you to be smarter, at least I like to think so. Maybe I didn't do such a great job after all. Pride goeth before destruction and—"

"An haughty spirit before a fall. Proverbs 16:18, King James Version. I'm surprised you didn't follow grandfather into the ministry." Zen patted his cheek and then kissed it.

"Humph," was his only response.

James had a brief coughing spell that quieted him. Then he drank from the steaming cup of tea with honey and lemon Enola had brought for him. Zen pulled the knitted throw up and tucked it farther up his chest. She sent up a silent thanks to whatever had helped him recover from pneumonia. Cold wind rattled bare branches just outside the window of her parents' home in Mitchellville, Maryland. Her mother was in the small kitchenette they'd created upstairs. A convenience so that they didn't have to climb the stairs to the full kitchen on the first floor. Her father loved his upstairs study. The windows gave a view to the wide backyard and woods just beyond. She walked over to gaze out. Zen and Alexis, Lexi to family and close friends, had enjoyed exploring them. Summer or winter, it didn't matter the time of year. Snow didn't keep Lexi inside. Zen had to go along on orders to look after her little sister. Over Enola's objections, James had built them a tree house, complete with solar panels. Their private hidey-hole, he and her father's youngest brother called it. Uncle Monroe had helped James with the construction. Zen could see the roof in the distance just beyond a stand of loblolly pine trees. James's gravelly voice broke into her thoughts. Zen hadn't realized he'd left the chair to stand beside her.

"She loved hanging out there. Probably because your mother isn't the outdoors type. Gave Lexi freedom." James sighed and put an arm around Zen.

"Mama hates bugs. And the possibility of facing wildlife in those woods kept her away." Zen laughed at the memory of her mother's reaction to camping out on the land behind their home.

"You'd think we were living in the wilderness miles from civilization." James chuckled.

"Lexi couldn't be roped in, not even by mama," Zen replied.

"Enola had to be really mad to go out there," James said. "You girls knew you were in big trouble if she marched through those brambles."

"Nothing struck fear in our hearts like Mama pushed to the limit. She'd stand at the bottom of that ladder and yell, 'If I have to come get you!'" Zen imitated her mother's threatening tone, her Louisiana Creole accent more evident when she was furious.

"Lexi wouldn't let it show. They were too much alike. Same nose. Same eyes. Same fiery, defiant tempers," James said.

Zen turned from the window and faced James. She put both hands on his shoulders. "Thanks for not taking it down, Daddy."

"Your mother insisted at first. When we went to clear out the furniture and toys, she stopped me. Said she could feel Lexi's happiness still surrounding the place."

Zen blinked at him in surprise. "Mama agreed not to tear down the treehouse? I didn't know."

James hugged Zen; his cheek pressed against hers. "It's a terrible thing to bury your child."

"To lose a sister," Zen whispered, her throat tight with the effort not to sob into his shoulder. "Mama's been the strong one, huh?"

Her father pulled back to gaze into Zen's eyes. "Not as tough-skinned as you think, Zenobia."

"I didn't mean to say she was cold-hearted." Zen winced at the memory of their clashes, made worse after Lexi's murder.

James coughed once. Then he returned to his chair and sat down with a short grunt. "Enola lost her parents young, had to take care of six brothers and sisters. No time to feel sorry for herself, she always says. Your mother handles grief in her own way, Zenobia."

"I guess, Daddy." Zen sat on the sofa across from him. She sipped from her own cup of tea.

"You're more like Enola than you like to think, too. Your mother felt guilt about Lexi's death. Like you." James leaned forward and placed a hand on Zen's knee. "You're both wrong about that, sweetheart."

"I'll get it. Must be Maisie about Rev. Wilson's anniversary celebration," Enola called when the phone rang. She must have looked at the caller ID display. "Yes, just what I thought. Hello, miss lady. How are you? Okay, let me get my notes."

James smiled with affection at the sound of Enola talking on the phone. Her voice faded as she went downstairs to the library. "Keeping busy has helped us both."

"I know," Zen whispered. She pushed against anguished thoughts crowding in on her. She patted the back of his hand and sat straight. "Work and parenthood keep me running like crazy."

"Ah, my grandchildren are a blessing. Astra is such a delight. And thank the Lord both your brothers had the sense to finally settle down." James's eyes brightened and the deep furrow of his brows eased into a smile.

"Blunted the shame of me as the unwed teenage mother, huh?" Zen covered her grin with the cup of tea.

"We were never ashamed of you, just concerned about your future. I'm sorry things didn't work out for you and Jordan. He's a good man. A good father."

"Yes, he is, but we're not getting back together. Divorce is the reason we're on good terms, Daddy. Don't pull a Mama on me with talk about the advantages of a two-parent home." Zen finished her tea and put the cup down.

"Fine. Be the career woman then. Speaking of which, what the hell happened in Madrid? Don't give me some generic answer, either," James added before Zen could speak.

"I was going to say—"

"And spare me the speech about it being best I don't know. I'm retired, earned my pension for sure. Your loose-cannon antics can't hurt my career." James fixed her with a hard stare. His frown said he wouldn't tolerate being treated like a frail senior citizen. Indeed, he looked anything but physically weak despite his recent illness.

Zen cleared her throat. "I tracked Navarro to Madrid after I matched his travel history to at least three of the murders. He has dual citizenship. It wasn't hard to get background information on him since he obtained clearance to work at NASA."

"Our security background checks are thorough. Go on."

"Our? Did you just give me a little speech about being retired?" Zen teased. She knew that once in business, former operatives never truly left those habits or ties behind.

"You said Navarro raised red flags because of his obsession with flash dancers."

Zen shook her head at the memory of visiting those clubs in Miami. Flash dancers used high-tech special effects in their acts. Flashing laser lights, holograms, and simulated sex acts made for the new version of stripping. Legal porn in three dimensions. Still, some dancers earned extra money by having 'dates' with patrons who could afford to pay. The prices weren't cheap, either.

"He's a rough-rider."

"Daddy!"

Zen grimaced at discussing the sordid details with her father. Law enforcement and sex workers used the term to describe customers who enjoyed violent sex. Even in the now mostly legal sex industry, assault was still a crime. Still, some women and men specialized in taking a beating. Transdermal implants blocked pain signals and caused injuries to heal quickly. Another reason the price for 'rough' services were high.

James's laughter at Zen's embarrassment brought on another coughing fit. He waved away Zen's attempt to fuss over him. He drank the last of his tea and then cleared his throat. "I was investigating crime before you were born. I know what goes on in those places. Bang bots aren't enough for some of those creeps."

"Not as satisfying as a warm kill," Zen said, referring to the act of beating a biological human to death.

Advanced humanoid robots were used to "satisfy the most exotic needs of special clients," as one such business said in its ads. In street language, robots used for sex were called bang bots. Those used for rough sex were called punching bag humps. An activist movement against the practice had grown as the robots began to look more like people. They argued that the androids had rights, too. Even more, sanctioning violence against machines made it more likely human victims would be next. Sex-work conglomerates countered they were providing an outlet that prevented rape and murder against the living.

"So, your source in the Miami strip club business led you to Navarro. I assume you did a search on sexual offenders, thinking the murders were sexually motivated. Narrowed it down to suspects who were in the area. Since none of their DNA matched forensics from the crimes, you figured it had to be someone with no arrests or convictions." Her father rattled off the investigative trail she'd followed as if he'd been her boss.

"Orlando. He started close to the base in Cape Canaveral. But he'd travel to Miami to party, too. But yeah, my source gave me a couple of names."

"Zenobia, this wasn't your fight." James held up a palm to stop Zen when she started to object. "Two of the victims were connected to the space program, one an Air Force pilot trainee. I know."

"She had a bright future. Her father is devastated," Zen said.

"And she was the same age as Lexi when she died," her father said in a gentle tone.

"I was helping to analyze crime data when I noticed the pattern."

James drummed his blunt fingertips on the armchair. Zen could feel his eagle-eyed gaze on her, his even sharper mind turning wheels. They rarely talked about her. Alexis Lynn Batiste went away to Mount Holyoke College at age seventeen. Zen would joke she was a late bloomer compared to her older siblings. They'd graduated from high school at fifteen or sixteen. Still, Lexi was no slacker. She'd been accepted for a dual-degree program—a bachelor of arts degree from Mount Holyoke and a bachelor of science degree in engineering from the California Institute of Technology. Lexi loved tech. Lexi loved partying just as much. She'd met her murderer at one. Most days, Zen could lock away those painful facts in a corner. So could her father, she suspected. The ability to compartmentalize helped them cope. And not talking about Lexi too often or too long. Today would be no exception.

"Okay. Skip to the part where you ended up in Madrid." James crossed his long legs and crossed his arms.

"You know from your buddies still in service," Zen countered. She returned his steady gaze with one of her own.

"I want to hear you tell it. Humor me."

Zen knew his investigative technique. Never assume you have the facts. Don't ask questions you don't have answers for already. Have the witness, or suspect, repeat their story. Pick apart the details. Hone in on inconsistencies. The cushioned sofa suddenly felt like the hot seat.

"I came to check on you and Mama, not be interrogated."

"Zenobia." James's basso tone reverberated in the room.

Enola came in at that moment, her own teacup in hand. "I swear, Maisie is acting like we're planning the Queen of England's Jubilee instead of pastor's fifth anniversary. I admire the young man, and he's done good work since he was installed, but..." She sat on the sofa and sighed.

"How is Mrs. Holcomb?" Zen jumped in, relieved at the distraction.

"Ordering everybody around as usual."

"Not you, I bet." Zen grinned at her mother. She avoided glancing at James.

Enola finally appeared to read the room. "You know me well. Now what are we talking about?"

"Zenobia is about to tell me about Madrid," James rumbled.

"You didn't tell me you took a trip, honey. Work or pleasure?" Enola raised both eyebrows at her husband as she spoke.

"Work. Sort of." Zen gave her father a stiff smile; a silent request to drop the subject.

"Not a sanctioned trip though," James replied with relentless determination.

"Hmm, then I definitely got Maisie off the phone in time. Go head, Zen." Enola settled next to James, cup in hand.

Most knew of her mother as a talented musician and music teacher. She'd traveled the globe before and during her marriage. Few knew she'd acted as an intelligence operative as well.

"My plan was simple. I took a couple of weeks off from work. I tried working with the local police and the Air Force special investigator. He was stuck on Lt. Shannon's ex-boyfriend, a civilian," Zen said with a grunt of scorn.

"Tunnel vision," James put in.

"Exactly. Nothing linked him to the crime. The fact that he didn't have a solid alibi wasn't nearly enough. Anyway, I made the connections. Long story short, I found out Navarro had attended parties with two victims. The other woman, a civilian Air Force employee, knew Lt. Shannon. They all knew each other. Navarro had narrowly escaped charges for assault when local police realized the victim was a humanoid robot. They look so real. Anyway, his DNA profile is a match, so I turned out to be right. That and the trophies I found in his Madrid apartment." Zen crossed her arms to match her father's stern pose.

"You illegally accessed his security clearance records to get your hands on his bio signatures—fingerprints, body chemistry profile. Flew to a foreign country to investigate one of their citizens in violation of an international treaty. When your plan hit a snag, you involved a local agent, who got shot." James ticked off Zen's crimes on the fingers of one hand.

"I didn't hack into his files. I explained to the personnel guy that I needed it for a project," Zen protested. "I was looking at data on employees at one point."

"Your DOJ badge and a pretty smile will get you in anywhere, huh?" James said.

Zen grinned at him. "Sometimes it works, sometimes it doesn't. This smile got me into two of his apartment buildings."

"Yeah, and look what else it got you into. A crap load of trouble." James scowled at Zen.

"How bad?" Enola asked her husband.

"Disciplinary note in her employee record and reassignment."

"Another agency?" Enola leaned toward him.

"Hey, you two. I'm right here and can answer for myself. I'm not twelve years old," Zen broke in.

"Hmmm." Enola settled back again and sipped tea.

"Not another agency, I don't think. Unless you know something." Zen shot a sharp glance at her father.

James waited a few seconds before he shook his head. "Hasn't been decided yet."

Zen felt a stab of anxiety at her father's reply. "I like my job at the DOJ."

"Then I suggest you act like it and stop making waves," James shot back.

Enola turned to Zen. "You've always been your own worst enemy. You won't move up if you keep going around your boss, making him look like a fool—"

"He *is* a fool," Zen mumbled.

"She's determined to ruin her career. Never listens." Enola let out a hiss of exasperation.

"The plan was solid," Zen snapped. "I got into Navarro's second apartment, where he really lived, found his trophies, mailed evidence and his address to the local police. Then the package delivery folks went on strike. So, I had Nino go to the drop box to get it. Navarro followed him and..."

Enola looked at James with a slight frown. "Nino?"

"Balduino Silva. He doubles as a local police officer who also does work for Spain's intelligence agency. Zen got to know him when she was in Portugal on assignment a few years back. Astra came to stay with us that summer," James said.

"Oh yes. I remember. Her father wasn't happy about it either." Enola nodded.

"So, you let her spend three weeks with him and his girlfriend." Zen glared at her parents in turn.

"Jordan has joint custody, and Astra wanted to go." Enola was unruffled by Zen's lingering anger over the incident.

"You didn't object at the time. He married the woman," James added.

"And divorced her a year later," Zen said.

"You're going to judge him? People in glass houses, as my grandmother used to say," Enola drawled, her Southern accent coming through despite years on the east coast. "You moved on. Several times, I might add."

"Most mothers side with their children in a divorce, Mama." Zen bristled at her mother's ceaseless disapproval of every move, every decision she made.

"Jordan stepped up, married you while you were both in college. He's been an attentive and loving father. It just didn't work out. Isn't that the speech you gave us when you announced you'd left him?"

James broke in to head off the familiar debate before it got more heated. "Let's not get sidetracked, ladies. Why didn't you send the damn package via drone delivery?"

"Because they snap a photo of the sender. You helped develop those security protocols," Zen said.

"Oh, yeah." Her father lifted his chin with pride at the mention of only one of many career highpoints.

"So, I dropped it into a self-driving mailbox. Every one of the damn things was disabled remotely by employees when they went on strike." Zen grimaced.

Although package delivery locally was largely automated, humans still had to sort large deliveries. They also maintained the equipment; drones delivered smaller packages. Self-driving compact vehicles carried mail to office buildings, including those that housed government agencies. Packages were dropped off secure docks and robotic devices received them. Electronic notifications for pickup were then sent to recipients. All of the machines had security scans for explosives and illegal drugs.

"You seem very friendly with Mr. Silva, or Nino as you call him. Enough that he didn't hesitate to help you create an international incident." Enola sipped tea.

"He was loyal, tried to keep her name out of it. But still, I wonder if they're pals since she got him shot," James said in his typical blunt way. His scowl softened at the stricken expression on Zen's face.

"You're right. I put Nino in that bullet's path." Zen squeezed her eyes shut against the image of Balduino hooked up to medical devices.

"He's recovering just fine, sweetheart. He's young and in excellent physical shape," James said, patting Zen's knee.

"Yes, he is. Thank God," Zen replied with a nod. When she opened her eyes, Enola was looking at her with both eyebrows raised.

"Plus, I understand he's undergone bio-enhancements. He'll heal quickly," James said. When both women turned to him in surprise, he cleared his throat. "That's all I can say."

"Spain is using its law enforcement and security agents as lab rats? I can't believe..." Zen's voice trailed off as she gazed at her father. "You served on the Global Security Council. Aside from package screening with the new robotics, I seem to recall there were rumors about creating super-soldiers. Not just technologically advanced weapons and equipment."

"Each nation and the EU had access to resources. Countries chose which ones they wanted to implement. But about ten were adopted in all countries by agreement," James said.

"Nino could almost sense the moves I'd made, what I was thinking." Zen felt a flush of warmth at the sensational sex they'd had. Apparently, he hadn't simply improved with age and experience.

"Really? Judging from that dreamy look in your eyes, those upgrades have other benefits." Enola tilted her head to one side as she gazed at Zen.

"I don't know what you mean," Zen said and affected a blank expression.

"Zenobia is an adult and her private life is none of our business."

"And by that he really means it's none of *your* business, Mama," Zen added.

"Back to the important thing, how this little episode will affect your professional career with DOJ," James said.

Zen shrugged. "I can survive sitting at a desk staring at data, sending reports, doing charts and graphs for a few months."

"Or years," Enola shot back.

"Ouch." Zen suddenly needed a sip of something stronger than hibiscus tea with elderberry.

"I'm sure it won't come to that. You caught a serial killer, after all. The press coverage boosted the department and made you a hero. Your boss can't punish you too much. Would only make him look worse." James smiled at his view of the bright side. He looked at his wife. "Her instincts were right. She gets that from me."

"Instinct. Another way of saying you would go around proper channels, ask forgiveness rather than permission. Bucked authority. You could be the head of global intelligence, which includes the CIA, by now." Enola pointed a finger at her husband.

"Daddy was rewarded for his initiative more than a few times, mama. Blame the nationalists," Zen said in his defense.

"His resourcefulness did take us around the world. Your father beat them at every turn. But I don't miss the grind and pressure." Enola's disapproving expression smoothed into a smile. She rose and gave James a hug. Her father touched Enola's cheek with affection. Then she gathered up the now-empty cups to put them on a tray to return to the kitchen.

James frowned. "Nationalists can't accept the reality or obvious advantages of global cooperation. Climate change continues to reshape the Earth. Terrorism continues to be a challenge. Income inequality, political oppression. We need to address them as a unified world."

"I don't know all factions, but racism is the subtext of every speech and social media post. It's the dog whistle that unites them. I don't care what they say," Zen said.

"At least we're keeping them on the margins. Not that we'll have a global governing system anytime soon. Nations still have their own interests. We have our own histories, languages, cultures—"

"And national interests," Zen said, finishing his thought. She grinned at her father. The engineer, history buff, and intelligence expert.

"Which brings us back to Spain and the EU. They're pissed, mostly embarrassed that a US operative solved the crimes. The Spanish and EU newscasts made them look like idiots." James scowled at Zen in the same way the committee members had.

"I didn't plan on such a blow up. Damn postal union."

"I was bold as a young special agent, but daughter, you take the cake."

"Technically, I had international probable cause to enter his residence. After determining that lives were endangered and time was of the essence—"

"Don't quote the exceptions to me, young woman. I helped write them," James snapped. One of his innovations once he rose through the ranks was protocol exceptions available to senior special agents. The regulations were a nod to a common problem. Field agents with real skills versus superiors in top jobs due to family and political connections.

"I had no way of anticipating the mail technician strike, Daddy. Of all the things I could have checked... I mean, they didn't even vote to stop work until a day after I was on the ground." Zen got up and went back to the window.

"I know. I had a few of my own close calls. There were steps you could have taken, even so." James heaved a long sigh at the look she gave him. They'd talked about Zen's boss more than once. "Yeah, Kenneth has solid connections up the chain of command."

"Then you know he would have been tipped off. I've documented his missteps before. Ignoring clear data that complicated investigations, making decisions based on his nationalist leanings." Zen came back from the window and sat again.

"Which he's vehemently denied. Careful taking that tack," James said, dropping his voice low. "The seriousness of such an allegation..."

"That's between us, don't worry." Zen waved a hand at him. "Not that it had anything to do with the Navarro case. Kenneth didn't want to listen to anything from *me*."

"Well, we're here now. A wild card landed you in hot water," James said, using two more of his favorite old-fashion expressions.

"A crazy quark," Zen replied, using the modern version. "Guess I'll have to deal with it. I have a meeting with Kenneth Monday."

"Daughter, you need to own up to the trouble you've caused and—"

"Keep my mouth in check and my head down. I got it." Zen beat one hand on the sofa cushion. She had all day Sunday to prepare. If Enola had been in the room, she'd have advised her to spend those hours in prayer.

———⧓⧓⧓———

ZEN ARRIVED AT THE anteroom where Kenneth's administrative assistant sat. She knocked after taking a deep breath and opened the door without waiting. The young man was on the phone. Grayson eyed her as she entered

"Kenneth Spaulding's office. Yes, ma'am, I'll let him know."

Grayson ended the call by tapping his headset and entered notes on a digital note tablet. He didn't look up at her. Zen didn't like Grayson any more than she liked her boss. Grayson and Spaulding were a matched set of arrogant entitlement. Seething resentment of Zen's family connections and accomplishments always simmered beneath the surface of their exchanges. Zen sat down in a leather chair. She made a show of scrolling through messages on her phone. They both looked up when the recessed door to her boss's office swung open. To her surprise, Clive Anderson stepped out, followed by Bertice Illinois. Zen snapped to her feet. She quickly jammed her phone into the pocket of her suit jacket.

Sir, ma'am," Zen said in a crisp, respectful tone.

Ms. Illinois nodded to her. "Have a good day, Agent Batiste."

"You, too, ma'am."

Zen studied the woman for non-verbal clues to what she meant and came up empty. Ms. Illinois's tone and face gave nothing away. Clive Anderson beckoned to her, turned, and disappeared into the office without waiting. Grayson looked at Zen, a smirk pulling his thin lips up at one corner. His porcelain skin, icy-blue eyes, and reddish-blond hair made him look almost like a doll—an evil one from a horror story.

"Yes, Ms. Batiste. As good a day as you can after that meeting," he murmured when she strode past. He hissed when Zen gave him a one-fingered salute as the last word.

She shut the door behind her after entering. She crossed the fine Moroccan wool rug to stand in front of Spaulding's desk. Back straight. Chin up. Hands clasped behind her back. Her father's advice came to her. "If you get in trouble but got a good result don't whine or grovel. And for God's sake don't crow about showing up the boss," James had said. The voice of experience, Zen mused.

Spaulding looked at her as he tapped his expensive pen on the polished wood. A file sat in front of him. "Batiste."

"Sir." Zen nodded at Anderson, who stood to one side of the room, as a greeting.

"Madrid turned into a shitshow, and you had the starring role." Spaulding used the pen to point at her.

Zen didn't respond immediately as the two men observed her for a reaction. Seconds ticked by before she replied. "An unexpected turn of events that I should have anticipated."

"Your mastery of understatement is astounding," Spaulding clipped.

"The circumstances were unique to say the least. I'm not sure anyone would have checked on the delivery workers union," Clive Anderson cut in smoothly.

Spaulding's mouth still hung open for a few seconds. Then he snapped his lips together. A sour expression settled on his broad face, accented by a flush of pink. Anderson walked over and gestured for Zen to take a seat. Then he sat next to her in a matching leather chair. They both faced Spaulding's desk.

"The strain on our relationship with an ally complicates—"

"Ms. Batiste has had the consequences of her independent investigation explained to her, Ken." Anderson smiled at him.

Zen glanced from her boss to Anderson. She could read the room but was still confused. Spaulding wanted his pound of flesh, a way to save face. He hadn't had a chance to castigate Zen, not even in private. He needed to as a balm to his scarred ego, to re-establish that he was large and in charge. Anderson seemed determined to thwart such a display.

"Diplomacy and quid pro quo have mitigated some of the damage, Batiste," Spaulding pressed on with a grimace at Zen.

"Understood, sir." Zen nodded to Spaulding.

Her boss leaned forward with both elbows on the desk. "Understand? What about an apology and humility?"

"I'm very sorry Agent Silva was injured. And I'm grateful for the efforts of the department to explain the circumstances to our Spanish counterpart. Agent Silva will get credit for solving two murders as well," Zen said. "I don't need to have my name on any public mention of the case."

"No mention. How generous of you!" Spaulding sputtered as he slapped a palm on his desktop.

*Don't brag, girl!* James Batiste's bass rang in Zen's skull as though he stood invisible at her shoulder. "I didn't mean it that way, sir. I know my actions caused potential problems with Spain."

"And the European Union," Spaulding put in, jabbing a thick forefinger at her.

"It's been handled by a competent team from my office and our embassy in Brussels," Anderson inserted. He and Spaulding stared at each other in silence for a few beats. Zen's boss looked away first.

Zen wondered at the tension between the two men. "Thanks for the update, sirs. I had no intention of harming international relations. I'm sorry."

"Your position will change." Spaulding's jaw muscle jumped.

Anderson transferred his gaze from Spaulding to Zen. "You know about the additional moon colony, I assume."

"Uh, I... Yeah. I mean yes, sir." Zen blinked with puzzlement at the subject shift. "Though to be honest I haven't kept up with the latest news feeds about it."

"Too busy plotting ways to cause an international crisis," Spaulding muttered.

Anderson heaved a sigh, but didn't address Spaulding's sarcasm. "Goddard has built the second colony, first one operated by a private company. As of last week, they have ten people up there and want to send ten more. That's added to the twenty people in the NASA colony."

"I see." Zen didn't see at all, though. "You're going to exile me on the moon as punishment?"

"Not a bad idea," Spaulding wisecracked. He flinched when Anderson squinted at him.

"No, Batiste. You caught a globe-trotting serial killer, after all. There are those who think you should get a commendation." Anderson's voice cut through the air like a flinty blade aimed at her boss.

Zen let the heavy silence stretch for a few seconds. She relished the way Spaulding fidgeted but maintained a poker face. "Yes, sir."

Anderson cleared his throat and turned to Zen again. "Your dissertation addressed the complexities of culture in special environments, the emergence of aberrant or criminal behavior. Specifically, on space stations or colonies."

Zen frowned at his reference to her long-ago academic pursuits. She'd started her research in grad school while pregnant, hence her daughter's name. That Astra's father would later train as an astronaut seemed prophetic.

"Yes. I posited that even in space, those with sociopathic tendencies would find a way to exploit new systems. Or that pressure from an alien environment would create new crimes, or at least twists on old ones. All theories back then. An intriguing academic exercise." Zen's combined interest in mental health and forensic sociology had led to her unconventional choice of a doctoral thesis.

"Well, it seems you're once again ahead of the crowd, Dr. Batiste. And you work for us." Anderson's hazel eyes twinkled with delight.

"Sir?" Zen blinked at him rapidly, looked at Spaulding and back at Anderson again.

"You're coming to a new department, a division of the DOJ in concert with NASA. We need your expertise," Anderson said.

"There's a crime problem on the colonies already? I hadn't heard—"

"We want to get on top of understanding... the dynamics of these new space cultures." Anderson seemed to be choosing his words with great care.

"Okay," Zen replied. She sensed Anderson held back because of Spaulding's presence.

"With Kenneth's consultation and agreement, of course." Anderson shot a glance at her boss.

"Right," Spaulding added, his expression stiff.

Anderson gave Spaulding a crisp nod and then stood. "Let me show you to your new office."

"Uh, sure. Great." Zen glanced at Spaulding for a clue and got none. She followed Anderson to the door, feeling like she was stepping into alien territory already.

# Chapter 3

Monday afternoon, Astra swept in through the kitchen door, a sixteen-year-old whirlwind of motion. Fall sunshine slanted through windows as the day slipped into evening.

"I've got band practice and my last paper due. A few research details to nail down. Loni is picking me up in forty-five minutes to give me a ride, so you don't have to worry."

Zen watched her sling the designer backpack onto the bench cushion. She pointed to the line of hooks above it. A shelf above and wicker baskets beneath were for extra storage. "Hang up your things."

"Oh, and I need you to sign for the end-of-the-term trip. Check your school DM app. Can't wait until I'm eighteen and don't need parental permission to breathe." Astra washed her hands at the sink.

"Where is it this time?" Zen sat at the table with a glass of red wine.

"Back to the National Archives. We'll get access to documents from the nineteen forties, maybe even earlier. I'm going to dig into what they have on UFO sightings," Astra tossed over her shoulder as she dried her hands on a dishtowel. She threw it onto the counter. At Zen's hiss of reproach, Astra sighed and hung it on a hook attached to a nearby cabinet.

"See? Only took a few seconds. And your dad dropped serious cash for that backpack you abuse so casually."

"You're sounding like grandmother more and more." Astra didn't slow down as she pulled out the fixings for a sandwich.

"Now that's downright mean," Zen tossed back with a grin.

"You started it," Astra shot back and stuck her tongue out. Then she giggled. "Honestly, you two fight more than my friend Deeanne's parents. And they hate each other. Loni and I have bets on how long before they split."

"You girls... Honestly, Astra?" Zen put the long-stem glass down on the table with a thump.

"We support her, Mom. We really do. Of course, we haven't said anything to Carola. But it's painful going over there. Why do you think she sleeps over here and with us at Loni's all the time?" Astra took care to spread honey mustard, her favorite, on the low-carb bread slices she insisted on using. She licked a drop from her thumb.

"There are mixed veggies in the fridge. No fried chips," Zen said.

"Of course. Gotta eat clean to keep this flawless melanin beauty." Astra swept back her thick braids over a shoulder.

"At least you're humble," Zen joked.

Astra winked at Zen. "I get it from you."

Zen faked an angry scowl. "Smart mouth."

"That, too."

Zen laughed with her and sipped more wine. She watched her beautiful daughter, auburn hair in braids to her waist, move around the kitchen. Astra ate healthy thanks to her interest in training to be an astronaut like her father and uncles. Astra also loved playing volleyball and tennis. Recently, she'd taken up strength training. Zen monitored to make sure she wasn't obsessing about her weight. Slender and graceful, Astra looked like a dancer.

Her meal complete, Astra joined her mother at the table with her plate. She pointed to the wine goblet. "Rough day, huh?"

"Could have been better," Zen said.

"And you're home early. You usually nag at me via DM," Astra teased.

"Hmm." Zen forced a brief smile she wasn't really feeling.

Astra was about to take a bite from her free-range chicken sandwich but stopped. "Wow. How bad did you fuck it up?"

"Astra, language!"

"Sorry, it slipped out. So, is it 'temporary rough spot bad?' or 'asteroid hits the Earth, mass-extinction bad'?"

"Let's just say if I was a dinosaur, I'd be kind of worried right now," Zen drawled. "But you don't need to worry."

"Thank goodness I'm graduating soon. My school fees are paid. I guess condo living won't be bad if we have to sell the house. We should get a great price for it though. We could live off the money for a—"

"Whoa, whoa. Slow down. I still have a job."

"I told Loni when you left on that *business trip* suddenly that something was up," Astra went on. It was her turn to sound like Enola Batiste.

Loni's parents had been more than happy to let Astra stay with them for a few days. The girls shared an obsession with science and were frequent study partners. So, Zen hadn't felt guilty leaving Astra. Her daughter wasn't just beautiful and smart, she'd inherited the autonomy gene from both sides.

"I'm good. *We're* good, baby. And I'm definitely not selling our home. Until you're out of college at least. Maybe not then. I love Fairfax," Zen said. She drained the last few ounces of wine and got up to rinse out the goblet.

"I wouldn't mind if we moved back to DC. I could go to Howard U. instead of Xavier. Stay closer to home." Astra rose and crossed the kitchen to stand next to Zen.

"You're going to do an internship at the Space Center in Houston for a gap year and then decide which scholarship you'll accept." Zen turned to Astra and placed both hands on her shoulders. "Everything as planned. And I know you really want to attend Xavier University and see Louisiana. Thanks to Mama's endless stories about how fabulous it is."

"I loved it that time we visited Grandmother's sister. I want to attend a majority Black school for once. I mean, the atmosphere was... awesome." Astra's dark-brown eyes lit up.

"Yeah, Mama sneaked in a campus tour during that trip. Had me fooled with the whole 'connecting the child to her Louisiana roots' sales job." Zen shook her head.

"Bayous and alligators. The red beans, the shrimp po-boys. Oh, the hot sauce!" Astra jumped up and down like she was twelve again.

"At least you have your priorities straight," Zen said with a laugh.

"I'm so happy Grandmother and Grandfather are moving for me." Astra grinned.

"Not to burst your self-absorbed bubble, but Mama has been talking about going back to Louisiana for years. At least the last ten as she got close to retirement." Zen walked Astra back to the table, an arm around her shoulders.

"So, I don't have to pawn my stuff to keep us from being homeless," Astra quipped, but gazed at her mother. The concern beneath her attempt at a light tone came through.

"Astra, really. Sit, eat." Zen sighed when Astra perched on the counter stool but didn't touch her food. "Okay, okay. I'm going to be reassigned."

"Oh no." Astra's eyes went wide.

"Not a demotion or pay cut. Matter of fact I'll be making more." Zen frowned at the contradiction. Her job change felt like punishment because of Madrid, yet in some ways it didn't.

"You're going to move up? Cool." Astra hugged her mother and then took a bite of her sandwich.

"No, it's not a promotion either. Truth is I'm not sure how to describe it."

Zen had spent the rest of the day packing up her desk. Only one colleague had talked to her. The others avoided Zen, afraid to risk the ire of their boss. Petty and vindictive, Spaulding demanded loyalty. She'd finally tired of the strained atmosphere and left early to avoid cursing someone out.

"Hmm, well, if things go south, I'm willing to part with a few things. Just kidding," Astra added before Zen could reply.

"You're something else." Zen tugged on a few of Astra's braids and hugged her. The playful gleam in her daughter's eyes and restored appetite told her Astra was reassured.

"So, what is the job anyway?" Astra had her phone in one hand and the sandwich in the other.

"I think it has something to do with more specialized data analysis and psychological profiles," Zen said.

"Sounds pretty dry. You are seriously being punished, Mom," Astra murmured, her focus back on her own world of teen gossip, memes, and goofy videos.

"You could be right."

Zen gave her a pat on the shoulder and went to the fridge. She started preparing her own dinner. She stared out through the kitchen window but didn't see the view. Instead, she sorted the puzzle pieces of the last few hours. Clive Anderson hadn't given her more details. In fact, he'd left not long after their meeting in Spaulding's office ended. The ambiguity made Zen both anxious and eager to know more. She put the salmon filet back in the fridge and headed to her office. Once there, she turned on the computer and logged into the secure cloud. After a knock, Astra stuck her Got to head in the door.

"Loni's here. Bye, Mom. I should be back by seven," Astra said.

"Hmm."

Zen blew her a distracted kiss and continued the search for information on her new workplace. Seconds later she heard the thump of the front door closing. Then it opened again and Astra yelled from the other side of the door.

"Mom!"

Zen pushed from her chair and rushed out into the hallway. Jordan, her ex-husband, and his current girlfriend stood in the door. Astra still had her arm around her father's waist. Minji Hanson transferred her scrutiny from Astra to Zen.

"What are you doing here?" Zen blurted.

"Mom," Astra repeated, this time with a note of disapproval in her tone.

"Good evening to you as well," Minji said and cast a glance at Jordan.

Zen didn't miss that an unspoken message passed between them. Minji's cool exterior matched the stereotype of a dispassionate scientist. Zen knew that beneath the surface simmered white-hot passion. That her ex was the focus amused Zen. Jordan was smart, but he didn't have a clue yet.

"Sorry, I was startled. Working on a project and you're the last people I expected to see." Zen recovered and smoothed down her skirt. She walked toward them with what she hoped came across as an apologetic smile.

"Minji's here for a conference and convinced me to come along at the last minute." Jordan kissed Astra's forehead. "I tore myself away to see my most favorite girl in the universe."

"Daddy, let's go to the African-American museum again. You said the next time you were in DC we would. Just you and me." Astra held him tighter. Then she glanced at Jordan's girlfriend. "I mean, since Minji will be so busy."

"I don't know, baby girl. I have a couple of meetings myself." Jordan laughed when Astra affected a pout. "Don't be like that."

"Yes, we do have a packed schedule. As I'm sure you do as well," Minji replied with a tight smile. Astra's friend blew the car horn again as if on cue.

"Just a sec," Astra said and dashed outside.

"So, you're taking a break from training?" Zen said to fill in the taut silence.

"Just wrapped up the first phase. There's a real possibility I'll be on a mission soon," Jordan said.

"Oh."

Zen cast around for something more to say, at least in front of Minji. The woman studied Zen with great care. No doubt looking for signs of some emotional vibe still between her and Jordan. Astra's return saved Zen from more forced casual conversation.

"Whew, it's cool. Now, as I was saying, I always make time for the best father ever. Can't you pencil in your only child? Please, Daddy?" Astra laid it on even thicker. She topped it off by batting the thick eyelashes that framed her lovely brown eyes.

"Sweetheart, we'll only be here for three days. Between your father's meetings and our time there's hardly any space." Minji raised a perfectly arched eyebrow at him.

"Astra continued to look up at her father. "I'll take the train and meet you there to save time. We didn't get to see the exhibits on Harriet Tubman, our hero."

"It's a date," Jordan said. He grinned when Astra squealed in delight.

"Jordan..." Minji's eyes narrowed.

"Let me talk to my kid for a minute, okay?" Jordan glanced from Minji to Zen. "Come on, baby girl, I'll walk you out." He and Astra strolled down the paved path toward Loni's compact Tesla.

Minji faced Zen when they were a few feet away. "Maybe you can explain to Astra how important this trip is for her father. He's being considered for a short-term assignment on the Global Space Station. The meetings are at the Pentagon."

"A bit of advice—don't get try getting between Jordan and Astra. If he says he has time, then he has time," Zen said.

"Thank you so much, but I had no such motive," Minji replied with a fierce smile that didn't include her eyes.

Jordan walked backward and blew a kiss at Astra. With one last wave, he strode back to the open door. He glanced at his smartwatch and read as he walked.

"So, we better be going. Minji, if you don't mind, I need to have a quick word with Zen. Wait for me in the car, babe. I won't be a minute." Jordan gave her shoulder a pat.

"Sure. Until the next time." Minji nodded at Zen and walked off to their rental steel-gray self-driving taxi. The heels of her Louboutin pumps tapped out her anger on the stone walkway.

"Wow, that sounded like a combat challenge. Until the next time," Zen said, pitching her voice low. When she giggled, Jordan stared at her. "What?"

Jordan pushed her ahead of him into the foyer and closed the door. "Min isn't as bad as she seems. She gets intense about her career. *Our* career."

"Hey, I'm not judging. You'll have to deal with her later, not me." Zen's suspicion was confirmed when Jordan sighed and glanced over his shoulder.

"Look, I wanted to check that you're okay."

"Good God! Does the entire world know my damn business?" Zen shook her head.

"No, it's just... I do keep an eye out for you and Astra, even from Houston. Divorce or not, you're both still my girls. You know? So..." Jordan studied Zen hard.

"In other words, your pals are spying on me. Great, Jordan." Zen put both fists on her hips.

"You know it's not like that. About this section you're being assigned to—"

"Geez, you're like my father with his network of eyes and ears."

"Just keep your head up. It's all hush-hush. Kind of controversial but I haven't been able to find out why." Jordan frowned as he rubbed his square jaw.

Zen matched his frown with her own. "Which means it's probably a political bombshell. But it sounds so milk-and-white-bread dull."

"What have they told you so far?"

"Not much. I got the feeling Anderson didn't want to say much in front of my boss," Zen replied.

"Spaulding's head is so far up the current administration's butt he rarely sees sunshine," Jordan said with a snort.

"So, whatever it is Anderson doesn't want the president to know? That's crazy conspiracy talk." Zen started to laugh but stopped at his unsmiling dark expression.

"Maybe not the president. But Congress, the Pentagon, even NASA. P0litics mixed with global corporations and… I don't like the way space missions are being managed these days. The US has been pushing back the Outer Space Treaty of 1967 for the past ninety years. Nationalists are behind it."

"Russia and China have objections, too, though," Zen pointed out.

"Look at you keeping up space politics," Jordan said with a grin.

"I don't know much, just the bit I've read since getting hit with the reassignment news. I haven't been able to find out a lot about Anderson's new department. I don't have high-enough clearance." Zen lifted her chin to stare at him hard.

Jordan blinked back at her for a few seconds and then shook his head. "Oh, no. I'm not leaving a trail of electronic crumbs back to me. This is some deep shit, Zen."

"I could find out how to erase the trail. I've got a friend—"

"No," Jordan cut her off. Then he huffed out a sigh. "Look, I can ask a friend. Talk over dinner and drinks doesn't leave a trace. I trust Brian."

"One of your Alpha Phi Alpha brothers from Hampton, I suppose."

"Yeah, and we were in med school together. I'll let you know what I find out." Jordan stopped when his smartwatch trilled a tune. Minji's voice came through, reminding him of the time.

"Your cue to snap to it." Zen stepped to the window, looked out, and waved.

"She's just jumpy about the paper she's presenting. She and Astra will hit it off soon enough." Jordan planted a quick, friendly kiss on Zen's forehead.

"If you say so," Zen replied dryly.

"Thanks for the encouragement. Gotta run."

Zen stood in the door and waved them off with a smile. Minji's stone-faced gaze implied she was not happy. "That should be an interesting ride back to DC."

AFTER AN EARLY-MORNING run the next day, Zen had breakfast with Astra before she went off to school. She welcomed one last day off before the new job. Once she dropped a load of laundry in the washing machine, Zen settled into her office. She gave up on trying to do a deep dive into Anderson. Instead, she read up on space mining and the space station. She found a few articles on space colonies, their culture and how a closed society would be affected. Most of the comparisons were to isolated communities in harsh climates, like small settlements in Antarctica, the Arctic Circle, or tribes in remote jungles. She made a few notes, but then gave up. Too speculative, not enough information yet. So, she dressed to meet her friend for lunch at one of their favorite spots. Since it was close to the train station, Zen didn't have to take a car into DC.

The Capital Bistro buzzed with the lunchtime crowd. Chloé stood and waved with energy to get her attention. Zen navigated around tables to reach her. They shared a hug.

"Girl, it's been too long."

"We had lunch last week," Zen replied.

"Events move at light speed in this town." Chloé sat down.

Zen took the seat across from her at their two-person table. "Yeah, and not always in a good way. Stop gawking at me like you just discovered I'm from another planet."

"I was just thinking. See, you blend in. Not like me, which is why I'm a keyboard puncher and not a field agent."

"Gee thanks for the compliment," Zen retorted.

Almost six feet talk, Chloé towered over Zen. Her thick hair had been slicked back into a neat bun suitable for the office. Off work, Chloé wore her hair loose and down to her shoulders. With smooth, dark-brown skin, long legs, and a killer smile, Chloé had modeled to pay for college. She'd turned down offers to continue, opting for grad school instead.

"You know what I mean. My colleagues are dying to get the inside story on Madrid and the serial killer. Hey, that would make a fab title for a streaming series or movie," Chloé said.

"I'm not exactly supposed to be in the field either," Zen replied with a grimace.

"The fact that you went rogue makes it even more exciting. I smell bestseller and movie deal offers. I could be your manager. Business major, remember." Chloé grinned at Zen in delight.

"Trust me, it's not exciting or glamorous. Nino was in physiotherapy for months." Zen stared out at the traffic. After four months, she'd finally had a chance to talk to him. He'd tried to reassure her, but his voice was shaky.

Chloé reached across and squeezed her hand. "Sorry, girl. I'm spouting off like the pampered desk jockey I am. Meanwhile, you know it's real blood and bone on the street."

"I didn't mean to put anyone at risk."

"Hey, you don't have to convince me. Forever team Zenobia Batiste," Chloé said with fervor.

Zen tapped a lacquered fingernail on the tabletop. She'd been obsessed with data on serial murders since Lexi's death. Everyone, even her parents, thought her fixation was unhealthy. Jordan claimed it was part of what had pushed them apart. Maybe he was right. His practical advice to move past what she couldn't change had rankled. Yet she couldn't stop thinking about the details missed that might have saved her sister's life.

"I couldn't get federal or local cops to listen to me. Drove me nuts. It was as if they'd never heard of spatial and temporal mapping."

"I'll bet they listen to you *now*. My bestie is a world-famous sleuth." Chloé's expression brightened again. She broke off when the waitress came to take their orders.

Zen watched the woman leave and leaned forward; her voice low. "I'm not thrilled my name ended up in the news cycle, Clo. And my bosses didn't throw a welcome home party for me either."

"Yeah, the reassignment. I hear Clive Anderson doesn't just know where the bodies are buried; he put a few of 'em there." Chloé glanced around as if checking for eavesdroppers.

"He's a middle-aged white dude from Iowa. Sure, he's got lots of bona fides, but he's a bureaucrat. Been in an office most of his career."

Chloé shook her head slowly. "You've been reading the official bio for public consumption. I have a feeling you're about to get a glimpse into the shadow world."

"You do love drama. First Jordan and now you. Picture me rolling my eyes." Zen grinned at her.

"Anderson doesn't get involved in anything below security level three, Zen. Any section he heads up will deal with something *very important*."

"Psychosocial profiles of potential space colonists are important, but not exactly national security stuff," Zen replied. She broke off when the waitress returned with their food.

"Space mining is projected to be a trillion-dollar business. How many countries would rise to prominence with those kinds of resources? Africa, India, Korea. The balance of world power could shift. Think about if they get their operatives planted in space colonies." Chloé pointed her fork at Zen.

"You've really pushed the boundaries of speculation, Clo. Stop reading sci-fi thrillers. Look, if we're talking national economies and relations with allies, I should think that alone is important enough for Anderson to be in charge. And the balance of world power shifted fifty years ago."

"Which is why the nationalist movement has gained a foothold. Remember how folks lost their minds when

Obama was elected?" Chloé returned to her favorite topic, race and politics. "If his great-grandson decides to run for national office? Heads will explode in certain circles."

"That was almost seventy years ago. Yes, I know it took decades for real structural barriers to come down," Zen said when Chloé raised both eyebrows at her.

"And nationalists are busy building new invisible ones. The demographics have them in panic mode, Zen."

"Okay, but the nationalists are small in number and on the fringes."

"So was the Black Lives Matter Movement at first. Three young women holding meetings on the old social media platforms," Chloé countered.

"I remember my history lessons, thank you."

"Then think about a bunch of radical nationalists getting their hands on trillions of dollars. They only need a handful in the right places." Chloé picked a black olive from her salad and popped it in her mouth.

Zen waved away her friend's theories on political intrigue. "You have zero facts. I've heard the same gossip about who is and who isn't a nationalist in top offices. And what has any of this to do with my new job anyway? Girl, we've gotten way off topic. I need to worry about my career. I've got private college tuition to think about. Then maybe med school if she follows in her daddy's footsteps."

"Just stay alert is all I'm saying. You running in some hot circles now." Chloé stuffed a forkful of the kale and shrimp salad in her mouth.

"Are you and Jordan coordinating the effort to make me paranoid?" Zen retorted.

"Jordan?"

"He's in town." Zen ate a piece of grilled chicken on her own salad. She chewed slowly and thought about her ex.

"He came all this way to check on you, huh? That's sweet. Maybe you two will—"

"He brought his girlfriend. She's uptight and I think jealous of how much attention he gives Astra."

"How long have they been rockin' it?"

"Almost a year, I think," Zen said with a shrug.

"Okay. Ten bucks says he dumps her in two months or less." Chloé munched on her salad with a smug grin.

"She's lasted longer than the previous three women. Minji is smart and gorgeous, and he makes excuses when she acts a little..." Zen's voice trailed off.

"The word you're searching for is 'bitchy'," Chloé wisecracked.

"Insecure," Zen offered instead with a laugh. "Look, Jordan and I were high school friends and then college sweethearts. We still get along. I think she'd feel better if we despised each other. You know, the stereotypical battling exes."

"Damn, you gotta break everything down so clinical. You sound like you feel sorry for her."

"Her issues aren't my problem. But Minji better wake up or she'll lose him. One thing I know, Jordan won't put up with her going after Astra."

"Two months," Chloé repeated and stuck out a hand.

"Jordan's in love. I say six months, and they'll get engaged before he wakes up. Her possessive streak will kick into high gear. They'll never make it to the altar."

"Ooo, upping the stakes. It's a bet."

"Done." Zen shook hands with her as they shared a giggle at being catty.

"More tea, ladies?" the waitress said briskly.

"Yes, I—" Zen let out a small gasp and then recovered. She looked down at her plate.

"Another cola for me and she'll have another glass of sweet tea." Chloé wore a perplexed frown but waited for the waiter to leave. "What's wrong?"

"My new boss is sitting at a table with two other guys," Zen said low. Anderson hadn't seen her, she thought. Or maybe he had. "Speaking of being paranoid."

"Describe them."

"Balding. Reading glasses pushed up on his head. Wait, he's put them on to read the menu. Dark-blue suit, talking to an Asian guy and a Black guy. Table to your left, three away." Zen covered her mouth with a napkin as she spoke. She did not look in their direction.

Chloé brushed her hair with one hand to glance around casually. "Got 'em. Hmm, distinguished looking but not noticeable. Looks like a thousand other middle-aged government guys."

"Yeah, but only at first glance. I'll bet he used that to his advantage early in his career. His competition didn't see him coming," Zen mused. She fought the urge to look at Anderson.

"There you go again, diving deep into the man's psyche," Chloé quipped. She went back to eating her salad. "We're near government offices and this place is popular. Coincidence."

"Jordan shows up to give me warnings. Anderson is vague about my new job. And you spin conspiracy theories over lunch. Now he's here."

Zen drank tea and stopped abruptly. Anderson gazed at her steadily for a few seconds, smiled, and waved. She waved back. He turned back to his companions. All harmless. Nonchalant. Just three guys out sharing a meal before returning to the office grind. When Anderson glanced her way again, Zen realized she had continued to scrutinize him. She plastered on a smile and looked at her friend instead.

"I was talking about nationalists. Anderson doesn't have ties to them as far as I know," Chloé said, her concentration on her food. "I'm just saying, look for ties when you check out potential space colonists. Or those companies."

"Hmm."

"Stop looking his way every five seconds. He'll think you're up to something or hot for him," Chloé said with a smirk.

"Hot for... Oh please." Zen shook her head with a laugh.

"They've got your life history already. Why would he need to follow you? Besides, at his level he wouldn't follow you himself. He'd have someone assigned to do it. Someone you wouldn't suspect. Like me." Chloé popped a shrimp in her mouth and grinned.

"Not even close to being funny," Zen said. They went on to exchange light chatter. Yet Zen couldn't shake the feeling that she was taking a test of some kind.

WEDNESDAY MORNING ZEN reported to her new office. The building was nondescript. The beige stone exterior blended into the scenery. Within two miles of the Department of Justice headquarters, it would be an easy walk to reach. Zen wondered at the proximity and what it meant. Then she dismissed the train of thought during the elevator ride up. She found her assigned office. Her ID badge opened the door to what seemed like an investigator's wonderland.

Zen sat at her new desk and gazed at the technology of her dreams. The razor-thin computer screen before her automatically adjusted to room lighting. Wireless devices had the ability to project graphs and maps into holographic three-dimensional images. But what thrilled Zen most was the access she'd been granted to additional classified data. So fascinated with her new toys, Zen failed to notice someone was at the other desk across the room. Loud throat-clearing caused her to finally drag her attention away from the monitor.

"Nice to see you again."

Tall with dark wavy hair and a sun-kissed brown complexion, Malone Ramirez wore a contained smile. He crossed to her with one hand extended. His dark-gray pinstriped suit had sleek lines that followed his toned body. He moved with grace, a cross between a dancer and a trained athlete. Or maybe an assassin, Zen mused. She tensed up the closer he got. Zen barely touched the manicured hand before she let go. The palm had been rougher than his appearance suggested. Underneath the polished exterior was a street solider.

"Is it really?" she replied and made a show of looking at her screen again.

"Just something to say. We can at least be polite since we're working together now. At least it's official this time." Malone perched on one side of her desk. "On the job already, huh? Making points with the boss."

"I'm getting familiar with the systems we'll be using, if you must know. But why am I explaining myself to you?" Zen asked rhetorically and continued to swipe the touch screen. She tapped a few links and pretended to read.

"Yeah, you don't usually answer to anyone. Like going around official channels to track my suspect to his home country." Malone picked up one of her glass paperweights shaped like a bird. He examined it and set it back down.

Zen used one hand to move it away from him, gaze still on the words before her. "You and your colleague wouldn't listen."

"Let's see, a social worker shows up from DC—"

"Correction," Zen cut in. "A trained investigator with seven years of experience and a recognized court expert in three jurisdictions so far. Add five years of experience in mental health diagnosis and treatment. I'm your senior professional." At thirty, Malone was four years younger than her.

Malone's tight smile relaxed a bit. "You don't look a day over twenty-five."

Zen gave him a side glance. Then she ignored him, her fingers gliding over the touch-sensitive wireless silicon keypad. Malone didn't move from her desk. She pointed to the opposite side of the room. "No wonder you needed help. You've lost your way in only a few feet of office."

"Good Wednesday morning to all of you. Unusual to start a journey midweek, but then we're not the usual unit." A leggy blond woman beamed at them from the open door. "I'm Hadley Truman, Mr. Anderson's assistant. You can call me Hadley, of course."

Zen and Malone both gazed at her without speaking. Her hair was in a ponytail that bounced as she talked. She appeared to be somewhere south of forty, but her skin didn't give away much more. Obviously, she invested in facials and the latest anti-aging tech. She had both hands in the pockets of her dark-gray slim skirt. Zen exchanged a look with Malone and then back at Hadley.

"Good morning," Zen replied, mentally adding Hadley to her list of research subjects.

"Nice to meet you." Malone flashed a handsome smile and walked to her.

Hadley's brisk professional façade faltered for a second. But then she recovered and shook his hand. "Agent Ramirez. Um, this arrangement is temporary until we're set up. Things moved rather quickly after last week."

"Last week?" Malone raised a dark eyebrow at her.

"You'll have a briefing shortly. Anyway, you'll have separate offices, more spacious is the good news." Hadley smiled widely as if she could take the credit for it. "Agent Ramirez, your office is right across the hall from Dr. Batiste."

Malone faced Zen with a mischievous gleam in his dark eyes. "Sounds great to me. I look forward to being Dr. Batiste's shadow."

"Hand-holding the youngster. I can cope. After all, I'm raising a teenager." Zen gave him a sub-zero glare.

Hadley blinked as she looked from Zen to Malone and back again. "Uh, I sense—"

Clive marched in with a grim expression. He cast a quick glance around the room. "Everybody getting settled in? Good. Let's head to the briefing room."

He turned around and left without waiting or expecting a reply or objections. Hadley darted off in the opposite direction. Zen brushed past Malone to follow their new boss. Malone's soft chuckle floated after her.

The conference room windows look out onto the 12^th Street NW. The thick insulated glass muffled sound from light traffic. Clive went to the head of an oval table that could seat up to ten people. Hadley slipped in the door and stood against the wall to their left. A panel slid up without a sound to reveal a screen.

"First on the agenda, let's kill the elephant in the room. I expect you two to put the past behind you." Clive stood, legs apart, and stared at Malone.

"I'm good with... everything." Malone glanced at Zen.

"You're going to be better than 'good,' Ramirez. Dr. Batiste turned out to be right about Navarro. Your boss missed the signs that a brilliant psychopath was working on the NASA team. She dismissed Dr. Batiste's credentials, didn't take her seriously, and two more people died." Anderson drilled home each point in a cool but relentless manner.

Malone winced at his candor. Then he sighed and nodded. "Facts."

Anderson faced Zen. "Don't gloat, doctor."

Zen's slight grin evaporated. "I didn't... I mean, I wasn't. Yes, sir."

"You missed signs that Navarro had figured out someone official was onto him. And didn't check after you were on the ground that he'd hadn't take a flight back to Spain. Agent Silva ended up in ICU." Anderson's tone piercing like his assessment.

"Well, if Special Investigations had been any help," Zen murmured and let the implication hang.

"And if you hadn't gone outside of official procedures..." Malone put in.

"So, what have we learned, class?" Anderson crossed his arms to stare from one to the other of them.

"Cooperation is job one, and egos must be checked. Mutual respect for expertise is vital to success," Hadley offered from her position at the sidelines.

"Dr. Batiste?" Anderson prompted with a sharp glance at her.

"I'll learn to play nice with others. Sir. And call me Zen."

Anderson swiveled to Malone. "Your turn, Ramirez."

Malone sighed. "Wasting time on turf battles is not just dumb, but dangerous. And for the record, I tried with my boss."

Zen's view of him softened a bit at the admission. "Thanks."

Anderson nodded and pressed a button on the remote. Text appeared on the screen. "Our small section is a new animal. We're doing background checks on potential space colonists and station staff."

"She'll do the psychology bit. I'll do the clearance legwork. Got it." Malone looked anything but enthusiastic."

"Wrong. We're trying to keep a killer from making outer space his hunting ground." Clive looked at them all in turn.

# Chapter 4

In the interest of building a sense of team, Malone and Zen accepted Hadley's lunch invitation. They sat in the DOJ main cafeteria with a view to the Federal Triangle courtyard. Hadley dug into her cheeseburger and fries; a surprising choice given her runway model figure.

"Hmm, the fries are better at the Undercover Burger Bar," Hadley said from behind her napkin. She dabbed her lips and sipped soda. She pointed to Zen's plate. "How's your chicken salad?"

"Better than expected," Zen admitted. She savored a forkful and nodded in appreciation.

"I hear the cook that makes it got the recipe from her Louisiana grandmother. I thought you'd appreciate it." Hadley grinned at her.

"I almost said there must be a Black woman in the kitchen, but I didn't want to sound biased," Zen joked and shared a giggle with Hadley.

"You wouldn't have offended me. Some of our best meals were cooked by the housekeepers that worked for us back home in Charleston. My grandmother had a photo album with pictures of them going back three generations." Hadley took a bite out of her hamburger and hummed in satisfaction.

"Old family, huh?" Zen drawled.

Hadley gazed at Zen for a few seconds, chewing as if it helped arrange her thoughts. "Yes, and before you ask, some of my ancestors did own slaves."

"I wasn't going to," Zen replied in a mild tone.

"My parents live in assisted living now, but growing up we had a housekeeping service. Owned by descendants of an enslaved woman. My great-grandfather loaned his grandfather the money to start it. I'm proud of that. Thank goodness we've left the past behind. Most of it anyway." Hadley frowned and went back to eating.

"You mean the nationalists," Zen said. Charleston was home to an active cell of the movement.

"Hmm," Hadley said around a mouthful of cheeseburger. Then she swallowed. "Luckily, they're still on the fringes."

"I've heard they want to get their fingers in the space commerce pie, especially mining," Zen replied.

"We're going to be alert for ties to American Heritage, one name they go by. That's the DC chapter of the larger organization National Interests First. Supposedly a think tank. But they're not on the menu right now, so to speak." Hadley giggled at her own pun.

Malone finished his spinach salad as they talked. "So, they're not a serious contender for causing hitches in the space program."

Hadley's thin mouth turned down at the corners. She shook her head. "Like Mr. Anderson said in our first meeting, we have bigger issues right now."

"Well, that wasn't dramatic at all," Malone replied. He grinned at Zen and then Hadley. "A killer stowing away on a spaceship? Sounds, I don't know...."

"Too much like pulp sci-fi," Zen replied with a crooked smile.

"Exactly." Malone pointed at her.

"You laugh, but think about it. What better way to escape justice? Six to twelve months or longer off the planet. You know the one thing that hasn't changed in all the decades of investigations." Hadley looked at them in turn.

"The chances of catching the perpetrator drops exponentially after as little as forty-eight hours," Malone said.

"Criminals have kept up with technology and advancements parallel with us. We're up against some of the smartest around." Hadley went back to her lunch.

"My daughter will be thrilled to hear I'm a space cop," Zen joked.

"She's almost seventeen, huh?" Malone looked at her.

"You know all my details, I'm sure. I'll bet you even know the brand of toothpaste I use." Zen gave him a frosty smile and dabbed her lips with a napkin.

"Peppermint gel by PowerSmile, with only natural ingredients." Malone's level tone sounded like a quintessential cop who'd done his homework.

"Listen, you—"

"We're on the same side, remember?" Hadley, seated between them, leaned forward like a referee.

"I saw the contents of your cosmetic bag this morning. It was on your desk, open. Your kit to freshen up during the workday, I assume." Malone smiled at Zen.

"Well, at least we know your powers of observation have improved," Zen shot back.

Hadley heaved a sigh. "Really, kids. You've got to get this sibling rivalry out of your systems. A boat doesn't go forward if each one is rowing their own way. There is no *I* in team."

Zen put down her fork. "Seriously, Hadley?"

"I'll spout any number of clichés if it stops you two from bickering and nipping at each other," she said. Hadley's cell phone chimed a tune and she stood. "Time to go."

"See you back at the office." Malone drank more cola.

"No, you'll see me *now* because you're coming, too. Boss wants us. The files have all transferred." Hadley dropped a tip on the table and marched off.

Malone looked at Zen as they stood at the same time. "Things are moving fast, huh?"

"A killer on the loose sounds like a reason to cut your lunch break short," Zen retorted and strode ahead of him.

"You buying it, though? I mean, seems a bit iffy. I skimmed the report. Two deaths at the training camp in Chile's El Valle de la Luna. Autopsies show their injuries could have been from accidental falls." Malone caught up and they were side by side. He spoke low as they walked.

"One of the victims had a puncture would," Zen countered.

Malone waited until they were alone on the elevator. "They were rock climbing and carrying sharp tools. He might have fallen on one, or hit it on the way down the cliff face."

They arrived at the tenth floor and got off. Zen considered Malone's arguments. Goddard Space Corp had set up a facility to get employees ready for deployment to their moon colony. The dry, rocky Atacama Desert resembled the moon's surface, a perfect setting to get used to conditions. Men and women worked in space suits needed for exploring and mining the lunar surface. Most trained at night when the hot temperatures dropped.

"Good cover for a murderer, I'd say," Zen said.

Anderson came around a corner. "Conference room in five minutes."

"Okay." Zen threw a look at Malone, who grinned back. She rolled her eyes and left before he could say anything.

They arrived back at the conference room. Zen paused when she spotted Bertice Illinois and a grim-looking man in uniform. Malone seemed to stand at attention for a few seconds. He nodded to the distinguished-looking Air Force officer, a four-star general. With nut-brown skin and close-cropped gray hair, Zen thought he looked familiar. He and Ms. Illinois spoke quietly in a corner. The sixty-inch thin-screen showed tiled pictures.

Ms. Illinois spoke up. "Introductions first. I'm sure you know General C.W. Newton. General Newton is head of the new International Space Corps."

"Yes, ma'am. An honor to meet you, sir," Malone said in a crisp military-like tone.

Charles Walton Newton was the first of three Black astronauts on the first Mars expedition. He'd been there for fourteen months in addition to the six-month trips to and from the planet. Zen's father would be impressed at the company she was keeping.

"Lieutenant," General Newton replied with a nod.

"Dr. Zenobia Batiste," Ms. Illinois said when the general turned his attention to Zen.

"Madrid," was Newton's terse response.

Zen gazed back at him with her best unbothered smile. "Nice to meet you."

"Hmm." General Newton glanced at Ms. Illinois.

"Go on, Clive," Ms. Illinois put in mildly.

Clive gave a voice command to the smart speaker on the conference table. The picture changed and a section of the moon's surface in HD appeared. "There's been a death at the Goddard Corporation's G-Colony One. Surveyor Site IV. A crew member didn't return from a foray to get more details on a crater."

"Damn it." The general glared at the image.

"I told you we waited too long to form this task force," Clive said.

"Once again, it could have been an accident," Ms. Illinois cut in smoothly before the general could reply. "At least we thought so at first. But there's evidence his space suit was sabotaged. Expert job, because their commander almost missed it."

"So, the killer knows we know. Which means no one on the moon is safe," Anderson said and faced the screen, hands behind his back.

"Two SFs were sent from NASA's outpost to Goddard's site. Other than them, no one is allowed in or out of the colony. Their spacecraft will transport the entire crew back to Earth in six days," General Newton said. Security Force officers, or SFs, were the Air Force version of military police.

"You have all of the files, maps of both colonies. The details have been uploaded to your tablets," Clive said to Malone and Zen. "Hadley is creating a database, spreadsheets, and charts as we speak. That way we'll have info organized."

Zen gasped at the image that faded into view on the large screen behind Clive. Silvery-white domed modular buildings appeared. They looked like half-buried tortoise shells. "Amazing. Astra would love this."

"Astra?" General Newton frowned at Ms. Illinois.

"Dr. Batiste has a teenage daughter interested in our global space program. Very gifted. I hear college scholarship offers are pouring in."

"Thank you, ma'am. A few, yes."

Zen's smile faltered when she realized the implication of Ms. Illinois's answer. Background checks were routine. Still, Zen felt unnerved at the easy way Ms. Illinois rolled out her personal details.

"Robert Goddard is livid. The secretaries of Commerce, Energy, Defense, and the White House are all growling as a result." General Newton's deep scowl implied he was taking the heat.

"We'll deal with the politicians," Ms. Illinois said with confidence. It seemed clear that the "we" she meant was outside of the room.

"Couldn't the SFs conduct interviews on-site, ma'am?" Zen asked.

"They've done preliminary questioning, but they're not trained homicide investigators. At least not at the level needed," Clive answered instead.

Ms. Illinois turned to Zen. "Because of the two deaths on Earth, the isolation of the lunar colony, a decision was made to evacuate. Safety first," Ms. Illinois said.

"The last man standing would be the obvious number-one suspect," Zen said.

"I don't think their families would support that method of solving the crime. Agreed?" Ms. Illinois replied.

"No, I didn't mean... I wasn't suggesting—" Zen cleared her throat. "Of course, we won't risk more murders."

"Goddard Corporation is not happy about shutting down their first colony. They were gearing up for G-Colony Two. The expense, not to mention the economic impact, will be high. Two years of work put on ice. Literally," General Newton grumbled.

"They're going to freeze bio samples and lower the temps inside their modular building to preserve some equipment. Tech developed just for lunar use," Ms. Illinois explained when both Zen and Malone looked puzzled.

"Classified work," General Newton said in a guarded voice with a glance at her.

"We suggested that Goddard Corporation clear the decks and send up a new crew," Ms. Illinois said smoothly without looking at him.

"But their other space-ready employees are the crew in Chile, where two other suspicious deaths have occurred." Zen gazed back at her.

"You see the problem." Ms. Illinois gave Zen a brief smile of approval. Her grim expression returned. "Goddard had a medical research team working on new treatments. A few with military applications."

"So, we're talking commercial, medical, and national security? Whew," Zen murmured.

"Exactly," Ms. Illinois replied.

"The details of which you folks don't need to know. With the evidence and face-to-face access to employees, you should be able to wrap up your investigation soon." General Newton stood. "We expect to get G-One running again in eight weeks, and that's all we're willing to concede. Weekly updates, Clive."

Clive stood to face him. "Yes, General."

"I'm told with the budget we approved your team will have advanced investigative tools on hand." General Newton studied Malone first and then Zen.

"They're imminently qualified," Clive replied. His answer seemed to continue a debate that had taken place before.

"Good. I better get back to the Pentagon."

General Newton shook hands with Clive. Then he gestured for Ms. Illinois to follow him, which she did. Clive let out a huff of air as if he'd been holding it in. He frowned at the door as it bumped shut behind them.

"How many people are we talking about, sir?" Zen asked.

"Call me Clive. No need to stand on formal titles." Clive turned to study the wide screen again. "Thirty from the Goddard lunar colony. Fifteen in Chile."

"Forty-five suspects, evidence from the moon, and a two-month deadline. No pressure," Malone said with a humorless laugh.

Ms. Illinois came back into the room. "Your department is a joint DOJ and NSA operation. Your focus is clearing up the deaths on the moon and the space training camp. You'll also review the psychological profiles and personal histories of those selected to staff the lunar colonies."

"Which is why Zen, I mean Dr. Batiste, is here." Malone looked at Zen.

"I'll let you get to it then. Clive, a few minutes, please." Ms. Illinois went to the door and waited.

"Check with Hadley and start. We'll meet Friday so I can look over your plan," Clive said and strode off to join Ms. Illinois.

"Plan?" Malone blinked at him.

"Yes, a plan, Malone. We're not going to jump in without one, not on a task of this magnitude," Clive spoke over his shoulder. "Hadley will give you the time based on my calendar."

He and Ms. Illinois left; their voices muted as they conferred. Zen wondered what details they'd left out. She sensed a heavy unspoken consequence to their success or failure to solve the crimes.

"We need more staff," Malone called out.

Hadley appeared in the doorway as if on cue to address his declaration. "We have three junior special agents in training assigned. They're in the large office. Your things have been moved to your individual ones."

"When did that happen?" Zen stood.

"While we were at lunch and you were in this meeting. We needed space for the new agents. Files have been uploaded. They're searchable. I worked until after midnight merging them into our database." Hadley yawned behind one had to confirm her long hours.

"I'll make us a fresh pot of coffee. Looks like we'll need it," Malone said as they followed Hadley from the conference room.

"Already done," Hadley said. "This is my assistant, Irina."

A small woman with pale skin, freckles, and bright auburn hair appeared from a small office. "Hello. I have three messages for you, ma'am."

"IT, making sure our wireless access is secure," Hadley explained to Malone and Zen before she bustled off. "Let us know if you need anything."

Malone watched the two women leave and then turned to Zen. "Well, where do we start?"

"There are several accepted tools used to create psychological profiles. I'll start charting those results to look for red flags, including if maybe any were missed," Zen said and headed for her office.

"Okay. I'll start with a list of persons of interest to interview. Those closest to our victims. Find out who had beefs with them, who benefited from their deaths, and work my way from there. A plan." Malone stood in Zen's office tapping a fist against his thigh.

"Include rationale. Explanations on which employees are likely not involved, that kind of thing."

Zen's tablet was docked so that it was connected to system. A slender wireless keyboard sat before it. Malone had the same setup in his office. She swiped right and the screen came alive. A list of alerts, all from Hadley, greeted her.

"We should meet tomorrow morning to compare notes. You can tell me if you think anyone should be added or deleted from my preliminary list," Malone replied.

"Good idea." Zen looked up at him.

"Don't sound so surprised," Malone retorted with a grin and strode off. "It's a date then. You, me, bagels, my office, nine o'clock."

"I'll bring the coffee," Zen called after him.

"Only if you're sure. I don't want to be accused of misogyny," Malone quipped as he walked off.

"Oh, shut up."

"You females are so touchy in the workplace," he said without looking back.

Zen laughed. "You'll pay for that crack, Ramirez."

Then she turned her attention back to her tablet. She already had an inbox of emails from Hadley and her new assistant. Zen took off her suit jacket, hung it up in the small closet near her desk, and sat. She heaved a sigh as she logged into the cloud. Hadley had sent directions on the new database and other files she'd created. Zen was relieved to find that the reports of other investigators were included. Malone's task of creating a list of interviewees would be less torturous. Zen settled in to read the psychological profiles. Three hours later, she stood to work stiffness out of her back and limbs. Her blue-light eyeglasses helped avoid eyestrain from staring at the screen for so long.

She walked to the window to gaze down at the street below. As she did stretches, her smartwatch trilled Astra's favorite childhood tune. Zen tapped a text message, went back to her stretches, and the tune played again. Astra admonished her once again that she wasn't a baby, and yes, she could start dinner. A knock came and Malone stuck his head in her door.

"Hey, how's it going for you?"

"Tedious. None of the psychological testers helped us out by writing 'murdering psychopath' in the margins," Zen joked.

Malone laughed and came into her office. "Hey, nice view. This your daughter?" He picked up a photo of Astra.

"One and only," Zen said.

"She's a beauty, and got brains like her mother. Lucky kid." Malone put the photo down.

"You?"

"Two boys," Malone grinned for a second, but then his expression dimmed. "They're with their mother in Fulton, right outside Baltimore."

"Divorce?" Zen blinked in surprise. His agency bio still listed his family status as married, so the breakup was recent.

"In process. You?" Malone sat in one of two visitor's chairs and propped a long leg on one knee.

"Four and half years ago. Thank God we're not the battling exes cliché," Zen said and continued to stretch. She rolled her shoulders to relieve tension in them.

"Yeah, like me and Kylie," Malone said with a grimace.

"Sorry, I didn't mean—"

"It's okay. We didn't just grow apart. We sort of exploded in different directions." Malone shrugged at the look Zen gave him.

"Breaking up is hell no matter how it goes. Jordan and I had our tough times, too."

Malone waved a hand. "Hey, I'm not whining. Things will smooth out in the end. Enough about me. Your dad is a legend."

"I'll be sure to tell him you said so. He'll love that younger agents even know who he is," Zen replied. "You still reading up on me, huh?"

"Don't act like you haven't done the same," Malone retorted.

"Okay, okay. I may have skimmed it a few times," Zen admitted. She kicked off her low-heeled pumps and ran in place. "All this sitting is not healthy, and I have a feeling we're in for a lot of it."

"Let's make a pact to stay in shape. We can bring workout clothes, take run or exercise breaks to bust out the kinks. Clive will let us use his shower." Malone stood and joined Zen in stretching.

"Clive has a shower? It's good to be the boss."

"He was gracious with General Newton today. Us career military guys forget that civilians don't have to shout 'how high, sir!' when we say jump."

"Clive's got the power, huh?"

"He doesn't have to flex in public. Dude is judicious about showing his hand. I'm guessing Newton knows it, too." Malone glanced at Zen as she rubbed her neck. "Here."

Before she realized it, Malone stood behind her. His wide hands kneaded her neck first and then shoulders. Zen stiffened for a few seconds, but he worked magic on the tight muscles. She relaxed into the movement of his fingers.

"You got a second job doing massages?" Zen murmured.

"I was a kinesiology major in college. Worked for some pro athletes to pay for undergrad and my bills. Thought about going to med school, like your ex," Malone said.

"Why didn't you?" Zen let out a long sigh when he stopped. Her skin tingled where his hands still rested on her elbows.

"Joined the Air Force instead. More exciting."

"Hey, you two. I was just..." Hadley's blue eyes twinkled as she studied them standing close together at the window.

Zen started for her desk and paused to look down at her feet. She'd taken off her pumps. She glanced up at Hadley, cleared her throat, and sat down at her desk. "Just taking a break."

"Hmm." Hadley lifted a honey-blond eyebrow at the explanation.

"What can we do for ya, Miss H?" Malone said with good humor.

"Just a heads up. You'll get a calendar update for a meeting with Mr. Anderson Friday at eight-thirty, sharp." Hadley continued to gaze at Zen.

"Thanks. I think we'll be available." Malone wore a relaxed grin as he sat on the edge of Zen's desk.

"If you know what's good for you," Hadley tossed back. She came just inside the threshold, arms folded. "I'm glad you took our little talk about getting friendly to heart."

"I know how to toe the line," Malone replied.

"We're learning to work as a team, yes. That's it." Zen pushed his hip until Malone slid off the desk.

"Yay team." Malone chuckled at the heated side glance from Zen.

"Hmm," was Hadley's only response before she left.

"Don't get any ideas. And stay off my desk," Zen snapped and jabbed a forefinger at Malone.

"What? People paid good money for a session with me. You got some for free."

"Hadley thinks... I don't want her telling Clive I'm an unprofessional, love-starved divorcee." Zen huffed out a breath.

"One thing you're not is unprofessional. As for the other part..." Malone's dark eyebrows went up almost to his hairline.

"Don't even," Zen warned, her voice pitched low and dangerous.

"Fine. I'll set the record straight with her. Stop the gossip before it stops," he replied.

"Gossip? What gossip?"

"You know, that I think you're hot and you feel the same about me."

"Are you—" Zen sputtered, unable to find words.

"You don't think I'm hot? I mean, c'mon. Look at the goods!" Malone did a complete circle, arms out. His chiseled physique showed through the tailored fit of his dress shirt and slacks. His thin leather belt accentuated a trim waistline.

"You're okay. Just not my type," Zen retorted.

Malone staggered back, one hand on his chest. "You wound me, lady."

"Sorry I'm not overwhelmed by your charm. Look, to be clear, we're working together. My dad always said, don't shit where you live."

"Comparing me to a turd? Okay, now that's just damn cruel!"

"You know what I mean."

"Peace. I've got the message. And for the record, I wasn't trying anything with you," Malone replied.

"Good. Because you're more like the younger brother I never wanted," Zen joked.

"Little brothers love to harass their big sisters. I kinda like that dynamic even more."

"Keep it up and I'll whip your butt, kid," Zen shot back.

"I think you just might be able to make good on that threat. Hey, you know what this means?" Malone said, his hand on the doorknob.

"Yeah, what?"

"No more magic massages. You gonna miss these delightful digits!" Malone held up both hands and wiggled his fingers.

"Out." Zen yelled and threw one of her stress balls at him. She smiled at his playful laughter on the other side of the door.

LATER THAT EVENING Zen got a real surprise. Jordan arrived at six-thirty for dinner. Without Minji. Astra had invited him, and whispered an assurance to Zen that she hadn't excluded Minji on purpose. Zen didn't question the circumstances. She accepted it as a natural end to their father-daughter day. Astra and Jordan went over her schoolwork and talked college choices. Zen cooked grilled salmon, roasted potatoes, and broccoli with cheese sauce. All their favorites. She even managed to find yeast rolls in the freezer. Seated around the wide kitchen island, they talked about a variety of subjects over dinner. Zen enjoyed the obvious delight Astra had at being with her father.

"Well, daddy, I have to put the finishing touches on my paper for tomorrow and get to bed. Volleyball after school, so I need my beauty rest." Astra slid from the stool and planted a kiss on Jordan's cheek. "Thanks for everything today."

Jordan stood and wrapped Astra with both arms. "You're not seven anymore. I think your mama will let you stay up a little later."

"You two need time to discuss me while I'm out of the room. Enjoy." Astra glanced from Jordan to Zen with a wide smile. Then she bounced out of the room like she had as a little girl.

Jordan blew her a kiss and turned to Zen, a palm on his midsection. "Dinner was delicious. A nice break from restaurant food. What?" he said at the look Zen gave him.

Zen shook her head. She picked up their empty plates "You know what that's about."

He gathered the glasses and stacked the two empty serving bowls. Then he joined her as Zen loaded the dishwasher. "Enlighten me, dear."

"And don't let her hear you calling me that. Not to mention Minji," Zen drawled.

"Minji knows you and I are on good terms. I'm not going to pretend we're enemies to make her feel secure," Jordan blurted out with a scowl.

"Whoa, sounds like that was a convo at some point."

Jordan blew out a long breath. "Sorry to dump on you."

"I'm guessing the subject came up again on this trip."

"Yeah. But forget about that. What did you mean about Astra not getting any ideas?" Jordan leaned against the counter.

Zen programmed the smart appliance using the digital controls. Then she faced him. "Astra still has hope that we'll remarry. She planned our second wedding three years ago." Zen nodded at the look of astonishment on Jordan's face.

"Damn!"

"She had a digital scrapbook with my dress picked out, flower arrangements, the works. I found it on her tablet computer. We had a talk. Astra said she understood that Mom and Dad could love her even if we weren't married. Guess what she said."

"I won't even try," Jordan replied.

"She was thinking about our future happiness. She remembered how we enjoyed touching and kissing so much." Zen laughed when his eyes got even bigger.

"You don't think she walked in on us while we were—"

"If so, she wasn't traumatized, so relax."

"Jeez, I don't even want to think about it." Jordan gave a shudder.

Zen burst into laughter and slapped his shoulder. "The point is, even amicable breakups affect kids. She'd like us all under one roof again, even if she's going away to college."

"We raised a caring, amazing kid. Good job."

"We did." Zen grinned and they shared a fist bump.

"I'm gonna miss my sprout." Jordan sighed.

"When do you leave?" Zen went to the island with a microfiber cloth and wiped it down.

Jordan followed and took it from her to finish the job. "We leave Friday morning."

"Good trip, I take it. For both of you." Zen held up the coffeemaker. When he nodded, she retrieved a gourmet blend. "I'll make you a double chocolate latte. Our dessert."

"I'll say one final goodnight to our girl and be back." Jordan hung up the towel and started off when his wristwatch buzzed. "Sheesh, I forgot to unmute. Three messages from Minji."

"I'm not trying to get in your business but..." Zen pointed to his wrist.

"I know, I know. Hey, you're making it hard." Jordan walked back to Zen.

"I'm not in it, sir." Zen held up both palms.

"You're beautiful, smart, and famous for catching a murderer. Plus, you and I created a wonderful human being."

"Being perfect is so much work." Zen heaved a sigh.

Jordan laughed, then grew serious again. "So, I've been giving Minji space to adjust. I was planning a trip to DC alone. She got on the program of this conference when a colleague cancelled last minute." Jordan sat on a bar stool at the island.

Zen sat next to him and put a hand on his thigh. "I hope you can make it work, Jordan. I do."

"Me, too."

Jordan patted her hand. Then he slid from the stool and disappeared down the hallway to Astra's room. Zen put away extra salmon she'd take for lunch the next day. Then she packed healthy snacks for Astra. Ten minutes later Jordan returned to the kitchen. He arrived just as she finished their lattes.

"Fixing snacks for her like she was little, eh?"

Zen poured both cups full, spooned on the whipped cream, and sprinkled cinnamon on top. "She grumbled at first, but she has a high resting metabolism. Between sports, band, and dancing to pop tunes, she'd lose weight without them."

"She still loves karaoke and techno K-pop, huh?" Jordan grinned.

"My father did me the great favor of introducing her to the hip-hop genre. They've reached back into the nineteen-nineties music archives."

"One hundred years of Black American music. Sounds good to me."

"Then you don't know what hearing it for hours does to the nerves. Earbuds don't do the beat justice, she says. She likes the way it makes surfaces vibrate. And she and her best friend can choreograph better when it's blasting from speakers."

"Ouch, I can only imagine. I still miss having her just a room away though," Jordan murmured. "She's grown up so fast."

"Time marches forward, Dad. We're gettin' old," Zen joked and sipped latte.

Jordan followed her lead. After a swallow, he hummed his approval. "Girl, you still make the best double chocolate with whipped cream ever."

"Thank you, sir. Leave a generous tip." Zen grinned at him. His watch buzzed again and she raised an eyebrow at him.

He shook his head and tapped a short message out. Then he looked at Zen. "How was your first day at the new job?"

"Interesting, but nothing exotic. Why, you found out something?"

"I tried, but even my NSA pal was really cautious about the subject. Seems it's seriously sensitive. So, I switched tactics. Used my NASA and Pentagon contacts." Jordan finished his cup and put it down.

"And?"

"All they'd tell me was Anderson is in charge of fixing a problem with the private lunar colonies. I met him; you know—the boy genius Robert S. Goddard. Full of brilliant ideas and big plans."

Zen knew Goddard's background. His father and grandfather passed on fortunes to the younger generation. His ancestor, Robert H. Goddard, was a physicist who built and launched the first liquid-propellant rocket in 1926. Young Robert showed his genius early. While his peers were getting drunk at frat parties on yachts, Robert hung out in labs. By the age of twenty-three he'd patented three inventions. His use of satellites, launched by Goddard Corp., had revolutionized computer science and security. Combined with block chain tech, Goddard Corp. locked down dominance in the field.

"Let me guess, another arrogant billionaire born with all the advantages and thinks he's entitled to more."

"Actually, he was pretty personable when I met him. Like a kid excited to meet real astronauts. My boss says he's not bad to deal with, until he's told no."

"A word I'll bet he didn't hear much growing up in multiple mansions around the world," Zen said.

"His father's favorite. So yeah." Jordan took both now-empty cups to the sink and rinsed them.

Zen smiled at the easy way they'd fallen into old domestic habits. Dinner, him tucking in Astra, cleaning up after. Minji must have sensed the in-sync vibe between them. She decided not to remark on it, though. No need to complicate things.

"So, what did you find out?" Zen asked.

Jordan dried the cups, a frown on his handsome face. He hung them on the hooks of her decorative carousel. "That's it. Which is strange."

"Some operations are strictly need-to-know," Zen said.

"C'mon, Zen. We both have clearance." Jordan dried his hands on the towel and hung it up. He faced her with his arms folded. "You can trust me."

"It's not a matter of trust, J. You know how it works." Zen pointed a finger at him.

"Yeah, yeah. Some things I can't tell you and vice-versa, but..." Jordan rubbed his strong jaw, still frowning.

"No putting each other on the spot by asking too many questions."

"Unless it affects our family, and I'm beginning to suspect this might," Jordan replied.

"That's a stretch. I'm making sure people chosen are mentally suitable for the unique conditions of a space colony. Glorified human resources screening, really," Zen said.

"Nothing else going on?" Jordan looked down at her with a stern expression. "We know each too well. There's more. Wait a minute, those deaths on Goddard's first colony. They're gearing up for a the second one. They weren't accidents after all."

"I'm not saying—"

"Your specialty is forensic sociology, how crime affects communities. And..." Jordan tilted his head to one side as he gazed at Zen. "You showed up two investigative departments by catching a serial killer. Now you're assigned not long after two deaths."

"Jordan..." Zen shook her head.

He took his phone out, tapped the screen, and read. Zen started to speak, but he held up a palm to shush her. "Someone died at the Goddard space training camp in Chile. Too many accidents."

"There's no evidence yet that the deaths weren't accidental. That's what we're going to find out."

"We're both in high-risk jobs now."

"I'm strictly on desk duty now. No more chasing killers. I promise." Zen raised a hand as if taking an oath.

"I could be going to the moon in another year—or one of the space stations. You're tracking the first extraterrestrial murder suspect. On the lunar colony."

"I'll stick to being on the sidelines. No risky field work. Astra needs one of us if anything happens," Zen replied.

"Hell no. She needs both us. I'll see what I can find out within NASA. I've never been comfortable with giving so much control to private space companies." Jordan started to continue when his watch buzzed insistently.

"This conversation to be continued?" Zen gestured at it.

"For sure." Jordan gave her a quick hug and left.

Zen considered his points as she gave voice commands to activate her home's smart system. Her coffee pot was set up to brew. Their wake-up calls and the outside floodlights were preprogrammed, so no need to set them. Then Zen glanced at the panel again. They lived in a safe, quiet, upscale community with regular police patrols. She rarely set the security system. Zen gazed at the control panel as Jordan's words echoed.

"I'm probably being overly cautious, but…" Zen murmured to herself as she entered the activation code.

# Chapter 5

Thursday morning dawned gray and cold. Zen dressed in layers. She put on a dove-gray dress shirt, dark-blue sweater and matching blue slacks. Her favorite pea coat completed her chosen outfit. Astra's day started later, so their roles reversed and daughter sent mother off on her day. Only after Zen made her swear not to leave the door open. Astra had developed the habit when she was expecting Loni to give her a ride. Zen fussed at herself for letting Jordan's grim warning affect her still.

Zen used her bio-synced ID sequence to enter the building. An app in her agency-issued smartwatch, it only worked if she was wearing it. Each wearer's unique skin surface pattern, heartbeat, and body chemistry were synced to the device. A second screening by guards was quick. Zen stared at the app as she rode the elevator up. Having one for her home would be pretty darn cool, she mused. If only she had a cool extra thirty thousand dollars lying around. Then shook her head at the paranoia that had taken root.

"Thanks, Jordan," Zen mumbled.

"You're on time."

Zen jumped at the voice just over her shoulder. "Damn, you move around like the invisible woman."

"Just one of my superpowers," Hadley joked. She strolled beside Zen, holding a purple glass water bottle. "Digging up info even the best special agents can't find is another."

"I'll keep it in mind."

"Don't even think about it, Zen." Hadley tilted her head down to gaze over her eyeglasses.

Zen paused outside her office after opening the door halfway. "Why whatever do you mean?"

"I prefer playing by the rules. If the day comes that you decide to go off the grid again, don't expect *me* to join you." Hadley's soft tone had just the hint of a distinct Southern burr.

"You should help out a fellow Southern girl," Zen teased with a crooked grin.

"You grew up in DC and Maryland."

"Summers down south count. Despite what you may have heard, I'm a team player. All the way." Zen shrugged out of her coat and tugged her sweater into place.

"Hmm."

"Again, with the cynical attitude. I'm hurt." Zen affected a fake sad face.

Hadley laughed. "Maybe I'm not old enough to be your mother, but take my advice. Don't cross Clive."

"I like Clive, and he listens to me." Zen avoided the taboo of bad-mouthing her old boss. Besides, Spaulding's shortcomings were well known.

"Don't let his kindly uncle demeanor fool you. Clive can be ruthless when necessary." Hadley's playful smile faded.

Zen's skin prickled at the ominous subtext. She gazed back at Hadley. "Duly noted and saved in my permanent file."

"Good."

"And you look ten years younger than your age. You must be filling that water bottle from the fountain of youth." Zen tapped the touch screen of her docked tablet.

"Just sensible skincare. New data uploaded in time for your meeting with Malone. You've got just enough time to review it." Hadley smiled and waved bye before vanishing.

Zen stared at the empty place where Hadley had just stood. Then she shook her head and sat to begin reading. One hour later she joined Malone in his office. He looked tired and harassed already.

"Morning." Malone covered his yawn with one hand.

"Partying on a school night is not a good idea, Malone. You're young, but you ain't that young," Zen joked.

"Ha-ha." He stood and stretched. "What the hell is it about turning thirty? Ten seconds after midnight on your birthday you feel old."

"Don't shop for reading glasses and a rocking chair just yet. Anyway, being newly single can go to your head. Slow it down." Zen sat in the chair facing his desk.

"Damn, they left psychic out of your bio," Malone said with a laugh. "And anyway, why would you assume—"

"You're lonely, reasonably attractive..."

"Hey!" Malone crossed his arms.

"Just pace yourself is all I'm sayin'."

"Personal experience?" Malone raised both eyebrows at her.

Zen looked down at the tablet computer in her hands. "We've got a heavy load and a deadline. You'll need your beauty sleep to keep up with me," Zen tossed back.

"Neat sidestep. Okay, fine. And for the record, I was up late talking to my soon-to-be ex-wife." Malone's square jaw tightened.

"Oh." Zen didn't have to ask. "Talking" probably meant arguing.

"Yeah. Anyway, on to a lighter topic. Murder."

"Maybe, maybe not. Anyway, I didn't see any major red flags in the psychological screening results." Zen swiped to the right to get the chart she'd made. "A few yellow ones, but nothing screamed a potential for violence."

"They're not likely to say, 'Yeah, doc. I think about beating folks with a blunt object every now and again.' I have a hard time putting much stock in those kinds of tests."

"They're more sensitive than you think. Multiple items pick up subtleties. Skillful interviews combined with questionnaires make them effective tools," Zen replied.

"Humph. I made a list of Goddard employees with minor criminal arrest records. Nothing big. A few were from juvenile records. Mostly property crimes like identity theft, minor drug dealing." Malone swung his screen around so Zen could see it.

"Juvenile records are sealed." Zen leaned forward to peer at the names of twenty-two men and women.

"Not to us. Anyway, I think these people are a good place to start. I say we interview the last seven at the end. They worked directly with the victims more closely than the rest." Malone tapped the screen with a forefinger.

"Why?"

"Let them get a bit anxious wondering about what's coming. We'll keep it simple, the basics the first round. Then call these seven in first on a second round."

"Okay with me," Zen agreed.

"Hadley is doing an even deeper dive for info. Our two agents-in-training reviewed security video from both camps. I gave them a list of things to look out for, like accessing locked storage more than needed for their jobs; anything that looks suspicious."

"I'm going to assume they'd be too smart to get caught on video, Malone," Zen said dryly.

"Probably, but with emotional crimes people slip up. It's worth a look."

"For sure. We'd be nuts not to. Hmm." Zen looked at her tablet then back at his screen.

"See something? Please tell me you've solved it already. Then I can get back to my regular life." Malone clapped his palms together as if praying for a miracle.

"Like it's gonna be that easy," Zen retorted. Then she leaned forward again to show him her tablet display. "Every one of the seven are on my list of yellow flags. Of course, a few more who aren't in your group have them. But it's giving me pause."

Malone sighed as he gazed at the list. "Great."

"It narrows our focus. Which is good news, I think. What?" Zen gazed at his long-faced expression.

"We should go to Chile to investigate and interrogate on-site." Malone rubbed his forehead.

"Makes sense. Oh, not a great time for you to leave," Zen said when she noticed his grim expression.

"Kylie's main complaint was me being gone from the kids a lot. At this stage she'll use it as ammunition when it comes to custody and visitation." Malone leaned his head back to stare at the ceiling as if answers were there.

"I could go alone. I mean, we could tell Clive we're dividing up to save time," Zen offered.

"First, Clive will see through that thin explanation. Second, you know the team approach on-site will be more effective. And in the long run, more efficient."

"Um, yeah. We can check each one, compare observations of facts, non-verbal reactions, and have each other's backs." Zen nodded. All important assets in such an unusual investigation.

"Plus, it's harder for suspects to manage obfuscation when more than one interviewer is there to watch." Malone smoothed down his silk tie and shrugged. "Gotta be done, partner."

"Agreed. What are you going to tell your wife?" Zen went back to studying her computer monitor.

"Ex-wife. That this is a career-making assignment and she'll be able to hit me up for more alimony," Malone said with a snort.

"I suggest you keep that as a joke and not actually *say it*," Zen replied with a side glance at him.

"Damn, you've gotten to know me too well already. Best get back to work." Malone stood.

"Yeah. Hey, let me know if I can do anything with the load." Zen studied him.

Malone had his special agent game face on again. "Don't worry. I'm not going to get distracted by personal drama."

"I didn't mean... You're right. I won't worry. You learned to read me fast, too." Zen shook her head with a half-smile.

"I think we're going to make a great team and crack this mutha fast. I'll get a big promotion, send my boys to the best private colleges, and live happily ever after." Malone flash a cocky grin.

Zen laughed as she gazed up at his six-foot-one frame. The cool confidence combined with his smooth good looks equaled drop-dead gorgeous. She predicted he'd add a sexy new wife to complete his recovery fairly soon.

"From your lips to God's ears, my child," Zen quipped and went back to the data. His jaunty whistle as he left made her laugh again.

FRIDAY MORNING ARRIVED bright and cold. Too cold for Zen. Bundled up in layers once again, this time a thick red turtleneck sweater over dark-gray slacks, she was the first to arrive in the conference room. She wrapped both hands around her paper cup of hot coffee. Her maternal grandparents in Louisiana had gotten Zen hooked on café au lait. In Spain, she loved café con leche. She sipped and thought about Nino. He'd texted her updates on his recovery, for which she was grateful. And guilty. He wouldn't be enduring physiotherapy if she hadn't pulled him into her unofficial case. Malone strode in looking rested. He winked at her as he sat across the table.

"Morning, beautiful." Malone wore tailored black wool slacks, a dove-gray shirt, and a red-wine silk tie. He looked fit and ready for action.

Hadley arrived a few seconds later. She moved with brisk efficiency to get the equipment ready. She synced her tablet with the television. "Morning, everyone. I took the information you sent me this morning and voila."

The digital whiteboard came alive with a highlighted summary of the plan Zen and Malone had developed. She had the names of staff they prioritized to interview first on a table. Their names were on the first column. The top cells listed attributes that explained why they were persons of interest above all others.

"All have the physical capability of causing the injuries sustained by the victims. So, I didn't need to consider that." Hadley stood looking at her work, hands resting on her slim waist.

"Yep. The oldest members of the crew are in their mid-forties, and they're in good shape. I checked their medical evals. Goddard is thorough," Malone added.

Hadley nodded, her gaze still on the list. "They've got a mixture of people that makes sense. There are veteran workers to put the brakes on youthful enthusiasm that might spell trouble. The younger members will push the old guys to innovate, see beyond what they know. "

"Hmm, you're making me feel like one of the 'old guys.' Some of the trainees are fresh out of school. A handful are under twenty-five," Malone said as he swiped through the tablet screen in his hand.

"The youngest three are twenty, twenty-one, and twenty-three. All exceptional kids who've been in space training since they were barely in their teens. Astra would love to be out there with them." Zen joined Hadley in staring at the screen.

Astra had been straining at the leash to be in of the specialized high schools for such training. Space mining and colonies had become viable in the past thirty years. For her daughter and the youngest Goddard crew members, a career in astronautics as a choice was normal. Even at her age, Zen barely remembered a time when manned space exploration was more science fiction than fact. Permanent colonies on distant planets had been considered within reach during her childhood.

"The new hot profession," Hadley said.

Clive marched in holding a thick folder. He dropped it on the polished wood surface of the conference table. "Morning, everyone. You people look far too rested to have something for me."

"We're ready, sir," Malone replied.

"Just kidding. I had no doubt you'd deliver," Clive said, his back to them as he regarded the whiteboard.

Zen and Malone exchanged an amused glance. Clive's response implied there would be dire consequences otherwise. He was a man used to having his instructions obeyed to the letter.

"As you can see, the employees with opportunity because they shared duties with the victims are cross-referenced with possible motives," Hadley spoke up.

"We've already checked flights to Chile. We'll hire a local company to drive us out into the Atacama Desert. It's the driest nonpolar desert on Earth. Great place to get a crew ready for the moonscape," Malone added.

"Yes. NASA has done space rover tests there for years. The terrain is an almost perfect replica of conditions on the moon and Mars. Goddard builds equipment out there, too. Mining and life-support gear that can withstand dust and lack of moisture." Clive faced them with his arms crossed. "When do you leave?"

"We haven't booked yet. We wanted to make sure you would sign off on the travel and our plan," Malone replied.

"That you need to go to Chile is a given. Make the arrangements." Clive gave a sharp nod and turned back to the television.

"I'll do it once we leave the meeting," Malone said.

Hadley's forefinger tapped the screen of her ten-inch iPad. "Done. You sent me the flight details, hotels, and contact for the transport company. I've confirmed. The agency payment app for expenses on the ground are on smartwatches."

Malone blinked at her. "Okay, then, we fly out Sunday. Monday morning, we drive to the camp. Did you pack my favorite jammies, too?"

"Very funny," Hadley replied, her tone as dry as the desert they'd see in a few days.

"Any theories of the crime yet?" Clive said, cutting into the light banter before it could take root. "I know it's early. Still, first thoughts, please."

"Given the isolation of both places, personal conflicts or even work rivalries seem logical. Goddard is one of three global companies that have a successful private space program," Zen said.

"And they're at the top of those three, which is damn impressive," Malone put in.

"Exactly. So, there's a lot of money to be made. Or to develop a new process or product. Millions in salary, compensation, stock options," Zen added.

"Job competition as a motive for murder?" Hadley's slender nose wrinkled into a skeptical expression.

"Not just a job. Fortunes will be made. A global reputation and influence with powerful governments. And the business world," Malone said. "People kill for less. Way less."

"Point made," Hadley replied quietly.

"A space colony, or camp in the middle of a desert, is like a small town. Small irritations can rub raw when you can't get away from others. Seeing the same people twenty-four seven for months." Zen looked at her tablet as she spoke. She swiped the screen to scan her summaries.

"Your dissertation on theories of social interactions in extraterrestrial colonies, closed societies," Clive said.

"That's part of it." Zen looked up at him. "Criminal behavior springs from three basic factors: social, psychological, and biological. We're in new territory when it comes to space. How does being on an alien world affect all three? Basically, the colonists are beta tests. We owe it to them, morally and ethically, to anticipate negative psychological and sociological consequences."

"We have data on how the body and brain are affected by months in space." Hadley looked at her tablet.

"Not nearly enough. Remember what happened on the first Mars colony," Zen replied as she continued to read.

Hadley tapped the screen of her own tablet. "I pulled six scholarly articles of interest for you. Check your inbox."

Zen nodded. "They didn't mention Mars. The researches who wrote them are the top experts, so if they've had access to—"

"Classified," Clive broke in.

Malone looked from Clive to Zen with a frown. "Sounds like we need to know what happened on Mars. Or at least the rest of us, since you and Zen seemed to have the story."

"Yes, how do you know?" Clive rumbled as he sat down next to Zen.

"The reports were given to me two years ago after their classification was lowered, which meant I was authorized. Right now, I'm the only forensic sociologist and social worker studying the field. I was asked to do a postmortem on the incident," Zen said smoothly. She met his gaze without blinking.

"Hmm." Clive thumped his blunt fingertips on the smooth surface of the conference table.

Zen had practiced, with coaching from her father, how to answer the question. If Clive was as much in the know as she suspected, then he had more details. James Batiste used his influence to get his daughter the information she wanted. He hadn't broken any laws or agency regs. Technically. Zen's analysis became a guide for preparing future space colonists and space crews. Including how to screen applicants.

"Then we can discuss the Mars colony 'incident' as you call it, the aftermath, and Dr. Batiste's findings," Hadley said. She pivoted her chair to face their boss.

"Yeah," Malone put in.

Clive looked up to find three sets of shrewd gazes studying him. He pulled out his own mini-tablet. After almost three minutes of tapping in codes and login verification, the television monitor brought up a grainy image. Three domed modular buildings formed a triangle on the surface of Mars. Two space rovers sat parked in the middle of their makeshift courtyard. Other equipment was visible.

"General Newton and Bob Evans were the survivors. Two other crew members had issues. One medical. The other..." Clive's voice trailed off. He stood to stare at the buildings. They gave no clue of the chaos that months in space had caused.

"But wait a minute. All four returned." Malone looked at Zen. "There were celebrations. NASA officials gave interviews."

"But only two of the astronauts talked to the media," Hadley said. She stared at Clive. "At the time, it didn't seem strange. Newton, who wasn't a general yet, and Evans were the commanders."

"No way. Not even the NSA could have hidden the fact that four people left and only two came back," Malone blurted out.

"The two had no close family connections, part of the reason they were selected. AI simulations could have provided video of them had it been necessary," Zen said.

"How do you know—" Clive heaved a sigh and waved a hand. "Never mind. Kenya Orji suffered a brain aneurysm and died within three months after their return. In a secure psychiatric facility."

"She stabbed the other crew person, El Haddad, in a fit of rage over coffee. Their conflict had been building for months. First, they were lovers, then estranged, and finally..." Zen shook her head. "The truth was concealed because El Haddad had a husband. She would have lost face and honor had her bisexuality become public."

"This isn't the nineteenth century." Hadley blinked at Zen.

"Many deeply held customs endure, Hadley. Thousands of years of tradition don't disappear so easily," Zen replied. "Anyway, crew member Orji injured General Newton as well when he intervened in the attack. Unfortunately, Haddad didn't survive the return trip."

"Her husband was content to let her simply disappear?" Hadley looked at Clive for the answer.

"As Zen said, they didn't have close family connections. He'd been somewhat estranged from his family because they'd never accept Haddad," Clive replied.

"She was from a low caste in Pakistan, and her skin too dark," Zen said with a grimace. "Yes, colorism has also endured. Her obituary twenty years later was accurate, except for the date she died."

"But—"

"They reported their divorce a year after the crew returned. Her husband remarried and had children. Haddad wasn't an important member of the crew. Newton got most of the glory. He earned it, though. That part isn't fake," Zen said.

"None of it is *fake*, Dr. Batiste," Clive said in a sharp tone. "For reasons of security and the future of the space program, the details remain classified."

"Damn, that was a well-planned scrub," Malone murmured and rubbed his jaw. "And thorough. I gotta give it to NASA. Thirty-two years later and no loose ends."

"Except a doctoral student with a father high up in intelligence and global space authority circles," Clive said.

"NASA is preparing for a second trip to Mars," Malone put in before anyone else could answer. He grinned when they all turned to him. "I do know a little something. NASA and the Air Force have a timetable for another Mars expedition. Eighteen months from now if there are no glitches."

Hadley looked at Zen. "Hopefully, we've learned from the experience?"

"Better protocols for preparation have been developed since. Biological and psychological postmortems gave clues. Provisions for simulated Earth sunlight, plants, even insects and birds have been added."

"Birds and bugs? Interesting," Malone said, sounding anything but.

"Our ecosystem is intricate in function. Not that I'm an expert, but yes. Birds and bugs play a role in nature," Zen replied.

"Bees are necessary for a variety of crops. Birds control insects and carry seeds. Dead insects provide material for topsoil," Hadley added. "Biology major before I joined the diplomatic service. I advised several countries on agriculture."

"In Situ Resource Utilization is key. That means create oxygen, food, and other resources in the environment using what's there. With the right equipment and supplies from Earth, colonists could generate what they need. Provide what's missing on the planet. Even a few familiar things like plants, trees, even bugs, the better it is for mental health. Seven months to Mars, then twelve months or more there before you leave. Living on an alien planet added to being stuck with the same people all the time. Very stressful even for the most healthy or stable mind." Zen gave them a very condensed version of theories on long-term space mental health.

"Especially if you don't like your neighbors," Malone joked.

"I enjoy your simple sense of humor," Zen shot back with a grin.

"Ouch." Malone pretended to be in pain.

Clive's solemn frown hadn't been eased by their levity. "The training camp just may be a case of accidental deaths. Nothing sinister or no pattern linked to the deaths on the lunar colony."

"Are there reasons to think there is? A pattern, I mean," Zen said.

"That's what we're going to find out." Clive looked at Malone and then at Zen.

"I think, 'Yes, sir, we sure will' is the right answer," Malone said.

"As usual, Ramirez, your military training comes in handy." Clive stood. "Keep me updated."

"Will do, sir." Hadley stood but didn't follow him out.

Zen stared at the place their boss at stood a second ago. "Your military training to follow orders. A subtle message that I better not... innovate, so to speak."

"Indeed," Hadley said in a dry voice. "As you can see, the stakes are huge."

Malone let out a soft whistle. "This isn't as routine or boring as I thought."

"TWO EVENINGS WITHOUT Minji," Zen whispered aside to Jordan as they stood at the stove. He'd come over for dinner again. They'd extended their stay and would fly back to Houston Saturday.

"Don't read into it. She had a thing with two top researchers at NIH. A business dinner. I begged off. She understood." Jordan spooned mixed vegetables into a serving bowl.

"You two conspiring against me again?" Astra called out as she set out napkins and silverware for them. Then she approached to get glasses from a cabinet. "Hey, let's have wine."

"No alcohol," Jordan said, using his 'that's final' dad voice.

"Almost seventeen. Anyway, I can wait. Plenty of time to party like it's 1999," Astra walked back to the kitchen island with a sassy swing of her hips.

"What?" Jordan blinked at Zen, waiting for an explanation.

"Her grandparents are sharing vintage Black music from the twentieth century. Prince. *Purple Rain*? '1999' is the name of one of his big hits. When kids were partying at the end of the twentieth century." Zen shook her head at the expression on his face.

"Who?"

"Prince, Jordan. Sheesh, didn't your parents teach you *any* Black history?"

"Harriet Tubman, the Civil Rights Movement, the fight for the federal Reparations Act of 2045. Not party songs." Jordan shrugged.

"Daddy was too busy studying and playing sports, keeping in shape for the big game," Astra called out. She giggled when he gave her an exaggerated scowl.

"I was cool. Ask your mother. Go on, defend me." Jordan poked Zen in the side with an elbow.

Zen brushed his arm away. "Your bookish nerdism is what I liked about you the most, Jordan. No need to be ashamed of it."

"Girl, you better quit. I had my share of fun and—" Jordan broke off. He joined Astra and put the dish of lasagna on the kitchen island. "Wait a minute, I was set up. I won't tell you stories about me partying hard in college."

Astra affected her best wide-eyed innocent kid expression. "I wasn't doing any such thing."

"You, heart of my heart, will concentrate on your studies. End of discussion." Jordon jabbed a forefinger at her nose. When she scrunched up her face, he laughed and kissed her forehead.

"Hey, D-Day put out a remix called 2099. You know how my generation will party when the twenty-second century arrives. We might be toasting with champagne on a space station, Mars, or even farther out." Astra smiled. She looked at her father and nudged him. "Speaking of long trips..."

Jordan cleared his throat. "Astra says you'll be going out of the country on business, huh?"

"And speaking of conspiracies," Zen retorted.

"I figured he'd need time to get my plane ticket," Astra replied. She gave great attention to cutting up lasagna for all three plates.

"Hmm." Zen squinted at Jordan.

"Instead of giving Loni's mom an early heads up, she wanted to give me one. Astra can come home with me."

"I see," Zen said and transferred her scrutiny to Astra.

"I have four vacation days saved up. We can have one hell of a father-daughter visit. She can teach me all about Prince and *Red Rain*." Jordan winked at Astra.

"Groan. Purple *Rain*, Daddy. Sheesh." Astra performed the classic teen girl eye roll.

"Whatever. I can give her a tour of the new launch facility."

"I thought it was a restricted area," Zen said. With global competition in the space industry, governments and private companies weren't above espionage.

"There are parts open for limited approved tours. Not to brag, but I think my pull will get you in." Jordan stuck out his chest.

"You're such a *dad*, Daddy." Astra giggled at him once again.

"He certainly is." Zen stared at him.

"So, it's a plan then." Jordan cocked his head to one side.

"Great. I'll finish packing." Astra jumped from the bar stool. She took a big swallow from her glass of sweet tea.

"You'll finish your food first. Your stomach gets upset when you rush," Zen said.

Astra was halfway across the kitchen when she answered. "I'll heat it up in a few. So excited."

"Young lady." Zen put both hands on her hips.

"C'mon, Mommy. Spending time with her father is essential for the emotional health of a girl."

"Astra—"

"And I'll have a chance to pursue my interest in space. I finished my coursework almost. Distance learning means I won't miss anything. I'll be back in time for prom." Astra looked at Jordan.

"I'm coming for her graduation ceremony anyway, so we'll be back by then. And you won't have to worry if Astra is okay. She'll be more than okay with me." Jordan looked at Astra with a soft smile of love.

"You two cooked up this game plan real quick."

"But can you argue with it?" Astra countered.

Zen heaved a sigh and crossed the room to hug her. "No, I can't. You've earned great grades, followed house rules, and I love you to pieces. So, finish packing."

"You're the best." Astra squeezed Zen hard and darted off singing Prince lyrics.

Zen turned around to face Jordan, hands on her hips again. "Slick."

"A dad's gotta do, what a dad's gotta do," he joked. Then his expression turned solemn. "I'm glad we're alone. Let's talk."

"Okay, but you're scaring me. You're not sick or something. I mean, that's not why you want to spend time with Astra." Zen sat next to him; her meal forgotten.

Jordan shook his head. "I'm healthy as can be. Better with the training."

"Don't let them use the latest bio-enhancements on you, Jordan. I know you're excited to go back to space. But—"

"Stop jumping to conclusions. I wouldn't risk not being here for Astra until she's married and giving me grandchildren. The tech of space travel is more advanced and safer than ever." Jordan studied Zen.

"We're still learning, though," Zen said, her meeting with the team flashing back.

"This is about your new department and the trip to Chile. I kept probing."

"Look, don't take any risks. We're dealing with highly sensitive—"

Jordan nodded. "I know."

"You know," Zen echoed warily.

"General Newton is friends with my uncle. Did I ever tell you that?" Jordan lifted a dark eyebrow.

Zen frowned as she searched her memory. "Yeah, yeah. You did mention it. You were trying to impress me. Back when we first started dating."

"It worked, didn't it?" Jordan flashed a brief grin.

"Yeah, it kinda did." Zen slapped his shoulder.

"My friend, a doctor with the NIH, says there's some research project called Lodestone. Details on it are above his clearance level, so he doesn't know much else now. They're recruiting him and he hasn't gotten his security level upgraded yet."

"Still vetting him." Zen shrugged. "Sounds routine."

"Yeah, but he told me because I'm in training. Sounds like Lodestone has some kind of implication for astronauts. A new training protocol, or some ill effects we need to know about. Not sure yet." Jordan started to say more when his cell phone buzzed.

"The boss?" Zen craned her neck as if trying to see the display.

"Don't start," Jordan muttered and tapped a text reply. "Look, just keep your ears open about Lodestone."

"Doesn't sound like anything related to my work investigating deaths."

"What if it explains what happened?"

"Not the deaths at a training camp here on Earth. Look, most crime is personal. I'm leaning more and more toward the usual explanations. If there's been a crime at all. But thanks for the info. I'm pretty sure Lodestone doesn't mean anything to me. Clive would have said so," Zen said.

"Would he?"

Zen laughed. "Damn, you've become a cynical government employee."

"Who knows better than us what they get up to," Jordan said. "But you could be right. Sounds more like my problem than yours."

"Companies like Goddard are looking to ramp up the size and number of space colonies. Rocket rides for regular people. You'd be able to profit big time with your expertise as a neurologist and astronaut." Zen winked at him.

"No thanks. I'll take my chances with the feds. Private companies are even more ruthless," Jordan retorted.

"Dude, you need to work on those trust issues."

Zen saw Jordan off after he reassured Minji, kissed Astra one last time, and left. The taillights of his rental car faded into the night. As Zen finished cleaning up, she considered her gut feeling. Her first assignment was an iceberg—a small peak visible but much bigger beneath the surface. And her boss knew more than he was telling. Later at her computer, she logged into the secure cloud and typed in Lodestone.

# Chapter 6

Zen joined Malone in first class of their flight to Chile before midnight Eastern Time on Sunday. She settled into the comfortable seat. She glanced out at the pavement, her thoughts on Astra. Zen wondered if Jordan was using time with Astra as a way to escape Minji for a while. She asked him directly, and he denied it. But she knew him well. Maybe he didn't realize it yet. And maybe she shouldn't have agreed to let Astra go. What if her little girl got caught in the middle of a relationship meltdown? Then Zen shook her head and sighed as she stared at the activity of the runway. Malone's deep voice broke into her thoughts.

"Kid got off okay with the male parental unit?" Malone wiggled into a comfortable position against the seatback.

"Yeah."

"At least she's older. They don't miss us as much at her age. My boys—well, my ex—is right. They need me more." Malone stared ahead, his thoughts clearly on his sons.

"How old are they?" Zen asked with a smile.

"Six and ten. Into soccer, AI virtual games, and keeping their rooms in chaos," Malone said with a laugh.

Zen heard the suggestion of hurt in his words. Based on what little he'd said, and how most contentious divorces played out, his wife had accused him of caring about his career more. "I'm sure they know how much you love them, Malone."

"Yeah. Anyway, your girl wonder is sixteen going on twenty-five, I hear. Got her foot in the door of some prestigious university. Right?" Malone said, switching the subject away from him.

"She's still deciding, but I'm pretty sure it will be Xavier," Zen said. She rolled her shoulders to ease the tension.

"Lost her head over a boy yet?" Malone stretched out his legs. They'd scored seats with extra room.

"Crushes, but nothing that sidetracked her from school or the rest of life. Thank you, Lord," Zen added. She laughed at how much she sounded like her mother.

"It's coming, especially when she meets all those guys at college. It's like an all-you-can-eat buffet. You remember." Malone took out his phone and swiped through screens.

"Thanks for the pep talk, partner."

"You're welcome," he said with a wicked grin. "Hey, you know she's got her head on straight. And her dad is probably schooling her on dealing with players like I was in school."

Zen laughed. "My daddy and older brothers filled me in."

"At least I don't have to worry about having a girl."

"You're just a bundle of reassurance this morning."

Malone's soft chuckle was his only reply. He closed his eyes as the flight attendants droned out safety information. Zen joked that she'd pay attention and save him. They traded more easygoing barbs until beverages were served. Malone drifted into a nap, no doubt brought on by a late night with his lady love, Zen mused. For her part, Zen couldn't relax.

Strange. She hadn't experienced such jitters on her way to Madrid to track a serial killer.

Instead of a movie or music, Zen pulled up their itinerary. They would fly into Santiago, Chile, and then take a two-hour flight to San Pedro de Atacama for one overnight stay. From there was another hour-long drive to the small town of Calama. They would spend the night there and then drive another two hours to the training camp. She stared at photos of the landscape for a few minutes. Then she turned her attention to Hadley's succinct summary of what they should expect. The camp director, Nyla Richards, had made arrangements for their sleeping quarters and the interviews. Zen looked at photos of the staff. Richards wore her brunette hair cut short, a fade on the sides. Then Zen turned on her wireless earbuds. Once again, she watched the recorded video of investigation interviews. Nothing jumped out at her. The third time was not a charm in this case. Or the fourth. No clues. No mention of Lodestone.

Zen glanced at Malone. He shifted positions but didn't open his eyes. She hadn't mentioned Lodestone to him, of course. That Clive wouldn't tell them everything was SOP, standard operating procedure. When it came to classified information or investigations, certain super-sensitive details would be withheld. Besides, Jordan's information was vague and it didn't fit. The deaths in the desert wouldn't be related to space travel. The trainees hadn't left Earth yet. She checked. None had previous lunar colony or space station assignments.

The Lodestone Program description sounded standard. Doctors compared medical evaluation data from astronauts going back fifty years. The reports included mental health and cognitive functioning studies. There were implications for potential benefits for the treatment of various medical conditions. Physiotherapy, occupational therapy, medications, and advanced hyperbaric interventions were found to help rehabilitate astronauts returning to Earth. Lodestone researchers were expanding their projects to psychological effects brought on by changes in the brain. Very interesting, but there was no mention of violence being a side effect. So, they were in familiar territory. Means, motive, opportunity. Confirm accidental deaths or catch the culprit. Then move on to the Lunar colonists when they returned. Her new job didn't seem like punishment after all.

Malone stretched, stood, and walked along the aisles for exercise. Zen was still working when he returned, having done the same herself twice while he slept.

"I see where Astra gets her work ethic. Pace yourself. We've got a long trip before we get there. Plenty of time for homework."

Zen finished a paragraph of one report and looked at him. "What do you know about new training protocols for space flight and extended stays?"

"I briefly considered training myself. But I got engaged and Kylie talked me out of it," Malone said and yawned. "Hey, I wonder if it's too early to get a cocktail. Hell, it must be five o'clock in evening in some time zone."

"We've only been in the air for six hours, Malone. You haven't slept that long. Now get serious and answer my question." Zen put her tablet on the side tray of her seat and leaned back.

Malone got the attention of the flight attendant and asked him for a cup of coffee. The attendant offered a selection of blends with a smile. Then he left to fulfill Malone's request.

"Perks of upgraded flying, huh?" Malone grinned at her. He blew out a sigh at the look she gave him. "Ask me again. I got distracted."

"I was wondering about the flight training for space. You were at Cape Canaveral. Any rumblings about strange adverse physical or mental effects?"

"You mean from stays longer than a few days or months. Like when General Newton and his crew went to Mars." Malone broke off when the attendant returned. Once he was settled with the paper cup, he sipped and nodded in appreciation.

"We'll be serving breakfast soon," the attendant said and left again.

"Can't wait. Hey, I smell sausages."

Zen jabbed his side with a finger. "Focus."

"I'm used to military planes, stripped down with lumpy seats. If they had any cushioning at all. Up at dawn to run obstacle courses. All-protein meals for nutrition but horrible taste. Let me enjoy a few luxuries, please." Malone sipped coffee and moaned approval.

"Good Lord," Zen mumbled and let her head fall back.

"You'll feel better with one of these. It's gourmet."

Malone held up the cup. He grinned when Zen finally nodded assent and told the passing female flight attendant. Cup in hand, Zen took a sip. She ignored Malone's complaint she would spoil the Colombian brew with sugar and coffee.

"That is good," Zen said.

"It would be better if you hadn't ruined it," Malone teased.

"Hey, my parents are from Louisiana and served café au lait when I was a kid. This is the *only* way I drink coffee."

"I need to get down to New Orleans. I hear they throw one-of-a-kind parties there."

"All over the state," Zen said with a grin. "I'd spend summers with my mother's sister in New Orleans one year. The next I'd be in New Iberia with Daddy's parents. So much fun."

"My kids love visiting my folks in Palmetto Bay."

"How did the news of you leaving town go over?" Zen looked at him. His slight frown provided part of the answer.

"The boys were excited. I email them maps of the countries I visit. And I always get them souvenirs, too."

"And Kylie?"

"She was excited for a different reason. One more negative data point for her divorce lawyer."

"Being bitter and out for payback doesn't help you move on. Not to mention the effect on the kids. I'm glad Jordan and I got over the anger fast."

"Not to change the subject from my misery, but yeah, let's change the subject. You asked about training. Did your ex tell you something?"

"We mostly talked about our daughter's future," Zen said, dodging an outright lie.

Malone studied her as he sipped coffee. The flight attendants came down the aisle serving breakfast. Zen selected the fruit and yogurt option. Malone had sausages with hash browns. The meal also came with a small brioche loaf with butter and marmalade. He made happy noises as he ate. Zen shook her head at him in amusement.

"Sure you don't want this last sausage? I haven't touched it. Promise." Malone stuffed the last corner of bread in his mouth.

"No thanks. I need to eat light when I'm flying." Zen patted her midsection.

"Humph." Malone didn't try to convince her further. He savored the last link.

Ten minutes later the attendants moved with efficiency down the aisle and collected the trash. Sunlight above the clouds brightened the interior of the electric plane. So far, the flight had been smooth and without air turbulence. For which Zen was grateful. A bumpy ride was the last thing her anxious stomach needed. She'd tried not to let Jordan's intimations affect her. After all, her point had been right. His friend's information was vague and had no connection to her assignment. Going to investigate suspicious deaths at a remote location in a foreign country didn't help.

"Okay, back to your insistence that we *work* before our feet touch the ground." Malone seemed fully alert. He rubbed his chin. "I know NASA has been studying physical changes of astronauts for sixty years or more. We've made changes to the tech on space stations and for the colonies, to the living quarters, I mean. Changes that minimize the effects of prolonged stays in outer space."

"Our bodies are adapted to gravity, certain levels of oxygen, and other chemical elements on Earth. Any studies on the brain?" Zen leaned toward him with interest.

"Not that I know of, but then I haven't thought about space travel for a long time. Definitely haven't followed it. Jordan told you something." Malone had lowered his voice and put his head close to hers.

"Nothing specific." Zen didn't want to pull her ex-husband into their investigation as a source.

"We're partners, Zen. I don't run blabbing to the boss the minute I learn something. For one thing, we should nail down theories first," Malone said, his deep voice quiet.

"So we don't look like over-eager rookies chasing crackpot hunches," Zen replied softly.

"I've had ten years as an Air Force cop. Nobody can call me a rookie. But a crackpot, maybe," Malone said with a grin. Then he grew serious again. "Well?"

"Jordan talked to a friend. He mentioned research being done on long-term space stays. But it seems related to NASA astronauts that have logged months in space. Nothing specific because it's considered sensitive. I only found a few short study summaries online." Zen brought up the information on her tablet and showed it to him.

Malone read for a few minutes. "All on animals. Nothing about astronauts."

"Results on human subjects is protected health information."

"Good old HIPPA laws. Even more strict since the advancement of genetic science. I have kept up with security breaches that led to scandals. Especially when it affected members of the military," Malone replied.

Zen nodded. "Foreign governments mining for weak points in our computer systems. But private conglomerates have been caught misusing information, too. Sometimes against their own employees, to discriminate or to beat their competitors."

"Our current president based part of his campaign on improving privacy protections. So, everybody is very touchy on the subject of security and confidentiality. Add in a top classified level and..." Malone gazed at Zen.

"Yes. Heads would definitely roll. Jordan wouldn't want his friend to get in big trouble. Not that he told Jordan much anyway."

Malone studied the tablet screen again. "Humph. Those articles don't say a whole lot."

"They're abstracts, so they wouldn't," Zen said with a frown at the scant details.

"Well, you know we've got access now. The advantage of being part of a hush-hush new operation," Malone replied, his voice barely above a whisper.

"And Hadley could help." Zen smiled at the thought of Clive's sharp assistant.

"Yeah. But you know space-crazy won't explain the training camp deaths," Malone said.

Zen grimaced at him. "Seriously, Malone? Space-crazy?"

"Hey, you can use it in your next academic paper but give me credit."

"Trust me you'll get *all* of the credit," Zen said and poked his side again with an elbow.

"Ow! Did you torture your ex, too?" Malone pretended to be in serious pain. He laughed when Zen poked him again. "Alright, alright. Message received."

"Let me school you on the RTD-RS philosophy," Zen said.

"Huh?"

"Respect the Difference and Respectful Speech. Just because someone has challenges or are different in any way doesn't mean they're due respect. That includes pejorative labels."

"Thank you for the lesson, Miss Social Worker and Justice Advocate."

"You're welcome. Besides, we don't know there are any links between our cases and concerns about prolonged space stays." Zen went back to searches on her tablet.

"Even more, we don't know that there are such effects. All we have are vague rumors. First rule of criminal inquiry is..." Malone held up a finger as if he was a professor prompting a student.

"Let the facts shape your theory of the crime, not your theories shape the facts," Zen replied without pausing her search.

Malone squirmed around in his seat to get comfortable again. He closed his eyes. "And if anything puts billions of dollars at risk, you can bet the evidence is buried deep. You won't find it that way. Hadley can excavate at the subterranean level. Or so she says. Let's put her to the test."

Zen clicked her tongue at the meager results of her search. "You're right."

"Relax. Enjoy the journey." Malone perked up and leaned toward her. "Hey, we won't have much time once we hit the ground. Look for places close to our hotel where I can get cool souvenirs. Something a kid would like."

"Might as well." Zen smiled at the "dad" version of her two-fisted partner.

For the next twelve hours they completed their journey. They finally landed in Santiago, Chile. Both checked their messages and read summaries while waiting for their connecting flight to San Pedro de Atacama. Clive had worried over the almost twenty-four hours of travel time. Yet he also knew that they needed the two overnight stays to rest. They needed to be sharp for nonstop interviews of almost twenty people.

Once they landed in San Pedro de Atacama, they checked into the guesthouse Hostal Lickana. True to his word, Malone dropped his bags and headed out to explore. Zen dropped her body onto the bed in her room for a nap. An hour later, she woke up refreshed. She met Malone for a dinner, and they strolled around together. He bought a few more items. Zen found a small bookstore that was also a coffee shop. There, they both bought books about the region for their children. Later, a friendly staff person served them as they sat at a table outside.

"Clive answered my message to Hadley," Malone said.

"Oh yeah?" Zen flipped through one of the books she'd bought. She admired photos of the desert and surrounding mountains.

"Yeah. Hadley replied to the first one. I'd forgotten that name you gave me. So, I sent a message specifically asking about Lodestone. That's when he answered." Malone took a sip of coffee.

Zen looked up from the pages. Something in his tone rang an alert bell. Yet his expression remained blank behind his aviator sunglasses. "Lodestone got the boss' attention. Interesting."

"Hadley thought so, too. More for what she wasn't able to find out than what she could. Clive stepped in to use his access to get more info." Malone lifted his dark eyebrows above the metal frames.

"Which means somebody already knows what went wrong at the Goddard lunar colony?" Zen dropped the book into the shopping bag, her purchases forgotten.

"Maybe. But you know our outfits are all about secrecy. And not just because info is classified, either," Malone replied.

"Information is currency," Zen said, quoting her father.

"The richer you are, the more power you have. Power eventually equals money." Malone pursed his lips.

"Some people value power above profit, though, Malone. My father taught me that." Zen thought back to the redacted anecdotes her father had shared with her over the years.

"Yeah, well, I'd bet on this being about money. But we need to concentrate on the mission at hand. Our feet are still on good old Earth."

Zen pulled out her phone at the alert chime. She smiled at the text from Astra, answered, and put it in her pocket again. "Agreed, but it's still intriguing. Anyway, I talked to the camp director, Nyla Richards. She's got two rooms set up. We can split the first round between us. Save time."

"Yeah, let's tag-team the ones we narrow down to being likely suspects," Malone replied.

"Or who have the best information to support an accidental death. Richards made the case for a fall. Where they train is pretty rough terrain. I mean, that's the whole point, to simulate the rocky conditions on the moon," Zen said.

"True. And Mars. Goddard is looking ahead." Malone stretched out his legs. He pulled a cuchufli out of a bag. The Chilean wafer dessert was filled with manjar, caramel, and dipped in chocolate.

"So are governments of leading world powers." Zen shook her head when he offered one. She stared off into the distance. The mountains looked serene and beautiful far away.

"Picturesque, huh? And treacherous. Tatio geysers are the third-largest group in the world. Then there are meteor craters, the Lascar volcano, and the mountains. All kinds of ways you can get killed." Malone savored the sticky treat.

"Gee, I'll sleep so much better tonight. Thanks," Zen retorted and went back to looking at a book. This time she browsed one on the local cuisine with recipes.

"You don't look like the cooking and homemaker type," Malone teased.

"Astra and my mother bond over cooking. They've collected recipes from other countries based on places my father visited. My sister used to do that as a kid. I'm not big on it." Zen turned more pages.

"You have a sister?" Malone looked at Zen.

"Had. And don't pretend you don't know." Zen closed the book, losing her interest in a recipe for Chilean sea bass.

"If you don't want to talk about it..." Malone let the words trail off.

Zen sighed. "I'm snapping at you for no reason. Nice technique, by the way. Introduce the subject as a question and let me lead."

"I'm not working you like a case, partner," Malone said. His deep voice held a tender undertone.

"I know. So, my profile had the usual family background details. Two older brothers, Brian and Elliot Batiste. One younger sister, Alexis Batiste, deceased." Zen rattled off the details of her own life.

"Sorry."

"The case went cold, so we don't know who killed Lexi or why. And no, I'm not hunting down murderers to sublimate a desire for revenge or justice on my sister's unsolved murder," Zen said in a fierce tone. Try as she might, the rawness of losing Lexi always returned.

"I didn't say I bought into that hypothesis." Malone looked away.

"Ah, there is it. Acknowledgement of the general thinking about my motives for going to Madrid. Probably the reason for this new job. They don't want my flaw to mess up more investigations." Zen tapped a fist on one knee.

"Or maybe you won't give up on finding the truth. You know what it's like for a family to not know," Malone replied.

"So, they put me in a department with a boring objective. Glorified human resources." Zen looked at him with a frown.

"Ms. Illinois sold your reassignment to the committee that way, yes. Only..." Malone pushed his sunglasses down to peer at her over them.

Zen gazed at him for a few seconds, deep in thought. "The deaths mean there's more to Clive's new section than meets the eye. You're saying she knew. Which means Clive knew."

"But the other committee members don't, or they didn't then. I'm guessing they're in the process of finding out. Too late though." Malone grinned and pushed the sunglasses back up.

Zen put on her sunglasses and leaned back to mimic Malone's pose. "I'm feeling better about this job change a little bit every day."

"Just think, the bonus is you get to work with *me*." Malone smiled behind the aviators at the loud snort Zen made.

TUESDAY MORNING, THEIR car, a battered Jeep, arrived at six-thirty. Zen and Malone were waiting outside. Malone talked to the middle-aged man. Malone spoke in Spanish, to the delight of the driver. The man switched to English to describe the journey, for Zen's benefit. Then he trotted off for a trip to the men's room before they left.

"Is this thing going to make it?" Zen walked around the Jeep. Its olive-green camo-styled finish had seen much better days.

"The engine sounds good. Bruno has taken great care of it. Look at the inside." Malone swung his and Zen's backpacks into the Jeep's rear.

Zen couldn't complain. Except for dust, understandable in the dry desert, the interior was well maintained. One or two places on the upholstery had been patched. "I'll ride in back. More leg room up front for you."

"So considerate." Malone pulled out another cuchufli. "Sure you won't take a bite?"

"I'm still stuffed from that breakfast burrito or whatever it's called. Tasty, but I shouldn't have eaten the whole thing."

"You need the nourishment. Brain food for getting to the truth," Malone quipped around crunches.

"How many of those things did you get?" Zen put on her seat belt.

"Not enough. Gonna miss 'em." Malone leaned against the jeep and savored the last bite.

Bruno strode up with a small tray. Three paper cups of coffee sat on it. He gave one to Zen and to Malone. He put one in a cupholder near the driver's seat. The hotel housekeeper, who had followed him, took the tray. She left after a wave and friendly smile.

"We are ready, yes?" Bruno glanced at his passengers. "One hour, thirty minutes. Tops.

"Sounds good," Malone said.

Zen settled in for the ride, her khaki jacket zipped closed. With the temperature still in the low fifties, the morning air felt invigorating. A cooler with bottled water sat in the rear next to their backpacks. The desert landscape rolled by as they drove down the packed-earth road. Shades of reddish-brown and tan surrounded them. They passed tall hills with taller mountains beyond. The rocky surface was both beautiful and stark in the early sunlight. As the sun rose, the orange tint of the night sky gave way to bright blue. Zen could see why training camps for the moon and Mars were placed here. The rocky, dry mountainous terrain most closely matched both. She'd expected the ride to be boring, an expanse of sameness. Instead, Zen could not look away from the arid beauty of the scenery.

Zen managed to reach her bag to pull out the camera she'd brought. She aimed it at the majestic Andes as they drove. Bruno slowed and even stopped twice so she could get a shot. Astra would be excited with photos of an actual meteor crater. They arrived at the Goddard camp just before nine. Three domes the color of sand sat like mushroom tops on a valley. Rock formations surrounded them. Bruno pulled up to one of the small ones and parked. A compact man dressed in camo shorts and a beige t-shirt stood outside. He strode forward when Malone exited the Jeep.

"Hola. I'm Javier Belmont, operations chief. You must be Mr. Ramirez." He stuck out a hand. "Hola, Bruno."

"Hola. I report in." Bruno strolled off, lighting a small cigar as he left.

Malone shook hands with Belmont. "This is Zen Batiste."

Belmont paused to gaze from him to Zen and back again. "I didn't know you would bring an assistant."

"Dr. Batiste is also a special agent with our department, Dr. Belmont." Malone glanced sideways at Zen.

"We'll both conduct interviews. I assume you've set aside space and we can get started immediately." Zen shook his hand and put on a tight smile.

"My apologies for assuming... I mean, er. Yes, right this way. Nyla is talking to the crew now. I'll take you to her office. She should be here any minute." Belmont started off.

Zen pulled Malone back as they followed him. "Richards wasn't supposed to tell the staff we were coming."

"They've had time to get their stories together already. If there's anything to hide, that is," Malone whispered.

The short walk brought them inside the building. The interior was surprisingly roomier than Zen expected. Two windows brought in sunlight and provided stunning views. Belmont led them past desks with computers and an old copier.

"Wow, they still make these?" Zen looked at the relic.

"Believe or not, they're useful. That one connects to our network. We can print out charts for training, for example." Belmont wore a jittery smile. "Have a seat. I'll let Nyla know you're here. And right on time, too."

"Thanks, Dr. Belmont," Malone replied.

"Oh, please. Call me Javier. I'll get Nyla." Belmont darted off. Moments later they heard him talking to another man.

"He's seems jumpy. Or is it just me?" Zen said low.

"The scary smile you gave him probably has the guy on edge," Malone quipped.

"Your assistant." Zen was about to go on when another man appeared.

"Can I get you something? We still have breakfast and of course coffee. Or tea?" The short man wore an apron around his waist.

"No thanks. We're good," Malone said with a smile. The man nodded and disappeared. When his footsteps faded, Malone turned back to Zen. "But yeah, I think our visit should rattle them. I mean, they thought the investigation was done."

"We'll see."

Zen glanced around the office. A couple of photos sat on a small bookcase. One was of a handsome man with blond hair and a small boy. The other was the boy and a Shih Tzu. Both seemed to be posed and smiling for the camera. A tall brown woman strode in. Her short-sleeved safari shirt was tucked into slacks, a brown belt around her slim waist. Her brownish-red hair, longer than in the photo, was pulled into a short ponytail.

"Good morning. I'm Nyla Richards, but I'm sure you've seen my full bio," she said with a crisp nod. She looked at them and waited.

Zen gazed back at her. "You have a doctorate in geological research. Married, one son. Originally from Los Angeles."

Richards's expression tightened a bit more. "Dr. Zen Batiste, famous for catching a serial killer. Ex-husband is an astronaut."

"Now that we've gotten intros out of the way," Malone mumbled and cleared his throat.

"You're Malone Ramirez, Air Force security," Richards said with a glance at Malone that went right back to Zen.

"Goddard headquarters has kept you informed. Good," Zen clipped.

"Except for a full explanation why our schedule has to be interrupted again. I assumed the government and corporate got the report. We're devastated by what happened to Robert, but it was an accident," Richards shot back.

"And the other employee?" Zen took out her tablet to consult it.

Richards replied before Zen continued. "Lee Franzen, and that was a good eight months before Robert's death. And it was clearly an accident as well."

Zen looked up from the tablet. "Well, we're here to make it even clearer."

"Given events on the Goddard Lunar Colony, we want to be as thorough as possible," Malone cut in, his tone conciliatory.

"Your company is just as eager to wrap up any loose ends so they can get back to business," Zen added. The reference to her Goddard bosses had the desired effect.

"I apologize for my abruptness. It's just... We finally got back to some semblance of order and now losing Rob." Dr. Richards rubbed her forehead with one hand.

"We will minimize disruption, but we've got our job to do. Your cooperation will expedite this process," Malone said. He stood tall with a stern face. His subtle change from "good cop" signaled he was all business underneath.

Within seconds Richards squared her shoulders and nodded. "Of course. We've set aside two rooms for you. This way."

They followed her to another hallway. A staircase to a mezzanine surprised Zen and Malone. They exchanged a glance but said nothing. Down another hallway to the left were three rooms. Two sat on the north side and one larger across from them. Pocket doors provided privacy if needed.

"They're small, but functional. Are these okay?" Richards watched as Zen made a short circuit of the rooms.

"These will do just fine. We can use the larger one, too, I hope?" Malone peered inside and nodded.

"Anything you need," Richards replied.

"This building is bigger than I expected from the outside." Zen touched the walls for a feel of the smooth material. The modular structure stretched back farther than what was visible on first approach.

"We use the same type of housing that will be assembled on the moon, and hopefully Mars in the not-too-distant future. Our buildings are embedded in the soil." Richards seemed to relax more with the subject change to her work.

Zen faced her. "Fascinating. You expect to be assigned to a colony?"

"Not for some years. Once my son is older, and if I'm in good health. I plan to keep in shape in the meantime."

"Yes, being separated from your children is tough. My daughter is sixteen and very independent, but she still needs us," Zen replied, and went back to examining the room.

"My husband gave up his job in the states and moved our family to Santiago. All so I could take this once in a career kind of opportunity. What we're doing is historic," Richards said.

"You don't live here at the camp?" Malone had subtly shifted into investigation mode.

"Most of the time. I even have family quarters so they can stay with me sometimes. When Phillip gets a break from the university." Richards smiled at the mention of time with her husband and child.

"Goddard Corporation is very accommodating," Zen said.

"Yes, but it's also part of our work. You see, one day families will be on colonies as well. So, we've made some adaptations based on how my son, Drayton, reacts to the camp. My husband provided feedback as well. Naturally, we can't simulate conditions of being on an alien world completely."

"You were onsite when both deaths occurred?" Malone went to the desk in the room and put down his backpack. Then he turned back to Dr. Richards.

"Not when Rob had his mishap. I was taking a weekend break. A rare vacation. My parents had flown in from New Mexico. I'm given more time away since I'm not going to the colony. Otherwise, the rest of the crew, the ones going to the second lunar site, stay here throughout the ten to twelve months of training." Richards arranged the four chairs around the table and checked surfaces for dust.

"I see." Malone unpacked his tablet. He then put both their backpacks in a filing cabinet.

"Our trainees are chosen because they're adventurous. They sign on because they love a challenge," Dr. Richards replied.

"Rock climbing, scaling mountains. Camping in the desert," Malone said.

"Yes, bungee jumping, cave diving, and more. They don't take foolish risks, but danger is part of the job. There's no way around it." Dr. Richards wore a somber face.

"Might as well start," Zen said.

Dr. Belmont appeared as if on cue. "I'll get them for you."

Malone looked at Zen. "Since he's here, why don't we start with Dr. Belmont?"

Zen nodded. "Okay, then we'll take a tour of the camp."

"Me?" Belmont squeaked and stepped back.

# Chapter 7

Malone went toward him. "That a problem?"

"I just, I mean my schedule. Nyla, can we talk for a minute?" Belmont swallowed hard and forced a smile that stretched his face in strange ways.

Dr. Richards looked from him to Malone and back. "Um, we have some time-critical tasks to complete. Reports to do. We were going to meet this morning and... We won't be long."

"Sure," Malone said after a few beats.

Richards and Belmont strode off. They'd barely gotten down the hallway before their muffled voices floated back. The crew member with the apron reappeared from nowhere. Another crew member, this one with a vacuum cleaner, showed up. The grinding hum covered background noises.

"Gotta keep dust out of here. Messes with the office equipment," the apron wearer said. "Sure we can't get you anything? I make a mean cup of coffee. The company even got us some Jamaican blend."

"We'll be fine for the duration. One of us will come find you if we need anything. But from now on we shouldn't be disturbed." Malone, his tone firm with official authority, walked toward him.

"Sure, understood. Just trying to be hospitable. Not a social visit. Got ya." The man matched Malone's step but in the opposite direction to keep distance between them.

"And you," Malone barked at the woman several feet way with the vacuum. "Cut that thing off. We know your office equipment has been designed for rough conditions. Lunar simulation."

The motor cut suddenly. The woman exchanged a brief look with her co-worker. Without another word, she moved on with the battery-powered cleaner. Zen joined Malone in the hall to observe them both. The two crew members scurried off through a second exit door.

"What the hell was all that about? Belmont turns to nervous jelly and what looks like a planned distraction shows up seconds later," Zen said, still gazing in the direction Richards and Belmont had gone.

"If Belmont wanted to avoid suspicion, he's doing a shit job of it," Malone murmured low.

"Yeah. He knows more than the reports imply." Zen looked up at Malone. "Smart gut feeling you had that I should talk to him first."

"He seemed too, I don't know, eager to get this over with. I'm guessing he's at least one weak link." Malone stopped talking when Richards and Belmont returned.

"I'm sorry for the delay," Richards said with a smile. "Get started with Javier. The rest of the crew expects to get called in. Might take a few minutes. We told them to carry on with their work."

"Sounds good," Zen added.

They also knew from reports that Dr. Belmont had been first on the scene of the accident. Seemingly, his alibi was airtight. He was on his computer sending messages when it happened. But he'd had a chance to make observations before anyone else.

"Uh, okay. I'll let Leslie know she can go back to the lab for the moment," Belmont said.

Zen held up a hand to stop him. "I'm sure Dr. Richards can do that. Right?"

Richards paused to exchange a glance with Belmont. "Sure."

"And in the meantime, I'll take that tour while they talk." Malone walked over to Dr. Richards and gestured for her to go first.

Richards and Belmont both looked flustered by the loss of control. Zen suspected they'd planned to choreograph her and Malone's movements. The wild cards her partner had dealt caught them off guard.

"I thought you both wanted a tour." Richards wore a slight frown.

"Sure, I'll get my first interview going once you show me around. Then Dr. Batiste can take one with Javier. Like we said, saving time." Malone smiled at her.

"Okay." Richards gazed at him for a few seconds. She cleared her throat and walked ahead of Malone.

Once they were gone, Zen slid the pocket door closed. The action muffled the sound of satellite phones ringing in another part of the building. She pointed to a chair and sat without waiting for Belmont.

"I assume you were informed that we'd record?" Zen asked. He nodded assent and she activated the recorder app on her agency smartwatch. "It's October 20th, 2085, and this is Special Agent Zenobia Batiste with the Joint DOJ and NASA unit speaking to Dr. Javier Belmont at the Goddard Training Camp at Ell Valle de la Luna. You understand this interview is being recorded."

Belmont cleared his throat and leaned forward. "Yes. I have no objections," he added before Zen went on.

"Good. Just sit back and speak normally. The mic is sensitive." Zen gave him a brief smile and launched into her questions.

She took him through the sequence of events that day. She asked him about the camp routine, if anything was off or unusual about that morning. Belmont said no, just as he told the first investigators. The camp had a day to sleep later than usual since it was a Sunday. Yet sleeping late only meant they got up between eight and eight-thirty instead of five. Breakfast was over by ten o'clock. Even on the rest days, certain activities went on. This was in keeping with what would be expected on a space colony. Certain life-support functions, water creation and air quality, had to be monitored or maintained round the clock. Zen noted that they seemed to be pretty strict with the routine. No more than five crew could go roaming farther than a half-mile away on their days off.

"As you can imagine, seeing the same few faces in a relatively confined area can be a bit much. Past trainings found it helps to build in capacity for private time and the ability to simply get away. With safety precautions, naturally," Belmont added.

"Did Robert Hunter and Tanner Martin have any disagreements or tension between them?" Zen rested both elbows on the table.

Belmont paused for a beat before answering. "No, nothing serious. I mean, Rob and Tan were friendly most of the time."

"But there was something." Zen nodded as if she already knew the details.

"They had some kind of beef, but that was weeks before the accident. And I'm sure it was an accident. Something about getting the last piece of bacon. Then they argued over a card game."

"So twice they got into it. I see." Zen tapped notes into her tablet and looked back at Belmont.

"We all have. Nothing that amounts to a motive for murder." Belmont pressed his thin, dry lips together as if to cut off saying more.

"Tension could mean they neglected to check equipment. Maybe distracted by the stress and monotony of long days in desert isolation," Zen replied.

"Yes, yes. You see what I'm getting at," Belmont blurted. He seemed relieved she'd given him something to pounce on.

"What about closer to the incident? How did they seem toward each other?" Zen put the tablet down and looked at him again.

"Fine." Belmont held himself still for a few seconds. Then he swallowed hard.

"You saw them together the day Hunter died?"

"Only for a few minutes in the dining area at breakfast. They were talking. They looked normal. You know."

"They weren't arguing, didn't seem to have any friction."

"I wasn't paying that close attention to be honest. But nothing stands out in my mind," Belmont replied.

"Walk me through the day then." Zen sat against the chair back.

"Routine stuff until, you know Tan called on the walkie-talkie. At first the crew heard him asking Rob if he was okay. Then he shouted in pain. He fell trying to get to him, broke his ankle." Belmont blew out air as if he'd been holding his breath.

"What next?"

"Leslie got him to slow down because he was talking fast. He gave us directions based on landmarks. We put out a few around the camp up to three miles away. So as not to get lost. Rob was at the bottom of a gully. Stupid mistake. They decided to push themselves, look for pre-Incan petroglyphs." Belmont stopped and rubbed his thigh with both palms. "Tan blamed—blames—himself."

"Was the victim able to speak?" Zen leaned forward.

Belmont shook his head. "I scrambled down to Rob while the others looked after Tan. No, he was in pain and groaning. Nothing intelligible. I wasn't concentrating on asking him questions."

Zen studied Belmont as he seemed lost in the memory. She decided to give him some space. Recounting a traumatic experience could bring back more details. After a few more seconds she leaned forward again.

"Understandable. He was in bad shape when you saw him," Zen said.

"I tried to comfort him. Tell him we had help on the way. Not much we could do. Not just the fall. He hit jagged rock on the way down."

"I've read the postmortem. He had extensive injuries." Zen nodded.

"Yes. Awful day. Awful." Belmont frowned. "Three of our trainees are trained medics. A firefighter and two certified as emergency medical techs. Just like on a lunar or Mars colony, we're stocked with medical supplies. Only enough to stabilize someone with serious injuries. Nyla arranged for a helicopter from the Calama Airport. It was obvious Rob needed more."

"Did you talk to Martin?"

"He wasn't making much sense. He was in pain, asking if Rob was dead. We were all in shock. This is one of the most dangerous deserts in the world, you know. In the top five." Belmont sighed.

"Hmm. So, Martin wanted to know if his buddy had survived the fall, huh?"

"Like I said, we were all pretty upset," Belmont replied.

"Try to remember Martin's exact words." Zen studied his every move down to the twitch above his right eye.

"Something about Rob should have listened, or kept his mouth shut. It didn't make much sense. He probably meant Rob wasn't watching his step. I mean, in hindsight." Belmont's thick eyebrows pulled together as he stared down at the table.

"What else?"

"Nothing. That's all I can remember. As you can imagine, it was chaotic. Our main focus was getting them both medical attention."

"Did you have any reason to think they'd had an argument or—"

"Look, the other investigators dragged us through these gruesome details. They made us relive what happened to Lee. They were thorough, so read their report." Belmont's voice rose with each word. His Belgium accent deepened with anger.

"Believe me we've gone over all of the information with great care," Zen replied in an even tone.

"Good. Then you won't need to be here long. Now if you'll excuse me, I have a lot of things to do." Belmont stood.

"Dr. Belmont—"

"I've cooperated. Put that down in your notes. However, you are not police. Correct?"

"No."

"Then you're basically on a fact-finding follow-up visit. I've given you all I know and I'm free to get about my work. Good morning." Belmont's stubborn expression contrasted with his genial welcome.

Zen stood to face him. "I'm not police, but my agency represents the government that regulates space travel. Your work will be dead in the water if Goddard Corporation can't establish another lunar colony. Our findings are critical to decisions that will be made."

"I've no doubt you'll confirm what the first investigators concluded. Rob died of injuries from a fall, a tragic *accident*."

Belmont turned to go just as Dr. Richards slid the door open. He almost bumped into her.

"Javier, is there a problem?" Richards looked at him.

"I-I've answered her questions. Now I will leave. Three of our people will be doing work in the low-gravity simulator. I need to monitor their progress." Belmont gazed at Richards for a few seconds. When she nodded, he left.

Zen studied Richards for a few seconds. "Dr. Belmont seems on edge about the morning Robert Hunter died."

"He watched a man, a colleague, die that day. Naturally, it's stressful going over such things again." Richards crossed her arms.

"Were they good friends?" Zen gestured for her to take a seat.

"Oh, so it's my turn under the hot lights." Richards let her arms fall and she sat.

"I get that this isn't the most pleasant topic to go over again." Zen stopped when Richards held up one hand.

"We're under enormous pressure. We have million-dollar equipment to maintain, a brutal schedule, and the head office wanting results yesterday. Now with two deaths. So, yes. Javier is on edge. As is everyone on the crew. Surprised?"

"Did Dr. Belmont have a close relationship with Hunter or Martin?" Zen said, her tone calm.

Richards heaved a sigh of resignation. "They weren't buddies, if that's what you mean. And no, they never had any kind of arguments. Look, we're stuck in a harsh place in the middle of nowhere. All of us have gotten on each other's nerves at some point. But if you're asking if Tanner pushed Rob off a cliff, there's no evidence he did."

"No evidence." Zen tapped the screen of her tablet and then looked at Richards.

"None." Dr. Richards's gaze shifted away from Zen.

"The crew spent months together before you got here. Then months here as well. You've had time to observe interactions, the group dynamic. If you have any insights, now is the time to share them."

Dr. Richards looked at Zen. "I have a degree in geological engineering with a minor in mathematics. Not psychology."

"You've managed three teams in past jobs. That's why Goddard recruited you six years ago. As a leader, your skill set is in managing people as much as engineering. You have to get to know each person, but also the personality of the group. How their individual strengths and weaknesses play out as they work together."

"Minor arguments aside, nothing leads me to think we've had anything more than tragic accidents. Now, like Javier, I've got a lot on my plate. And you mentioned interviewing everyone. So, I'll let you get to it." Richards started to stand but stopped when Zen waved her back. "What?"

"I didn't say we were done. Where were you when Hunter was hurt?"

"Oh, give me strength!" Richards blurted. "I was in another building going over the results of two experiments. And yes, I have a witness. Rob was unconscious by the time they brought him back to camp. I didn't try to interrogate two seriously injured men. No, I didn't have any kind of unresolved conflict with Rob. Or Lee."

Zen gazed at her for a few moments before tapping a quick note in her tablet. "Okay then."

Richards let out a long breath. "Listen, it's nothing against you. I've had a total of six messages and a long phone call, and it's not even lunchtime yet. My boss back in California is on my ass."

"Goddard has a lot riding on the success of these lunar colonies. So does NASA. We all want the space program to succeed. Crews like yours have developed amazing medical advancements and technology. The USA—hell, the world—has benefited from the kind of work you do. The safety of you and your people is just as critical. Worth a few hours of answering more questions, I think. Don't you?" Zen studied the effect of her speech on Richards.

"Yes. Of course. I apologize for being brusque or dismissive." Richards folded her hands on the tabletop between them.

For another twenty minutes, Zen walked Dr. Richards through a series of questions. Zen's goal was to get a feel for the daily operations from her point of view. Then Richards left. Zen interviewed two more crew members. They had been at the camp, nowhere near the site where the fatality occurred. She talked to them for about thirty minutes each. When the last woman left Zen checked her watch. It was two o'clock in the afternoon. She hoped Malone had made good progress as well. He walked in as if her thoughts had conjured him up.

"Please tell me you solved the case, sent in our final report, and we're going to have an expensive meal to celebrate," Zen muttered, still scrolling through her notes to check them.

"I think we should spend the night. In fact, I've made the arrangements. You can guess how well that's gone over with Dr. Richards and company." Malone wore a lopsided grin.

Zen gaped at him for a few moments. "You're kidding."

"Something ain't right here, Zen." Malone slid the door closed and faced her again. "I've been to North Korea and China. Those official tours they give are planned so you don't learn information. I have a feeling they've got a script that they stick to."

"Goddard is very touchy about its proprietary information. North Korea, China, and a couple more countries have tried to hack their networks," Zen said. "Big corporations just as serious about their classified info as we are."

"Yeah, but my instincts say we don't have the full story."

"And you think sleeping on lump camp cots and eating bland food will shake loose the facts," Zen retorted.

"I've seen the sleeping quarters. They're pretty comfy." Malone gazed at her. "You found out something, too. Or you get the sense there's more. Admit it."

Zen huffed. "Yeah. Belmont got irritated when I pushed him for answers, especially when I asked if Hunter or Martin said anything."

"Bruno has gone back to Calama and he'll be back in the morning. I mean, we might finish up earlier tha—"

"You sent him away, set up for us to stay, and didn't bother to consult me. Now I understand what Nyla Richards meant." Zen squinted at him.

"Meant how?"

"About being trapped with annoying people," Zen replied in a deadpan tone.

AFTER A SHORT LUNCH, Zen and Malone got back to work. The stretched out the interviews with the purpose of making more of the crew members nervous. Malone tackled Tan Martin. Meanwhile, Belmont managed to keep clear of them for the rest of the day. They didn't even see him at dinner. Malone and Zen exchanged chitchat while they ate but observed those around them. Malone left first, leaving Zen with Dr. Richards. The woman was taciturn, barely saying more than a few forced answers. Then she excused herself while Zen was in the middle of a sentence. Zen met Malone outside at a small patio. A man and woman sat on a bench on one end. Malone lounged in a chair at one of three café tables. He stared at his phone as he tapped messages out.

Zen made a circle of the patio. The floor was crushed stone. Two more tables sat spaced out. The floodlight attached to the building created an arc of illumination. Parts of the patio were shadowed, giving it a cozy, intimate look. Zen stared up at the night sky filled with stars, fascinated by the worlds they represented. After ten minutes she joined Malone and sat in the chair across

"Find out anything more?" Malone mumbled without looking up.

"No way. Richards rushed off like her butt was on fire." Zen watched as the man and woman left the bench and walked into the night. "Beautiful, even if it's a bit chilly. I'd think more people would be out."

"I don't think we're popular around here," Malone said. He put his phone on the table with a sigh.

"Things okay back at the ranch?" Zen asked with a smile.

"My eight-year-old got into a scuffle at school. His mother, of course, blames me for not being there. Talking to him on the phone from across the world isn't enough." Malone drummed his fingertips on the tabletop.

"I take it that's a direct quote." Zen looked around at the landscape. Mountains were dark shapes in the distance.

"Just kids teasing that turned into a spat. Didn't help that he quoted my dad wisdom. I taught him to stand up for himself, don't get bullied. Kylie is of the 'run and tell a teacher' school of thought."

"He got suspended?"

Malone grinned. "No, he convinced the assistant principal to see his point of view. My boy."

Zen laughed. "Sounds like you have a future politician on your hands."

"Hey, take that back!" Malone pretended to be horrified, which made Zen laugh even harder. "Bruno is coming at two o'clock tomorrow. I finished up the interviews. I'll talk to Tan Martin again."

"What did he say?" Zen waved a signal at Malone when a crew member approached.

"Excuse me, ma'am. I thought you guys might like an after-dinner coffee. Special blend called Colombia

Supremo." The cook, one of the female crew members, set a tray down on the table. "It's smooth. Brought real cream, too."

"Thanks." Malone took a cup and sipped. "Mmm."

"Wow, a pretty patio and gourmet blends. Goddard is good to its employees." Zen smiled at the woman.

"Kylie arranges special touches for us. She's smart and doesn't miss much," the woman replied in a controlled tone. Then she flashed a tight smile. "Enjoy."

Zen watched leave. "She didn't come out here to bring us coffee."

"Wanted to let us know they're united and loyal," Malone replied. "Humph, this is perfect. That custard for dessert wasn't bad either."

Zen gazed around at the neat domed buildings. No roughing it for these folks."

Malone drank more from his cup and sighed in appreciation. He glanced up at Zen when she stood. "Hey, you're not going to have your coffee? It's smooth as silk going down."

"You have it. I'm going to turn in." Zen gestured at the cup.

"Don't mind if I do." Malone filled his empty cup with the contents of the one meant for Zen.

"Yeah. No need in both of use going down if they put something in it," Zen quipped as she strolled off. She giggled at the choking sound behind her.

Zen spent two hours on her tablet going over her interview notes. She cross-checked details in them with reports about both deaths. Then she read messages from

Hadley about the Goddard lunar colonists' evacuation. Goddard appeared to be dragging out the process. NASA sent reps over from the US colony to goose them into complying. It was clear the delays were deliberate. After sending messages to Astra and her parents, Zen got ready for bed.

With water being at a premium, a short shower had to suffice. She'd been given toiletries from the camp's storeroom. A plastic bag contained a small tube of tooth gel, a toothbrush, deodorant, liquid shower soap, and body power. Wearing an oversized man's t-shirt, Zen got settled onto the small bed. Not quite a cot, the firm foam mattress was comfortable. Microfiber sheets made it even more so. Soon, Zen drifted off to sleep.

Sometime later, a pressure on her chest woke her.

"Don't move or yell," a voice whispered.

Zen froze, resisting the reflex to strike out. Something covered her mouth. Not a hand. She must have been sleeping soundly to not have felt it. Her head felt fogged up, but from more than sleep. Maybe something had been in the coffee. No. She didn't drink it.

"You have to take me with you when you leave. I need to get out of this place."

"Whaa—" Zen couldn't move her lips beneath the binding. She strained in the dark to see the dark figure looming over her.

"I'll tell you what I know, but you gotta promise," the voice insisted and pushed down on Zen for emphasis.

The sensation of increased weight triggered anger in Zen. Her own training kicked in and she bucked hard against the load. Since her arms weren't secured, Zen used both palms pressed flat on the bed to push up. Surprise must have been on her side. A yelp followed a release of what held Zen in place. Using the brief advantage, Zen struck out. Her fist connected with something solid. A grunt of pain encouraged Zen to swing again. Battle-induced adrenaline must have overcome whatever had drugged Zen. She kicked out at the lump crouched near the bed. The fight had caused the motion sensor lights to blink to life. Zen didn't wait before striking again. The noise roused others. But the sliding door had been locked by the intruder. By the time Malone kicked until the lock popped off, Zen had used the top sheet to wrap up her attacker. Dr. Richardson, wearing pajamas with her hair loose, stood in the doorway with her mouth open. She quickly recovered and, along with Belmont, blocked more of the crew from approaching.

"Get me something to tie her up," Zen barked at them.

Belmont gasped with eyes wide. "But we don't—"

"Now, damn it!" Zen shouted.

She glared a warning at them not to argue. They must have seen the danger in her eyes. Both vanished. Malone helped pull the bound figure to an upright position on the floor, her back propped against the camp bed. She squirmed a few seconds until Zen shook her hard. Then Zen pulled the sheet from over her face. Malone stood over them, hands on his waist. He wore camp-issued pajama bottoms and a long-sleeved t-shirt.

"What the hell—how did you start a fight in the middle of a desert?" he said and blew out air.

"I decided to get some exercise in the middle of the night," Zen retorted. She scowled at their prisoner.

"Here. Zip ties we use to secure equipment." Dr. Richards handed them to Malone.

"Handy," Malone replied and took them. He and Zen wrestled the woman's arms behind her.

"I'll slap you into next week," Zen growled close to the woman's face when she continued to struggle.

"I just wanted to talk. Goddamn!"

"Yeah, by sneaking into my room and sitting on my chest. Nice way to start a conversation."

Zen stepped away and swiped a sheen of sweat from her forehead. She leaned against a small metal desk. Three deep breaths later her heart rate started to wind down. Malone stood, legs apart and head cocked to one side. They both studied the woman. He'd herded the crew members away so they could talk to the intruder alone.

"Iesha Lenae Franklin, twenty-six; native of Detroit, Michigan. Earned a scholarship as a teenager despite her troubled past. She dropped out of college. Yet mentors worked hard to guide her away from the streets. She impressed her supervisors during an internship at a Goddard research lab at the University of Michigan." Zen rattled off a condensed version of the background from her personnel file.

"You finally got your BS degree with a concentration in biology. Finished an engineering course by the age of nineteen. Smart, but you make dumb choices like dating a drug dealer." Malone crossed his arms.

"And attacking a federal agent who could put her away for years," Zen added. She winced and rubbed her shoulder.

"I said I only wanted to talk. I really need to leave or—" Iesha broke off and twisted as if trying to get free.

Zen kicked the sole of Iesha's boot. The blow made the woman get still again. She frowned at Zen. "Or what?"

"Look, I'm trying to help you out and this how you treat me." Iesha looked at the door. She lowered her voice to a soft whisper. "Check the hall. See if anybody's out there listening."

"Maybe being tied up and on your way to prison isn't a clue. You don't get to give us orders," Zen snapped.

Malone held up a palm to quiet Zen from more threats. Then he walked to the door. It was partially open. The small lever that served as a handle hung crookedly thanks to Malone's powerful kick. Richards and Belmont stood a few feet away. Both seemed startled when Malone appeared.

"Could you give us a minute with the prisoner. Maybe get something to fix this door," Malone called to them. He shot a side glance full of meaning at Zen.

"The locks are made to give easily, for emergencies. Just enough to give privacy, but easy to pop if we need to get in," Belmont said. "Um, but we might have to check if there are cracks."

"We have tools to open the lock as well. We could have used them if..." Dr. Richards spread her hands out.

"Yeah, well I wasn't going to wait while my partner was getting tossed around. Anyway, get those tools. Is there any place secure we can put her later? After we finish interrogating her, that is."

Belmont exchanged a look with his boss before answering. "We have a locked room in the lab, building three."

"With the research animals, Javier?" Richards frowned at him. He shrugged as a response and she sighed. "Where is she going to go? We're in the middle of a desert. I'm sure we can secure Iesha in one of the small offices."

Zen marched past Iesha. She pointed a finger at her as a warning not to move or resist again. Then she went to the door. "Dr. Richards, you have two off-road vehicles and a moon rover. She knows the camp well and could take one. Just do as we ask."

Something in Zen's expression must have impressed the director. She clenched both hands into fists at her side, but spun away. Her footsteps pounded on the particle board flooring as she left.

Belmont gazed after his boss for a few seconds and turned back to them. "Umm, I'll go clear out that room. It's really a storage closet. Won't take long."

"Do it, then, Dr. Belmont. Check he doesn't hide somewhere," Zen whispered to Malone as she went back into the room.

Malone gave her a slight nod of acknowledgement and then waved at Belmont. "They're gone."

"Make sure nobody else is around," Iesha said low.

Malone slid the door shut. It shuddered on the track and didn't close all the way. "They might have to do more than fix the lock."

Zen crossed her arms and looked at Iesha. "Now get to talking. For somebody that went to so much trouble you're being shy,"

Iesha stared at her hard. "Look, I don't want to go home in a body bag like Rob."

"You're saying his death wasn't an accident?" Zen glanced at Malone.

"I'm not saying much of anything until we're gone from here. Don't you get it? You're outnumbered and they've got stuff to hide," Iesha blurted. Then she flinched and lowered her voice. "I want out."

"Listen to me." Malone crouched down and softened his tone. "We want to understand what's going on and get at the truth. But you gotta give us *something* first."

"And quit wasting our damn time," Zen added. She leaned into her role as "bad cop."

"I can see you're scared, and you didn't really hurt Dr. Batiste. That counts for something," Malone said.

"Yeah, maybe ten years less of a sentence," Zen snapped.

"You're pretty freaking cold for a social worker. Don't look so surprised. We did our homework on you two," Iesha said when Malone and Zen looked at each other. She nodded to Malone. "You're an Air Force cop. Worked at the space center in Florida. Helped crack a case with some soldiers stealing in 2081. They were selling equipment on the black market to Chinese agents."

"How did you get this info?" Zen sat on the one chair in the room.

Iesha shrugged. "Wasn't hard to find with a bit of digging. We do have internet access, ya know."

"Damn news media," Malone grumbled with a grimace.

"Two examples of why the government needs Goddard more than they need the government. That's the general feeling with upper management." Iesha chuckled at their scowls. "Yeah, I know. Goddard has sucked in a lot of taxpayer bucks for its space program."

"Some, but it's a billion-dollar company. Goddard has invested heavily in its space program," Zen said.

"How do billionaires get so rich? Answer, use other people's money. But hey, it's the way the world works. All of these fat careers depend on Goddard having a squeaky-clean public brand. You got me?"

"Which has what to do with our investigation?" Zen asked.

"Rob and I were close. Very close."

"You were having an affair. I would have thought Goddard had rules against that sort of, uh, team spirit," Malone said.

"Nyla and Javier didn't care as long as we got the job done and didn't cause problems. Condoms and contraceptives are part of the supplies. Anyway, Rob confided in me. He knew Tanner before, like ten years back. And what he knew probably got him killed."

"Well, go on," Zen said after a few moments of silence.

"That's all I'm gonna say. If the others know, and I think they do, then you should want to leave just as much as me." Iesha pressed her full lips together. She stared at them and then at the wall.

"You're saying Drs. Richards and Belmont are in on the death of Rob Hunter?" Malone's frown deepened as he looked at Zen.

"I don't know for sure, but I don't want to take any chances," Iesha said.

"We're going to take you into custody no matter what," Zen replied.

"Richards and Belmont are going to want to know what she said and how it affects Goddard, the camp. Everything." Malone raised an eyebrow at Zen.

"I was scared you found out I had some weed stashed away and I've been stealing experimental drugs," Iesha said.

"They'll never buy you broke down and confessed so quick. Even I know you're tougher than that," Malone retorted.

"The cook caught me smoking one night, and she saw me coming out of the storage lockers behind the kitchen. Tell them you saw the report on missing inventory and Ellen snitched. She doesn't like me much, so they'll believe it. She had a thing for Rob." Iesha's words rushed out as the sound of footsteps got closer.

Zen grunted. "Girl, please. Like we're going to take direction from *you*."

"What's your plan? What are you gonna do with me?" Iesha's eyes went wide.

"Not offer your weak-ass story for one thing," Zen retorted.

She bent down to pull Iesha to her feet and Malone stepped in to help. They took her to the room Belmont had told them about. He'd moved boxes and equipment, set up a field cot, and even installed a portable potty. A small window in the door allowed a view inside. Zen looked in at Iesha Franklin. The woman paced for a few second then spun around to glare back at Zen. Malone managed to fend off questions as they secured their prisoner. Once Iesha was locked in, Dr. Richards wouldn't be put off any longer.

"As the director of this operation, I should have a complete explanation of what the hell just happened." Dr. Richards blocked the door leading from the lab. Two crew members stood behind her.

Malone studied her for a few seconds. "This camp is a designated foreign mission. Which means as federal special agents we're law enforcement. Ms. Franklin is now in our custody."

Zen spoke up. "She panicked, thinking we'd uncovered her petty thefts. I can't say more for the moment."

"But that doesn't make sense," Dr. Richards shot back.

"I've sent messages to our agency. We have full authority. You want to see the email from your VP of Goddard space operations?" Zen held up her tablet and opened the screen.

Dr. Richards glared at her without reading it. After a few beats she stepped aside and nodded to her staff. "I expect a full report shortly. I intend to discuss this with the head office, too."

"Arrange for Bruno to come early. This area is off-limits to everyone except us until we leave," Zen said to Dr. Richards. The director stomped off with the two crew members following.

"So much for getting sleep." Malone looked around the lab.

"Iesha can't get out, and Richards and Belmont won't try anything. Their bosses know. Plus, security footage." Zen pointed to cameras tucked into two corners of opposite walls.

"You said the story about thefts was too weak." Malone yawned and stretched.

"It'll get us through the next few hours."

"Until then we're in hostile territory," Malone replied.

"Yeah." Zen walked over to the locked door and put her face close to the small window. "She better have a damn good story."

# Chapter 8

Four hours later Bruno arrived. Sunlight had just begun to paint the landscape a pale yellow. Oddly enough, Zen had gone back to sleep again without much trouble. She woke to the sound of her smartwatch beeping a wake-up call. Malone arrived just as she pulled on her hiking boots. He grumbled a good morning, a paper cup of coffee in one hand. Without much fanfare, they packed Iesha into the SUV. Dr. Richards repeated her complaints. Malone assured her once again they'd send information later. As they pulled away, Malone showed Zen two dispatches Clive had sent him during the early-morning hours. She read silently and they didn't discuss the contents. Once they were on the road to Calama, Malone heaved a sigh. He glanced at Iesha seated on the third row behind him. They'd untied her hands.

"What a day already. At least they let us take breakfast for the road," Malone said. He turned to Iesha again. "Hey, sure you don't want a bagel?"

"I'm not putting anything from that place in my mouth," Iesha replied. "Thanks for not making me wear handcuffs for the trip."

"Making a run for it in the middle of the desert wouldn't be so smart," Zen retorted.

"Hey, I'm your best chance to find out what's going on," Iesha complained.

"I had them print me out a copy of inventory checks and supply lists." Zen pulled out the pages. She scanned them. "So, items have gone missing. That part wasn't a lie."

"You took part in the thefts?" Malone asked Iesha.

"Just get me out of here and back home," came the terse reply.

Neither Malone nor Zen tried to question her again. Bruno drove them to the local offices of the Carabineros, the Chilean national police. They handled most day-to-day crimes in the country. Clive had arranged for them to take Iesha there for more questioning. The United States and Chile had cooperative law enforcement agreements. Also, the status of the camp as a foreign mission afforded it limited diplomatic privileges. The thefts onsite were within the jurisdiction of the US, so Zen and Malone could be in charge. The police chief arranged for one of his female officers to get Iesha breakfast. Once she'd eaten, Zen and Malone sat across from her in the room set up for them.

Iesha patted her lips with a napkin. "That wasn't bad. Y'all got my stuff from the camp? I had a bag—"

"This isn't a hotel, and we're not your concierge," Zen said in a dry tone.

"We have your personal belongings," Malone replied, moving into his good cop role again. "Don't worry about it. Now, tell us the whole story."

"I came up rough in Detroit, you know. Back when I was eleven my mother left us. Daddy did his best, but you know. Drugs." Iesha shook her head.

"We don't care about how you skinned your knee in the fifth grade, okay?" Zen squinted at her.

"For a social worker you sure come across hard." Iesha stared at Zen with distaste.

"Ms. Franklin, let me explain the situation you're in," Malone said in a patient voice.

"Oh, I know what *situation* I'm in. You can believe it," Iesha clipped back. "I'm the only one that can spill what's going on at the camp. Maybe at Goddard and their whole space program."

"Which is?" Zen let skepticism drip from her tone.

"If you let me tell it my way, you'd have it," Iesha replied with heat.

Malone waved a signal at Zen. "We've got time. Go on, but it needs to be relevant."

"Thank you," Iesha replied to Malone and cast a mean side-eye at Zen. "Goddard has this thing for disadvantaged youth, a special program. They identify smart but poor kids, some with juvenile offense records. A kind of special STEM diversion program."

"And that's how you got involved?" Malone asked.

"Eventually. Not just kids, but college students. I didn't realize they recruited at adult prisons. Not until I finished school and started working for them full-time. Rob and Tan are two. They both had criminal records. Even smart ones get caught." Iesha shrugged.

"Minor convictions, we know." Zen gazed at Iesha.

Iesha smirked at them in turn. "No, you don't. Goddard Corporation has clout. I guess they can even keep stuff from the feds."

"Stop the game and say what you mean," Zen replied.

"Look, what I'm about to tell you is a bomb. It could get us all blown to bits. How do you know Goddard hasn't paid off the local cops here?" Iesha had lowered her voice and leaned forward.

"If there's a killer still at the camp, you owe it to your former co-workers. Their lives are at risk. They have families like you," Malone said.

"He's not gonna try anything. The only threat to him ended up at the bottom of a dry ditch in a desert," Iesha said and shivered. "Except for me. That's why I had to leave. He knows I know. Or suspects I do."

"You're safe here. Now, take your time and tell us what you know," Malone said.

Iesha fidgeted for a few seconds. "Yeah, I guess. But Goddard and the government didn't know about Tan."

"Enough of this bullshit. You're going to a jail cell." Zen pushed back her chair as if to stand.

"Wait a minute! I'm all you got to get at the truth," Iesha yelped.

"I'll tell you one truth, missing drugs and equipment. I have the inventory lists and the reviews," Zen shot back.

"You mean the medicines? You can't get high off that crap. Most of it was for pain or sunburn. Except some experimental stuff. Look, I didn't take no equipment. Okay, maybe a few of those high-tech ink pens." Iesha's words came out in a rush as her gaze darted from Zen to Malone and back again.

Malone's stone-faced expression seemed to convey he'd lost his patience as well. "Talk."

Iesha flinched at the single word command. "Rob and Tan were in the same prison. Rob stole from a couple of stores. I just assumed Tanner was in for something similar. But then Rob told me he'd been up on more serious charges. A couple of times witnesses were too scared to testify. Tan used to joke about it when they were locked up."

"Okay, so..." Zen gestured for her to keep talking.

"Goddard execs assured the government no one with a record of violent offenses would be on the crews." Iesha blinked at them when neither Malone nor Zen responded. "He slipped through because he didn't have *convictions*."

"I can't believe with all of Goddard's resources they didn't know," Malone said after a few beats.

"You're saying Martin killed Rob Hunter to cover up his violent past?" Zen frowned at Iesha. Not because she didn't believe her, but the motive sounded shaky.

"Rob knew too much for Tan to risk his job. See, Tan had gotten in good with Nyla and Javier. The bosses were impressed with his skills. He's good at fixing things."

"I don't get how him being such a good handyman is so special though," Malone said.

Iesha shook her head. "He's a lot more than your everyday Mr. Fix-it. Tan can handle complicated devices. All he has to do is study the schematics, boom, he can maintain or repair anything. He even came up with improvements. Remember, there are no dummies picked for these jobs."

"Humph." Malone rubbed his jaw.

"Look, let me lay it out. Tan has a real shot at moving up to higher-paying positions. Rob made the mistake of bringing up Tan's past one day when they were reminiscing.

Nobody else was around, but Rob got more and more nervous. Tan started giving off scary vibes. Next thing, Rob turns up dead. An accident with Tan being the only witness."

"And Rob confided in you," Zen said.

"After the first 'accident,' when the bucket of a mini-excavator just missed Rob's head. Guess who was at the controls?" Iesha tapped the tabletop with a finger.

"Tanner Martin," Malone answered.

"Bingo. That's when Rob told me everything. Tan stalked two previous girlfriends. He was an enforcer for a local gang, but nobody was brave enough to testify against him. Rob always told me, it's not the stuff a guy's gone to prison for you have to worry about. It's the stuff he did and got away with."

"If Goddard knows all this, then Martin would have no reason to hurt him." Zen glanced at Malone.

"Yeah, but—" Malone stopped at the knock on the door. An officer came in and they spoke to each other in Spanish. Then Malone left with him.

"What's going on?" Iesha twisted around to stare at the door.

"Let's continue. All employees had detailed background checks done on them by Goddard Corporation. They have a security division." Zen spoke up to cover the sound of muted voices outside.

Iesha continued to stare at the closed door. "I don't know how they missed it. What are they talking about?"

Malone opened the door and gestured to Zen. "A minute. Just relax, Iesha. We won't be long."

"Hey, I have a right to know what's going on. I'm sticking my neck out for you people," Iesha yelled.

"You've got your own worries based on security footage. Now settle down," Malone replied.

Zen joined him and the chief in the hallway. "I'm just as eager to know what's happening."

"Martin hijacked the one Land Rover from the training camp. He's on the run," Malone said.

"Our officers will find him, no worries," the chief said. She followed with more rapid-fire Spanish to Malone. Then she marched off with more of her officers.

"Okay, I caught random snatches of that," Zen replied. "If he gets to Santiago he'll get lost in the crowd."

"Chilean police are good. And he's in the Atacama Desert. GPS is very unreliable. But..." Malone huffed out air.

"But?" Zen frowned at his expression.

"He made his getaway before sunrise, "Malone said. "The electric motor on it was modified not to make much noise."

"Let me guess. Mr. Wizard is the one who came up with the improvement."

"Maybe he meant to run even before last night." Malone gazed at the door to the interview room where Iesha waited.

"His backup plan. Now what?" Zen looked up at him.

"Even if the Carabineros don't catch up with him, he can't hide forever. We need to check if he's got any contacts in this country." Malone held up his smartwatch and tapped the screen. "I'll message Dr. Richards at the camp."

"Or neighboring Argentina," Zen added. "I'll contact Clive to get the wheels grinding with Interpol and the CIA.

They'll issue alerts, coordinate with the Chilean and Argentinian authorities."

"He won't get far. I don't know why he thinks running will help." Malone read the display on his smartwatch with a scowl.

"He didn't have a lot of options. I'll let you break the news that she'll be sitting in a jail cell. She likes you more than me," Zen said.

Malone grunted. "No surprise there. I get to be bad cop next time."

"Yeah, it's kinda fun." Zen grinned at him.

"She's right. You're pretty tough for a social worker." Malone continued to read and tap short messages.

"Being underestimated is my secret weapon," Zen quipped.

Malone shot a side glance at her. "Duly noted. Okay, Richards says based on his file Martin shouldn't have any connections locally."

"Not reassuring. If Iesha is correct that means Goddard has gaps in their records on crew members. Ready?" Zen nodded at the interview room.

"Wish I had earplugs to blot out the screaming we're about to suffer through," Malone joked.

Zen placed a hand on his shoulder. "Hold up. You play the part of the disappointed friend. I accuse her of helping Martin escape, that this was an act to create a diversion. Pretend I've all but convinced you."

"Um, I don't see it. Might be better if we don't tell her about Martin." Malone wore a confused frown.

"We need to confirm her account. Maybe she had an affair with Tanner Martin, not Rob. It's possible. Watch her reaction," Zen said.

"Worth a shot. You don't think he'll try to get her out?"

"Even if they were a couple, I doubt he's the knight in shining armor type." Zen reached for the door handle. "Here we go."

As expected, Iesha howled in protest. She quieted down when told Martin was on the loose. Malone peppered Iesha with questions about Rob, Martin, and the missing inventory. As Zen suspected, Iesha had seen the value of selling high tech equipment. She'd hoped the small tools wouldn't be missed or would be counted as lost. Some Rob reported as damaged out in the fields, dropped into deep valleys. She and Rob had used the money to party in local towns when allowed breaks from the camp. After another hour of sweating facts from Iesha, she was escorted to her temporary home. The cells at the local jail weren't so bad. Not that she had a choice. Malone and Zen met with the local head of the Carabineros, Director Hector Lòpez.

"So, our working theory of motive is Tanner Martin didn't want his criminal secrets to get out. Rob Hunter talked too much, especially when he was drinking. He gets him out in the desert and gives him a not-so-gentle push." Malone stood with his arms crossed in the director's office.

"Sounds plausible." Zen wore a slight frown. Means, motive, and opportunity. It all lined up, if you looked at it sideways.

"It is a routine murder investigation. We could handle it, of course," the director said. He spread his hands out. "But since you wish to take charge of your citizens, who are we to argue?"

"We've arranged for our federal marshals to transport Ms. Franklin back to the states. As a material witness, not a suspect. At least for Hunter's death. Same for Martin when he's caught," Malone said.

"It won't take long; I can assure you. He doesn't have local people to help and his Spanish is limited. He'll be very noticeable. And my officers are good at what they do." Director Lòpez smiled at them. Except for the uniform, the silver-haired Lòpez looked like a calm, genial uncle.

"Great, sir. Now we'll get back to the camp," Malone said with a crisp nod.

As they left the office, Zen grinned at him. "I thought you were going to salute the guy."

"He reminds me of my commanding officer back at the first base I was assigned to. I don't doubt his officers will find Martin. I just hope they give him to us in one piece. Don't let the friendly smile fool you. The Chilean national police are no joke," Malone replied.

"If he's got any sense, Martin won't try to fight his way to freedom." Zen took out her tablet. "Clive sent me the ID photos of the two special agents on the way. Director Lòpez should have them by now. Back to the camp?"

"Back to the camp."

They found Bruno waiting for them at a café a block from the police office. After a brief respite to get water, they were on the road. Malone read several updates from Director Lòpez on sightings of Martin. They didn't talk much on the ride. The driver dropped them off outside the main building.

Richards and Belmont were waiting for them when they arrived.

"Is Iesha okay?" Belmont spoke first.

"She's fine. You think we tortured her or something?" Malone joked.

"The national police have a reputation, but no. We're sure with you here she'll be fine," Richards said with a side look at Belmont.

Belmont still looked jittery. "The courts here can be harsh, and the prisons very rough."

"Director Lòpez isn't eager to get involved in a murder investigation involving foreigners. He's not questioning how far the alleged crime happened away from the camp." Zen put away her tablet and studied him.

Malone faced Belmont. "You seem especially concerned about Ms. Franklin."

"She's young and made mistakes. The things she took aren't high value. Nothing that interfered with our work. And Rob influenced her," Belmont replied with conviction.

"Twenty-five is a bit old for the hanging-with-a-bad-crowd defense." Zen continued to gaze at him steadily. "But I'm sure she'll be okay. Our special agents will be here tomorrow."

"Maybe I'll visit her. I mean, she's still a Goddard employee. And we're not going to press charges." Belmont looked at Richards. When she gave a reluctant nod, he strode away without saying good-bye.

"No charges?" Malone raised both eyebrows at Dr. Richards.

She gazed after Belmont for a few seconds, blinking hard before she turned back. "Like Javier said, what went missing isn't worth the trouble. She'll be reprimanded and have pay withheld to compensate for the cost."

Zen exchanged a surprised look with Malone. "That's awfully forgiving."

"Ms. Franklin has an otherwise-spotless work record with us. And she's very talented, though still a bit immature. She's part of our corporate mentorship program. Believe it or not, Iesha has come a long way. What she did was minor. And she's cooperating with your investigation I understand." Dr. Richards gestured for them to follow her inside, which they did.

"Speaking of which, Bruno is going to drive us to the scene of Hunter's death again. We'll take more pictures," Malone said once they were in Dr. Richards's office.

She closed the door and faced them. "Has Iesha provided information about Rob's death? We're still assuming it's an accident."

"Martin ran. Usually an indication of guilt," Zen said.

"Listen, this is a closed society. I'm sure you, Dr. Batiste, understand the implications of such a disruption. I read a synopsis of your work on the social dynamics of space colonies," Dr. Richards replied.

"But you're not in space," Malone put in.

"We can only simulate the environment of space in a limited way, naturally. But we do try to create the same conditions as much as possible."

"Right. Crew members wear spacesuits to collect samples outside and inside for several hours at a time," Zen said.

"Not only that. We encourage a sense of community, of interdependence among the crew. My point is the rest of my team is worried about both Iesha and Tan."

"He was with a crew member who ended up dead. Some might call the circumstances unclear at best. Tanner Martin runs away and ..." Malone spread his arms out and gazed at Richards.

"But you're still convinced it was an accident," Zen said.

"Tan and Rob were known to hide liquor in their water bottles. We always take two or three with us since it's so dry out here. Nothing harmful, just a bit of fun. We don't leave the camp often. Tan's probably scared because they weren't very careful, and he feels bad about Rob."

"They've done that before?" Malone asked.

"Yes, a couple of times. I didn't mention it to the investigator that came out before because—" Dr. Richards broke off and sat. "We're under a lot of stress to get ready in a short amount of time. I've pushed the crew hard. Maybe too hard."

"You didn't want your bosses to know about minor incidents like drinking or sneaking off to party in town?" Zen looked at her.

"I reported everything to the VP of space colony operations. I didn't cover anything up. We have to monitor all of our people's behavior, especially with the very real isolation of a lunar colony. The only outlet will be vising another Goddard camp or the NASA site. They have a café of sorts onsite. Our company knows boredom, Earth sickness, and interpersonal tensions will take a toll. And yes, I'm still quite sure it was an accident," Richards insisted, her chin up.

Malone cleared his throat and frowned at her. "We're going to start over with you telling us *everything*."

"I've told you everything already," Dr. Richards said in a tone cold as steel. She returned his glare with one of her own.

"Except you left out sneaking drinks, slipping off to party, Iesha and Rob's affair," Malone clipped.

"We'll need to speak to your cook again, and the guy who shares quarters with Hunter. Then we'll go to the site one last time. Make the arrangements, please," Zen added the last word in a firm tone.

Richards stood and strode to the door without speaking. She yanked it open hard enough that it bounced back on its hinges. Malone faced Zen and blew out a long breath once her bootsteps faded.

"You believe this crap?" Malone blurted and combed his fingers through his thick, dark hair.

"If she's telling the truth and her bosses knew, then maybe Goddard is covering. They could be keeping these blips from us, meaning the government. NASA in particular." Zen continued to gaze at the open door.

"Yeah, well, it doesn't say much for their screening process either," Malone said.

"You really think Goddard didn't know about Tanner Martin? I find that hard to believe," Zen replied.

"Maybe, like Iesha, they overlooked his past to give him a second chance. Hey, it's happened with the military. You heard Iesha and Richards. They're into rehabilitation, especially when it comes to talented people."

"It's just... like my granddaddy in Louisiana used to say, 'somethin' just don't sit right. I didn't recognize the names on some of those pill bottles." Zen glanced around the director's office as if looking for a clue.

"Huh?"

"Nothing. I'll dig into it later." Zen looked at him with a crooked grin. Hey, you gave up good cop, partner."

"Richards got on my bad side with the attitude. Let's take a look at the crime scene again." Malone jerked a thumb toward the exit.

They found Bruno outside leaning against the Range Rover. He shared gossip from locals about possible sightings of Tanner Martin. Bruno assured them that even with modern satellites, GPS could not be relied on in the desert. The general consensus was he'd either die from heat and thirst or get caught soon. Zen hoped it would be the latter. Martin had answers they needed, if he gave them up.

Bruno drove for about twenty minutes over what he assured them was a path. Even with great shocks, the SUV jolted them around. The driver took the rough ride in stride. They arrived at the line of rock formations where Rob Hunter took a fall. A series of yellow flags still marked the site. Bruno parked away from the scene to keep from disturbing it more. He settled in with a bottle of water and newspaper to wait for them. Malone and Zen struck out to trace the path Martin had told them they'd taken. The wind picked up and Malone zipped his jacket.

"I thought deserts were supposed to be hot like the sun," Malone said. The landscape was reflected in the mirror surface of his sunglasses.

"Good thing Hadley did her research to bust our preconceptions. Bless whoever invented thermal undies."

Zen trod ahead of him over rocks. She stared up at the tall mini-mountain. Malone stood in the shadow of one portion. The warm tan color of their surroundings was starkly beautiful. Even wearing her own sunglasses, Zen shaded her eyes as she gazed up.

"They decided to rock climb out here with iffy radio contact and not a lot of experience," Malone said as if he could read her train of thought.

"According to Martin. Now we know not to believe what he told us. Look." Zen pointed. "It tapers down to the west."

"You're not suggesting we climb," Malone complained.

"Why do you think we're wearing hiking boots? I brought climbing equipment." Zen trotted back to the SUV without waiting for Malone.

"You've got to be kidding me," Malone yelled after her.

"Quite whining. It's a way for you to warm up," Zen called back and laughed at his string of curses.

Bruno helped her pull out the ropes and two helmets. Malone uttered a few more expletives when Zen handed him one. Then they set off for the formation again.

"Fighting off suspects, climbing five-story rocks. They teach you that in social work school?" Malone said as they stood looking up at their target once more.

"Thanks to my father I did sports, gymnastics, and obstacle courses. Oh, and rock climbing in gyms and on vacations in Texas. My dad has two brothers there." Zen snapped the chin strap of her yellow helmet.

"Sounds like he wanted you in the military." Malone rolled his shoulders.

"Yeah, but I got interested in psychology. I'm not a total disappointment since I worked for the DOJ." Zen pointed. "See? It widens farther up. Notice I didn't bring harnesses. I won't ask you to go over the side."

"Thanks. My least-favorite part of training. Too many ways to get killed." Malone stared down. He waved at Bruno, who flapped both arms in response.

"A lesson Hunter learned the hard way," Zen replied.

They both huffed from the effects of the altitude. They kept conversation to a minimum after a while. The climb required concentration and caution. Rocks could suddenly shift. After five minutes, Zen reached the right spot first. She gazed around to admire the view and catch her breath. Malone stopped to take a long drink of water.

"Remember to hydrate." Malone waved his bottle at her then clipped it back to his belt.

"Good idea," Zen yelled back, realizing her throat was indeed dry. She quenched her thirst and put her own bottle back in the shoulder holster. "Okay, so from the position of where he landed, this is about where they were."

"Beautiful. I can see why anyone would like taking it all in." Malone looked around and then down.

"This is remote and dry. Why not head for the coast? A day on the beach would be even better. Or at one of the lagoons around here. I'd be looking for water all the time."

"Yeah, well, you grew up in Maryland not far from water and Louisiana, the land of bayous. Could be they wanted a different—" Malone stopped and knelt. He took off his sunglasses.

"Ah, the boy wonder has found evidence that solves the case."

Malone looked at her with a grin. "I may have, smartass. Just give me a minute."

Zen found a semi-flat section of the formation and took a seat. She watched him walked a few paces in one direction. He shook his head and retraced his steps going past her. Malone stopped and took pictures of something Zen couldn't see. He took small knife out of a jacket pocket and scrapped pieces of stone. Then he put a large pebble in one small evidence bag and dirt in another. Bruno, a smaller dot in the distance now, seemed curious. He stared in their direction, interested in his passengers.

"Well?" Zen stood and dusted off the seat of her pants.

"Blood. Sure of it. I can only think of one reason why blood would be up here." Malone handed her the bags.

Zen stared at the contents of the polycarbonate bags. The material was one of several made from minerals mined from outer space. The tan rock had what looked like two black spots on them. She then looked at the bag of dirt. At first, she missed it. Then she saw the hair.

"Hunter was already hurt when he went over the side," Zen said.

"Here, and here, and here." Malone pointed. He handed the compact forensic camera to Zen and walked away.

While he continued to look, Zen followed his cryptic instructions. She took more pictures of the rock from different angles. After another twenty minutes of walking the crest, they scrambled down again. As they walked back to the SUV, Zen and Malone talked freely while they could. Then they directed Bruno to drive them back to the camp—with one diversion. Zen convinced Bruno to take them to one of the briny lakes nearby. Her request was rewarded. Chilean pink flamingos dotted the sandy shoreline. She spent fifteen minutes talking photos of the lovely birds. Malone waited patiently while Zen delighted in getting close-up shots of the relaxed birds. They ignored her, intent on looking for brine shrimp. Meanwhile, Malone managed to get a connection and send updates to Clive as they drove.

Back at camp, Zen went off to interview the crew member, one of two who cooked their meals, who disliked Iesha. Malone found the man who shared sleeping quarters with Rob Hunter. An hour later they met up again outside to compare notes.

"The woman definitely doesn't like Iesha," Zen said once she and Malone were alone. "She pretty much called her a lying slut. According to her, Iesha had sex with every heterosexual male she came across."

"Harsh." Malone chuckled.

"I got her to admit that Rob traded her in for Iesha. Aside from a chance to vent about her love rival, she didn't add much."

"The roomie didn't give me anything new, either. Still says Rob didn't seem worried or upset on the day of his death or the days before," Malone said.

"So, if Tanner Martin was a threat Rob didn't see it coming," Zen replied.

"I think we're pretty much done here. I want to get these samples back for analysis." Malone started to say more when the camp director walked in.

"Can I see you both in my office before you leave?" Richards left as if she expected them to follow.

Malone clenched his jaw and exchanged a look with Zen. She waved at him as a signal to keep it cool. Then they walked to the larger building housing her office. Crew members were upstairs on the landing, talking low. They stopped when Zen and Malone entered. Three sets of steady gazes followed them to Richards's office.

"We know our investigation has been a bit of disruption—" Zen began and stopped when Richards raised a palm.

"A bit? More like an earthquake. My crew can't seem to talk about anything else. My orders not to spread rumors is a joke." Richards crossed her arms.

"The problems started *before* we got here. Two people are dead," Malone replied, his voice raised but not to a shout.

Richards blew out air. "Of course, you're absolutely correct."

"Thank you," Malone retorted.

"We found out things that needed to come out. The safety of the entire crew could have been at stake," Zen said.

"I've busted ass to get us ready for the colony. We've done several successful experiments. Now all my boss can talk about is 'getting the train back on the tracks. Like it's my fault. I'm not in charge of screening potential colonists." Richards paced as she spoke.

"Let me guess. Your boss handles screening and selection at the initial stages," Zen said, her tone sympathetic.

Richards stopped and faced Zen. I'm not going down for his screw up."

"A lot is at stake, especially with the first colony in trouble. Now these issues with the crew of the second colony means Goddard won't have a footprint on the moon," Zen replied.

"Which means another space corporation will fill the gap. NASA and the White House doesn't want to lose momentum, or the potential flow of dollars," Malone added.

"So, Goddard will try to fix this problem fast. Find someone to blame, dump them, and provide assurances the issues are resolved." Zen paused to let the implication sink in with Richards. The director was more than halfway there already. "Recent events might help you see something in a new light. Something you might not have thought had much significance before."

Dr. Richards huffed out a breath and stood straight. "I apologize for the meltdown. My boss is under as much stress as I am, maybe more. My outburst was more frustration. I'm sure we'll pull together and weather this temporary storm."

Zen glanced at Malone. Their window of opportunity had passed to get inside scoop on the inner workings of

Goddard Corporation. Richards probably remembered being a team player would benefit her much more.

"Yeah, right." Malone pressed his lips together.

"Let Iesha know she's still part of our family. We don't write off people after one mistake," Richards said. She appeared to be back in full control again.

Malone tilted his head to one side. "And Tanner Martin?"

"Obviously, his situation is more... complicated, and how we'll deal with him depends on your investigation."

"You won't deal with him if it turns out he's a murderer," Malone said.

"There are no conspiracies or killers here, Agent Ramirez," Richards said.

"Recent events suggest otherwise," Malone replied in a mild tone.

Her satellite desk phone trilled before she could go on. Richards picked up the handset. "Hello, yes Coronel. No, of course not. I don't— They're still here."

Zen accepted the handset when she held it out. "*Hola. No, ciertamente no lo hicimos.* We're on our way. Thanks."

Malone looked at Zen. "Developments?"

"Two men impersonated federal marshals and tried to take Iesha Franklin from the station. Shots were fired." Zen faced Richards again, both hands on her hips. "It seems someone is anxious that we not talk to her or Tanner Martin."

"Martin?" Malone asked Zen.

"Not any more. They found him dead on a side street in Santiago."

# Chapter 9

The next eight hours were fast-paced and exhausting. The real US Marshals arrived, a man and woman, and took charge of Iesha. Through the 2055 International Police Treaty the United States had with dozens of countries, extradition was much less complicated than in the past. Broad cooperative law enforcement agreements across world borders were one feature anti-globalists criticized. The world had moved closer to an international governing body. The United Nations continued to transform, with more legitimate power to take action. Notable holdouts clung to the nationalism of previous centuries. China, Russia, a handful of African nations, and three Asian countries being the major ones. Proponents of transnationalism argued the fruits of jingoism: corruption, poverty, and war.

Political battles were far from Zen and Malone's minds for the moment. A short stay had stretched into four action-packed days. Now, they were more concerned with getting their witness back to the states in one piece. Zen and Malone spent almost an hour convincing Iesha they were real. Finally, Zen went back into bad cop mode and assured her she could stay in the Chilean prison system. Iesha quickly chose the better option.

Malone accompanied them to the airport. Colonel Lopez allowed Zen to use a small office at the station. There, she completed electronic international paperwork in less than thirty minutes. Through treaties, governments allowed great latitude to foreign law enforcement. However, classified reports had to be filed with all the countries involved. Then she debriefed Drs. Richards and Belmont via remote video conference. Her summary to them left out sensitive details. They knew it and weren't happy. After a tense fifteen-minute conversation, Zen signed off. Then Zen completed the grim duty of arranging transport of Tanner Martin's corpse to America. By that time Malone had returned. Afternoon shadows lengthened as sundown approached.

"Let's get the hell out of here," Zen blurted out when he walked in. She stood and massaged the tight muscles of her neck.

Malone glanced at his smartwatch. "Almost six-thirty. I could use a solid meal right about now. C'mon. My treat."

Zen put on her jacket to ward off the evening chill. "You mean the agency expense account."

"Don't nitpick," Malone quipped.

They opted for Italian food at Lucertole, a restaurant with a lovely courtyard. It had been built around old tree trunks that rose up from the floor to the ceiling. The soft lighting and calm atmosphere were a soothing contrast. Malone ordered ribs and pasta. Zen chose linguini and Chilean sea bass.

"Did Iesha do okay with the Marshals?" Zen asked and stuffed her mouth. She only realized how hungry she was once they'd been handed menus.

"Humph," Malone replied around his own mouthful of ribs. He chewed for a few moments. "That female marshal? Remind me to request her the next time we need them. She got Ms. Franklin's attitude in check real quick."

"Good. Unexpected plot twists, huh?" Zen took dainty sips of pinot grigio and sighed with pleasure.

"Um, yeah. A few. Glad you got to tell Clive all the good news." Malone winked at her.

"No wonder you were fine with driving the marshals and Iesha to the airport." Zen kicked him beneath the table.

"Dealing with Chilean police and airport security was no picnic, partner," Malone said and pointed his fork at her. "They triple-checked everything. Then repeated the process."

"If I hadn't done all the e-forms, it would have been worse. You're welcome," Zen countered.

"So, is our boss nursing a migraine because of the stuff we uncovered under desert rocks?" Malone continued to dig into his food.

"I can see how concerned you are," Zen quipped. Then she sighed and leaned back, wine glass in hand.

"Hey, we earned this. And a good sleep in comfortable beds before we fly out tomorrow. Just try not to cause more drama before we get out of Chile," Malone joked with an impish twinkle in his eyes.

"Oh sure."

"I don't know, Batiste. Trouble seems to follow your cute little rear end."

Zen shook her head. "They can't blame this mess on *me*. Goddard execs got some explaining to do. I wouldn't want to be on their side of the meeting table. Clive says the big guy himself will be meeting with the agencies."

"Which ones?" Malone finished off his half-pint of beer. He signaled for and got a refill.

"NASA, NSA, DOD, DOJ. A host of letters," Zen joked.

Malone sat forward and lowered his voice. "I get the feeling we only know a small piece of how big this thing is."

"We're going to peel it like an onion. The more we uncover, the more Clive will have to tell us," Zen replied.

"Uh-uh. I'll bet Clive starts to handle more. And some other top NSA or CIA agent," Malone replied and went back to his ribs. "Our agencies are paranoid about leaks."

"Even with the events in Madrid, the NSA controlled the public media accounts. We've both proven we can keep our mouths shut. Clive wouldn't have chosen us otherwise," Zen argued. "Besides, we turned up a lot of serious issues. What more could there be?"

"We still have the Goddard lunar colonists to interrogate," Malone said.

Zen winced at the prospect. "Damn, maybe Clive will give the junior agents-in-training the experience."

"Seriously?"

"Yeah, at most they'll do initial fact-gathering. The heavy lifting will be up to us. At least they have a few more days to decontaminate. That means we'll have the weekend off." Zen clinked her glass of wine against his in a toast.

"I love your youthful optimism. How much you want to bet Hadley is drawing up our to-do list as we speak?"

"Don't spoil the mood," Zen whined.

Malone laughed and they moved on to mundane topics of what they'd do once home. Astra had opted to stay longer with her father. She assured Zen that her schoolwork had been kept up. Not that Zen worried much about it. Astra had inherited a zeal for learning from both sides the family. She was also relentless when it came to finishing what she started. Malone had already set up a day of fishing with his boys. He swore an oath not to answer messages that might pull him into work.

They went back to the hotel, warm showers, and bed. At five a.m. the next day, Zen rose for an early-morning run. Thirty minutes later she crossed path with Malone. They completed cool-down stretches together. After cleaning up they were on their way to the airport. The flight home was long, but uneventful. Zen caught up on news. Malone alternated between flirting with the pretty female flight attendants and reading both their notes. They arrived at Obama National Airport across the Potomac River outside Arlington at ten o'clock Friday night. With only their small carry-on bags, they quickly went to the transportation hub. Zen would take the monorail home. Malone opted for a self-driving car to his condo.

With the real prospect of Saturday and Sunday to herself, Zen booked a spa appointment online. She sighed with happiness when the taxi stopped in front of her house.

She'd barely dropped her bag on the floor of her kitchen when her smartwatch trilled a tone. Her father's face flashed on the call ID screen. She hit speaker.

"Hey, are you okay? Mama okay?"

"Good evening to you, too, daughter," James Batiste rumbled on the other end. "Switch."

Zen blinked at his face for a few minutes. Hours of travel and the pieces of the investigation puzzle caused a mental logjam. Her father's pointed, dark-eyed gaze finally got through. They had a code when she needed to use the secure app on her smartwatch. She tapped the screen and ended the call. Then she used her house phone to call him back. James Batiste knew all too well that her agency-issued devices weren't secure, at least not from the NSA, CIA, FBI, or Secret Service. Her employers had the right to examine her call and text history at any time. Even those of a personal nature. Her father picked up on the first ring.

"We're both fine, Zenobia," James said without saying hello.

"It's just you don't usually call so late. You know what Grandpapa Chatelain always says. Messages after ten at night are always bad news." Zen felt the tension drain from her shoulders. "What's up?"

"Jordan called. And Astra's fine, too," her father added quickly. "We need to talk about the space colonies. I've found out something worrisome."

Zen took the cordless handset and went to her office. Then she turned on the video display on her desk. "How worrisome?"

"An eight," James replied, using their inside ten-point scale.

"With the potential to go up, I'm guessing," Zen replied. She tapped the slender keypad that brought her computer to life.

"Politics and money. A nasty mix. You and your dashing partner uncovered problems with Goddard Corporation. By the way, Ramirez has a reputation for—"

"I'm not attracted to him, Daddy," Zen broke in. She entered her three-step login as she spoke.

"You know what I always say," James said.

"Yeah, yeah. I gave him the speech. He's a big fan, by the way."

"Then he knows I'll cut off his head and his balls if he messes with my daughter," James retorted.

Okay. I'm in. I see the information."

Zen had logged into her computer, then into the encrypted block chain cloud. Her father had long used it to store family documents. Once Zen started working for first the DOJ and then the NSA, he used it to communicate with her at times.

"Goddard will be meeting with a lot of heavy hitters this weekend, right?" James said.

Zen smiled at his image. "You already know you're right, Daddy. You probably have a copy of the agenda."

James grinned back. "You won't be offered up as a sacrifice. I made a few calls."

"Why would I be in hot water for finding out the facts? Hell, that's why I went to Chile."

"You know how these things work. We got your back," her father said.

"We?"

"Never mind. Rob Goddard is going to show up in person, which is a very big deal. A true measure of how seriously they're taking the situation." James's expression turned solemn again.

"I'm no threat to their trillion-dollar investment in space," Zen said and turned to the read the screen.

"Scapegoats assure the powerful that the government is serious about appeasing them. A public display of commitment," James said.

"One or more high-profile Goddard employee will be punished. Our government will reciprocate and do the same to me." Zen clicked her tongue.

"Normally you'd be perfect for the role. After Madrid, I mean. Which is why I've always told you—"

"Yes, Father. I remember. Don't make mistakes and give them an excuse to go after you. Lives were at stake, and I had a Plan B," Zen clipped.

"Fortunately, you came out a hero. You won't get blamed for exposing the flaws in Goddard's trainee program."

Zen gave a snort of disgust. "Instead of fixing problems, the focus becomes punishing the person who discovered them."

"Our government does both. Except you have a habit of being untouchable. Drives upper management a bit nuts."

"I don't do it on purpose," Zen retorted. She went back to reading. "Okay, so Goddard left out details about their work with ex-prisoners and young people with juvenile records. Well, glossed over them."

James nodded. "Turns out over half their lower-level space trainees have criminal histories. Here's what's interesting, though—they're not garden-variety ex-offenders."

"All of them have high intelligence and/or extraordinary skills," Zen put in.

"You figured it out. They, Goddard's recruiters, have identified some of the brightest minds the prison system has to offer. Pretty genius when you think about it. In theory it's even laudable. Giving a second chance to gifted young people. Lifting them up out of poverty in some cases." Her father frowned. "Wish I'd thought of it."

"Yeah, then you'd be in a meeting with a group of very annoyed powerful government officials."

"The US, indeed the world, is too far in with Goddard to do more than express their deep displeasure. Remember what else I taught you."

"Make sure your allies have as much, and preferably more, to lose than you," Zen replied, reciting one of her father's many lessons over the years.

"You, my child, are in the enviable position of being valuable to your new department. Which means *you* are in a unique position to become a boss." Her father grinned at her. "Damn, you're a magician."

"Mama would say I've found God's favor." Zen laughed with her father.

"Well, I'm not religious like your mother. But if this keeps up, she just may have a convert on her hands," James joked. Then he grew serious again. "You still have to tread with great care. You're going to be tasked with finding out what went wrong."

"I'll be assigned to monitor them or review their risk-management protocols?" Zen switched to using the touchscreen. She swiped to a new page. Her name didn't appear in the emails.

"Pretty sure that's the plan," her father replied.

"And you told me poking around in people's heads was a waste of a good education," Zen teased. She went back to browsing the documents her father had sent. Goddard employees had already floated ideas on tightening procedures.

"Those were your mother's words, not mine. But I did think the hard sciences offered better career opportunities. I'll admit you had greater foresight than your parents," James said. "Happy?"

"I just recorded the admission for posterity. What else did you find out?"

Her father sighed. "I suspect..."

"Come out with it, Daddy," Zen prompted.

"Maybe I was allowed to find out enough to fit into hidden agenda." Her father frowned, his gaze far off as he lapsed into thought.

Zen stopped reading to stare at him. "I don't understand."

"It's just... I can't put my finger on it. You know the feeling—the sense that you haven't been as clever as you think."

"You're hella clever in my unbiased opinion," Zen replied.

"So are Clive Anderson and Bertice Illinois." James reached from something off screen and then turned back to face Zen. "I'll keep probing, but change tactics."

"If you see a ghost in the machine, then I'll be on the lookout, too. I hate politics. I want to find the facts and keep more people from being hurt. Period." Zen grimaced.

"Wheels within wheels comes with intelligence work. You don't get to choose."

"Thanks for the heads up, Daddy. And the words of wisdom." Zen blew him a kiss.

Her father's expression became a combination of stern and worried. "One last thing, since you seem to be listening to me for once. Don't go maverick again. The outcome might be worse next time."

"Rules were made for a reason. Look for the reason, including the hidden ones, before you break them," she said, quoting him once more.

"I know why you do it. I wasn't disappointed you didn't choose law enforcement."

"Daddy—"

"One day we'll find out who killed Lexi." James flinched when he said his youngest child's name. "It's only a matter of time."

Her father had kept in touch with the detectives working Lexi's murder case. No surprise that he knew the current status, beyond it being unsolved, that is. The working theory of a serial killer should have led to a break. It hadn't. Two people known to be responsible for multiple murders had died in the past ten years. Detectives were convinced one of them killed Lexi, despite lacking solid evidence linking either. Zen couldn't look past all of the holes in their theory.

"Following the damn rules hasn't done it fast enough," Zen replied. When her father's frown deepened, Zen added, "I'm not sticking my fingers in the investigation."

"Good. Give my granddaughter a hug." James's face gradually relaxed into one of affection. His mood always lightened when he talked about his grandchildren.

"Sure will. Love you."

"Oh, and I heard the unspoken word 'yet'. Stay out of the way of those DC cops. They haven't officially closed her case." James' voice rumbled again like thunder. He went from paternal indulgence to firm disciplinarian at light speed.

"Yes, sir," Zen replied dutifully and saluted.

Her father heaved a deep sigh right before his image blinked off. No doubt Zen would be the subject of a late-night parental conversation. She would love to eavesdrop on what her mother would have to say. Enola Chatelain Batiste was known not to bite her tongue. Mother-daughter battles seemed to run in the family, at least on that side. Zen grinned at the memory of her grandmother firmly putting Enola in her place, one of only two who could. The other being James.

An hour later a chime alerted Zen that a message had come through; a calendar entry for a meeting with Clive at seven Monday morning.

"Surprise, surprise," Zen mumbled as she clicked on the confirmation button.

"GOOD WORK, TEAM," CLIVE said.

He sat at the end of the oval conference table. He drummed his blunt fingertips on its surface. He didn't seem happy despite his words. All four of them studied the LED max-definition screen. Three-dimensional images of the Goddard training camp in Chile faded out. They'd just ended a vid-call with a general of the Chilean national police. Hadley had taken notes to be entered in the digital files. Malone and Zen had mostly kept quiet while Clive and the general did most of the talking. The built-in AI translator had made their consultation seamless, though the general's English was pretty good.

"Raise your hand if you think Tanner Martin was the victim of a robbery," Malone said and looked around at the others. No one moved.

"Not much we can do here. The president of Chile is very cooperative, but turning over an investigation completely to us? That was a polite 'Hell no,' " Clive said.

He continued to use his tablet to swipe through pictures. Photos of the crime scene in Santiago appeared. Zen winced at crisp images of Tanner Martin's corpse on a side street. Blood, turned black, pooled around his torso. Two shots to the chest, one to the head. The killer made sure Martin would not get up again.

"He didn't have much to steal, did he?" Hadley got up and walked closer to the screen. She studied the picture with clinical interest.

"He'd taken a Goddard debit card with him. But all trainees had them. And they were well-paid, by the way," Zen said.

Clive nodded. Then he repeated what the Chilean police had told them. "He used substances mined by Goddard from space, material they were testing at the camp. Then he set up his own designer drug. An exotic new way to get high courtesy of an asteroid."

"I don't believe it," Malone said. "How did he have time to make connections in between his duties at the camp? He was way out in the desert."

"They had short breaks, and they weren't cut off from communicating. Maybe his pals from home hooked him up." Zen looked at Malone and then back at the television display. Another photo appeared of Tanner Martin with his bio next to it.

"Check out his known criminal associates. His brother and a sister have arrest records, too," Clive replied. He swiped through pages of a report on his tablet. "Saw it somewhere in here."

"I'll follow up," Hadley said. She studied Martin's face for a few seconds. "He's movie star handsome. Look at that bone structure."

"If you want a date, you're gonna need one of those ghost whisperers," Malone joked.

Hadley turned to face them with a grin. "I do love a bad boy, but that wasn't my point. I'll bet he has ex-lovers willing to talk about his flaws."

"More than his partners in past crimes, probably," Zen said.

"I'll wrap up with Batiste and Ramirez," Clive said, his tone heavy with meaning.

Hadley, taking her cue to leave, stood up. She beamed at Zen and Malone before she quietly left. "Welcome back."

Clive waited for the door to whisk shut after her. Then he leaned both arms on the table and faced them. "You somehow turned a simple assignment into a wild ride."

"Goddard Corporation's training program is a nest of trouble," Zen countered, both eyebrows raised at him.

"You're being generous, partner. They screwed up and created a shithole of petty criminals doing work for NASA," Malone said with blunt force.

"Except they're not so petty. Martin had a history of violence, if Iesha Franklin's information can be confirmed," Zen added.

"Her hearsay account, you mean. The two men who could give direct evidence are dead," Clive replied with a frown as he rubbed his chin.

"Pretty convenient." Malone rose and walked to the HD screen. He switched it to touch mode and scrolled through photos. Then he went to the document view to read a few paragraphs. He turned back to them, one forefinger pointing to a sentence.

Clive studied Malone in silence for a few beats. "Are you about to posit a conspiracy by the biggest single federal contractor in the world?"

"Martin slipped through the cracks. Hunter knew it. He had to die. Then the real problem child had to go as well. Classic cleanup tactic," Malone said with a shrug.

"For a drug cartel or major organized crime syndicate, sure. And they think *I'm* the loose cannon," Zen said.

"Goddard didn't become a trillion-dollar company while being good little boys and girls."

"Business sharks are one thing, but you're talking about murder, Malone," Zen argued.

"Sharks go in for the kill. We've all read the Goddard Corporation profile. They've annihilated four heavy-hitter rivals since 2037. The current Goddard family member in charge has boyish good looks and private school manners. That doesn't mean he's different from his father and grandfather." Malone looked at Clive for a reaction.

"What are your impressions of Dr. Nyla Richards?" Clive asked in a mild tone.

Zena exchanged a look of surprise with Malone before she answered. "Stickler for following protocol. Dedicated to the work they're doing out there. She and Belmont are both scientists to the core. I don't see them engaging in corporate intrigue, much less planning two assassinations to cover up a company mistake."

"On the surface. Hadley could do a deep dive," Malone said, his steady gaze still on the boss.

Clive went back to drumming his fingers for a few moments. "Fine. Tell Hadley to explain to any sources that her questions are routine after an incident."

"Are we worried about making Goddard and his top people angry?" Malone asked after shooting a side glance at Zen.

"Until we know for sure they're culpable, yes. Let's not kick the hornets' nest any harder until we absolutely have to. Got it?"

Malone started to say something but stopped. "Got it."

"Yes, sir," Zen said. Clive reminded her of her father in that moment. He was a reasonable man. But when he gave an order it was best to comply.

"You two will shadow Goddard's internal review of what happened at the camp. The junior special agents will prepare summaries. In about ten days, you'll interview the lunar colonists. Let me know immediately if there is any sign the deaths there weren't accidents."

"Will do," Zen said.

"Right," Malone added.

"Goddard is on the defensive." Clive hunched his shoulders forward, causing creases in his expensive suit jacket. He frowned at the wall as though seeing something he didn't like.

"I can't believe they'd knowingly make mistakes to put so much at risk. Maybe we're dealing with ambitious decision-makers rushing to make an impression. Glossing over problems. Either missing the warning signs or minimizing them." Zen stopped when she realized Clive and Malone were staring at her.

"That's exactly the thinking from the White House and NASA. They're giving assurances to the UN International Space Governance Council," Clive said and stood.

"Kinda soon to make definitive statements, don't you think?" Malone transferred his gaze to Clive.

Clive smoothed down the front of his jacket. "You both did a fine job in Chile. We've found the glitch. Now clear up the lunar colony incident and the private space program will be back on track."

"But sir..." Malone seemed to search for words.

"Arrangements will be made to quickly and efficiently deal with any complications uncovered. Do we understand each other?" Clive looked from Malone to Zen and back.

"Yes, sir," Zen and Malone said in unison.

With a sharp nod, Clive tugged on his already-perfectly aligned tie. "I have meetings most of the morning. I want to start getting reports after lunch."

"The first will be on Chile, of course. We're almost done," Zen replied quickly.

Clive's serious expression cracked into a tight smile. "Glad to hear it. Carry on."

They watched him stride out of the conference. Zen followed him down the hall with Malone close behind. They watched Clive until he stopped to talk to two men. Then all disappeared around a corner. Zen and Malone faced each other.

"Your office or mine?"

"I've got coffee and breakfast for us," Malone said with a grin.

Twenty minutes later they sat on opposite sides of the round table near his desk. Malone had gotten yogurt for Zen, pastries, coffee, and apple juice. Zen savored the mix of fruit in her yogurt. Malone polished off a pineapple-topped pastry and half a mug of coffee. They had discussed their report, but it only needed a few edits. Malone had transcribed most of it during the trip from Chile.

"Are we gonna talk about what just happened?" Malone rose and poured a cup of coffee for Zen. He put the mug in front of her but didn't sit.

"I'm good."

"Zen, c'mon. You saw," Malone insisted.

"All I see is a special agent about to screw up his well-paying gig."

"Clive pretty much just told us we're working on a cover-up," Malone said, dropping his voice low.

"That's not what I heard, Malone," Zen shot back.

"The bottom line is no matter what we find, someone is going to dress it up. Make it look pretty and presentable for the powers that be. Which apparently includes the International UN Space Authority. I don't want my name on several pages of lies."

"You have leaped to a pile of unwarranted conclusions. NASA and all the other agencies want to fix these problems. Agreed?"

"Yeah, but—"

"Let me finish," Zen cut in. "Of course, they want to put the best spin on what's happened. Clive didn't ask us to alter our findings. We're going to make sure Goddard cleans up its crap. Then we're going to make sure they put in controls to prevent more crap."

"Okay." Malone's skeptical frown didn't go away.

"The boss didn't ask us to lie or gloss over any facts," Zen insisted.

"Yet."

"Jesus, be a fence!" Zen groaned and fell against the chairback.

"Huh?" Malone blinked at her.

"It's from an old African-American gospel song, it means... Never mind. Stop being paranoid." Zen got up to get a donut then changed her mind and sat again.

"Clive jumped on your rosy line of reasoning double quick. You made him happy. Or did you pick up on what he wanted to hear?"

"I'm a mental health professional, not a psychic, Malone," Zen shot back with a snort. Then she glared at him. "Wait a minute. You think I'm in on the conspiracy."

"I didn't use the word conspiracy."

"You used the other 'c' word. Cover-up," Zen whispered.

"That's two words. And why are you whispering? I'll tell you why. You're thinking the same as me," Malone replied.

Zen returned his gaze for a few beats. "Fine."

"I knew it."

"And it's to be expected with important heads on the chopping block. Not just at Goddard, but in multiple federal agencies. The private space companies, especially Goddard, are too big to fail." Zen stood and paced as she talked. "Malone, we're *not* going to cover up murder."

"But like you said, too big to fail," Malone replied in a grim tone.

"People know what we found at the Atacama Desert training camp."

Malone sat rubbing his chin for a few seconds. "Okay, I'll concede your point. And if Clive had concerns about us, we'd be out."

"What?" Zen stopped and looked at him.

"Clive knows we're good at what we do and we send official reports. Nothing left out or finessed. But he didn't reassign us. Which opens the door to us finding out even more dirt."

"Thank you. At last you're talking sense." Zen retrieved her coffee mug, drank from it, and scowled. "Ugh, cold coffee is the worst."

"Okay, I'm going to say something else that will upset you."

"Then don't." Zen went to get a refill. When he didn't reply, she let out a groan. "But you're going to anyway."

"Clive didn't argue with my theory about Tanner Martin being killed as part of a cover-up," Malone said.

"There's that phrase again," Zen complained.

"He knows or has a suspicion just how deep this thing goes," Malone pushed on.

"Which means something ain't clean in the milk." Zen frowned as she took a sip from her mug. The implications increased her sugar craving. She eyed the pastries again.

"Okay, I think I get what you mean. Where the hell are you coming up with these clichés?"

"Comes from hanging out with my Southern elders," Zen replied.

"I gotta hit you with some sayings from my *abuelo*," Malone said with a grin. He rubbed his hands together. "So, we about to get on it. Follow the facts no matter where they lead. Clive will thank us."

"Humph, you *hope*," Zen retorted.

"If I've read him right, Clive will provide cover for us from political blowback. Look, let's protect the integrity of the space program." Malone stood with both fists planted on his slim waist, the picture of a man ready for action.

Zen sighed and put down the mug. "I hate when it when you make a convincing argument. I'm trying to stay out of trouble."

"Let's stir up some good trouble, partner." Malone gave Zen a cheerful pat on the shoulder.

"He said as he led her over a cliff," Zen drawled.

# Chapter 10

Friday night, Zen wandered the aisles of the market. The giant store featured organic, free-range everything those dedicated to eating clean could want. Astra would be home Saturday evening. She'd decided to become a vegan. So, Zen shopped for ingredients to feed this latest teen girl whim. She had a variety of recipes for meatless casseroles and other meals. Determined not to spend a fortune, Zen figured commitment would last maybe a week. She expected Astra to miss bacon fairly soon.

After a week of long hours, Zen looked forward to thinking about something other than Goddard, Malone's theories of intrigue, and her own sense of unease. Jordan's summary of their time together seemed full of forced cheer. Astra dropped a few cryptic hints about domestic drama. Their video call had definitely piqued Zen's curiosity. She felt a tinge of guilt about looking forward to gossiping about her ex-husband. Then a flash of a familiar distinctive black coat caught Zen's eye. A wide-brimmed, dark-gray wool fedora obscured the face. She'd seen the same figure twice before. Zen pushed her basket along while keeping an eye on the woman. When she turned left and black coat turned right, Zen sighed and shook her head. *Seriously, Batiste. You let Malone get into your head.* Her grin faded when the woman confronted her in the artisanal bread section. The look of determination on the stranger's face made Zen's pulse pick up speed. There were alone. In fact, muted voices seemed to indicate they were isolated. Other shoppers were scarce since it was only forty minutes until closing. When the woman glanced over her shoulder, Zen moved fast. She placed the shopping cart between them. When the woman looked at Zen again, she blinked at the change.

"Nice selection, huh?" Zen glanced down at her purse. It lay next to a bottle of orange-infused dish soap in the cart.

The woman followed Zen's gaze. "I'm not a panhandler or a thief."

"You're here for the sourdough or multigrain?" Zen calculated how hard she could shove the metal shopping cart. The surprise element might take her down like a bowling pin.

"I waited at your house, but I didn't want to freak you out," the woman said in a sharp whisper. She looked around once more.

"Shadowing me among the veggies and grass-fed beef seemed a better idea, less freaky." Zen looked at her purse again. The top of the leather hobo bag was snapped closed. Who knew she'd need a stun gun in the health food store?

"I'm not going to harm you, Dr. Batiste. You want to hear what I have to say," the woman said, her voice dropping to an urgent hiss.

"Wait, you know my name? Where I live? What the hell—"

"Meet me at High Note around the corner. Ten minutes. Fifteen minutes tops. I won't wait longer."

"Not unless you tell me why. And maybe not even then," Zen snapped.

"I've got a lot on the line talking to you." The woman pulled up the collar of her coat.

I'm not following some weirdo to a druggie hangout," Zen replied. "I don't care if they are legal."

The woman stamped one booted foot in frustration. "They have security. Not that they need it. A bunch of mid-level managers and their bougie girlfriends. They just sit around pretending to be cool."

"You sound pretty familiar with the scene." Zen scanned the woman from head to toe. "Pull that scarf down."

"Fifteen minutes, or you can spin your wheels on dead ends. Tetra and Goddard will bury the truth."

The woman marched off. Between the scarf, collar, and hat, most of her face was hidden. Nothing unusual in the freezing cold temps of March in the DMV region. Not suspicious at all to a casual observer. Zen stood staring after her, mouth open. She jumped at a voice behind her.

"Need something, ma'am? Those loaves were baked fresh this afternoon," a store employee said. The young man with pale skin and red hair wore a restrained smile. Then he glanced at the digital time display on the wall.

"I'm done, but thanks." Zen headed to checkout.

Anything else she meant to pick up was forgotten. On the way she grabbed an insulated tote and a complimentary bag of ice. That would keep her two packs of meat cold for a good hour. The cashier had to get Zen's attention three times. She couldn't focus on coupons or store rewards programs. Zen glanced at her watch. Seven minutes to grab her bags, stash them in the self-driven taxi, and walk around the corner. She tapped the taxi's digital dashboard, programming the address and a wait time.

"Thank you. I'll meet you at 2790 Upper E. Tolliver Drive in forty-five minutes," the male AI voice said, its dulcet customer service tone a soothing purr.

"Show up with an automatic pistol and I'll kiss your virtual lips," Zen wisecracked.

"To notify local police, say 911 and your location will be sent. No need to take further action. Zippy Taxi cannot assure response times. We accept no liability for—"

"Never mind for now," Zen broke into the automated sequence before things went too far. The AI would call them if she didn't respond, assuming she was in danger and couldn't talk.

"Thank you. Trip rate will be adjusted," the voice said.

"Yeah, this trip has been adjusted in more ways than one," Zen said with a grunt.

She pulled up the chocolate-brown knit scarf around her ears. As she walked, Zen stayed alert to her surroundings. She pulled her herringbone tan and brown wool coat tight against the cold. She walked a few yards around the corner. Soft blue neon lights glowed the words High Note above the trendy-looking bar entrance. Inside, the mostly Caucasian middle-class crowd all appeared to be in good spirits. Soft mood lighting added to the chill atmosphere. Neo-soul and blues music played in the background. One section featured a hookah lounge to the right of the entrance. A traditional bar with bottles of alcohol stretched down the center. To the left a door led to another section.

A female hostess with a diamond stud in one nostril approached.

"Hello. Your party is waiting this way please." The young woman flipped a hand as a gesture for Zen to follow.

"How did you know I was meeting someone?"

"Your friend described you perfectly," the hostess replied with a welcoming smile.

The hostess led her around tables. As they walked, Zen noticed the building was larger than it looked from the outside. More long and narrow than wide. Couples mixed with groups. Not a sinister looking face in the bunch. But looks could be deceiving. Malone had definitely rubbed off on her. They arrived at a booth away from the windows. The woman watched them approach.

"Here you go. Tyra will be you waitress. She'll check to see if you need anything in a few." The hostess flashed a professional smile at them and left.

Zen stood looking down at her stalker. She wore her brunette hair tied back in a long ponytail. She still had the hat on. She'd taken off her coat and scarf. Nude lipstick outlined a pouty mouth. White female, between twenty-five and thirty years old, approximately five feet six inches, sturdy but not overweight. She gazed back at Zen from brown eyes with smoky eye-shadow. Her gray turtleneck sweater was pulled up as though she still wanted to hide.

"The makeup and wig aren't much of a disguise Miss..." Zen waited for her to fill in the blank.

The woman sipped from her goblet. She brushed blunt bangs to one side. "Have a seat. I ordered wine. Hope that's okay."

"None of this is okay," Zen clipped.

"You're here because you want to know what I know. I paid for the drinks and Tyra will bring over food. I ordered a tray of heavy hors d'oeuvres. Ah, speaking of which."

The woman stopped when their waitress returned with a tray. It held a variety of light fare; chicken winglets, small oysters on crackers, cheeses, and more. The woman ate while Zen huffed out a sharp breath of annoyance. They were in a public place and she didn't feel vulnerable. So, she unbuttoned her coat and sat. The food smelled good, but Zen didn't touch any of it. She continued to study her companion.

"I eat when I'm nervous. Working out helps. Bread?"

"Who are you?" Zen snapped.

"You're going to get hot with that on," the woman replied around a mouthful of oysters. She pointed to Zen's coat. "They've got a good heating system in here. You don't need it."

Zen swiped away small beads of sweat on her forehead. But she didn't want to concede anything to this odd stranger. "Look, this isn't a wine and cheese social."

The woman patted her lips with a napkin and sipped more wine. "I've driven hours to meet you. At least be civil. As you can see, this is a legitimate business with a nice class of customers. No seedy drug dealers in back rooms. Relax."

Zen scanned her surroundings yet again. The woman was correct. Marijuana and several synthetic drugs created in space had become as ubiquitous as liquor. As with any drug, there were still those who became addicted. Yet social use had been popular since 2027, the year they were decriminalized nationally. The well-dressed patrons of High Note looked like a normal after-work crowd.

"Mood lighting and cute décor doesn't make it less damaging. But I'm not going to debate the subject of party drugs." Zen stared at her hard. "Talk or I walk."

"I'm not the enemy."

"Friends don't get creepy and follow me around. You were about to explain so I don't call the police." Zen crossed her arms and glared at her.

"Fine. I don't blame you. To business."

The woman wiped her fingers on a moist towelette provided by the café. She drank more wine and signaled to the waitress. Ordered more, and then looked at Zen's full glass. Before she spoke, Zen shook her head.

"Well?" Zen barked. She wound up to tear into the stranger. But she both stopped when Tyra returned with two glasses of wine. "I didn't want more."

"Hold that thought until you hear what I have to say." The woman raised one palm to forestall more questions. She drank deeply and sighed. "I may need more before the night is over."

"You know what, don't worry about it. I've lost interest in your little game." Zen slid from her seat and stood.

"You want to know why the space program is on meltdown. Why colonists ended up returning to Earth in body bags. Don't you? I assume you do since that's the whole point of IPA."

Zen blinked at her for a few seconds. "IPA?"

"Interplanetary Policing Agency, your new department. At least that's what they call it in classified documents. Small, but mighty. Your boss has major clout. He speaks, people listen." The woman gave a short grunt and drank more wine. "They haven't told you yet. Typical government bullshit."

Zen eased back onto the dark-green faux-leather booth bench. "Who the hell are you?"

"Wrong question. You should be asking why NASA, the White House, and the DOJ need space cops about now, right?" Zen squinted at her.

The woman waved away the waitress when she swooped in again. "Drink, eat. I'll tell you a story."

Zen took a drink from her goblet. "I love a good story. Let's see if it's fiction or fact."

"Oh, it's fact alright. You wouldn't have met me if you hadn't heard of Lodestone already." The woman took in a deep breath and let it out. "I work... never mind. I've been part of the space program for twenty-five years. My father and grandmother both worked for Interstellar Unlimited. Long family tradition of looking to the stars. I have degrees in astrophysics and astronautical engineering. Mostly hands-on experience. Passed the tests without much classroom time."

"Wait, you're telling me that you're at least in your fifties?" Zen gaped at the woman's smooth, white complexion.

"Thank the good Lord for anti-aging cosmeceuticals. You do know about medical research done on the Sagan ISS, right?" The woman smiled at her.

"Advances in gene therapy to combat dementia, treat cancer, and more," Zen said, reciting reports she'd read over the years. Sagan International Space Station had been launched in 2055, one of four in operation.

"Like throughout history, incidental discoveries have been commercialized. The beauty industry is one example. My great-great-aunts founded a cosmetic company using space-developed products." The woman leaned forward to stare at Zen.

"I see." Zen turned over the scant facts she had so far.

"You won't figure out who I am from a bit of family history. Their company was bought out before we were both born. Doesn't exist anymore, and it was one of dozens that sprang up around that time."

Zen studied her for a few seconds. Cosmetics to alter the appearance had also been developed. Actors used them, but so did crooks. The effects lasted a few days at best. She guessed her companion looked very different. So much so that Zen might not recognize her on the street.

"And you know about Lodestone," Zen replied.

"How did you hear about it?" the woman countered.

"A friend came across information in reports."

"And thought you might want to know about Lodestone because of your new job. Makes sense." She nodded and stared at the tray of food. She selected a round cracker with brie cheese on it and ate.

"Seriously?" Zen blurted.

"Hey, I haven't eaten much at all. Okay," the woman said between chews. Then she swallowed. "Tetra Corporation is a research and development consortium. They hire the top experts in a variety of fields. Those men and women have invented or created products on spec for the government for decades. Defensive weapons for the military. Advances in space vehicles. They helped Tesla and Edison Corporations perfect self-driving vehicles over three decades ago. Electric airplanes, new medical devices. You name it, they've done it. The UN depends on them a lot, too. But they also contract with major non-governmental organizations.

Zen shrugged out of her coat. Her stomach rumbled a complaint of hunger. She selected an oyster and a stuffed mushroom. "Why haven't I heard about them before?"

The woman pushed a large paper napkin across to her. "That's the point. They prefer being in the background. Invisible, if possible."

"And Lodestone is..." Zen placed a hand over her mouth full of food and gestured for her to keep talking.

"Advanced research and clinical trials using deep transcranial magnetic stimulation. Since the mid- and late-twentieth century, it's been used to treat Parkinson's disease, depression, obsessive-compulsive disorder, and more. The human brain is infinitely complex, but since the nineteen nineties, medical science has learned more about neural signal patterns." The woman warmed to her topic like a professor giving a lecture.

"Okay." Zen squinted at her.

The woman heaved a sigh. "You need this background information. Context, Dr. Batiste."

"Continue." Zen decided she might as well eat another delicious mushroom.

"In the last twenty years or so returning people have been staying in space longer and longer. Technology has developed to allow for the physical changes. Things like loss of bone and muscle mass, even genetic changes. But also changes in the brain. Motor functioning, but then behavioral changes."

Zen paused in the act of polishing off another appetizer. "Such as aggressive behavior."

"Yes. Areas of the brain that involve self-control and moral reasoning are affected in some. Deep transcranial magnetic and electrical stimulation began to show positive though inconsistent results."

"If astronauts and long-term colonists have become violent, that would be big news," Zen said.

"For several decades the changes were small. Irritability, a deterioration of pro-social skills. Nothing dramatic," the woman replied.

"Like murder," Zen said, lowering her voice.

"In 2033 a twenty-two- year-old woman on the first private lunar colony stayed for eighteen months. She came home for a three-month furlough. Then she went back for another twelve months. The effects became pronounced, so much that she couldn't function as a team member. Three months after she returned, she killed her entire family. Her new husband, her mother, and her two teenaged brothers."

"Are you saying that's why the first private colony stalled? I always heard it was because the company went bankrupt," Zen said.

"They did. The three governments that backed them pulled their contracts. The files on that colony were buried. Tetra has had access to them for decades. Her brain was studied, along with colonists and space travelers since. Transcranial brain stimulation, using procedures developed in space, treat those effects." The woman downed the remaining wine in her goblet. "Let's have more. Neither of us is driving. I left my vehicle at the rental."

"You work for Tetra." Zen studied her for a reaction.

The woman shook her head. "Not exactly. Their employees are chipped like pets and swear a blood oath of secrecy. I wouldn't be here if I was one of them."

"C'mon," Zen said with a snort.

"A bit of an exaggeration, but not by much. All you need to know is I have credible information." The woman flagged down their waitress and ordered a vodka martini.

Zen searched for connections. "So, the deaths at the Goddard colony are connected to living long-term in space. Wait, you said there are treatments to counter the brain changes."

"Correct. The implications for wider treatments were studied for ten years. Then in the 2040s clinical trials were done on convicted criminals. The results were encouraging. The trainees at Goddard's camp in Chile."

"Their program for rehabilitated youth and adult offenders. You're saying those folks have had this transcranial brain stimulation?"

"Those convicted of more serious crimes, yes." The woman looked around and hunched forward. "Some of the most brilliant minds in the world. A physicist who killed his wife for insurance money. An astronautical engineer who helped pioneer oxygen creation in space. He raped and strangled his date. And more."

"They're not common criminals. Like the Goddard trainees." Zen blinked as the implications sank in.

"Exactly. Targeted brain stimulation, or TBS, offers hope that lives can be saved. Keep the genius and get rid of those nasty habits. Like rape and murder. However, for reasons they're still studying, not every 'patient' recovers."

"And they can't predict which ones will recover and which ones will revert to their violent ways," Zen replied. "Oh shit."

"Some of the women and men are living great new lives, have been for years. I've kept quiet because of them. Tetra, the feds, and state governments don't want the public to know. I mean, when a crime is committed, we're still lovers of vengeance. Think of victims' advocacy groups and how they'd react."

"Okay, but some of the criminals must be high profile. If they're released from life sentences, someone would know. Parole and pardon boards must be involved. Victims or even the families of the convicted would be notified," Zen said.

"The media and the public move on after a while. Bigger stories dominate the news cycle. And then there's relocation and re-identification programs. Goddard pioneered it. New identities, even a new appearance. Death certificates. Bob is laid to rest. Dave emerges to the new life." The woman nodded at the look of skepticism Zen wore.

"Now you're talking science fiction, or fantasy."

"Millionaire psychopath goes to prison. Commits 'suicide.' Because he's a violent pedophile or a murderer, his family is happy he's gone. They get a body. A low-key funeral. Life goes on. Even better for those with zero close ties. It hasn't happened often. Three times in the last forty years that I could dig up."

"Hunter and Martin weren't millionaires. Though they did have specialized skills. And they hadn't made it to space."

"A cosmic stroke of bad luck for Goddard Corporation. Too much digging into the deaths at their lunar colony and the Earth training camp would be... inconvenient," the woman replied.

"They're scrambling to salvage the situation. The training camp investigation can be tied up with a neat bow. Case closed."

"Except you brought up Lodestone. Dr. Zenobia Batiste, mental health clinician, forensic sociologist, and catcher of serial killers." The woman leaned forward again and spoke softly. "And you know about TBS as a treatment for depression. Remember your intern days at the psych hospital?"

Zen's eyes went wide. She'd met Jordan, then a neurology resident, at J. Biden Medical Complex in Baltimore. Her grad school internship was in the behavioral health clinic. "They were doing brain stimulation implants for depression and OCD back then."

"You won't dig up more about Lodestone and Tetra on your own. I decided to help." The woman gulped more martini.

"Why?" Zen gave the woman a once over examination, looking for clues. She didn't find any.

"The program is way over the line. They're willing to sacrifice a few lives to make money. Granted, a trillion bucks or so ain't nothin' to sneeze at. But still." The woman went silent for a few beats. "I can't put a price on being able to look at myself in the mirror or sleep at night."

"I know you're scared, but maybe we could help," Zen said and placed a hand on hers.

"Right, like you helped Iesha Franklin. She's dead," the woman whispered in a flat voice. She snatched her hand away from Zen.

"What? No way. I'd know if she—" Zen stopped.

Her smartwatch was on silent still. She hadn't checked for messages since leaving the office or while shopping. She pushed back the sleeve of her sweater to stare at it. Several messages glowed in red, the indicator they were urgent. Zen had been so intent on their conversation that she'd ignored vibrations from the device. She entered her code and the screen popped up with a display. Malone had texted "911" twice, the second time followed by the words "damn it!" Clive had left a voicemail. Hadley had left a cryptic message to check her inbox. When Zen looked up the woman had put on her coat.

"Now you know. If you believe what they tell you, then I gave you too much credit."

Zen pulled her back when the woman tried to stand. "I need to verify what you've told me. Get more details for my boss."

"Get to it then. I'm out."

"At least tell me how to contact you if I need more details. I'll keep it secret. Even from my boss. Trust me," Zen hissed low.

"Yeah right. The lies start at the top." The woman peeled Zen's fingers from her arm and jerked away.

Another insistent buzz on her wrist made Zen look down. Malone's face appeared. Zen pulled her wireless pod in one ear and connected. "Hold on."

When she looked up, the woman had vanished. Zen pushed from the bench and dashed to the exit. She scrambled past a knot of people waiting for a table. Once on the sidewalk, Zen glanced around. She saw the back of the woman's coat just as she slid into a taxi. The vehicle idled on the opposite side of the four-lane busy street. Playing dodge ball against speeding traffic would have deadly. Zen let out a yelp of frustration. Then cold bit through Zen's sweater. Shivering and rubbing both arms, Zen went back into the café to the booth. Their waitress turned, almost colliding into Zen. She held Zen's coat and bag.

"I was coming back to pay," Zen said and took them from her.

"Oh, no worries. Your friend paid for everything. I just didn't want you to leave your things. More wine?"

The cold air combined with bad news had settled a chill in Zen's spine. "A large hot chocolate, please. If you have it. If not, coffee will be fine."

"Our hot chocolate is the best. Be right back." The young woman bounced off.

Zen plopped down and scooted into the corner of the booth. She made sure no one seemed to be watching her. She sighed with relief to find the booths vacant on either side. Only then did she answer Malone's call.

"I'm back. It's been a damn night. You're calling to tell me Iesha Franklin is dead. Right?"

"Holy sh—No! Why the hell would you think Iesha is dead?" Malone's mouth hung open. He brushed tousled hair back from his forehead.

"Long story. Can't tell you all of it right now." Zen stopped and accepted the steaming mug from the waitress.

"Get your ass home, Batiste. Clive has pushed back the time because we couldn't get in touch with you. Ten-thirty. You know what to do." Malone gazed back at her with a frown. "You need me to come?"

Zen looked at the time display. The numbers glowing above Malone's image showed it was nine-forty-five. "I'm not far from home."

"Then leave now. I have a feeling we should talk before the damn meeting. Get a to-go cup."

Malone's face disappeared. Zen did indeed get her hot chocolate switched to a large paper cup. Moments later she stood outside. The taxi pulled up. Its AI voice pleasantly prompted her to pay the increased fee due because of the extended wait. Zen complied. Seconds later the sleek sedan moved into traffic. Fifteen minutes later she arrived home. She called Malone while putting away the meat and milk in her fridge.

"What's happened?" Malone said. "Wait, you stopped to go grocery shopping?"

"I'd finished by the time she caught up with me," Zen replied, out of breath from rushing around the kitchen. She continued to put away the rest of her purchases.

"Who?"

Zen glanced at the time again. "Can you talk?"

"Yeah. My date just left. Probably the last one since I practically pushed her out the door," Malone said.

"And your phone?" Zen shook free of her coat. She marched to the hall closet and hung it up. Then she went to her home office.

"Safe," Malone clipped.

"A woman I don't know, never seen before, followed me in the market. I met her at a café. She says Goddard has a lot to hide about their space colony program. It's connected to an outfit called Tetra and Lodestone. How much do you know about deep transcranial stimulation?" Zen glanced at the time as she logged into their encrypted video program.

"Not a damn thing. Lodestone?" Malone had pulled on a shirt and was now seated at a desk.

"People with criminal tendencies, including convictions, are treated using it. Changes their impulses to be violent or make immoral decisions. Medical research has refined areas of the brain that relate to violence and judgement. I'm wondering how much of this Clive knows already." Zen sighed when the agency seal remained in place. Clive and Hadley hadn't started the video feed yet.

"He just delayed another ten minutes. You think he's calling to tell us Franklin is dead." Malone stared back at Zen with a grim expression.

"My informant says some of Goddard's recruits are killers. Convicted killers with little-to-no remorse. TBS doesn't always fix the glitch," Zen said.

Malone's brows pulled together. "TBS?"

"Targeted Brain Stimulation. She didn't know for sure if the deaths on the moon are because the treatment failed." Zen opened another screen to search the topic.

"But she suspects so."

"Yeah. I think she feels responsible somehow. Anyway, some of the people working for Goddard are brilliant, but they're high-profile killers. I'm guessing local prosecutors and judges would never agree to them walking the streets again. Which means Goddard bypassed them somehow."

"Iesha Franklin is in protective custody. A federal detention facility near Quantico," Malone said, switching back to their witness.

"If my informant is right, then..." Zen looked at Malone.

"We're not going rogue, Zen. We have to trust Clive. From everything I know about the guy—" Malone stopped and looked away. "To be continued, partner."

Zen nodded and ended their call. The agency seal had winked off on her computer monitor. Clive's broad face filled her screen. Malone and Hadley appeared in smaller squares. A digital whiteboard made up the right side of the screen. Short text summaries had been entered.

"Good evening. The Goddard colonists have completed quarantine. The timeline was quicker than we thought. Enhanced protocols have shortened the required isolation period. We'll regroup at eight-thirty Monday morning. Interviews will begin Tuesday. Goddard insists their people be able to reconnect with social supports quickly. For mental wellness," Clive said.

"Never mind a killer might be on the loose," Malone retorted.

"We don't know that yet, Ramirez," Clive said promptly. "Anyway, we need to hit the ground at top speed Monday. We'll be in briefings most of the day. I want us to report to the Secretary that we're ready with a game plan."

Malone sighed. "Which means Zen and I need to work this weekend."

"We'll all be working. And my wife has expressed how she feels about it." Clive paused with a pained expression and his own deep sigh. "No long weekend in the country."

"We're almost done with our report on Iesha Franklin's information," Zen said. She studied Clive's reaction to the name.

Clive rubbed his jaw for a second and nodded. "You two have a head start then. We were prepared for events to move quickly anyway. I'll press Goddard's team for results on their internal review."

"They're expecting a call, sir. I've already established communication with the head of their quality assurance director," Hadley said.

"I've got my notes pulled up already. We can meet here in my home office, Malone. Lunch on me," Zen said.

Malone gazed back at Zen for a few seconds. Zen felt her heart beating hard in her chest. She could almost hear the debate in his head. Say something or keep quiet. Clive appeared intent on reading something before him.

"Problem? I can help out if you need me," Hadley said.

"We've got this, but thanks. Right, Malone?" Zen held her breath as he continued to gaze back.

"Yeah. Right. Like Clive said, we anticipated the need to move fast. Especially after the Iesha Franklin statement."

"Good. Unless you need me before, I'll see you all Monday." Clive nodded. His face winked out.

"See you Monday, Hadley." Zen forced a smile.

"Right. Are you two bickering again? This is not the time if so." Hadley's eyes narrowed. She looked like a disapproving school principal.

"We're good," Zen replied. "Hey, who likes to work on a weekend? Not to mention we just got back from Chile. Fun times, eh, Malone?"

"Yeah. Woo-hoo," Malone added.

"Okay then." Hadley continued to scrutinize them for a second. "See you at the office Monday."

"Sure, bye," Zen and Malone said together, which prompted another quizzical look from Hadley.

Once they ended the video call on the agency's server, Zen's private vid-phone lit up. Malone's scowl greeted her.

"What the hell, Zen?"

"He didn't mention anything about Iesha. Not one word. What does that tell you?" Zen replied.

"That your informant is wrong. Or she has some other agenda," Malone shot back with an annoyed grunt. "The longer we don't tell Clive, the worse the consequences for our careers. I don't know about you, but I like being well-paid and trusted."

"I'm not saying Clive is a bad guy, but he didn't blink when I said her name. Maybe he doesn't know she's dead yet. That could mean someone is keeping info from him."

"Listen to yourself. An unknown woman follows you around, feeds you some wild stories, and you believe her but not our boss. Oh, and by the way, she wouldn't tell you her name or how she supposedly knows all this stuff."

"Well... when you put it like that..." Zen frowned. "She knew Iesha's name and about the Lodestone program. Does that sound like she's a random unreliable source? She didn't sound unstable. Just scared."

Malone pulled a large hand over his face. "Look, I'm going to get some rest. I'll see you at nine in the morning, if that's okay. It'll give us time to get a lot done before Astra gets home."

"Yeah, okay." Zen's mind continued to work through the tangle of events.

"And partner? Don't do anything impulsive like follow clues on your own." Malone pointed a forefinger at the camera.

Zen blinked back from her musings and grinned. "I'll never live down Madrid." He groaned at the reference and terminated the call.

# Chapter 11

Monday morning Zen arrived at the office at before seven, the first one in. She started a fresh pot of coffee for the others. Then she went to her office. Her boost was a large cup of hot chocolate from the cafeteria. Astra had, with her typical teenaged energy, gotten off to school on the bus for once.

Zen got to work on the leads her mysterious stranger had provided. She dug deeper into Tetra Corporation. Founded in 2009, its history included a long list of important scientific and technological achievements. And no wonder. A string of Nobel Prize-winning researchers had worked for or with Tetra for almost eighty years. The public face of Tetra as presented on the website seemed straight-forward enough. Yet the descriptions of their programs were broad. No mention of Lodestone.

Malone strolled into her office, coffee mug in hand. He glanced at his watch. "Wow, you got here early. You better not be starting trouble."

"Ha-ha. Preparing for our meeting. What else?" Zen said.

"We need to tell Clive about your little visitor *before* he tells *us*." Malone was about to go on when Clive walked in behind him, followed by Hadley.

"I already know, Ramirez. I'm going to overlook the fact that you didn't tell me immediately. You were going to check to make sure the woman wasn't some screwball malcontent with an axe to grind." Clive stared at Zen with his chin tucked into his collar. "Right?"

"Exactly, boss," Malone put in.

"No excuse," Hadley put in and crossed her arms. Her olive-green tailored suit gave her a take-charge look. "I have more resources to locate the woman. Did you keep her drinking glass or anything she touched? I could have run her DNA and fingerprints. Three hours to have her identified."

Zen looked from Clive to Hadley. Then she retrieved a paper sleeve from her tote bag. She'd taken an appetizer fork the woman had used. "Malone didn't know."

"Your protection of him is admirable," Hadley clipped.

"I asked him to let me do more digging before we mentioned anything," Zen replied evenly. She didn't flinch at the formidable gazes from Clive and Hadley. "But that's beside the point. Is Iesha Franklin dead?"

"Sharing *complete* information with this team is very much the point, Dr. Batiste," Hadley said, her voice like steel.

Clive held up a palm to avert more of Hadley's lecture. "I agree, Hadley. But in this case let's call it *initiative*. I don't plan to micromanage my agents. We have to trust their judgement."

Zen nodded. "Thanks."

Malone tugged at his collar and wore a brittle smile. "Well, glad we cleared that up."

"One more thing. I'll come down hard if you jeopardize a case or cause anyone to get hurt." Clive spoke in a cool tone, but the weight behind his words came through.

"Understood," Zen said.

"Got it, boss," Malone added in a subdued voice.

"Iesha Franklin's death has been listed as self-inflicted, at least that's the preliminary cause of death. She used a shirt to hang herself," Clive said.

"Nothing she did or said indicated suicidal tendencies. Not when we talked to her." Zen looked at Malone and he nodded assent.

"Yeah. She was relieved to find out Hunter was dead. That meant he wouldn't be around to take revenge on her," Malone said.

"Her mother has relapsed on drugs. Their first phone call was mostly her mother demanding money. A younger brother was recently sentenced to twenty years for attempted manslaughter. She only found out two days after coming back to the States. Her career at Goddard was over. They made it clear she couldn't come back. With her record, getting re-established wouldn't be easy. To say the least." Hadley recited the somber facts with grim efficiency.

Malone shook his head. "Damn. A lot of hard knocks piled up at once."

"I talked to her about her life, Clive. Her mother had relapsed before. She'd resigned herself to the fact that she couldn't rescue her family members, save them from themselves. Iesha's death is too damn convenient for Goddard Corporation and Tetra." Zen stood up.

"Tetra?" Clive frowned and glanced at Hadley. When she shrugged, he turned back to Zen.

"They're running the Lodestone clinical trials, transcranial brain stimulation. The informant said—"

"Georgina Preston. She's a biophysicist and considered a leader in bioethics. She also specializes in the effect of space travel on humans and animals. I didn't need the fork," Hadley said. She wore a slight smile of satisfaction when the other three stared in admiration.

"A clear illustration of why you should keep me informed," Clive rumbled. "And your next question is how did I find out so fast."

"Um, yeah." Malone cast a quick side glance at Zen.

"The person watching her was being watched," Clive replied in a calm voice.

"By someone who reports to you," Zen said.

"You mentioned Lodestone, which led me to Tetra Corporation. Georgina Preston wrote several letters to her superiors about Lodestone. Goddard took the research in a direction that concerned her." Clive put both hands in his pants pockets. "Tetra's clinical trials were promising. As is the usual practice, Goddard took their data and applied it."

"For their rehabilitation program?" Malone wore a puzzled expression.

"Goddard has a substantial non-profit foundation for philanthropical purposes. It's common for private companies to benefit from research done by Tetra. Of course, most don't have billion-dollar budgets."

"Let me guess. Goddard Corporation hired top medical professionals and continued the clinical trials on human subjects," Zen put in.

"They did animal testing first," Clive said.

"How awful. I thought that kind of monstrosity had been outlawed." Hadley wore a look of disgust, no doubt thinking of her beloved labradoodle at home.

"They complied with best practices and humane guidelines. They used animals slated for euthanasia after attacking people or other animals," Clive replied and patted her shoulder.

"Only because we've invaded their habitats or mistreated house pets," Hadley insisted.

"Let's save the animal rights discussion for later." Malone seemed not to notice the heated look Hadley gave him. He gazed at Clive. "Back to why Preston was being followed."

"Goddard hired her away from Tetra. Preston quit in protest and went back to her previous job. That's when she continued to send memos to her colleagues at two influential IERBs." Clive took a hand out of his pocket and glanced at his watch.

"Influential whats?" Malone cocked his head to one side.

"Interagency Ethical Review Boards," Hadley put in.

"They review research experiments and clinical trials. The goal is to protect the rights and welfare of human subjects. Several include review of how animals are used, in keeping with animal welfare policies," Zen said.

"In short, Preston thought Goddard was going too far, even fudging the data on outcomes." Clive turned to Zen. "Who first told you about Lodestone?"

"Why?"

Clive's eyes narrowed. "I'm sure your father explained what it means when someone answers a question with a question."

"Is this an interrogation?" Zen shot back.

"I have a meeting in forty minutes with people who want answers, Batiste. People above my pay grade who are chronically short on patience," Clive snapped. "Much like me."

"I did extensive searches on space colonists recruiting. Obviously because of the two investigations of deaths on the moon and in Chile at the space training camp. I cross-referenced with Goddard's trainee selection process. Saw the abstract about their research on rehabilitation and made the connection." Zen spoke in a calm, even tone.

Clive stared at her in silence for several tense minutes. "Malone, finish preparations for interviews of the lunar colonists. Hadley, check in with Goddard's team. I'll talk to you both later."

"Zen and me—" Malone flinched when Hadley jabbed him with an elbow.

"We'll have updates by the end of your meeting. Come on, Malone." Hadley herded Malone out of Zen's office.

The door closed as they left. Their intense whispered conversation faded down the hall. Clive faced Zen with an impassive expression. Zen lifted her chin. At five feet ten inches, Clive wasn't that much taller than her. He still managed to be a commanding physical presence. Even Malone at six-foot-two backed down when Clive asserted authority. Though her pulse sped up, Zen was determined not to show fear. She'd had plenty of practice with two formidable parents.

"About the time you mentioned Lodestone, your ex-husband was in town. He's been in astronaut training for some time. He visited friends here." Clive gestured at the two chairs that faced her desk. Zen sat and he joined her.

"I don't mix work with family," Zen replied in a cool tone.

"Zen..." Clive raised his bushy eyebrows at her.

"Fine. You've proven not much happens in this town that you don't know about. Jordan's got nothing to do with our investigations. Trust, remember?"

"I'm not going to throw his name around. Besides, I can make your impromptu explanation plausible. Now reciprocate my trust," Clive said.

Zen considered potential moves the way a chess player might. The game board seemed just as tricky. But she had to rely on what she knew about her boss so far. "I was already starting to think Goddard had crossed some line. Even before Georgina Preston cornered me. Malone thought I was reading too much into the facts."

"He's Air Force, but also a cop at heart. The simple explanation is usually the right one," Clive said with a smile.

"Except politics combined with intelligence work rarely equals simple." Zen gazed back at him.

"He'll learn in time. The distance between his previous experience and working in DC is more than just miles." Clive's faint smile faded. "The President's Chief of Staff and Robert Goddard will be at the meeting."

"The big man, Robert S. Goddard himself?"

"You've stirred a very big pot, Batiste," Clive said. "You better make sure you have all of the facts. He doesn't play nice."

"A dead witness and another one in jail. I pretty much figured that out, Clive," Zen retorted.

"I have an agent posted at your daughter's school. He'll be at your home tonight," Clive said.

Zen came up out of her chair. "What?"

"Look at your inbox," Clive said in a grave voice. He nodded to her desktop. "Use that instead of your smartwatch."

She strode over to the wireless keypad and tapped in her code. Zen ignored the list of messages and went to one with "Unknown" as the sender. She clicked it opened. Two photos appeared. One of Astra getting off the bus at school laughing with her schoolmates. The other was a zoom shot through a window. Astra sat in one of her classes. Zen slammed a fist on the desk. A tone indicated she had a new message, same source. She clicked to open it and saw her mother in front of her favorite coffee shop. Clive joined her in staring at the computer monitor.

"Your father already knows. They're both safe, Batiste," Clive said and put a hand on her shoulder as reassurance.

"I'm not scared. I'm very, very pissed off." Zen drew in and let out a shaky breath. "Okay, both."

"Don't upset your daughter."

"She needs to know what's going on. She's had self-defense classes, gone on camping trips with Daddy, her uncles, and Jordan. More like military survival courses. With the work we're in, Daddy has always insisted we know how to take care of ourselves." Zen paced as she talked. Nervous energy prickled through her like an electric current.

"Expecting the apocalypse, is he?"

"Daddy calls it being a realist about the world we live in. Those messages aren't threats, though. I think they're letting me know they have a long reach."

"They're counting on you withholding information from me. That you'll be triggered by Iesha Franklin's supposed death."

Zen tore her gaze away from the photos. "And go off on my own, like Madrid. Wait, you said supposed."

"She was in a coma, but came out of it. Franklin was given medication that induced suicidal thoughts. A young woman separated from family, troubled as it was. Locked up with her only promise of escaping poverty gone."

"And the pills pushed her to the edge and over." Zen felt rage tilt the scale to outweigh fear. "Attempted murder."

"We can't assume, Batiste." Clive studied her.

"I'm going to prove it."

Clive studied her for a few seconds and nodded. He turned to leave. "Update me when you can."

"Clive," Zen called out and he paused. "Make sure Iesha is protected."

"She's been transferred to Bethesda Naval Hospital. Their security is tight," Clive replied.

Once he was gone, Zen called Astra's school. When the principal appeared on her screen, Zen forced a smile. "Good morning, Mr. Carter. Please have Astra excused from class for a video call. It's an important family matter."

The principal wore a concerned frown. "A federal agent just left my office. Only my assistant principal and Astra's teacher know. I don't want the entire student body and faculty in a panic."

"I assure you there is no danger to the school. Precautionary only."

Zen put as much reassurance in her tone as possible. The principal's expression didn't relax, so she could have saved the effort. Moments later Astra's face popped up on her smartphone screen. Murmuring in the background was followed by the sound of a door shutting. Astra didn't wait for Zen to say anything.

"Hey, Mom. I can talk." Astra hunched forward with an excited wide-eyed expression and rushed on. "Are you about to close another case? Daddy called threatening to come back. Grandfather called him. Papa James is such a worrier. But don't be mad at him."

"Astra, this isn't a game. Okay? And I'm going to have a chat with Daddy about calling Jordan." Zen frowned. She would have talked to Jordan, but not so soon. The last thing she needed was her ex swooping in to play protective father. He'd just get in her and Malone's way.

"Yeah, well, don't worry. I talked to Dad and got him calmed down. I reminded him that I have a brown belt and swing a mean softball bat," Astra said cheerfully. "Plus, our security system is the best. Auntie Chloé helped with that. Not to mention our nearest neighbor is a retired Marine, and his hobby is sharpshooting."

Zen had been concerned about the taciturn gun lover when they first moved. Estranged from his own family, he'd become a grumpy uncle to Astra over the years. Under Zen's watchful eye, of course.

"Can't believe I'm grateful to have him next door," Zen drawled.

Astra giggled. "Mr. Youngblood is sweet. And a crack shot. Okay, tell me what's really going on."

"You know I—"

"Can't discuss an active investigation. Just trust you that everything will be fine and I'm safe," Astra filled in before Zen could finish her speech. Then she executed a perfect teenage girl eye roll.

"Astra, listen to your mother. Nothing will happen. Remember what Daddy taught you."

"Be aware of my surroundings. Change my pattern. Notice anyone or anything out of place. Scream if I feel cornered or threatened. Forget being embarrassed. Better safe than sorry." Astra ticked off the lessons on fingers as she spoke. "Did I miss anything?"

"Quoted your grandfather to the letter. Good girl." Zen began to feel better about Astra's well-being.

"The agent you sent is cute. A little old for me, but still cute." Astra wiggled her eyebrows at Zen.

"Very funny. Seriously, honey. You shouldn't be scared. Finish the school day and let the agent bring you to my office."

"This is so exciting! No wonder you enjoy your job. Maybe I'll join the NSA, CIA, or FBI instead of the astronaut program. Hey, military intelligence." Astra snapped her fingers.

"Having to deal with criminals isn't a fun occupation. Law enforcement officers see people on their worse days, victims and perpetrators. It's sad—heartbreaking even," Zen said. "Human beings can do terrible things to each other."

Astra studied her mother's gloomy expression. "Yeah, like sheesh. Time to grow up, huh? Anything else I should know?"

"We'll move up taco night. Throw in some nachos with jalapenos," Zen said with a grin to lighten the mood. They typically had Astra's favorites on a Saturday, if they were both at home.

"Yay for Mom!" Astra blew a kiss. "See ya later, alligator."

"After while, crocodile," Zen replied. Another joke her father had passed down from previous Louisiana generations.

Malone poked his head in the door after a brief knock. "Safe to enter?"

"My rear end is intact, if that's what you mean. The boss didn't tear me a new one," Zen wisecracked and motioned for him to come in.

"Glad to hear it. Hadley lectured me on the importance of keeping you out of trouble." Malone closed the door and sat in one of the chairs facing her desk. He held his own tablet.

"Did you break it to her that I've already corrupted you?" Zen scrolled through search results on the touch screen of her computer.

"Nah, I didn't want to destroy her hopes so soon," Malone quipped. "Look, I've got the list of colonists we should interview. One of the agents-in-training sorted through all those with solid alibis. The ones who were nowhere near site of the lunar accident. If it was an accident."

"Great. Now we need to do really good background checks on each one."

"Done. I brought Hadley up to speed. Five of them have criminal backgrounds. Two felonies, one had her record expunged. The other three had misdemeanor convictions." Malone consulted his tablet as he spoke.

"Did any of them know Martin or Hunter, or serve time at the same correctional facilities?"

"Looking into it. We should know in a few hours." Malone looked up with a frown. "Astra okay? I sent the special agent to her school."

"She's fine. Even with Hadley and the two agents helping us, we've got a ton of data to review. Looks like no tacos for us. Long night ahead."

"Tacos?" Malone blinked at her.

"I promised Astra a treat. Really to distract her, make her think there's no cause for alarm." Zen rubbed her already-tired eyes and relaxed into her chair. "My mother may have been right. A boring job in academia is looking good right now."

"My soon-to-be ex-wife makes delicious tacos, and she's former Air Force. No slouch when it comes to a fight. Between her and the agent standing watch, you won't have to worry," Malone said.

"Your ex would babysit a teenager she's never met? And on short notice at that?" Zen gazed at him in surprise.

"Kylie is used to my work. I told her all about you, your dad, Astra. Don't look so shocked," Malone said with a laugh. "We can actually have conversations that don't turn into arguments. Sometimes."

"She wanted to know if you and I were mixing off-duty pleasure with business," Zen retorted and sat forward again to continue searching.

"Wait, you think…" Malone gaped at Zen.

"She'll be happy to pump Astra for details about your new female partner."

"Kylie's not jealous, trust me. She's got a new man in her life already." Malone wore a slight frown as if unsure how he felt about it.

"Are you?" Zen looked at him around the monitor.

"What? No. It feels weird though. Anyway, I won't call her if you want to make your own arrangements. But you're right. We've got a long day and night ahead."

Zen was about to reply when her desk phone pinged an incoming call. The ringtone she'd given to identify her father. She used her headset, careful not to put him on speaker mode. "Daddy, everything is okay. Astra is fine."

Malone lowered his tablet to study her face as she listened. Zen assumed the role of dutiful daughter. Her parents would worry themselves into a frazzle otherwise. Arrangements confirmed and assurances given, Zen ended the call.

"What time do they get here?" Malone wore a crooked grin.

FOR THE REST OF THE morning, Zen and Malone pored over information they'd looked up and reports given to them. They'd finally moved to the conference room. Notes on the case rapidly filled up the digital whiteboard.

Her mother had called once they arrived at Zen's house. Astra knew to go straight home. Her grandparents had the evening planned out with military precision. Delivery food, including dessert. Homework. Classic Black horror films—*Tales from the Hood* I through IV and Jordan Peel's entire catalog. With her mind relieved, Zen could focus on the puzzle pieces in front of her. That's what each report and search result looked like. She knew the answers were there.

Malone glanced at the digital time display in one corner of the whiteboard. Eleven fifty AM. He rubbed his flat midsection. "No wonder my stomach is complaining. Almost lunchtime. I haven't eaten since before the crack of dawn."

"Let's finish the last report first."

"Starving ourselves won't help. In fact, research shows concentration and cognition improves when we feed the brain." Malone gave her a pat on the back.

Zen stood in front of the whiteboard, both fists on her hips. She shook her head in frustration. "I feel like it's staring right at me and I can't see it."

"You will; we both will. A change of scenery might help us see clearer. Let's go to that new little restaurant off the quad. I hear it's good."

"Talk to me," Zen murmured to the writing before her.

"It is, Zen. The board is saying, 'Let's eat,'" Malone joked in a stage whisper. Then he turned toward the door. "Boss, come join us for a quick lunch."

Clive walked in and waved away the suggestion. "Batiste, you're in the one-thirty briefing with me."

Zen exchanged a look with Malone. "Sir?"

"Robert Goddard flew in for the meeting. He specifically asked for you to be there. Straight from the top." Clive frowned at no one in particular.

"Me?" Zen crossed her arms.

"He wants to talk to you about Iesha Franklin." Clive held up a palm before Malone and Zen could finish their protests. "I've made it clear what subjects are off limits. Supposedly, he wants your mental health expertise. Something about refining Goddard's rehab program for youth."

"Their charitable foundation has professionals who consult. He doesn't need me," Zen argued. "No rich ex frat boy is going to order me around."

"No, but the assistant attorney general of criminal division can," Malone replied with a side-eye at Clive.

"As usual, Ramirez goes straight to the point. Goddard is a major power broker. He's even met with the President on space commerce," Clive said with a huff. He sat down in one of the chairs. "Have food delivered."

"Let Malone go," Zen said, and heard the whine in her voice.

"Don't throw me under the bus. Besides, you're the authority on crime in space," Malone said. He pulled out his tablet. Moments later the menu for the restaurant appeared on the television monitor.

"Goddard mentioned an article you wrote on the social context of space colonies. Implications for crimes committed in space, I think you is how you put it," Clive said.

"Damn it," Zen muttered and sat down.

"Even if you could get around orders from on high, which you can't, he's got you there," Malone said. "What does everybody want?"

Zen put her forehead on the conference table. "A new identity and a place to hide."

"Right, a chef's salad for Zen, extra ranch dressing on the side. And a large raspberry lemonade. Boss?" Malone looked at Clive, who lifted an eyebrow. "I've gotten to know her well. Creature of habit."

Clive ordered a roast beef sandwich. Malone chose to go with a low-carb mini-pizza. Fifteen minutes later the food arrived. Malone and Clive indulged Zen as she ranted about her work being interrupted by politics. Clive reminded her how important private space companies were to NASA. Hadley arrived just as they finished.

Malone wore a guilty look. "Sorry, Hadley. I sent you a message, but—"

"I had a protein shake, thanks. You two have about fifteen minutes to prepare. Check your inboxes. I sent you both a summary. Yes, it's mostly what you already know but includes updates. Iesha Franklin is improving. Breathing on her own."

"What?" Zen looked up at her from the salad.

"She had breathing problems. They're not sure why. So, the medical team put her on a ventilator, but only for twelve hours. Fortunately, she's young and healthy," Clive said.

"Ms. Franklin had a bad reaction to the meds they gave her," Hadley added.

Zen wiped her hands on a napkin and picked up her tablet. The information had been uploaded to their encrypted project management app. Malone and Clive joined her in reading. No one spoke for ten minutes. As usual, Hadley's report was succinct but thorough. Iesha had been in protective custody at Cumberland, a medium-security federal prison with a minimum-security satellite camp.

"Who ordered the anti-depressant and antibiotics?" Zen looked from Hadley to Clive and back.

"The mental health team did a screening. Based on her history, she was given the meds. She'd had two suicide attempts before. It all makes sense, really," Clive replied.

"Except in addition to become more depressed, she suffered serotonin syndrome. Sometimes antidepressants cause a dangerous elevation of serotonin," Hadley said.

"As a lunar colony trainee, she had extensive medical tests. Any reactions should have been listed. Her psychological profile would have been available as well." Zen pushed aside the empty plastic bowl.

"She became agitated, crying. The staff aren't sure if the history of drug reactions was missing or got missed. Goddard uploaded her records a day or so after she arrived at Cumberland." Hadley pursed her lips.

"Okay, I'll say it. Someone told them what meds to give with the goal of shutting her up for good." Malone looked around at the others.

"But she'd already told us enough to put us on the right track," Zen said.

"Unless there's more," Malone replied in a dark tone. "She's off the ventilator. I say we delay interviews with the lunar colonists and go see her."

"I agree." Zen stood as though ready to leave right then.

Clive shook his head. "No. We need to start talking to those folks yesterday."

"I'll have the agents-in-training start. They're excellent. I've been observing them. That way we can say the interviews have begun." Hadley looked at Clive for a sign.

Clive drummed his thick fingers on the conference table for a few seconds. "Only because it won't take you long to get there. She's at Arundel Medical Center in Annapolis. They're moving her from ICU later today."

"Right," Zen said and smiled at Malone. "I'll even let you drive."

"How generous of you, Batiste," Malone retorted. "We can take the metro in. Then rent an SUV. I'm tall and manly, you know."

"Right, the speed trains will get us there faster than slogging through traffic." Zen grabbed the remains of their lunch, empty bags and containers. "I'll toss this stuff out. Meet you in your office—"

Clive stood. "Batiste, you're coming with me. Meeting in..." Clive glanced at the clock. "Less than ten minutes. Enough time to wash our hands, freshen up, and walk over to the briefing room."

"But boss, this is critical. An urgent development in the investigation. One that'll get them answers sooner than expected." Zen gave their boss a hopeful smile.

He strode to the door. "I'll get there ahead of you and explain you'll join us shortly. Very shortly, Batiste."

"Yes, sir," Zen mumbled to his back because Clive didn't wait for an argument or an answer.

"Well, you gave it a try anyway," Malone said. He held up both palms when Zen scowled at him. "Hey, don't take it out on me. You're the one who took up space crime and caught a serial killer. You gotta expect some celebrity perks with that combo."

Hadley stood. "Take a few minutes to get your game face on. Being in a room with so many top people can be a bit much."

"Who will be there?" Zen followed Hadley out.

"The assistant attorney general, three top NASA officials, and—"

"And Robert S. Goddard, the billionaire with low friends in high places." Zen stood tall and smoothed down her jacket.

"Lose the attitude, Zen," Malone said. "Hell, you're a star in your own right. Own it, baby."

"Don't call me baby again, Ramirez," Zen snapped over her shoulder without looking at him.

Hadley kept going past Zen's office. She faced them both. "We'll regroup after the meeting. Mr. Anderson's orders." Then she marched on.

Malone turned to Zen, palms out. "Deep breaths in, deep breaths out. Center yourself and don't go off like a shotgun. I'm not the enemy."

Zen pushed through to her office and paced in a circle for a few seconds. Malone watched her. When he tapped his wristwatch a second time, Zen blew out air. She smoothed down her wool and silk-blend suit jacket. She fiddled with the mock neck black sweater she wore beneath it. Then she took out the cosmetic mirror from a desk drawer.

"You've got just enough time for a jog to the ladies' room." Malone brushed her shoulders.

"Being summoned to this meeting doesn't feel right, Malone," Zen said.

"You've got a chance to look this Goddard dude over up close. They'll be watching you. Here's a chance for you to watch *them*."

Zen stood straight and stopped rubbing her hands together with nervous energy. Two women had put themselves at risk and their trust in her. "You're right. Focus, Batiste."

"Anybody who goes to a foreign country to track a perp and bags him can handle a meeting of suits. They're not all that smart. I've been in the room with those types before. Not impressed." Malone gave a snort of scorn.

She put her arms around his neck and pressed a cheek to his without thinking. "Thanks, partner."

Malone swallowed hard when Zen pulled back to grin at him. He wore a shy smile. "Careful. Don't want anyone to think you like me too much."

"I don't," Zen wisecracked with a laugh. "Okay, on to the lion's den."

Malone nodded and watched her leave. She took Malone's advice and ducked into the women's restroom; nerves having activated the urge to go. *No harm in making sure*. They could wait. After all, she was merely the sideshow for Goddard. The new century space magnate wanted to meet a minor celebrity. At least that was his cover. One last look in the mirror. A check to make sure her hands were completely dry after washing them. Wouldn't do to have damp palms when shaking hands with the bigwigs.

Zen made the short walk across the courtyard to an adjoining building. She went through the usual security process. She picked up her tablet and keycard on the other side of the checkpoint. Then she headed to the elevators to the eight-floor conference room. Men in dark suits strode back and forth with great purpose. Probably rushing to the break room for donuts, Zen thought. She smiled at the silly joke, but it worked. The jitters at the pit of her stomach eased. Zen slipped into the meeting and pressed her back against a wall and scanned the room. Six men and four women sat around the polished oak table. Clive, head bent close to the woman next to him, didn't look her way. He seemed intent on listening to his companion. The woman tilted her head in Zen's direction. Clive followed her gaze. Zen suppressed a sigh when he gestured for her to join him. She kept close to the wall as she walked to the chair beside him. No one else appeared to notice Zen. After a few minutes of muted side conversations, a man Zen recognized got everyone's attention. The administrator of NASA, Ed Giancarlo, welcomed them all.

He went through other subjects, summarizing the current status of three space projects. The others in the meeting exchanged discreet glances with each other. Zen could tell they were waiting for the main event. Then her gaze settled on the man sitting between the NASA administrator and the assistant attorney general. Robert Goddard listened to the administrator with an expression of respect. Zen felt a firm nudge in her side. She glanced left at Clive.

"They're getting around to us," he whispered and looked at Giancarlo.

Zen looked in the same direction. Goddard, seated one down from Giancarlo, gazed at her. He flashed a brief smile before he turned back to the administrator. When Zen looked at Clive, his eyebrows pulled together in one thick line. Just as he'd said, the topic had swung to the lunar colony sites. Clive cleared his throat. His basso voice held a grave note as he delivered a summary of their investigation so far. Then Clive responded to questions from all sides of the room. Zen sat next to him, content to let her boss do the talking. Furtive glances darted at her as Clive talked.

To her surprise, the assistant attorney general made a few remarks and the meeting was over. Before she could escape, Goddard headed straight for her. He stretched out a hand.

"You're the main reason I came today, Dr. Batiste. I was assured we'd be able to meet for a few minutes. Thank Ed and Frank for me," Goddard said aside to Clive. Frank Newsome was the President's chief of staff.

"We understand how busy you are. And our meeting lasted longer than expected." Clive moved closer to Zen.

"My schedule is clear for the next forty minutes," Goddard replied without glancing at the time.

Clive pasted on a smile. "Excellent. I don't know if we can use this room, though."

"This is my PA. Arrangements have been made?" Goddard said aside to a young man who appeared at his shoulder.

"Yes, sir. We have the room for another twenty minutes or so," the assistant replied.

"Excellent," Clive replied in a smooth tone.

Zen didn't bother forcing a smile back at Goddard. She sat down, ready to be scrutinized. Goddard took the lead, asking quite informed questions as it turned out. Clive deftly guided him back to their team as a whole when Goddard tried to probe Zen. After thirty minutes of verbal gamesmanship, Goddard took his leave.

"Wonder if he got what he wanted?" Zen watched him saunter like the king of the hill.

"Just a friendly chat. He's curious about you. Madrid," Clive replied. "They all are, Batiste.

"Goddard wouldn't use his clout to meet a minor government employee. Even one that made the news for a minute."

"You've developed a psych profile of him already, huh?" Clive gave a gruff chuckle as they headed out of the building. When Zen didn't laugh with him, his face settled into a grimace. "I was joking, Batiste."

"Why? It's such a great idea," Zen replied.

# Chapter 12

Monday evening Zen and Malone went to the hospital. Malone insisted on going along. "Just in case," he said. Zen gave up trying to talk him out of it. He checked in with hospital security while she went to see Iesha. She'd been moved from ICU to a private room.

Zen looked down at Iesha in the hospital bed. "How are you feeling?"

"Dumb for opening my big mouth," the young woman croaked, her voice still cracked from the ventilator. She gently rubbed her throat for a few seconds.

Zen looked around for the water carafe, found it, and filled a cup with a straw. She held the cup while Iesha took tiny sips. A nurse came in to check Iesha's vitals. After entering data on her tablet, the nurse looked at Zen.

"Fifteen minutes. Ms. Franklin is still weak."

"Understood," Zen replied with a nod.

Iesha waited until the door whisked shut behind the nurse. Then she pushed to sit higher on the pillows at her back. "Where's that fine ass partner of yours?"

"Outside checking in with the security department," Zen said.

Iesha went still. "You mean somebody might try to kill me?"

"We're in the business of being cautious. You gave us a good scare. Why did you try to hurt yourself?"

"I don't know. These thoughts kept repeating in my head like an audio loop. Saying I was useless. My life was and always will be crap." Iesha sank against the pillows with a sigh. "More water."

"Had you been thinking about suicide before?" Zen shifted into therapeutic interview mode.

"When I was fifteen, I took a bunch of pain pills I had bought off the street. I got sick and my foster mother slapped me around for being stupid. Didn't take me to a doctor or nothing. Only 'treatment' I got," Iesha said.

"I'm so sorry."

"But I wasn't thinking about it in Chile. Antidepressants, at least some of them, mess with my head." Iesha stared at the ceiling. "The prison doctor said that's what happened this time."

"Yes, it seems so." Zen smoothed the blanket down across Iesha's lap. Then she helped her drink more water.

Iesha settled against the raised bed again. She gazed at Zen. "You think I got that med on purpose."

"You were clinically depressed, based on your symptoms. Feelings of helplessness, hopelessness, and insomnia," Zen replied with care.

"My personnel profile from Goddard includes detailed medical info. I'm pretty sure reactions to meds would be in there. Someone either left it out on purpose or bought off the medical staff. A male nurse brought me the pills one evening. So, you tell that sexy cop to be really thorough with security."

"We've found no evidence to suggest a deliberate attempt to harm you." Zen sat in the chair and pulled it closer to the hospital bed. "Did you see or hear anything to suggest otherwise?"

"Humph, you think they're stupid? I was in a nice cushy holding cell. Remind me to commit a federal offense if I slid back to crime again," Iesha said with a sly grin. Then she grew serious again. "But it's still being locked up, right? I was feeling down. My mom... She swore to me she was straight. No more sweet gig at Goddard."

Zen put a hand on her arm. Iesha's eyes had become glassy with unshed tears. "You're still under the influence of the medication, Iesha. It's going to take time to metabolize out of your system. The fluids will help."

Iesha held up the other arm with the IV tube inserted, her cocky grin back. "I'm gonna piss it out, huh?"

Zen laughed. "Something like that. It will take a while. You're on another antidepressant, one of the new ones. Then you'll be eased off of it, too. Or maybe you should keep taking it."

"At least that voice of doom is out of my head." Iesha winced as if the memory caused physical pain.

"Who told you about Hunter?"

"I heard the police in Calama talking about it. I picked up enough Spanish to understand. A robbery or a drug deal gone bad, they said. You believe it?" Iesha grabbed Zen's hand and held on tight.

"There's no evidence—"

"Oh c'mon! Don't give me that lame official line. Rob knew too much. He dies. Tan knew too much. He's dead.

All too damn convenient and tidy." Iesha glared at Zen as if daring her to contradict the logic.

"Which is why we're making you won't have unauthorized visits or treatment decisions." Zen stared back at Iesha.

"Until you get evidence. Fine. That's all you can tell me." Iesha blew out a breath and settled into the white sheets.

"We're making sure you're safe. Do you know a Georgina Preston?" Zen asked.

"Never heard of her. Who is she?"

"Her name came up as someone who might have information on the training process," Zen said.

"Goddard is a big company. Even the space division has a few hundred employees. Just make sure Robert S. stays away." Iesha looked at Zen.

"You've met him?"

"Yeah, I'm small fry but the space program is his passion project. Goes back to his great-great whatever. And like a lot of wealthy folks, he likes to meet his charity cases. Excellent company PR," Iesha said with a cynical grin.

"Robert S.?"

"To keep him straight from the other Roberts in the family. A couple of uncles, a cousin. It's a tradition to name a kid after the founder. They think it helps them end up being the boss of it all." Iesha chuckled.

"You know a lot about the Goddard folks." Zen cocked her head to the side.

Iesha looked at her for a few seconds and changed the subject. "Mama will go into treatment again. My brother has done time enough times. He'll be okay. Gonna take him wanting to change."

"True," Zen said.

"I had one decent therapist when I was in foster care the second time. She helped me develop a recovery plan. I get down, but I always manage to bounce back. I don't want to die."

Zen took Iesha's hand again. "I believe you."

"I'm counting on you and handsome to keep me alive." Iesha inhaled deeply and blew out air. "Okay. I had a short but fun ride with Robert S."

"What the... I did *not* see that one coming," Zen said with a low whistle.

"What, you think I'm too basic for the rich white guy?" Iesha arched a brow at Zen.

"Please. You're pretty and smart. I figured you wouldn't go for the spoiled, arrogant trust fund kid," Zen said. "You'd eat him for breakfast."

Iesha laughed too hard. It brought on a coughing spell. She sipped more water. "I almost did, girl. I knew the deal. No wedding bells and intros to the family."

"You got accepted into the prestigious training program."

"My brains and hard work got me into the program. I didn't need Robert S. smoothing the way for me. Anyway, screwing him came later."

"Gotcha," Zen said with a grin.

"Look, Robert S. is like his father and the rest of them. Ruthless as hell. He's not gonna risk a trillion-dollar payoff on his investment."

"He's in DC now," Zen said, her tone quiet. She thought Iesha would become terrified, but she didn't react as expected.

"You're about to figure out stuff way more damaging than what I know. Which isn't much. Watch your back," Iesha said and gripped Zen's hand tighter.

"But your affair..."

"His second wife doesn't care. Or is she his third? What gets his attention is any threat to being on top. He didn't beat out the other private space companies just on his charm."

"We have a special agent working with security," Zen said.

"Make sure the nurses and staff have been working here awhile and haven't been contacted by Goddard employees." Iesha let go of Zen's hand. She relaxed into the pillows and closed her eyes.

"Maybe you should consider applying for a job in law enforcement," Zen said with a grin.

Iesha opened one eye. "Not with my shady record."

Zen grinned at her but became serious again. "I'll check on you later."

"Humph." Iesha covered a wide yawn with the back of one hand. She drifted off to sleep in seconds.

After sitting with Iesha a few minutes, Zen left the hospital room. She went to the nurses' pod nearby. The nurse assured her they had instructions on visitors. Zen went off to find Malone, got turned around in the maze of hallways. A male nurse stopped to give her directions. Finally pointed in the right direction, Zen headed for the main security office.

An elevator opened up in the seamless wall as if by magic. After a voice command, Zen arrived on the first floor. Another set of instructions from a different employee helped her again. She rounded a corner and almost collided with Robert S. Goddard. His warm expression of delight made it seem like they were old friends.

"Dr. Batiste. I hoped we could meet again." Goddard wore an affable grin.

Zen glanced at his companion. The assistant that had accompanied him now looked like a bodyguard. Tall, and lean in a muscular way, the man did not smile. Goddard's brunette hair and skin with a hint of olive contrasted with the cool blondness of the assistant. The assistant swept Zen with an appraising full-body gaze. Both of the men's attitudes touched a nerve.

"What are you doing here?" Zen clipped. She shifted her slim crossbody bag to the side. The "assistant" followed the movement with cool grayish-blue eyes.

"My family has been a donor to the medical center's foundation for years." Goddard held onto his smile even as his hazel eyes studied Zen.

"Interesting." Zen pursed her lips to keep from blurting out more.

"Isn't it? And that I would bump into you, literally." Goddard glanced at the assistant with an amused gleam. He seemed not to notice the man didn't share his good humor. "I hope you're in good health."

Zen let out a deep breath. She wanted to slap the smug, handsome face. His assistant moved closer to Goddard as if he read her mind. "I'm fine."

"Ah, visiting a friend then?"

Zen flashed a smile. "A close friend. One whose well-being I'm very much invested in."

"Friends are a precious thing. I can understand why you're so protective." Goddard let out a sigh as if contemplating the importance of relationships. "I have a lot of friends—well, useful acquaintances, really. Hard to find people you can rely on."

"True. Then again to have a true friend, you must know how to be one." Zen watched his smile waver for a split second. Then he pasted it back in place.

"Mental health access is a particular interest of mine. We're helping the center expand outpatient services," Goddard replied.

"How generous of you, Mr. Goddard. How did you come to care so much about the field—family history?" Zen put on her best earnest expression.

Goddard blinked but recovered. "I had college friends who had issues. I've seen the devastating impact when left untreated."

"Also relevant to your space program. We're only just beginning to learn about the stress of space isolation," Zen replied smoothly.

"My company has plans to expand our lunar program."

"Along with plans to establish a colony on Mars within the next decade. You're already ahead of other space companies on asteroid mining." Zen gazed back at his intense hazel eyes.

"You're on the team that will review our internal investigation." Goddard gave his assistant a side glance.

"Near completion and will be very thorough," the man said on cue.

"Good to hear." Zen let her gaze flicker to the blond and back to Goddard.

"We're sure the death at G-Colony One was a tragic accident. Great risk is the price of great progress. Space travel and colonization are dangerous occupations," Goddard said in a suitably grave tone. "Naturally, Goddard Corporation will provide for the next of kin, financially, that is."

"Ah, they're highly insured then. I'll note that in our files." Zen matched his pose with her own somber expression. She pretended to check her watch twice.

Goddard's jaw muscle tensed until his smile pulled into a rictus. "We both have the aim of improving safety in space. Please, set up a meeting with me. Your expertise could be invaluable. I have an entire section working on the design of space colonies."

His assistant pulled out a business card and extended it to Zen. The man's impassive expression didn't change. Zen returned his gaze for a few seconds before she looked at it. She snapped a photo with her smartwatch. The information transferred into her contacts securely.

"I'm afraid we can't meet, as it would be a conflict while our investigation is in process. But thanks for the card. I may need to speak directly with you later, or an executive member of your space team." Zen saw Malone approach from an adjoining hallway around a curved wall. She tried to send a message with her eyes only.

"Hey, I was just about to call you. Whoa." Malone stopped short, stared at Goddard first and then the assistant.

"Malone Ramirez is another special agent on our team. This is Robert S. Goddard and ..." Zen looked at the blond.

"Mikal," Goddard put in before the man could speak. "You're Dr. Batiste's supervisor, I take it, second in command under Clive Anderson, as it were. Nice to meet you."

"We're partners," Zen snapped and then was annoyed at allowing Goddard to push that particular button.

"Special Agent Ramirez has more field investigative experience. I've done my homework, too. But forgive me for making an assumption." Goddard smiled as though satisfied.

"Mr. Goddard is a big contributor to the Arundel Foundation. He's here to..." Zen pivoted to face Goddard again. "I'm sorry, you didn't get around to telling me why you're here."

Goddard's lips slipped at the edges into an almost frown. "An impromptu meeting with the board. And as it happens, I have a friend being treated here, too. Two birds with one stone, to use an ancient cliché."

"Visiting hours are closed," Zen replied in a terse tone. She stared at the rich man as a challenge to be contradicted.

Goddard studied Zen for a few beats before his expression relaxed. "Ah, well... meeting with the chief of medicine, the CEO, and the foundation president will have to suffice. For now. Pleasure to meet you, Special Agent Ramirez."

Malone looked at Goddard with a bemused expression. "Sir."

"I look forward to consulting with you in the future, Dr. Batiste. We've had a wonderful tour of the center, but best not keep our hosts waiting. Mikal."

Goddard glanced at his assistant, who gave a barely perceptible nod in reply. He pointed toward the bank of elevators leading up to the administrative suites. The two men headed off. Malone and Zen watched them until the doors whisked shut.

Malone faced Zen, his voice a low, whispered rush of words. "What the hell just happened? What was he doing here? Coincidence? Nah, even I don't buy that and we know I don't do conspiracies."

"Let's do one last check on Iesha, and don't mention Goddard's in the building," Zen said.

They walked to the elevators that went up to the hospital floors. Malone tapped a fist on one thigh and fidgeted. They couldn't talk because of others on the elevator. Nursing assistants chattered about going on break. Two women whispered about the condition of a relative. The ride to the third floor seemed to last forever. Once they stepped into the hall, Malone led the way to the east wing. The main nursing station formed a large circle broken by openings on three sides. A beefy male nurse supervisor looked up as they approached.

"Back again? Look, we always want to cooperate with law enforcement, but medical care is the priority." At least six-foot-five, the man towered over them both.

"Right, right. We just want to make sure Ms. Franklin hasn't had any other visitors," Malone said.

"She's good." The man frowned and exchanged a look with his female colleague. "Should I be expecting trouble?"

"Call us if anyone tries to see her or asks about her condition," Malone replied.

The nurse pointed to a panel. "Monitors alert us if her door is opened without a hospital code. Staff that go in swipe their ID. A video feed is saved to the cloud. We don't lock the doors because in an emergency seconds count. I used to be a correctional officer, so I know security. Satisfied?"

Malone nodded as he stared at the panel. "And you have video for the last twenty-four hours or so?"

"Video is triggered only if there's no ID scanned. Patient privacy. And we only set it up when there are special security concerns. Like with Ms. Franklin. No one has been in her room. I double checked."

"What about on the floor?" Zen asked. Screens showed the hallways.

"Some guy was wandering around. He'd gotten lost. I walked him to the elevators to re-direct him," the female nurse spoke up.

Zen turned to her. "Had the man been here before?"

"Nope. If he had, I would have told Damon." She nodded at the male nurse.

"Like I said, security talked to us," Damon added.

"Was it one of these men?" Zen held up her agency issued smartwatch. Two images came up in a slide show fashion. Both nurses studied the pictures.

"The blond guy. He's handsome. Great body, too." The nurse shrugged at the look her fellow nurse gave her.

"You're sure he didn't go into any of the rooms?" Malone said.

"See for yourself," Damon replied. He tapped the slim keypad. "Jai, assistant security director, showed me how to review video recordings. Tell me the time you saw the guy, Jenn."

"Within the last hour, hour and a half. It was after I'd done my eight o'clock rounds," Jennifer said. She leaned forward to peer at the screen. She pointed to it. "There he is."

They all watched as Jennifer emerged from around the corner. The man slipped something inside his suitcoat. At least that's what it looked like to Zen. Then he faced Jennifer with a baffled smile. She smiled back, they chatted, and then they walked off together.

"I went with him to the elevator. Just to make sure after getting briefed by security. He looked harmless enough. You think he was up to something?"

"He works for the same company as Ms. Franklin. And we don't want him talking his way into her room," Malone replied.

"Send me the pictures of them. I'll make sure security and nursing knows," Damon said.

"I'll go say good-bye to Iesha one last time," Zen said. She walked away while Malone, Damon, and the female continued to talk.

Iesha sat up when Zen entered her room. "What's happened? You're not back just to tuck me in."

"We're super thorough. You know how government types can be. Check and double check," Zen said.

"I bet someone from Goddard showed up, maybe Robert S. himself. They're *thorough*, too. They want to know what I know and if you know it now." Iesha's pretty brown face pulled into a grimace.

"But they aren't sure how much you know," Zen countered in an effort to reassure her.

"Enough for them to want me dead," Iesha. "You should look real close at the Goddard space colony program. I don't know what they're hiding, but it's gotta be big."

"Yeah. Try to rest. I'll come again when I can." Zen tried to sound upbeat.

"Get me out of here. I'm not taking any more pills, and the only thing I'm eating is stuff out of the vending machine."

Zen spent another fifteen minutes assuring her about hospital security. She also got the big male nurse to come in and explain their safety measures. Iesha was too sharp for anything less. Damon's solid physical presence helped. Iesha appeared to be more relaxed, though still wary. Zen and Malone left after making sure they'd covered every possible contingency. They didn't speak until they were in the agency SUV.

Malone got into the driver's side. "Well, this turned into a way more interesting trip than I thought it would. I'll bet Goddard was surprised to see us."

"Maybe. Maybe not. Remember he's got connections," Zen replied as she put on her seat belt.

"Our department is too new. He hasn't had time to plant an informant. I personally checked out the agents-in-training assigned to us." Malone tapped the button and the electric engine purred in response. He steered the vehicle into the flow of traffic with ease. He set the location of their office in DC and let the SUV take over most of the work.

"But you didn't know to look for a connection to Goddard Corporation. Did you?" Zen gazed at him.

"I eliminated anyone who might have ties to one of the private space companies."

"Damn, you're good." Zen punched his muscular bicep playfully.

"I've been trying to tell you, partner. No conflicts of interest that I could uncover."

"This from super-rational Special Agent Malone, who doesn't buy into conspiracies," Zen teased.

"We both know that rich and power people with government connections think ahead. Apparently, Clive and your friend Ms. Illinois planned ahead as well," Malone said.

"What do you mean?"

"They already knew trouble was brewing on the moon. And Goddard has influential allies. Let's not pretend everyone who works for the government is pure like us," Malone said.

"I don't think Iesha is in any danger now. Goddard is on notice we're watching."

"Makes sense. How'd you get those two to pose for a photo?" Malone turned to Zen.

"They didn't know. I pretended to check the time with my handy-dandy secret agent watch. What I actually did was take pictures to show the staff. Which reminds me." Zen sent hospital security an encrypted email with the photos.

"Damn, you're good," Malone quipped.

"I've been trying to tell you." Zen grinned at him.

ZEN AND MALONE WORKED late into the night preparing for interview questions. She checked in with her parents several times. Malone scanned his emails. He hadn't gotten anonymous photos of his family. Zen's father called her twice.

"He's retired, but still connected. I don't know if you'll be able to keep him out of it. I'd do the same in his place."

"You're right. He's quietly pissed, and that's not good."

Malone stood and went through stretching motions. "Meaning…"

"Daddy isn't the type to make a lot of noise when he's angry. He tends to be cool and methodical when faced with a problem. Says getting worked up is counterproductive. When he's really angry, he's like one of those stealth missiles. Just because you don't hear or see it coming, doesn't mean you're not about to get hit."

"Remind me not to make him angry then," Malone joked. "I'm going home. Let me walk you out."

Zen glanced at the digital time display. She yawned and stood. "You don't have to, Malone. But I appreciate the offer. I can—"

"Take care of yourself. Everybody needs backup sometimes. We don't know what Goddard or whoever is capable of. Now come on."

"Your offer to be my bodyguard is cute but unnecessary."

She retrieved her leather tote and followed him out. Despite her words, she checked to make sure her office door was locked. Then chided herself for being silly. AI security covered the building. The Federal Protective Services Department provided patrols after hours.

"Yeah, well, indulge me anyway. I'll be able to sleep better if I put you in the taxi. Better yet, let me drop you at the train station."

"Oh c'mon. You're tired and I'll be fine," Zen protested.

They had a brief verbal tug-of-war about it. Malone won. He drove her to the station, which allowed them more time to discuss their next move. When they reached the Metro Center Station, Malone pulled into a drop-off lane. His Tesla SUV hummed as it shifted into park.

"Text your parents your ETA. Get—"

"I've already scheduled my taxi. I won't share it with strangers to save a few dollars. I'll be aware of my surroundings. Check, check, and check. I didn't just ride into this town on the turnip truck you know," Zen quipped as she opened the passenger door. She got out and leaned in to grab her bag. "Drive safe."

"You and those old sayings. Fine, you're prepared. You don't mind if I watch you walk in, do you?" Malone's lips tugged up at one corner.

"Fine. Overprotective." Zen shook her head.

"Yeah, but you think I'm cute. It's a start." Malone winked at her.

Zen rolled her eyes and pushed the door shut. She ignored the sound of his muted laughter inside the SUV and walked away. The trip home was uneventful. Nothing looked out of the ordinary. But then experts wouldn't stand out if she was being followed. Robert S. Goddard had more than enough money to hire the best.

By the time the train pulled into the Falls Church station, her eyes felt heavy. In spite of her bravado, she only felt truly at ease once inside the taxi. She texted her father, who stood in the door waiting when Zen emerged from the sedan. To his credit, her father didn't pepper her with questions. Zen greeted her mother. Astra was already asleep. Then she went to her bedroom to shower and change. Her mother had prepared a light supper of sliced roast beef and asparagus.

"I'll let you two talk. The mattress in your guest master suite is wonderful. You did right buying a home with four bedrooms," Enola said. "I thought this house was too much at first."

"Yes, Mama. You made your opinion clear. At some length and repeatedly," Zen muttered.

"I was giving you the benefit of my wisdom. Not that you listen to *me*. My granddaughter seems to be thriving at least."

"Two compliments. I thought those flying objects I saw on the way home looked like pigs." Zen placed a hand on her chest in mock disbelief.

"I don't nitpick everything you do," Enola complained. She stared at Zen.

"No, ma'am. I'm teasing you. Goodnight, Mama." Zen pecked Enola's cheek.

"Hmm." Enola turned to James. "You're here as a grandparent to offer support.

Stay out of anything else, James," Enola said. She left them, her satin lounge dress billowing around her as she walked.

Zen sat at the kitchen island and drank from the glass of sweet tea beside her plate. She could feel her father's heavy presence. He sat across from her pretending to nurse his own drink, two fingers of bourbon. Except what he did was watch her eat. His glass stayed full.

"I knew you'd be happy for a chance to be here, back in DC," Zen said. "Astra had the agent shadowing her. She could have gone to her best friend's house and been fine. Not that I don't welcome a visit with y'all. Mama's critiques keep me humble."

James's grunt rumbled deep in his chest. He went to the dishwasher and unloaded it. He seemed perfectly at ease putting away plates, cups, and pans. He knew where they went. The strong, dignified man performing household chores was an incongruous sight. But her father had always said no one was above menial tasks. His father and grandfather had taught him that back in Louisiana.

"How much do you know?" Zen pushed since he didn't seem in a hurry to talk.

James placed one last pot away in a deep drawer that rolled closed. "Your mother still cooks a mean roast. Our meal delivery service is excellent. Still, nothing like a home-cooked meal."

Zen put down her fork. "Seriously? We're going to talk about beef?"

Her father sat across from her again. "I spoke to a few people, including Clive."

"My boss. You talked to..." Zen leaned away from him with her arms crossed. "Mama is right. Stay out of my business."

"Zenobia—"

"No, I don't want to hear it," Zen snapped.

"But you're going to anyway because it's critical. I didn't raise you to react emotionally. I have information you need," James said.

She tapped a fist on the quartz island surface. He was right. Zen sighed. "Share what you know and then go home."

"Zen—"

"I mean it, Daddy." Zen glared at him.

James gazed back at her. "Okay, then. You've got conditions. So have I. Let Astra stay with us or her father for a while. Until you're done with Goddard."

"What does that mean?"

James gestured for Zen to follow him. They went to her home office and he again pulled the door shut. "You know I worked on the early international space agreements."

"Of course. You're going to tell me you worked with Goddard?"

"His father, Ian. Funny how he's not a Robert, too. He told me his mother stuck to her guns. Named him after her father because she said that name was cursed." James let out a dry chuckle. "Not based on their bank accounts though."

"He's retired, the father," Zen said.

"Let's say he's semi-retired."

"Like you?" Zen squinted at him. He waved a hand, a gesture she couldn't interpret. A denial or conceding that he still worked for the government in some capacity? She decided to let it pass. "So, the senior Goddard still has a say-so in how the empire is run."

"There's been a gradual transition of control. Robert wanted to develop the space program more than Ian. He proved to his father how viable and profitable it could be.

Ian was encouraged that he could take the reins. The oldest son has issues. Alcohol. Brilliant but troubled, as they used to say. The youngest one mostly wanted to party and sleep with other men's wives. He died seven years ago in a speed boat accident."

"Interesting family history," Zen said in a sardonic tone. She sat on the sofa across from her desk. "

"Relevant," her father rumbled. He scowled at her in admonishment.

"I'm sure you're getting to the point."

"Ian Goddard is powerful, but Robert has taken influence to a whole other level. He's looking to the future. America isn't the global eight-hundred-pound gorilla anymore. Most of our leadership just doesn't know it. The smart ones, like Clive, know. Over a hundred years of arrogance and a false sense of superiority has taken its toll." James looked off as if a world map was before him. He frowned as he pronounced his assessment in a deep, prophetic tone.

Zen suppressed a groan of frustration. His years working in various intelligence agencies, added with studying abroad, gave him a long view. And James Batiste didn't like most of what he saw. Not for his children but especially his grandchildren and beyond. Zen felt a lecture coming on. One that she wanted to head off.

"Right. Racism, classicism, and a desperate clinging to past glory days. We can discuss your view of what this country has become later. What has that got to do with murders on the moon?"

James snapped out of his pondering, his dark eyes sharpening into focus again. He looked at Zen. "The US is still among the top global leaders, though diminished. One of four powerful countries that are committed to Goddard's success. His program is 'too big to fail.' Martin was a murderer who got poetic justice in a rough neighborhood. Case closed. The deaths on the moon were tragic accidents. Nothing more."

"I'm going to follow the facts," Zen said carefully.

"Those are the facts. You know the guiding wisdom in criminal investigations. Simple answers are always the best. Criminals, including killers, are pretty basic folks. Greed, sex, revenge. Hasn't changed in thousands of years. Don't chase ghosts when answers are right there in front of you." James reached out to her. His large hands swallowed her smaller ones.

Zen's eyes narrowed as she studied his piercing gaze. "You've talked to Clive? I don't think he'd be happy about me being content with the obvious."

"He's your boss. I'm your Daddy," James replied. He'd lapsed into a downhome Southern way of speaking, a soft trace of his Louisiana accent coming through.

"Okay. Well, I get it. The Goddard family has a long reach. I won't the bear any more than necessary. So far, all we have is pretty straightforward evidence." Zen assumed a relaxed pose.

"Good girl." James nodded and then smiled after a second or two. "With what you've done so far, you're going to move up. The right people are impressed."

"Whoopee." Zen affected a big yawn.

"I've kept you up long enough. Get some rest. Astra is pretty much done, her high school diploma in the bag. She can come home with us."

"Sure, Daddy. Goodnight, and thanks."

She accepted his paternal hug and peck on her forehead. Once he was gone, Zen turned on her computer. She typed a message to her friend Chloé. Hadley wasn't the only wizard at digging deep.

# Chapter 13

Tuesday morning dawned cold. A chilling rain fell as Zen rushed into the building at seven a.m. Five more minutes took her through security. The officers, knowing who she was, let her hold onto the cup of coffee. Zen smiled at the husky supervising security officer with dark-brown skin. He was usually affable. This morning he wore a focused grimace as people filed through.

"Hi, Kareem. Lots of people arrived early today. Anything special going on you can talk about?" Zen looked around as employees strode to elevators or the escalators with purpose.

Kareem stepped aside as Zen went through the doorframe detector. The device could detect metals, plastics used in 3D printing, and specific chemicals. Kareem stood next to Zen as she put her belongings in her tote again. He waited until another group of people went through.

"You would know better than me. The place is buzzing about spacers coming in. They're going straight to your floor." Kareem kept his voice low and his expression casual as if they were discussing the weather.

"Guess keeping it under wraps wasn't possible," Zen replied.

"You pull an entire crew off the moon after two deaths? Oh yeah, *somebody* gonna notice."

"Yeah." Zen moved closer when Kareem turned his back away from two HD cameras. They had two techs who could lip read.

"Anything I should know? Off the record." Kareem mumbled low. His genial smile never wavered.

"Accidents on the face of it. None of the crew seem implicated or with rough backgrounds," Zen replied. She pretended to laugh at a non-existent joke he'd told.

"Humph, wouldn't expect them to have dirty sheets," Kareem said, slang for a criminal or shady history.

"Goddard Corporation." Zen looked at him.

Kareem nodded. "Private space company. Let somebody slip through the cracks?"

"Something like that. Anyway, I don't expect trouble." Zen wouldn't break protocol beyond a certain point. Her discretion didn't faze Kareem. Plus, the big man was sharp.

"But just in case, I'll send an officer up there to do a special security check every twenty minutes or so. Might even make a round myself." Then Kareem's voice level return to normal conversational as he turned back. He told her a quick, funny story about his dog.

Zen's laughter became genuine. "A good one, K."

"I'll have more corny jokes for you next week. Have a great day, Special Agent Batiste." Kareem gave her a friendly wave. He pivoted in time to give another employee a jovial greeting.

Once on the elevator, Zen checked her smartwatch for messages. Nothing beyond a short text update from her mother. The message included a mention that there were no grits in Zen's pantry. Her mother concluded Astra wasn't being fed correctly. Zen exited the elevator, shaking her head. Malone emerged from a second one a minute later.

"Morning, partner. Got us some bagels." Malone shook one of the bags in his hand.

"You're perfect, Ramirez. Don't ever change," Zen called back over her shoulder. "Conference room in ten minutes?"

"See ya there."

Malone disappeared around a corner. No doubt heading for the small kitchen on their floor. She put away her things and grabbed her work tablet. Zen frowned when she tried to drink, only to discover the coffee was gone. Muttering, she tossed it in the trash can and headed to the conference room.

Like clockwork Malone entered the conference room. He put a large paper cup in front of Zen. The aroma of chocolate wafted to her. Then he handed her a saucer. He'd warmed and sliced the bagel. Beside it was a small packet of cream cheese. Out of another pocket he produced a tiny glass container of strawberry jam. Hadley walked in. Her eyebrows went up as she watched him serve Zen.

"Ready to rock early, huh, Hadley?" Malone walked past, her seeming not to notice the look she gave him. He grabbed the remote and turned on the digital whiteboard.

"I'm older than you two but I still manage to keep up," Hadley retorted. "Good morning to you both. I heard you worked late last night."

"Not too bad," Malone said before Zen could reply. "Long enough to get ready. But I still managed to get a good night's sleep."

"My parents came over. We had a nice late dinner. Malone was thoughtful enough to supply breakfast."

"Yep, had my hands full. Back in a minute." Malone left.

Hadley waited until he was gone and then turned to Zen. "You called former director Batiste about the photo."

"He already knew. Is he still on the job, Hadley? Tell me the truth," Zen added before Hadley answered.

"Old intelligence agents and cops never retire. Do they?" Hadley smiled. She leaned against the long table but didn't sit.

Malone returned with a paper platter filled with donuts and more bagels. His other hand held a large steaming mug with his name on it. "Fresh coffee in the kitchen, H. Special Agent Harris even brought an espresso machine, bless her. She's making café mochas, too. You did good in the hiring."

"Pace yourselves. Talk later," Hadley said. She grabbed a bagel on her way out.

"Such a suck-up." Zen performed a dramatic eye roll.

Malone put down the platter and sat, mug in hand. He studied Zen for a few seconds. "You seem a bit cranky this morning."

Zen walked to the door, looked out into the hallway, and closed it. She pushed aside her tablet and stylus. "Just between us."

"Personal or professional, my lips are sealed." Malone sat forward.

"I think my father is somehow involved in our investigation," Zen said.

"He wrote the book on international space agreements. He provided intelligence analysis for over twenty years on the space programs of other countries. Knows about spy satellite tech. The man's a walking library when it comes to—"

"I know his resume, Malone. He's a legend, blah-blah-blah. He's also supposed to be *retired*," Zen snapped.

"Whoa. Don't beat me up before I finish my second cup of coffee." Malone rolled his chair back as if afraid.

"Sorry. I was up until almost two o'clock thinking about it. He pretty much asked me to wrap up the moon death investigation fast. Even gave me a mini speech about the Goddards."

"Did he go into specifics?" Malone rubbed his chin.

"No outright warning. Just that I shouldn't look beyond the obvious answer, like in Chile." Zen broke off a piece of her bagel and lathered it with cream cheese.

"Martin had secrets that he was willing to kill to keep." Malone drank from his mug.

"I know, I know." Zen chewed as she turned over the facts in her head.

"We don't know anything different. I mean, aside from your secret informant—"

"Georgina Preston," Zen put in.

"Yeah, her. There aren't any dots connecting. Even Iesha Franklin believes shutting up Hunter was his motive."

"But what if Martin went through that treatment and it didn't work. And Goddard's team covered it up because he was too valuable to lose. What if the earlier camp death of that guy Franzen was no accident either?"

Malone sipped, nodded, and sipped again. "I see your father's point. No need to go around the world when the answer is sitting right in front of us."

"Maybe Goddard is nervous that NASA didn't know he was using ex-cons," Zen insisted.

"A lot of maybe, what if. Makes for a great mystery novel. Not good for investigators. And we have another long day ahead."

Zen blew out a noisy breath. "I know, I know. Seven interviewees from Goddard's G-Colony One."

"Nine. The agents-in-training put two more back on our list. Seems they came through programs for at-risk youth that Goddard's charity funds. And they both had arguments with the dead colonists."

As if on cue, Hadley entered without knocking. "The colonists are here, along with Goddard's chief project director for their lunar program. The interview rooms are set up. Clive is meeting with them first."

"As a group? That's unusual," Malone said with a frown.

"We want them as relaxed as possible. Guard down," Hadley said.

Zen shrugged. "Unorthodox, but makes sense. We don't have room to keep them all separate. It would take forever if they brought them here one at a time."

"And with everything happening, you couldn't fly down to the Florida NASA facility where they were housed. This way they can take flights to their homes after. Unless..." Hadley looked from Malone to Zen.

"We decide somebody needs to go to jail," Malone said. "Might as well have breakfast then. We'll go over our interview plan one last time."

"You can watch." Hadley used the remote to turn on the television. "Cameras allow for remote attendance."

"Cool," Malone said and took a large bit out of a sugary donut.

"Special Agent Harris will babysit them. They're being told not to discuss the events under review. She'll be there to make sure."

For the next hour Zen and Malone switched their attention from watching the live feed to their interview strategy. Then they stopped to study the lunar colonists; their body language and facial expressions. Nerves and tension were to be expected, though several of the colonists seemed at ease. Zen wanted get some insight into how to put them at ease, or shake them up, to get answers.

Zen and Malone spent the rest of the day on interviews. Some led to second and third rounds with the same colonists. Zen's eyes felt like tiny grains of sand had blown into them. Malone must have been feeling tired, too. They let all but three of them go by six that evening. Special Agent Harris still looked alert and fresh as she served them coffee. Malone and Zen studied the live feed on the screen of the two women and one man. They'd been returned to the room used as a waiting area.

Malone stood, legs apart, and did stretching exercises. "We got nothing. Looks like the deaths were accidents after all."

"I suppose it's too much to ask for a Perry Mason moment," Zen murmured as she continued to gaze at the widescreen.

"A who?"

"My great-grandfather passed on his love for detective fiction and televisions shows. Mid twentieth century. Perry Mason was a sleuth, and a lawyer, in an old mystery TV show. Perry would get one piece of evidence that would crack the case. My father called it a 'Perry Mason' moment, when suddenly the facts line up and you know." Zen walked closer to the screen; arms crossed.

"Oh yeah, like Franco on *Calor Nocturno* or *Night Heat*," Malone replied, still going through his moves.

"Who?" Zen looked back at him.

"Popular streaming series on Telenova. My sister and her friends love it. Mostly because the lead actor is handsome. Got my ex hooked on it, too."

"Hmm." Zen turned back to stare at the three colonists. "If only forensics would—"

"Ask and it shall be given," Hadley stood in the open doorway. Clive followed her into the room.

Zen's eyes went wide. "Seriously?"

Clive looked anything but pleased. He took the remote control and the widescreen display split between the video feed and the agency cloud. He went to the investigation folder. Then he opened an email from the FBI forensic lab. Another click and the feed vanished. The report spread across the screen.

"The first death at G-Colony One appears to be an unfortunate accident. Human error. The second one was deliberate. Two sections of the spacesuit were tampered with. Microscopic cuts in the hoses that led to the air and gravity systems caused the colonists to get disoriented and fall. Even the forensic tech almost missed them. A substance was used to dissolve the hose and make the hole bigger. Then fuse the opening to make it less visible again. Genius, really."

"Something developed for industrial application two years ago," Hadley added.

"Wonderful. Killers coming up with new ways to cover their tracks. Welcome to our brave new world. Two hoses though?" Zen frowned at the images.

"Overkill," Malone said. "The perp wanted to make sure. Those suits have fail-safes built into them. Any minor ding or glitch wouldn't be a big problem."

"Humph." Clive split the screen again. A zoomed image of a spacesuit appeared next to the report. "Whoever sabotaged the suit knew what he was doing."

"Or she," Zen pointed out.

"We've let go all but three colonists. Two are female," Malone explained.

"What were their relationships to the deceased," Clive said. He handed Hadley the remote.

They all sat at the table. Malone put his tablet, a ten-inch, in a dock on it. For thirty minutes they used the whiteboard. Zen brought up all of the colonists. She erased names as she detailed why they were eliminated and sent off. Names of the three colonists remained. Then she created a table with columns to cross reference connections.

"So, this woman was recruited in the same month as the victim. They're both from the Midwest," Zen said.

Hadley looked up from her own tablet. "They grew up about six blocks apart."

"Probably went to the same high school," Malone said, a cup of coffee in hand.

Hadley scrolled through her search. "They graduated a year apart."

"Any issue from the past?" Clive shook his head. "Sounds thin."

"Let's see if one of them was in a re-entry or at-risk program sponsored by Goddard." Zen used her tablet to open her and Malone's shared notes.

Clive frowned. "Well?"

"Hold on." Zen continued to scan through the profiles of each colonist. Then she heaved a sigh. "Shit."

"You haven't found a connection," Clive said.

"Nothing in here. But this colonist has a news article in her history about how she overcame obstacles. My gut tells me at some point she was in a program." Zen rubbed her tired eyes for a few moments. Then she sat straight. "Lodestone."

Malone turned to Zen. "We have all of their medical records."

"But do we though?" Zen looked at Clive. "We're waiting to get more information on Lodestone."

"Records on medical treatment, particularly forensic rehabilitative trials, are considered confidential. Since the mid-2020s, privacy has been a huge political and social issue. It took decades for laws to catch up to technology," Clive said.

"Right. Data collected by giant tech companies became big business. Information isn't just power, it's lucrative," Hadley added. She gave their boss a side glance.

"But I'm still working on getting what we need," Clive rumbled. His jaw muscled jumped as he spoke.

Zen looked at Malone, who kept a neutral face. "We'll talk to her. Tell her the other two have been sent home."

"You might need them." Hadley pointed to the chart on the whiteboard.

"We won't actually send them home," Zen replied.

"But she doesn't have to know it." Malone perked up. He stood, straightened his tie and drank more coffee. "Let's go."

"I'll observe." Clive stood as well. His frown deepened but he said no more.

"So will I. Guess we all should send messages that we'll be here a few hours longer."

Hadley looked energized. "My husband is used to eating alone."

Malone watched Hadley and Clive leave together. He waited until the door whisked shut behind them before he turned to Zen. "Clive had powerful push-back on getting Lodestone info in detail. And he's pissed about it. Which means..."

"Lodestone is a hot button, highly sensitive and classified. And it's connected to the space program." Zen tapped her stylus on the tablet's screen as she thought.

"He's not used to being told no. He doesn't drop the hammer often, but when he does? I feel sorry for whoever is standing in his way," Malone replied.

Zen stood. "I don't."

By the time Zen and Malone finished with the last colonists, their chief suspect had cracked. At least enough to let them know they were on target. Then she asked for a lawyer. By midnight, federal police officers had led her away in handcuffs. Clive asked for one last meeting at one o'clock Wednesday morning. Malone pulled a hand over his face and yawned. Even Hadley looked wilted around the edges. Zen slumped against the back of her chair with her feet propped on another one. She'd taken off her shoes. Formality got tossed aside at that time of the morning.

"I'm preparing the report. Finishing it up actually," Clive said. "Once I saw where your interrogation was going, I started writing it."

"The rivalry with the victim started before they launched. Friends turned to enemies. The victim sabotaged our perp's advancement twice," Malone said.

"Third strike and it was too much," Zen said, giving the condensed version of their case.

Clive tapped his fingers on the conference table. He gazed at the face of the now-arrested colonist on the wide screen. Details of her background and career were displayed next to her photo. Sinead Flannery seemed to stare back at them in defiance. Her blunt, honey-blond bangs gave her the look of an angry prep school cheerleader.

"She's one cute killer, I give her that much," Malone said, speaking aloud what probably was on the rest of their minds.

"Worst kind. I went to school with some of those girls. Ruthless," Hadley said. "I should know. I was one of them."

"I knew there was lava bubbling beneath that cool surface," Malone joked, which prompted a giggle from Hadley.

"I'm going home. My husband babysat our grandson, so I'm sure he's as exhausted as I am." Hadley stood, gave them all a tired wave, and walked out.

"Two accidents. Two murders. There's no pattern. No connection to Lodestone," Clive said.

"But sir..."

"I'll keep working to get more on Tetra Corporation. But for now, we've done our job. Good work. Carry on." Clive marched out without giving either Zen or Malone a chance to reply.

"Yes sir." Malone blinked at the open door he'd gone through. "You get the feeling he's headed to another meeting?"

"Yeah." Zen stared at her tablet. "It's all too damn convenient."

"The facts fit once we scraped through the layers of lies and half-truths."

"But there's more. I just know it." Zen looked back at him.

Malone grabbed his leather jacket. "All will be revealed after a good night's sleep."

Zen grabbed one sleeve of his jacket before he could put it on. "We missed it, Malone. And it's big. Something big enough that you got sent that photo of Astra as a warning. Goddard tried to low-key his visit to Iesha Franklin at the hospital," Zen replied.

"But he didn't know we'd be there. Surprise," Malone said.

"Or maybe it wasn't. Goddard put us on notice how easily he can get inside information, know our next moves."

"Whoa, I don't like the direction this conversation is taking. Are you saying the boss..." Malone glanced over his shoulder and then looked back at her. "Zen, if you're saying what I think you're saying, don't say it."

"Clive has to report up the chain of command." Zen spoke low.

"You're dangerous woman, partner. We've got two killers identified." Malone tapped a forefinger on the polished surface to the conference table.

"You want to play it safe, harvest the low-hanging fruit? Or do you want the truth?"

Malone stared back at her for a few beats. He draped the jacket over a chair again. "Which lead you gonna follow?"

ZEN HAD FINALLY CRAWLED into bed at three o'clock Wednesday morning. She felt like she'd been asleep two minutes when the wake-up alarm sounded. The beeps gradually grew louder. Six o'clock, the glowing digital clock informed her. The lights in her bedroom came on, a soft glow to mimic first sunlight. The smart bulbs became bright at her movements. She sat on the side of the bed for a few minutes. A message came through the speaker of her smart home assistant.

"Message from Clive Anderson," the mechanical female voice said. "You've earned a day off, Special Agent Batiste. I'll see you Friday."

"Humph." Zen stood and rubbed her lower back, stood, and yawned for a third time. Her phone rang. "Answer, speaker on. Good morning, Ramirez."

Malone's deep voice rolled into her bedroom. "You got the day off, too, I bet."

"Yep."

"What are you going to do?" Malone asked.

"Eat scrambled eggs, toast with Louisiana blueberry jelly, and then go back to sleep." Zen padded to her bathroom and gazed at the mirror. Red eyes stared back at her.

"Liar. Let me know what you find out." He ended the call.

"One of these days, Ramirez. One of these days." Zen scowled as if he would see and hear her still.

She hadn't lied about the eggs and toast. Then she went back to sleep for another two hours. But not before she arranged to meet Chloé for lunch. The nervous excitement in Chloé's voice gave her hope for answers. She arrived at Zen's house at twelve-thirty. Zen prepared two roast beef po-boys. Chips, Creole spicy pickle spears, and hibiscus tea rounded out the meal.

"Girl, I took the rest of the day off. My supervisor was so surprised, she asked if everything was okay. I rarely take a day." Chloé crunched on a bite of pickle. "God bless your people down south for sending you such tasty treats."

"My uncles have gardens. They say we need to keep land and the skills to work them just in case," Zen said.

"In case what?" Chloé said between chews.

"I don't know. The zombie apocalypse or something. You know old folks. Conspiracies—we're not that far from our history." Zen shrugged. "Anyway, what you got?"

Chloé wiped her fingers on a napkin. "Speaking of dystopian futures... How far do you want to go with this?"

"Oh c'mon. Not you, too." Zen rolled her eyes. "I love 'em like crazy, but my family skews toward eccentric."

"You won't be skeptical after you hear what I found out."

"Which is?"

"Tetra Corporation was founded in 1970 by a group of 'visionary scientists and businessmen.' That's straight from their website. Over the years, they've developed cutting-edge technology that became mainstream. Some stuff their researchers invented or created."

"How are they funded?" Zen sipped tea.

"Investment at first. Three founders were rich from their own patents. Then they got government contracts. Big contracts. Military tech. Their work improved manufacturing processes."

"Large corporations contracted with them as well. Including Goddard. Let me guess. They pioneered space mining techniques," Zen said.

"China launched the first so-called space mining robot back in 2020. Tetra poached Chinese scientists. It didn't actually mine asteroids. It tested technologies needed to capture small celestial bodies and perform orbital maneuvers."

"Interesting, but get to the part about Lodestone." She picked up her po-boy and took a bite.

"Here's where it veers toward sci-fi ominous. Tetra branched into medical research fifty years ago. Then behavioral research."

Zen dropped her sandwich and wiped her mouth. "Here we go."

"Lodestone came out of work done to refine deep transcranial magnetic stimulation or DTMS. It started out being used to treat Parkinson's disease and depression. The brain contains magnetic particles. Long story short, with more space mining, certain magnetized minerals found in asteroids and the moon enhance DTMS."

"Research for the past five decades has mapped the brain. Refining knowledge about which sections control different functions. That includes aggressive behavior. Which led to Lodestone and DTMS being used on people with sociopathic tendencies," Zen said.

Chloé held up a hand while she finished chewing. She swallowed tea and said, "I knew you'd see where this was going. I mean, you got a PhD in crazy."

"For the millionth time, stop saying that," Zen retorted and took a playful swat at Chloé's head.

"Hey, my mama is crazy and—"

"She's bipolar with episodes of psychosis," Zen murmured in reflex to correct her friend. They'd had this conversation repeatedly over the years. Zen's thoughts stayed on Lodestone.

"Crazy is shorter. I don't use it in a pejorative way," Chloé said with a crooked grin and went back to eating.

"Whatever." Zen squinted at her then went back to thinking.

"I don't get how they went from treating medical patients to inmates," Chloé said.

"Some people with Parkinson's become psychotic or violent. Anger and aggression can also be features of depression. But why did they start using it on violent criminals and then sending them into space?" Zen asked no one in particular.

Chloé shook her head. "Good question. I don't have an answer. There's no clear connection to space. Unless—"

"Goddard Corporation is one of the companies that buys tech and research from Tetra," Zen broke in. She looked at Chloé.

"You literally plucked the words right out of my head. Do you read minds as well as tinker with 'em?

"Goddard has a non-profit foundation. One program is to rehabilitate ex-cons."

"Like I said, I don't have answers for the space connection, but..." Chloé's expression turned serious.

"Why are you squirming all of a sudden? Wait a minute. You're considering how to break bad news or whether to lie. Spill it," Zen ordered.

"Your employer, the Department of Justice, helped fund the research on DTMS. There's been a trend away from locking people up or putting them on death row. Even for the most violent crimes."

"Yeah, a 'waste of human capital.' Big business wanted cheap labor."

"Not good PR if your minimum-wage employee goes on a killing spree though," Chloé said and went back to eating.

"Welcome to the new millennia form of chain gangs and..." Zen's voice trailed off. She blinked at the elusive thread. Her gut told her they were on to something. Her brain stumbled on identifying it.

"You'll figure it out, pal. After all, you're the 'Hero of Madrid who stopped the slaughter of innocents," Chloé said. "Straight from a news report. One of the more dramatic ones and a personal favorite."

"Just what I tried to avoid."

"Yeah, well bask in your fame. It might be useful someday."

Zen watched Chloé finish the last of her meal. "Good?"

Chloé patted the toned abs she worked hard to keep that way. "Girl, it's depressing to have a perfect best friend. Pretty, brilliant, famous, and can cook."

"Don't forget mind reader." Zen crossed her arms.

"What's that mean?"

Zen leaned close to Chloé with a forefinger pointed at her nose. "The real reason you got all jittery a few minutes ago."

Chloé gulped tea and blinked back at Zen for a few seconds. "Your dad's name popped up. Some of the Tetra research related to brain interventions involved interrogation techniques. Strategies used by military intelligence to extract information."

"Torturing prisoners? Oh God." Zen shivered at the chill that ran through her body.

"Using psychology to re-educate terrorists is the way he said it—your dad, I mean. In a declassified document. I wasn't searching his name. I stumbled on it. It's probably not as bad as it sounds, and they abandoned those plans anyway. Like it was twenty years ago." Chloé stammered into silence.

"We've had heated debates about the use of torture. But I didn't think he'd taken part in..." Zen clenched both hands into fists. "He didn't show up because of Astra. He wanted to find out what I knew."

"I'm sure he was concerned about her." Chloé forced open Zen's hands. "Breathe and think. Don't assume the worst."

"Find out if Daddy ever had contact of any kind with Goddard Corporation."

Chloé hissed out air. "Hmm."

"You already know. And now you're going to tell me the rest."

"Mr. Batiste and Ian Goddard served on the task force that led to the current international space treaty." Chloé flinched at Zen's grimace.

"Damn, and he never breathed a word," Zen said.

"Nothing I saw indicates they did more than sit in the same room. They might not have even *talked* to each other, well not directly," Chloé said in a rush of words.

"You through?"

Zen pointed to their lunch. A piece of pickle still sat on Chloé's plate. Chole hurriedly popped it in her mouth and chewed. She watched as Zen rushed through loading the dishwasher and wiping crumbs from the island's granite surface.

"We're not going to the 3D fashion show. Or the new space art gallery. Or have cocktails to end a perfect day of playing hooky, are we?" Chloé's whining tone ramped up as she talked.

Zen dried her hands on a dishtowel. She hung it to dry and faced Chloé. "We can if you get results fast."

"What?"

"You're going to put on your black hat." Zen nodded when Chloé shook her head. "Oh yes you will."

"Not against Uncle James. I want to use my powers for good," Chloé complained.

"You are doing good. Goddard may be using flawed treatments on dangerous people. Sending them into stressful isolated space colonies is a recipe for disaster. Someone has to expose what's happening. Let's go to my office. Get out that powerful laptop. I know you don't leave home without it." Zen strode off without looking back to see if Chloé followed.

"But he's your father, your daddy as you Southern folks say." Chloé grabbed her bag and scurried to catch up.

"I'm not going after Daddy. I'm going after the truth to prevent more murders." Zen pushed away the next thought. What if finding the truth hurt her father?

# Chapter 14

Chloé was right, to her great dismay. They never made it to the fun activities on Wednesday. Chloé went back to work the next day. Zen spent Thursday doing household chores and running errands. She told herself it was to catch up after so many hours working. What she really wanted was mental distraction, no sitting around thinking. There were too many unpleasant "what-ifs" floating around in her head. Zen went to the office Friday feeling drained. An early-morning phone call from her father hadn't helped. She strained against asking all the questions pushing to get out.

Zen went back to her first unedited notes from their trip to the Atacama Desert. The list of medications from the Goddard camp tugged at her attention again. She frowned as she grappled with why it bothered her. Rubbing her temples as she thought hard didn't conjure the answer. Clues skittered into dark corners of her mind, elusive. She hissed in frustration.

Malone strolled into her office. He held a mug with steam rising from it. "Good morning, partner. Ready to get up and at 'em?"

"We caught the bad guys. Remember?" Zen replied without looking away from the computer screen.

"Yeah, but even superheroes have paperwork. All you gotta do is put your e-signature on it and we're set. On to conquer new worlds." Malone sat across from her with a satisfied grunt.

"We solved all the world's problems and put a neat bow on top." Zen picked up her own cup. The rich brown contents had grown cold. "Damn it. Nothing worse than hot chocolate that's not."

"Somebody is in a mood. Which is strange since our agency is on a winning streak. Talk to me."

"It's all good. Guess I'm still tired or something." Zen avoided his gaze.

"I'm going to put my money on 'something.' Lodestone, to be specific," Malone said, his dark eyebrows raised.

"I'm just curious about it. Stop," Zen said with a scowl.

"I didn't—"

"You're studying me like I'm a lab specimen. I'm not under investigation," Zen snapped. She rubbed her forehead, counted to ten, and then looked at him. "Sorry."

"That bad, huh?"

"It's not about you. I just... have family stuff on my mind," Zen said and forced a smile that felt stiff.

"If Astra is upset or you've had another message, say the word." Malone sat forward.

"She's fine. Astra loves being with her grandparents. They treat her like royalty. When she was little, she'd be impossible to live after a visit with them." Zen gave a short laugh.

"Great. Glad to hear it."

"Yeah, it's a relief she's not rattled," Zen replied, still avoiding his gaze.

Malone rose, crossed the office, and closed the door. "Then it's your dad. I got curious, too. He knows Ian Goddard. And he worked on debriefing techniques based on research from Tetra."

"Lots of intelligence officers work on a long list of projects."

"C'mon, Zen. I'm on *your* team, which means I won't tattle to the teacher."

"Malone..." Zen heaved a sigh. She raked fingers through her thick hair pulled back into a curly ponytail. She hugged herself even though the deep green sweater kept her warm.

Malone came around the desk to sit on the edge of it. "I can help."

"I'm trouble. No, listen," Zen said quickly when he started to object. "I don't want your career on the line because of me. Madrid, right?"

He took her hands and closed his larger ones around both, resting them on his thigh. "I can't walk around like it's nothing when you're in danger. On any level."

Zen felt the warmth of his skin through the wool blend fabric of his slacks. Malone's dark gaze pulled her into a circle of shelter he wanted to give. And she knew it included Astra.

"Thanks. I mean it. A lot, but—"

"Shush, no 'buts' allowed," he said in a soft voice.

Hadley swung the door open, her tablet computer in hand. "Battle stations, troops. The boss wants to meet on the moon case. Is everyone okay?"

"Um, we're good." Zen pulled her hands back from Malone.

"Making sure there are no loose ends in our case summary report." Malone wore a relaxed expression as he stood.

"Right." Hadley gazed from Zen to Malone and back again. "We'll convene in the conference room. Clive is on a call now. Fifteen minutes."

"I'll freshen this up." Malone grabbed the mug from Zen's desk and raised it. "And meet you ladies there." He smiled at them both and walked out without looking back.

"Malone pretty much wrote the report. I'm just going over it. He's great at making it concise yet thorough." Zen tried to channel Malone's unruffled air. Yet she still felt like a teenager caught with a boy in her bedroom.

"He has many talents. Doesn't he?" Hadley tilted her head to one side.

"Hmm. So, any word on a new assignment? I mean, this one is over." Zen plastered a smile on that she didn't feel. Then she looked at her computer monitor as if reading important content.

"Not sure, but there may be one or two incidents we'll be asked to review. But this case is far from over. Let's focus on the task still at hand."

The last sentence yanked Zen's gaze to Hadley again. "Always."

The older woman seemed to perform a quick mental assessment of her. Hadley smiled, nodded, and walked out. Zen let out the breath she'd held in without realizing it.

Then she pulled it together for their meeting. She entered the conference room ten minutes later.

Clive sat the end of the oval table that faced the computer screen. A photo of the Goddard lunar colony was displayed in full color. Then another of the Chile space training camp replaced it. Seconds later a gallery appeared with the subjects of their investigation: Tanner Hunter, Iesha Franklin, and another woman. Zen recognized the shape of her face and eyebrows. Clive pressed a button on the remote and paused the slideshow.

"I have updates. First, I want to commend the entire team on a job well done. I'm not sure if you know this but we were under a microscope on this first investigation." Clive stood and walked the length of the table. Then he faced them. "We're a hybrid, something new. The FBI investigates crime at the national level. The DOJ handles investigations as well. The CIA and NSA deal with international security. Where do space colonies and space stations fit in? Well, that would be us now. We've closed the first case, not just solved it but quickly. Work on high-priority missions in space will resume with minimal impact. The NASA director and the White House are very happy."

"Nice to end a work week with good news," Zen said.

"We'll have a sweet weekend knowing Monday won't be hectic. And the updates?" Malone asked.

Clive's shoulders hunched beneath the fabric of his suit jacket. He didn't seem pleased despite his words earlier. Then he stood straight. "Iesha Franklin has recovered and been discharged from Arundel. She might even return to a job at Goddard, though a different division."

"But she doesn't want to. Ms. Franklin has offers from two other companies, Goddard competitors, in fact, who have their own budding space programs," Hadley put in.

"Excellent follow-up," Clive replied with a nod. "As long as she complies with the Goddard NDA, Ms. Franklin should have no problems."

Malone slapped his hands together. "Okay, we can stamp 'Done' on this. Moving on, what's next?"

"Wait a minute. Georgina Preston," Zen said and looked at Clive. "She put her career maybe even her life on the line."

"She and her attorney are working on a deal," Clive replied.

"What do you mean a deal, a plea deal? What law—"

"Corporate espionage." Clive picked up the remote, cleared the screen, and turned off the television.

"The Economic Espionage Act of 1996, to be specific, the federal law that deals with the theft or misappropriation of trade secrets," Hadley added.

"She didn't reveal any trade secrets. What she did was alert us to what could be a harmful science project."

"She shared information that could injure the owner. She also signed an NDA, so Tetra and her own employer could file a civil suit against her. Fortunately for her, they haven't made a move to do so," Clive put in.

"Am I the only one who sees this mysterious Tetra Corporation as creepy?" Zen shoved back her chair and stood.

"Easy, partner," Malone murmured.

"Tetra Corporation isn't mysterious or creepy," Clive rumbled in reply. "Tetra is a legitimate research organization that's an invaluable resource for public and private entities."

"You sound like a press release, Clive. Whatever Lodestone is doing doesn't work. In fact, they make people worse."

Clive looked at Zen for a few seconds in silence. He transferred his scrutiny to Malone and back to Zen. "Lodestone has nothing to do with our now complete investigations. Hunter killed his colleague to cover up his violent past. The death on the moon was the result of personal enmity. Evidence supports the finding that the other two deaths were accidents."

Zen mentally pulled the reins tight on her mounting anger. "Since we're quoting federal law, I think she's covered under the federal whistleblower act. It was expanded in 2026."

"You're not her social worker or her lawyer, Batiste. We have important work to do here. I'm ordering you to stand down. End of discussion." Clive's eyes narrowed to slits.

"But sir—" Zen stopped when his jaw tightened.

"I understand. You feel protective toward your sources. They're both landing on their feet. Ms. Preston will probably face less than five years in prison or a minimal fine. Even if it's not small, she's from a wealthy family. My point is, both of these young women will weather the storm."

"Good to know," Zen said. "Thanks sir."

"You two put in long hours and did great work. Lunch is on me. You're included, Hadley. Get out of the office for an hour, or two even. Being cooped up talking about dark deeds takes a toll. No one knows that better than me after thirty years." Clive smiled at them all and strode out.

"He had to leave for another meeting," Hadley said. "What about DC City Café? It's close by and has the best burgers in town."

Malone answered Hadley but gazed at Zen. "Sounds like a plan."

"Good. I'll make the reservation." Hadley stood to leave but paused. "Mr. Anderson is under a lot of pressure. Tetra Corporation hasn't just helped government agencies. They've created or contributed to literally hundreds of developments that have improved technology and saved lives."

"And generated billions in profits for companies like Goddard," Zen said. Hadley's nod of assent surprised her.

"Making money isn't inherently evil. Oh, and I can name at least ten tools you use that exist because of Tetra research. Like block chain tech that improved government secure servers exponentially. Or translator devices we use in places like... say, Madrid." Hadley smiled at Zen and Malone in turn. "Enough about work. See you in a bit for lunch."

"Everyone loves to throw Madrid in my face." Zen crossed her arms.

"Well, you did break a few rules, almost cause an international crisis, and—"

"Stop a killer. You're welcome, nobody." Zen picked up her tablet. She brushed past Malone on the way to her office.

He followed her. "So, where do we start?"

"What are you talking about?" Zen said over her shoulder.

"The search for dirt on Tetra, Robert S. Goddard, and Lodestone. You won't let this go. Not *you*." Malone's long stride allowed him to catch up to her. "I can hear those wheels turning."

Zen stopped at her office door and faced him. "You heard the boss. The investigation is over. I wouldn't dream of defying him."

Malone squinted at her. "Oh yeah?"

"See you at lunch." Zen affected a serene smile.

"Right."

Malone started to say more but a jazz ringtone came from his pocket. He answered his smartphone and started talking. He continued to glance at Zen even as he walked away, still responding to the caller. Zen watched until he disappeared into his office. Then she entered hers and closed the door. Her first call was to Jordan. The second to Chloé.

SATURDAY EVENING ZEN got dressed up and met Chloé at the National Gallery of Art. She wore a silk and cashmere-blend black sweater. She belted it at the waist over a black suede maxi skirt and matching ankle boots. Chloé was giddy with excitement at the invitation, a chance to be among the Beltway elite. Chloé wore a midnight-blue sweater dress over thigh-high silver boots. She tumbled into the self-driven electric taxi next to Zen and babbled away for the entire trip to the National Mall. They blended in with the other art aficionados.

"You came through, girlfriend." Chloé sighed happily and downed her third mushroom mini quiche

Catering staff moved with smooth efficiency through the crowd. They served guests food from silver-plated platters. Two waitresses carried trays of goblets filled with sparkling wine. The art exhibit featured virtual three-dimensional displays. Paintings that came alive, projecting landscapes or people as observers got closer. Another huge gallery held a rendering of the galaxy floating above their heads. Planets swirled with multi-colored gases. Asteroids spun in elliptical patterns past moons. Everyone gasped at the dramatic birth and death of stars.

"Whoa. I totally forgive you for the other day. You really know how to apologize, best friend." Chloé stared up in wonder. "I understand why people volunteer for space travel. I'm thinking of becoming a moon tourist myself. Maybe even Mars."

"That's the wine talking. We both know your feet will never leave Earth. No parties, no shopping, and a limited selection of potential lovers," Zen teased.

"Hey, I switch-hit. My pool of possible 'the one' is larger than yours," Chloé shot back, her wide-eyed gaze still out in space.

"You should settle down." Zen scanned the crowd as she talked.

"Like you and sexy Special Agent Ramirez? I feel the heat every time you mention him, which is a lot lately." Chloé gave Zen a gentle nudge in the side with an elbow. "Don't bother to deny it."

"You know my strict rule about office love affairs. Both your private and personal life explode spectacularly. Kinda like a mile-wide meteor hitting the surface of a planet." Zen pointed at a stunning flash above their heads.

"And sometimes people get married on a tropical island and have gorgeous babies," Chloé said with a sigh.

"You just said the magic word, babies. No more for me. I've got a kid headed to college."

"Astra would love a genius baby sister or brother. They could solve the world's problems together." Chloé spun in a circle to take in the full effect of the galaxy.

Zen snorted a laugh. She took the fluted glass from Chloé's hand. "Now I know you're drunk. No more wine for you."

"You killin' my vibe, girl." Chloé affected a pout. Her expression brightened when a passing waitress appeared. She grabbed a full wine goblet and stuck her tongue out at Zen.

"Your vibe is about to get you in trouble."

"You're not just rewarding me. Goddard Corporation and Tetra topped the list of sponsors. So, what are we looking for?" Chloé turned in a circle.

"I hadn't thought of any such thing. This is your reward for a job well done," Zen said with a smile.

"Bull."

"There may be a lecture in a few minutes about the art of discovery. Maybe Lodestone will be mentioned; some of the team might be here." Zen shrugged and sipped from her goblet.

"Ah, and you'll find a chance to chat with them. Maybe steer the conversation to probe deeper since some of them are disgruntled. I doubt Tetra sent any of them. They're on guard after…" Chloé looked around and lowered her voice. "Georgina Preston went rogue."

"I'm here to enjoy the evening."

"Uh-huh. You're right though. I deserve a little fun after a crappy week at the office and hours of dry eyes staring at the computer for *you*." Chloé downed her wine, grabbed a another from a smiling waiter, and gave Zen a defiant look.

Zen laughed. "Ok, ok. You did fill in way more blanks on Lodestone than my boss. Which makes me wonder if he kept info from me on purpose." Zen's amusement evaporated at the thought. She looked at her friend, but Chloé's focus had shifted to across the room.

Chloé swigged wine as she nodded agreement. "Look, there's a cute guy I met who works at the state department. Give me ten minutes."

"Chloé."

"Meet you back at the giant sculpture in the lobby. Damn, he's fine. Make that twenty minutes."

"Hold up." Zen found herself talking to an empty space.

Chloé weaved through and around knots of people. She was too intent on her target to look back. Zen considered chasing after her, but decided against it. Besides, ammunition to tease her about being thirsty for male attention would be too delicious later. She turned only to bump into an elegantly dressed man. Wine splashed from her glass.

"My apologies. How clumsy of me to collide into a lovely lady."

His British accent combined with dark good looks made female heads nearby turn. He wasn't tall, but the expensive fabric seemed to strain over muscles. He wore a black turtleneck sweater under a gray wool evening jacket. An alert waitress appeared. She wiped up the small puddle of spilled wine. Zen nodded thanks to her.

"No worries. I wasn't exactly paying attention myself," Zen said.

"How are you enjoying the exhibit?"

"Very impressive."

Before she could go on, the man took Zen's almost-empty wine glass and replaced it with another from a passing waiter. The motion was so smooth, she had no time to object. He moved like a magician pulling objects out of nowhere.

"Fascinating subject matter. Time, space, celestial bodies. To think at one time the United States had put the space program on the back burner. Money changes everything," the man said dryly, looking around him. He turned back to Zen. "Interesting mix, don't you think?"

"Of art you mean?" Zen enjoyed the fruity taste of bubbles on her tongue when she sipped.

"An eclectic selection from brilliant artists, of course. I meant our fellow partygoers. Quite a few people from NASA and private space companies," the man said with a smile.

Zen's spine tingled. "Which one are you with?"

"I work for a research company."

"Tetra Corporation, by any chance?" Zen leaned into him. His strong arm went around her. A man moved in, along with a tall woman with nut-brown skin. She was surrounded.

"Let's go somewhere private to talk, Dr. Batiste," the Brit purred.

"I'm with my friend." Zen's mouth felt full of cotton suddenly. Part of her wanted to push free of the trio, but her brain felt fuzzy.

"We'll make excuses for you. I'm sure her companion will make sure she gets home safe. She looks quite thrilled to be with him as well," the woman said.

Zen blinked at her, trying to catch the accent. Nigerian? She wore thick braids pulled up into a bun. Diamond earrings sparkled as she moved her head. Zen squinted against the light.

"What have you done to—"

Zen felt dazed but still steady on her feet. Pliant, that's how she felt. She tried summoning the will to resist even as part of her brain said to let go. They moved through the lobby. Then they were outside. A sleek black limo pulled up, and she found herself sitting on leather seats between the Brit and the woman. They talked casually around her, but Zen missed most of it.

"Will she remember? I don't know if this is a great idea," the woman said.

"Yes, Nikka, you've made the point a few times. This new formula is supposed to make her remember we talked, but details will be jumbled. At least that's what I've been told," the Brit said.

"I didn't sign up for this kind of thing, you know. Neither did you," Nikka clipped. She stared at him and then out the window at the passing city scene.

"Where are we going?" Zen managed to get out, cutting off his reply.

"Somewhere quiet to answer your questions," the Brit said.

"I haven't asked any questions yet." Zen swallowed hard at the dryness of her mouth. The man handed her a bottle of water. She drank.

"But you planned to, Dr. Batiste. You didn't show up at this exhibit by chance," the Brit said.

Zen tried to form another attempt to get information, but her mind wandered. She became distracted by the flash of streetlights as the limo drove on. Time passed; the vehicle kept moving. Zen didn't even feel the sensation of the limo pulling to a stop. When the Brit held out a hand, Zen took it and stepped outside. They went up steps into a mansion. Or was it a museum?

"Where..." Zen turned in a circle trying to get her bearings.

"No harm will come to you," the man said. Somehow his accent and the soft purr of his words made him seem sincere.

"Humph. You shouldn't make promises. The man is unpredictable at best," Nikka said, bursting the bubble of reassurance.

Before Zen could resist, the other man who'd shown up at the gallery moved in. She was flanked on both sides. Nikka brought up the rear. Minutes later they were inside a beautiful library. Floor-to-ceiling mahogany bookcases lined the walls. A fireplace had been lit. Two seating areas were arranged around it; on another end of the room sat a large desk. Chairs and sofas of rich leather dotted the room. A dignified woman dressed in a winter-white cashmere sweater and matching slacks appeared from somewhere. Her platinum-blond hair blended with the clothing. A rich tan set off the light colors. She could have been anywhere between forty and sixty years old. Maybe because she'd had work done? Zen worked to focus her attention and grab onto every detail. The effects of whatever concoction they'd given her seemed to be wearing off. Luckily, she'd only had one sip of the doctored wine.

"Thank you for coming, Dr. Batiste. I'm so glad to meet you. I've read your theories on the dynamics of space communities. I understand at least two space companies that plan to establish colonies have used them in planning. Everything from living spaces to social outlets. You've practically invented a new field of sociology," the new woman said.

She waved a hand at a smaller sofa that matched another across from it. The Brit sat and pulled Zen down with him. The second man remained standing. Nikka was about to sit as well when the woman shook her head. Nikka's expression tightened into a frown. The woman in white seemed unaffected. She nodded toward the door. Nikka and the other man left.

"Everyone knows my name, but I didn't get introduced to my kidnappers," Zen snapped. Adrenaline combined with anger sharpened her senses.

"She came willingly," the Brit said in a mild tone.

"After you slipped something in my wine." Zen felt the fire of outrage flare. She tamped it down once again. "Can I at least have a drink while I'm captive?"

"We're not savages, after all," came the smooth reply from the woman in white. She spoke softly, but not to the Brit.

Zen stared at her. A microphone. Her glasses most likely contained a communicator. Which implied that cameras were focused on them as well. Zen casually glanced around the room until she spotted the cams, two perched in opposite corners of the room. "Nice décor."

"Thank you," the woman said.

Nikka came in wearing a tight expression, no doubt peeved at being reduced to serving drinks. She threw a chilly glance at the woman in white. She extended a sculpted modern glass tumbler to Zen. "Here."

"I don't drink scotch," Zen said in a controlled voice and brushed invisible lint from her sweater.

"It's Rémy, the best of this year. Drink it or do without." Nikka glared down at Zen.

"Well in that case, I'll have to make do." Zen smiled up at the woman and accepted the glass.

"Choke on it," Nikka spat and then marched to the door.

Zen watched the straight back of the toned woman. A dark-gray sweater and form-fitting leggings outlined her shape. She pivoted and shut the double doors with a firm thump. "I don't know why she's so touchy. I'm the one brought here against my will. I must say, your hospitality needs serious work."

The Brit wore the ghost of a smile. He never glanced at Zen, though. Instead, he seemed to study his expensive leather shoes. The woman in white remained impassive as she studied Zen for a few moments. Zen gazed into the glass she held. Then she gave the contents a delicate sniff.

"It's only cognac, Dr. Batiste. We wanted to discuss your investigation of Lodestone," the woman said. Her tone implied they could change the plan.

"Forgive me if I'm skeptical. Arranging an appointment at my office would have been much less... aggressive. Don't you think?" Zen placed the tumbler on a glass table near her.

"We saw an opportunity and decided on an impromptu invitation," the woman in white replied in her silky contralto voice.

"Invitation," Zen echoed. "My agency still has infrared monitoring devices outside my home. Two mounted on either end of my block. Special agents at a satellite office could be at my house in ten minutes. And for all you know I'm embedded with a tracking chip as a backup."

"We scanned you twice for a bio-microchip."

"Signals would be blocked in any event. We're well equipped," the Brit said.

"So, let's discuss," the woman added.

"You do know my agency has the latest tech? We've reversed engineered blocking devices."

"Then we should get on with it before we're interrupted," the woman in white said and stood. She strode to a desk and came back with a tablet computer.

"Oh, what the hell. Might as well enjoy the pricey liquor. You know, on a government salary..." Zen grinned at the man. He covered his mouth with one hand but didn't reply as she sipped. Then she put the glass down again.

The woman in white held out the tablet to Zen. "In the interest of good faith. Here are answers to your questions."

"You don't know what questions I have right now. For one, what's your names? I only know Nikka's, but then that's probably fake." Zen gazed at the woman's face and not the tablet.

"I'm Ilyana Petrovich," the woman shot back with a slight grimace that implied she was losing patience. "Now let's put all of your dark theories to rest."

"Goddard worked fast. By the way, my friend will be worried that I've gone missing," Zen said.

"She's being happily entertained by a very handsome young man. You know the one, a State Department employee. They should be at her apartment by now," the woman in white said. Her thin lips lifted to one side. "You spoke to him when he got her a refill; a message that you were heading home and that she should have a good time."

"Did I? You people really did plan this one on the fly." Zen's pulse sped up.

"You're a creature of habit. We monitored the self-driven taxi service you prefer. And since we had staff at the exhibit gala to open the show..." The woman in white gave a slight shrug.

Zen took the tablet from her and scrolled through pages for several minutes. The woman and the Brit both waited without comment. Zen scanned pages of treatment protocols, clinical trial results, and study summaries.

"And this is supposed to convince me of what?" Zen said finally. She held out the tablet but the woman didn't take it.

"That your father and your boss are wise advisors, Dr. Batiste. You're an excellent investigator. You were expeditious in uncovering the truth behind four deaths. Results in little more than a month. Outstanding."

"Heartwarming to know I'm admired," Zen replied in a dry tone with a side glance at the handsome Brit.

He smiled. "I'm tempted to try and lure you away from the US government."

Zen tilted her head to one side. He was no fool. Flirting with him wouldn't make him lower his guard. Still, he radiated a heated response to Zen. She allowed a bit of thigh to show in the slit of her maxi skirt. Maybe a bit of distraction might get her out of there. Wherever "there" was.

"Who are you and who do you work for again?" Zen said to him in a stage whisper.

"My—"

"His name isn't important," Ms. Petrovich broke in. "The information I shared is available only to senior officials with the government," the woman said in a crisp response with an annoyed glance at the man.

"I'm honored," Zen quipped.

"Neurobiological interventions have been effective in reducing violent impulsive behaviors. In fact, those with less aggressive but sociopathic tendencies have responded as well. Like Iesha Franklin," Ms. Petrovich continued.

"Less successful with Tanner Martin. Tell me more about the conversations you've had with Clive Anderson and my father." Zen dropped the tablet on the sofa between her and the Brit.

"We can't control for every situation. Martin responded to an unanticipated trigger. A former prison mate who had more information on him than even we had."

"Bullshit," Zen replied.

The woman flinched as if the word had physically slapped her across the face. "Pardon me?"

"You orchestrated kidnapping me, planned ahead to get my friend out of the way. Which won't work for long. Chloé will be eager to tell me about her hot date. When I don't respond—" Zen stopped when the woman raised a palm.

"Again, we're not going to hurt you or keep you captive."

"All to stage this elaborate performance. Pretty good. The mysterious stately mansion and intimidating yet attractive minions are an especially nice touch. Like old spy movies my father loves to watch." Zen studied their faces for some reaction to a mention of her father. Real pros. Not even a twitch.

"Dr. Batiste, please—"

"But," Zen snapped, her voice loud. "It's still bullshit. For one thing, you don't work for Tetra anymore, Ms. Petrovich. Goddard Corporation headhunted you away from Tetra's subsidiary in London eighteen months ago. Did they know you're a former Ukrainian operative? Probably made you that much more desirable."

"Score for you," the Brit murmured, and went on studying his shoes.

"Thanks," Zen tossed aside to him and pressed on. "You did work on Lodestone, which is why Goddard wanted you. Or maybe it was his father, Ian. I figure he's still the brains behind Goddard. A brilliant physicist and businessman. A genius for taking scientific research, developing practical applications, and turning those into billions in profit. Junior is window dressing."

"Dr. Batiste, let's not get sidetracked," the woman said, dropping her cool façade.

"You sold your wares to two other governments. The scientific equivalent of a streetwalker," Zen barked at her in response. "Your superiors at Tetra had already begun to suspect you were up to no good."

The woman stood, both hands clenched into fists. She crossed the space to where Zen sat and slapped her hard. Zen's head snapped to one side. The Brit jumped to his feet and stood between them. He yanked Petrovich away a few feet as Nikka burst through the door. Zen worked her jaw as she rubbed her cheek.

"What the hell?" Nikka gaped at Petrovich.

Robert Goddard followed Nikka into the room seconds later. He walked over to Petrovich. They glared at each other in silence for a few seconds. Then Goddard shocked everyone when he shoved Petrovich hard enough to send her tumbling over the opposite sofa. He bent down over her out of sight because of the sofa. Blows and grunts of pain followed. Then Goddard stood again. He straightened his evening jacket and tie.

"Get her out. Upstairs in one of the guest rooms. Now," Goddard shouted at Nikka.

The woman glanced wide-eyed at the Brit but followed orders. She supported the slumped woman, half dragging her from the room. Goddard blew out a breath as he brushed at the sleeves of his jacket. The Brit gave Goddard a slight shake of his head and followed them out. The other man entered the library to replace him. Zen's heart beat faster. The new man appeared more than willing to follow Goddard's orders.

"Dr. Batiste. Let's start again," Goddard said.

He sat on the sofa with legs crossed. His relaxed pose held no hint of the explosion of raw violence he'd displayed. Zen shivered at the fear stabbing her spine. She knew danger when she saw it.

# Chapter 15

"Taking my smartwatch won't help you," Zen said as the man pulled it from her wrist.

"I've been observing the interaction. And let me apologize for my employee's lack of emotional restraint," Goddard said in a matter-of-fact tone.

"You're kidding. You just—"

"I was in total control." Goddard's steady gaze was a challenge.

Zen affected a restrained smile. She settled back into the upholstered chair and looked back at him. "Okay."

She'd called him a liar with one word. Her calm unnerved him, but he only displayed it in the tightness of his jaw muscle. Zen gathered up every bit of experience she had from working in prisons. Goddard showed the classic signs of a sociopath. Charming, attractive, and intelligent. Cold, manipulative, a total lack of empathy. Ruthless. His employees moved in and out of the room, whispering to him. No doubt reporting, but about what? Zen could only catch a few fragmented phrases. The Brit returned but said nothing. One valuable tidbit gave her confidence. Time was of the essence.

Goddard waved away his blond male assistant with a grimace. He loosened his black bow tie. "Here's our problem,

Dr. Batiste. May I call you Zen? You can call me Rob. Only a few people are allowed to use my nickname."

"I'm bowled over, but let's keep it formal. Dr. Batiste is fine," Zen replied. "After all, we barely know each other. I'd prefer to keep it that way."

Goddard regarded her in silence for a few seconds. "I can understand the insistence on being addressed as 'doctor.' You worked hard for the title. Years of study and sacrifice. Like your family. Pride in achievement is very important. You come from slave stock on your mother's side."

Zen didn't rise to the bait of Goddard referring to her ancestors as though they were cattle. She brushed a hand through her hair. "Hmm."

"Your father's family became free people of color around 1787, I believe. They—"

"Let me save you time, since you're short on it," Zen broke in. "Five points for doing homework on me."

Goddard nostrils flared but he smiled. "Only fair since you've done such exhaustive research into my affairs. I'm sure you even know what brand of socks I buy."

"Balenciaga." Zen brushed nonexistent lint from her maxi skirt.

The Brit covered his mouth with one hand and coughed. Then he sat straight. "Sir..."

Goddard glared him into silence. When the Brit sighed and said no more, he turned his gaze back to Zen. "Your boss won't support this obsession with digging into my space program. There's nothing to find. At most it's a minor nuisance."

"Really? All this attention seems to suggest otherwise, Mr. Goddard. Pictures sent of my daughter at her school. You popping up twice, the billionaire making time to stalk little old me." Zen gave a "what do I know?" kind of shrug. She picked up the glass, sipped, and put it down.

"You have no evidence. Don't throw away your career for nothing. We're on the cusp of huge breakthroughs. Based on work done by my great-grandfather, my company can generate water from small moons and planets. Rocket fuel manufactured on Mars or beyond. That solves one huge problem of space exploration. Working colonies not only will provide us with resources, but a Plan B in case this planet become uninhabitable."

"Or big corporations could work to not destroy the planet we've lived on for four hundred thousand years. Sounds more cost-effective and efficient, if you ask me," Zen replied.

"I didn't," Goddard snapped in his first show of temper since attacking Ilyana Petrovich. "We could ground you into dust. My father has been a power behind the scenes longer than we've both been alive. His father before him."

"Does he know I'm here? Tsk, tsk." Zen gave a slight shake of her head when Goddard's face flushed pink.

"Speaking of fathers, yours won't be able to save you." Goddard's knuckles went white as he gripped the armchair.

"Mr. Goddard, I think we should get to the point," the Brit said.

"Shut up—you work for me. I'm not done with this arrogant—"

"I work for your father. Be sensible, and he won't have to hear about this… misstep," the Brit replied in a measured tone. When Goddard stood, so did he. The two men stared at each other in tense silence.

Nikka pushed through the door. "We have a problem."

"You're damn right you do," Malone yelled as he strode in behind her.

He holstered his Remington automatic pistol in one motion and grabbed her wrists in another. Nikka was cuffed as she spluttered in rage. Three additional men followed Malone, one shoving the other man who'd been with Nikka when they snatched Zen. He had been cuffed as well. Voices outside indicated the cavalry had arrived. Goddard lunged at Zen in fury.

"You stupid bitch! You have no idea what you've done."

Goddard's profanity was cut short when the Brit punched his right jaw. Goddard's eyelids fluttered as he stumbled back, a hand on his face. He gaped at the Brit in shock. The Brit took time to straighten the sleeves of his evening jacket and his tie.

"Let me save you a stream of threats. You won't get me fired. Your father might even give me a raise for knocking you about a bit. Says he's wanted to do it for years, but he didn't want to live with your mother after." The Brit seemed unperturbed by Malone or being surrounded by federal agents.

The heir of a dynasty nursed a growing bruise to his right jaw. His gaze might have been murderous, but Goddard had the wisdom to restrain himself. He didn't make a move on the Brit. Zen concluded Goddard had made a smart decision. The Brit looked like he would wipe the fancy marble floor with the billionaire's son. And Malone would likely let him.

Malone shoved Nikka to a female special agent and rushed to Zen. "Are you okay?"

"I'm fine." Zen blinked at him. She looked as agents swept the room for hidden tech. Voices called the all-clear to each other from outside.

"You sure? You look rattled." Malone put a protective arm around Zen and pulled her close. "I would have come in sooner but—"

Clive marched in wearing a taut expression. "Tactical special agents, clear. One team, take our 'guests' in for questioning."

Malone's arm slipped down until his hand rested on Zen's waist. He returned Clive's steady gaze with one of his own. Zen pushed away until there was distance between them. She felt disoriented by the fast pace of activity around them. A female agent came in and murmured quietly close to Clive's ear.

"This is ridiculous. You have obviously forgotten who I am and what I represent. My father may have his little joke at my expense sometimes, but when push comes to shove..." Goddard stood tall and swept them all with an imperious glance. He smirked when no one, including Clive, responded.

"I've been followed, sent threats, been drugged, and had my evening generally ruined. Somebody tell me what the hell is going on!" Zen yelled. She strode over to Robert Goddard, Malone fast on her heels. She jabbed a finger into the front of his expensive white shirt. "And you're a lot less impressive than you think."

"You little—" Goddard pulled back a hand to slap her.

The Brit grabbed his arm and yanked Goddard away. "Trust me, *sir*. You don't want this agent's wrath."

Zen blocked Malone before he got to Goddard. "Take a breath."

"Ramirez, we've got more important things to do," Clive added. He placed a hand on Malone's shoulder.

"Yeah, like filling me in on this bit of drama I just went through," Zen snapped.

She started to go on when a familiar commanding figure stopped her cold. She blinked once to make sure she wasn't imagining things. Her father strode in, followed by a man she didn't recognize. The special agents standing by moved back as if in respect. Clive spun to face them, a look of thunder and lightning in his gray-blue eyes.

"Mr. Goddard will come with us," James said, staring at him. His brief gaze also included the Brit, who nodded.

"What's that old expression? Oh yes, heads will roll." Goddard smirked at everyone and strolled out with the Brit. The man with James seemed to afford him a measure of polite deference as they left. Zen grappled to take in the extraordinary scene as Clive and James went to a far corner. Their muted exchanged became heated in two seconds. Zen spun to face Malone. He held up both palms.

"Don't ask me," he said. Then he joined Zen in staring at the two men. "Wait, Zen. Maybe—"

Zen shook free of Malone's attempt to stop her. She walked over to Clive and her father. "You're retired."

Her father stopped talking to Clive to glance at Zen. "Give us a moment, Zenobia. This is important."

Before she could object, James and Clive walked away to continue their conversation. A female special agent moved in position between them and Zen. Her expression radiated a "back off" message to Zen and anyone else that might approach. The woman was doing her job, so Zen moved away.

"You ask about your dad's job status. Really?" Malone whispered over her shoulder.

Zen huffed in frustration. "I know, I know. It's the first thing that popped in my head. What the hell is he doing here?"

"Taking a break from babysitting?" Malone whispered back. He let out a soft grunt when Zen stabbed him with an elbow to the ribs. "Hey, a little joke to lighten the atmosphere."

"Pardon me if I don't get it," Zen retorted.

Clive returned with James staying in the background. "Goddard overstepped with this 'invitation' to Zen. His heavy-handed way to get a private meeting."

"Try abduction, intimidation of a federal agent—" Malone stopped when Clive raised a hand.

"Ian Goddard knows you've done a deep dive into their business. Which includes their relationship with Tetra Corporation, whose officials are also concerned. He's agreed not to press the issue," Clive continued.

"Let him try it, *sir*," Malone said with force before Zen could reply. "As a special agent, Dr Batiste has the authority to follow up on possible leads that pertain to an active murder investigation. Namely, Lodestone, a program that has ramifications for our space program. Since its subjects are being used to staff space facilities."

Clive hissed out a sigh and glanced over his shoulder at Zen's father. James had a cell phone pressed to one ear, intent on his conversation. "You been practicing that speech for a while, huh? Since Zen continued to investigate Goddard."

"I fight my own battles," Zen put in before Malone offered another defense. He pressed his lips together at the look she gave him. "Lodestone and whatever shortcomings it may or may not have goes far beyond our investigation."

"Not your call, Batiste," Clive clipped.

His deep voice caused activity to pause. Curious gazes shifted to them from the agents left to gather evidence. Then they went back to work after a few beats. One special agent approached, gave Clive a short report, and left. They heard voices coming from another room in the large house. Then the front door shut.

"Clive, a minute. And then I'll talk to Zenobia," James called from across the room.

"Right." Clive left them to have another muted back and forth with James.

"I have a bad feeling we're about to be told to back off and let the bosses handle it," Malone said.

"I'll tear this house down and kick whatever ass I have to before I walk away without answers," Zen snapped.

"Whoa. Follow your own advice and breathe." Malone rubbed the small of her back.

Zen knocked his hand away. "My father has been keeping secrets. I am pissed."

"I understand, believe me. But let's consider if attack is the best strategy. Your father wants to explain. Let him think you're willing to listen, then crack open the holes in his story." Malone kept his gaze on James as he spoke.

"No, I'll punch craters in it." Zen wore a wicked grin for a few seconds, then faced in her father's direction again.

James walked over to Zen with a grimace, both palms raised. "I know you're upset. Believe me, Robert will face consequences. No weapons were used to escort you here, correct?"

"The guy with a British accent is either working for you, or another government agency supplying information," Zen said, ignoring his question with a statement. "He's the reason that psychopath didn't go further in *kidnapping* me. Correct?"

James hung his head for a second before he looked up again. "Bobby is smart in his own way but..."

"How close are you to Ian Goddard?" Zen pressed.

"Being rich doesn't make him a master criminal, Zenobia. I taught you better about passing judgement."

"So, you became pals. Close enough that you call his kid by a nickname. Please tell me you're not his godfather." Zen glared up at James.

"So much for the soft approach," Malone muttered.

"Would you excuse us, Agent Ramirez?" James rumbled.

Zen grabbed Malone's arm and held him in place. "He's staying put. I'll need a witness for this conversation."

Her father glared back at her without speaking for a few seconds. "Ian Goddard and I collaborated on the early global space treaties. Six countries have become major powers in the past fifty years. Space is one more flashpoint that could have kicked off major conflicts, even wars. He was instrumental in early efforts to avoid consequences."

"His global companies contribute to the economies of ten countries," Zen put in.

"He talked, they listened. Our country owes him a debt of gratitude for those efforts. He didn't have to, you know. Ian Goddard could have let things play out and sided with whatever government won," James said.

"So now that his son is a major screw-up, you're committed to covering for him. To pay back Ian Goddard," Zen said.

"Straight to the point like your mother," James replied.

"You were a major player when it came to Lodestone, so you've got two big reasons to protect them both."

James's stone face eased into a smile. "You've followed the breadcrumbs, gathered intelligence like a real pro."

Zen ignored the expression of paternal pride. "Well?"

"You know the history of mass incarceration, the school to prison pipeline in our country's history. But vestiges of them remain. The effects have been generational. Our family has been committed to prison reform and rehabilitation for years." James nodded at them both as if his words would explain.

"Daddy, cut the history lecture."

He heaved a deep sigh and sat down in a chair. Malone and Zen followed his lead. They sat on a sofa. James waved to an agent who had remained behind. The woman closed the doors to give them privacy.

"Rob and his assistant are still here. Family-owned property. Dr. Petrovich probably won't press charges," James said.

Zen exchanged a glance with Malone then turned to James. "Why, of all places, put convicted criminals on space colonies?"

"It wasn't a plan, but... Grant Hubbard started it all. Damn him," James grumbled.

"Who?" Zen said with another look at Malone.

"Never heard of him," Malone said.

"Ah, you and Chloé didn't find that bit of history yet. Is she still fond of the darknet?"

"Grant Hubbard, Daddy. Answer the damn question," Zen said and slapped a palm on the sofa seat beside her.

Her father scowled a rebuke but didn't voice it. "Hubbard, born 2010. He developed the first viable process to extract water and minerals from celestial bodies. He pretty much invented the field of intercosmic engineering."

"Building in space," Zen said.

James nodded. "The man was a genius. Forget Leonardo Da Vinci. Hubbard was the real thing. He could do it all."

Malone stared at his smartphone. "He killed three people. Says here he—"

"We needed his brilliance. He was one of the first to take his family to an International Space Station in 2042." James sat forward in excitement. "He detected signals in the direction of at least three earthlike planets. He designed the first viable dome design for a Mars colony."

"The United States government in all its wisdom decided he was too valuable to lose. With trillions at stake, why let a little thing like murder get in the way," Zen said.

"It wasn't about money. Back then with climate change looming, many felt Earth was doomed. Billions of human lives at stake," James replied. He sat back.

"After we screw up Earth, we can move on to ruin new worlds," Zen retorted.

"Research into transcranial magnetic stimulation sped up when certain minerals found in space enhanced the procedure for people with Parkinson's and forms of dementia. Your mother benefited from those treatments."

"What are you saying?" Zen's heart thumped.

"You didn't notice she showed early signs of deterioration. Remember how you and the boys would joke because she'd put her keys in the refrigerator? Or the times she was late getting home? Enola got lost twice coming from work before I realized what was happening."

"You never said..."

"Your mother was terrified. She'd seen her own grandmother go downhill. But she had her pride. She made me swear not to say anything. I got Enola into advanced clinical trials. Otherwise, she would be in a special care unit needing round-the-clock supervision."

"Damn," Malone whispered softly. He rested a steadying hand in the small of Zen's back.

Zen swallowed against the lump in her throat. "Is she okay?"

"She has quarterly tests at Johns Hopkins. The last showed she's fine. So, yes. I helped Tetra Corporation and

Ian Goddard. They had the resources to treat Enola, and millions more."

"I can't find anything on Hubbard after 2057. What happened to him?" Malone asked.

"He went on to invent the first rocket fuel generator in space. His goal was to help in travel to the nearest exoplanet like Earth. Kepler-1649c. A global team worked on light speed travel," James replied.

"He lived happily ever after then," Zen said.

James cleared his throat. "He attempted to kill his third wife and a colleague. His wife had left him. The colleague won the Nobel Prize instead of Hubbard."

"Jesus," Malone muttered.

"The procedure for criminal and violent impulses has progressed since 2051," James added quickly.

"Yeah, we see how well it's working for Goddard's space program," Zen shot back.

"We've examined their records, done postmortem exams on the deceased colonists and Tanner, the space trainee. There were situational motives for the murders. The other deaths really were accidents. You two did fine investigative work."

"You and Clive kept details from us. You didn't mention looking for specific indicators during autopsies." Zen gave James a stone-faced glare.

"Or that space is being populated with sociopaths," Malone put in. "But being kept in the dark about my own damn investigation is what really pisses me off. What if one of them tried to kill us for getting too close?"

"We knew you could handle it."

"Thanks for the vote of confidence, Director Batiste," Malone said.

"Retired," James said with a slight smile.

"Doesn't look like it to me," Zen said.

James heaved another sigh. "I retired from the CIA. I work for the White House. I'm special counsel on space security and tech transfer. I have expertise in global intelligence, international space programs, and a relationship with Goddard. Ian, not Robert S."

The special agent came in so low key they didn't notice her at first. She stood several feet away. "Sir, Mr. Goddard and his staff have announced they wish to leave."

"Escort them to the Intercontinental Gold; it's a Goddard luxury hotel. We will debrief them before they go anywhere. No side trips to the airport when he has three private jets, Sonnier," James said, his voice ringing with authority.

"You must be psychic, sir. Mr. Goddard insisted he be allowed to retrieve luggage from his plane. For the extended stay they didn't expect, he says." The agent's skeptical cop tone came through loud and clear.

"Like hell. They go straight to DC," James shot back.

"Done, sir." The woman left.

"You know him well," Zen said in a dry voice.

"He's used that one before, in Brazil." James wore a sour expression.

Zen continued to stare at her father for a few seconds. "If everything is butterflies, bluebirds, and sunshine, why did Robert S. need to snatch me up?"

"He's impulsive." James stood and smoothed down the front of his deep-blue wool sweater. "If it helps, Clive didn't know about Lodestone or my involvement. He's just as pissed off as you, Agent Ramirez."

"Which means this thing goes high up," Malone said aside to Zen.

"We're working for the same government, the same goals. We need to develop space programs, ours and other countries', for a wide range of benefits to mankind. We're talking about the future for your children." James nodded to them. "Good work, both of you."

Malone stood as well. "Thanks."

"Astra is doing fine. I spoke to her school. She'll be able to march with her class even though she's already earned her diploma." James turned to Malone. "She wants to be with her classmates. You know kids."

"Yeah." Malone shot a side glance at Zen, who said nothing as her father went on.

"Her father promised she could join him and tour the new launch facilities in Corpus Christi. Her big graduation present, after she celebrates with us, of course. Oh, and Jordan will be flying in for the ceremony." James spoke like a typical father and grandfather relating family news. He kissed the top of Zen's pile of thick curls. "You look nice, by the way. I'll call you later. Agent Malone."

"Sir," Malone replied with a nod of respect. He shrugged at the side-eye Zen gave him.

"Good-bye, Director," Zen called after her father as he strolled off. He paused, looked back, and shook his head before leaving.

A tall young Black man wearing braids pulled back appeared. He cleared his throat and shifted from one foot to the other in nervous movements. "I'm in charge of the grounds. I'm just here to lock up."

Malone smiled at him and waved. "It's cool, man. We'll get out of your way so you can do your job."

The young man smiled back, visibly more relaxed. Still, he darted off as though more than happy to be dismissed. Swarms of federal police and special agents in black tended to have that effect.

"Is it just me, or did Goddard react like he still has something to hide?" Malone said. They walked into the cold night air through wrought iron entry doors.

"You up for finding out?" Zen caught his arm and brought him up short. She gazed into his dark eyes. They both knew what she was asking him to risk. Malone's slow smile was all the answer she needed.

# Chapter 16

Malone rubbed his eyes and then massaged his neck. "You find anything? I got zippo, nada, and a big load of nothing. In that order."

"Nothing yet," Zen murmured.

They were in his office in an otherwise ghostly quiet building. Night security didn't question why they were in the building on a Saturday night; now Sunday morning. Zen had called Chloé earlier to make sure she was okay. Her friend's husky whisper assured her that she was more than okay. Her handsome colleague was in a deep sleep. Chloé gleefully took full responsibility for his exhaustion. Assured her friend was safe, Zen could concentrate on the task at hand.

She scoured their notes, Hadley's reports, and secure databases they used for investigations. Still, Zen still didn't see any fact or detail that might lead to answers. She let out a groan and fell against the leather chair. Her silver and black pumps lay in a corner, abandoned for the comfy ballet flats she kept in her office. She'd shed the heavy sweater. The knit capped-sleeved blouse layered underneath was no longer tucked at the waist. Zen stretched and let out a noisy yawn. Malone chuckled as he stared at her.

"What?" She looked at him, down at herself, and then blushed. Her current state was a long way from an elegant evening look.

"Just occurred to me I've only seen you dressed for work. Dark suits, very special agent conservative. I like the earrings, by the way." Malone nodded at the silver double hoops that dangled from her ears.

Zen glanced away from the smoky look in his eyes. She became all too aware how alone they were, how close he was, and how good he smelled. "Thanks for showing up. How did you know though? Were you at the gallery with a date?"

He shook his head slowly. "I was keeping an eye on you. Had a gut feeling. Goddard had shown too much intense interest in you."

His comment pulled her back to their issue at hand. Zen tugged her blouse in place and sat straight. "Speaking of Goddard, he's a case study in privileged entitlement. The stereotypical rich frat boy who tortured freshmen pledges."

"God, you just triggered a flashback to my days at Penn State. There, I was the Irish Afro Brazilian kid who..." Malone's voice died away when he looked at Zen. "Found a clue?"

"Kind of. How much do we really know about Robert S.?" Zen's fingers moved across the silent keyboard once again. Soft clicks were the only sound of her search.

"The usual. No criminal history, if that's what you're thinking. I may have broken a rule or three poking around following digital footprints," Malone said.

"Oh no! Not Mr. Follow the Rules Would Never Go Rogue?" Zen pretended to clutch non-existent pearls around her neck.

"Mama warned me about hanging with the wrong crowd," he shot back.

"Sure, blame me. Anything in his health history, including psychiatric treatment?"

"Hacking into protected health records is above my skill level."

Zen called Chloé again. Her friend sleepily protested but went to the computer she used at home. Soon, all three were deep into the high anonymity proxy networks. Chloé appeared via live video on Malone's computer. Malone and Chloé forgot to be sleepy after a time. While they roamed through murky virtual hallways, Zen went back to her notes. One document caught her eye. She pulled up information on Lodestone again.

"Hey y'all, see if you can find info on Robert S. Goddard having surgery of any kind," Zen said.

"No problem. But why?" Chloé asked.

"I'll talk to Clive tomorrow morning." Zen glanced at the time on her smartwatch. "Tell him to set up a meeting with Goddard. I want to apologize for causing so much inconvenience to his space program."

"What in the hell—" Malone stopped as he studied Zen's face. "Oh man. Do I want to know the real reason?"

Zen grinned at him. "Probably best if you don't."

Monday morning dawned bright and crisp. Zen hummed to herself as she got ready for work. Astra had insisted on taking a short electric light plane flight home from Maryland Sunday afternoon. Too tired to argue, Zen had given in. Now Astra fussed over Zen. She cooked breakfast and kept shooting side glances at her mother.

"You really have earned sleeping late, Astra. You did all your schoolwork. Just chill." Zen munched on the edge of her cheese toast. The scrambled eggs had been done just right. She glanced down at her plate. "You've been taking lessons from Mama?"

"From Uncle Peter's farm down home in Wakefield. I brought home a couple of jars from Grandmother's pantry." Astra placed another slice of toast on Zen's plate. Then she put a large spoonful of the fig preserves next to it.

"Look, baby, I don't know what Daddy told you but I'm fine."

"He didn't tell me anything. I snooped and found out. I know when shit is going down, and no lectures about language. I'm almost eighteen."

Zen grinned and shook her head. "Seriously, you don't have to treat me like an invalid. I'm good. In another forty years or so you can take care of elderly Mom."

"Right now, I'm happy to have my mama safe," Astra said in a quiet voice and went back to the stove.

"What are you talking about?"

"I know the signs. You're about to take a big risk for justice and truth. Which means you could be out of a job. Not sure if Grandfather will use his influence to help either. He seemed more than a little annoyed with you." Astra took the cast iron skillet off the burner and over to put sausage links on both plates.

"Sheesh, you and Malone seem to have me figured out. Didn't think I was so easy to read. Better work on *that*," Zen said with a scowl.

"He's a good partner. You should ask him out. And after a suitable time introduce me to him." Astra winked and grinned at her. They both dissolved into girlish giggles like two middle-schoolers.

Zen's serene confidence withered away as she got closer to the office. Doubts crept in during the train ride into DC. She'd hoped a brisk walk from the metro stop would unclog the logjam of "what ifs" in her head. What if the darknet data was wrong? What if she'd left a digital trail while digging into legally protected health records? Had she put the careers of both Malone and Chloé in jeopardy? Or worse, put them at risk for prison sentences? Madrid had been different. She'd gone lone wolf to track a killer. But not this time.

Malone was waiting for Zen when she pushed through the automatic glass doors of their building. The first AI security scan cleared her for entrance. The regular security officer gave her a cheerful greeting. Pale sunshine slanted through vertical glass windows overhead. Zen smiled at Malone as she walked into the wide ground floor lobby. Malone gave a crisp nod but the tension didn't ease from his posture. He stood next to the long reception desk.

"I don't know about this, Zen," Malone said instead of good morning. He grabbed two paper cups and handed one to Zen.

"Hmm." Zen took a sip and looked at him in surprise. "Thanks for the café au lait."

"One of the guys at the coffee shop is from New Orleans. I got him to promise he'd make beignets soon." Malone walked close to Zen as they headed to a bank of elevators for employees only.

"You're spoiling me, Ramirez," Zen teased.

Malone faced her as they waited. "I will."

Zen gazed up into eyes the color of rich, dark toffee. For a few seconds the sound of early morning foot traffic faded as they looked at each other. Chatter from four more staffers broke the spell. They stepped away from each other and rode up to their floor. Hadley was waiting in the hall when the doors whisked open.

"Everyone is assembled. What are you up to, Zen?" Hadley's perfectly arched dark-blond eyebrows lifted.

"You make it sound like a packed house. It's just Clive and Goddard," Malone said.

"Five minutes, no more." Hadley glanced from Zen to Malone.

"Understood," Malone said. He shrugged out of his suede jacket and headed for his office.

"You don't need to go," Zen called after him. "This is all me."

"I'll see you in Clive's office," Malone yelled over his shoulder without looking back.

Zen heaved a sigh and headed to Clive's office. Malone slipped in behind her a few seconds later. Clive's eyes flickered surprise but he didn't object. Tablet in hand, Zen affected a calm expression. The room looked crowded, even as wide as it was. Goddard, his blond male assistant, and the mysterious Brit were there. Clive and Bertice Illinois stood across from them. Hadley placed cups of coffee on the large round table in a corner. After a whispered aside, Goddard dismissed his assistant. The man looked peeved but obeyed. He strolled past Zen with a smug expression as he left.

"Let's get started," Clive said, his deep voice heavy with the seriousness of their gathering. He waved at the table and waited until everyone was seated. "Dr. Batiste wants to set the groundwork for continued cooperation. A kind of closure on the... situation that affected Goddard Corporation's space program. She was doing her job, of course."

"By situation you mean our investigation into two murders and two accidental deaths," Zen put in.

Malone stood next to Hadley along one wall. He and Hadley had a discreet whispered exchange that lasted only a second. Their boss squinted in their direction but said nothing. His look was enough to quiet them.

Clive took a sip of coffee. "Exactly."

"And you did a fine job. Cleared up the unfortunate circumstances that none of us could have foreseen," Goddard said. No one answered, but his expression implied he didn't think they needed to. He stared hard at Zen.

"Hmm." The Brit tilted his head at Goddard as he looked at him.

Goddard seemed to ignore him by design and pressed on. "As Dr. Batiste pointed out in her doctoral thesis, we're in uncharted waters when it comes to space communities."

"I also gave the reasons why extra care and diligence in *how* colonies should be built. Planning the social infrastructure is as crucial as life-support facilities," Zen replied in a cool voice. "And who is selected to build them."

Ms. Illinois wore an uncertain smile as she gazed at Zen. "So now that we've cleared up any perceived differences, we're done."

"No, we're not," Zen put in, stopping Ms. Illinois before she continued.

"I'm confused," Ms. Illinois blurted out. She blinked rapidly through the lens of her tortoiseshell eyeglasses.

"I understand Dr. Batiste had something she wanted to say to me in particular," Goddard put in.

"Well…" Clive tapped a forefinger on the table's surface and turned to Zen.

"I looked at the supply lists for both the training camp and your colony, Mr. Goddard. The medications are missing." Zen set her tablet to display and projected onto the white wall of Clive's office.

"What kind of game are you playing?" Goddard snapped.

"Your staff isn't following protocols established by the Lodestone treatment team. Medications that should be given to people like Tanner Martin and others aren't listed. Trainees and colonists didn't have subsequent transcranial magnetic treatments as required," Zen went on. "Don't bother denying it. I spoke to Javier Belmont. He broke down. I have copies of the emails he sent expressing concerns that were ignored."

Goddard gazed at her for a few seconds. Then he nodded. "Very serious failures on the part of my employees.

I can assure you, Clive, and you, Dr. Batiste, that we'll get to the bottom of—"

"Orders to ignore the protocols came from the top, Mr. Goddard. From you," Zen broke in.

"Anderson, you seem to have lost control of your people," Goddard said.

"Initial treatments should be more than adequate in my experience. Medications blunt the mental concentration of brilliant minds. Anymore so-called brain treatments are no more than mental castration," Zen said, reading text from an email.

"Internal corporate communications are protected by the Space Program Act of 2077. I will definitely insist that you be charged with a federal crime," Goddard yelled and slapped a hand on the table.

Zen looked at his hand and then into Goddard's eyes. "You committed three assaults in college. In one incident, a young man pledging at your fraternity died. You took part in the hazing. In fact, another student stated you orchestrated the most brutal challenges, as they're called. A generous settlement to the family, an expensive lawyer, two million dollars to fund a university chair, and non-disclosure agreements. Poof. It all went away. And you, Mr. Goddard, after two more violent outbursts, entered a private hospital. Your treatment included deep transcranial magnetic stimulation."

"And it worked. I'm fine." Goddard glared at Zen.

"Where is your first wife, Robert? Her family never believed she stole from your first business and took off to parts unknown. The trail went cold in Belize," Zen said in a soft tone.

Goddard let out a scream and lunged across the table. His hands reached for Zen's throat, but she moved in time to avoid the chokehold. Instead, he grabbed a fistful of the front of Zen's sweater. She punched Goddard in the left eye and the nose in quick succession. His howl of pain mixed with rage. Malone pulled him back, but not before Zen landed another blow to the side of his head. Goddard slumped against the Brit. The man dumped the stunned billionaire into a side chair. Clive, Hadley, and Ms. Illinois stood gaping at the breathless combatants. Clive only moved when Malone pulled out flexible zip handcuffs.

"Wait a minute. Let's just... think it through." Clive frowned. He pointed to the Brit, who nodded.

Zen's father pushed through the door with a brawny man on his heels. "We'll take it from here. You come with us."

"If he wasn't already halfway gone, I'd hit him again myself," Malone panted. He looked like he might have another go at Goddard anyway, but Zen got to him in time to pull him away

James and Zen stared at each other in silence for a few seconds before he spoke. "I'll have a long talk with you later."

"I look forward to it, Director Batiste," Zen shot back. Her father spun and strode out.

"I'll follow-up," Ms. Illinois said to Clive and hurried out after James.

"No boring meetings in this job," Hadley said. She leaned on a chair as if needing support.

"Collect yourselves and meet me back here in an hour." Clive went to his desk, picked up the phone but paused to give them all a pointed glare.

"Um, yes sir." Malone straightened his tie and gestured to the women to go first.

"And try not to turn the whole damn world upside down until then," Clive shouted as they left.

One hour turned into three. Apparently, Clive had a lot more explaining to do than he'd anticipated. Hadley sent them secret cryptic updates about calls to and from the White House, DOJ heavies, and NASA. Zen and Malone had been ordered to prepare documentation to back up Zen's allegation. Hadley joined them throughout the morning to help. By lunchtime they'd pulled together a compelling summary backed up by evidence. Emails sent to Clive resulted in terse replies. Hadley read between the lines and interpreted for them.

"He's not happy to deliver unwelcome news up the food chain, including the White House. But Clive is dedicated to following the facts. Luckily for you, he's got the power to not only get their attention, but get results." Hadley chewed her bottom lip.

"You're still worried," Zen said as she studied the older woman's expression.

"Using that kind of capital has consequences." Hadley looked at Zen.

"Among them creating formidable enemies," Malone replied.

Zen swallowed hard as Hadley studied her closely. She could almost hear her mind working to arrange facts and assess observations of Zen. Hadley had known Clive for over thirty years. She cared about him. Maybe she wondered if Zen was a possible threat to his well-being.

"Ian Goddard is a man you don't want to cross." Malone rubbed his chin.

"She's not talking about Ian Goddard, Malone. She means my father," Zen said

"You can trust Clive, and to a certain extent, Bertice. You did what you had to, Zen. Next time consider letting us in on it," Hadley replied.

"Message received." Zen grinned at her.

Hadley gave her arm a final quick squeeze and stood. "I'm off to grab a quick lunch before we meet up with Mr. Anderson again. You two do the same. We've had an eventful Monday. I recommend plenty of protein."

Promptly at one o'clock they met in the conference room instead of Clive's office. Zen blinked in shock at the people assembled. Her father huddled with the Ed Giancarlo, the NASA administrator. Two other men she didn't recognized radiated authority. Malone pulled out a chair and sat next to Zen. The two men she didn't recognize shot curious glances at Zen but didn't speak. Clive didn't bother with introductions.

"The space programs won't be affected. Goddard is putting plans for additional colonies on hold—a chance to tighten procedures, get a change in leadership, that kind of thing." Clive skipped introductions and started the discussion.

The NASA administrator's grim expression lightened. "Fortunately, two other private partners are able to step up. They've been waiting in the wings, so to speak."

"The benefit of competition," Zen spoke up. She ignored the loaded gaze James aimed squarely at her.

"And more good news: Lodestone will continue. No need to overhaul or scrap the treatment program," Clive said to break the taut silence.

Giancarlo stood. "Excellent. The White House expressed relief at the outcome of your investigation. We have another meeting."

"Tee time Saturday morning at nine per usual, right?" James stood and shook hands with him.

"Wouldn't miss it. Thank God for golf, eh?" Giancarlo chuckled and left with the other two men.

"We could have had a leisurely lunch and missed the back-slapping ceremony," Zen murmured. She shrugged when Malone shushed her.

James spent a few moments in a muted exchange with the men before they left. Then returned to the table. "Goddard's space program needed a serious reset. You uncovered what could have been a disaster in the making. To say Ian Goddard isn't thrilled, though, would be an understatement. Even he can't avoid the aftermath this time."

"And Robert S.?" Zen said.

"He's entered treatment in a private and very secure hospital. The case into the disappearance of his first wife is ongoing," James added quickly when Zen started to speak.

"I sent notes to the chief detective here and in Belize City," Zen replied in a cool tone.

Clive darted a glance between Zen and her father. "I'll make sure both police departments have everything they need."

"Good," James clipped. His grave expression eased. "Your mother is having one of our old-fashioned Sunday dinners. Be there no later than five-thirty. Plus one if you like."

"I'll be there," Zen replied without acknowledging the tacit invitation to Malone.

"Thanks for everything, James." Clive shook hands with James and they walked out together.

Hadley blew out a dramatic sigh. "Well, no blood on the walls or body parts on the floor. Guess we're going to survive our first big test."

"A bit over the top, Hadley," Zen quipped.

"This team, this new section, is under an electron microscope," Hadley replied

"I think you mean telescope. Space program; moons, asteroids, planets. Get it?" Malone grinned at them.

"You two managed to pull a win out of a touchy situation this time. Malone will need that magic on his next assignment. The new intelligence team will have even tricker cases."

"New intelligence unit?" Zen blinked at her.

"Oh dear, I spoke out of turn. I was sure you'd told her by now, Malone," Hadley said with a frown.

"I got a really nice offer. Couldn't pass it up." Malone blew out air at the look Zen gave him.

"I have details to sort, reports to complete." Hadley backed through the door and pulled it closed.

"Gee, I didn't realize you were that ambitious," Zen said when they were alone. "No wonder you didn't bother personalizing your office."

"Opportunity knocked and I answered," Malone replied.

"And said yes, obviously."

"The good news is we won't be working together... so, let's have dinner tonight. And talk about anything except the case," he added fast before Zen spoke.

Zen stared at her shoes for a few seconds before she looked up at him with a smile. "I'm pretty sure we'll end up talking shop."

"You're probably right."

Malone bent his head low until their noses almost touched. They both pulled away from each other when the door swung open. Clive studied them for a few seconds with a look of speculation. Then he appeared to shrug it off.

"Ramirez told you his big news. We'll work hand in hand, so it's not like he's going far," Clive said.

"Really?" Zen faced Malone.

"Intelligence-gathering on international space spies and terrorism. Like those vintage Star Wars movies," Malone replied with a grin.

"I expect we'll get critical information from the team he's joining when needed."

"Great." Zen didn't bother to hide her delighted smile.

"Anyway, Batiste. You'll need a new partner. Someone with serious knowledge about astronautics, celestial mechanics, and astrophysics. And how it all relates to space commerce. Check your inbox." Clive pointed to her smartwatch.

Zen nodded and pulled up her encrypted work messages. She read for few minutes, then re-read the paragraph. "Peter Navarro. You're going to have me working side by side with the serial killer I helped put away?"

"He's one of only a select handful of next-level geniuses we can't afford to write off. Besides, the evidence of his guilt has been called into question. It looks like he may have been framed by a colleague. That man's been arrested in two murders that happened while Navarro was in custody. Full details are on the server."

"Sir—"

"Not my decision, not my choice, Batiste. But they make a strong case for him. He's been in intensive treatment for the past few months. TMS, I believe is the acronym," Clive said.

"Deep transcranial magnetic stimulation, to be exact. But sir, he has a history of—"

"I've been assured that he's stable, very calm, and has given us valuable input to NASA since he recovered. Your investigation proves that if the protocols are followed, the treatment works," Clive broke in. "Good job, Batiste."

"My investigation? No, sir, that's not what I set to... I mean, just because Goddard didn't follow the protocol doesn't mean it works for everyone when—"

"Read the background and we'll talk tomorrow. Knock off early, guys. You've earned it. More meetings." Clive didn't wait for a reply before he strode off.

"Like what the hell? I can't even..." Zen stammered into incoherence. She stared after Clive with her mouth open. Then she looked at Malone.

Malone stuck both hands in his pockets. "On the bright side, you won't be bored."

"Yeah. Real exciting. Now all I gotta do is investigate space crimes and prove my new partner is a murderer. Again," Zen replied.

# Don't miss out!

Visit the website below and you can sign up to receive emails whenever Lynn Emery publishes a new book. There's no charge and no obligation.

https://books2read.com/r/B-A-YISG-CHXKB

BOOKS 2 READ

Connecting independent readers to independent writers.

# Also by Lynn Emery

**Dr. Zen Mystery**
The Lodestone Puzzle

**Joliet Sisters Psychic Detectives**
Smooth Operator
Hunting Spirits
Dead Wrong
Dead Ahead
Die Trying
Spirited Sisters

**LaShaun Rousselle Mystery**
A Darker Shade of Midnight
Voodoo Lily
Between Dusk and Dawn
Only By Moonlight
Into the Mist
Third Sight Into Darkness

Devil's Swamp
LaShaun Rousselle Mysteries Books 1-3

**Triple Trouble Mystery**
Best Enemies
Devilish Details
Pretty Dangerous

**Standalone**
After All
Louisiana Love City Girls Boxset
A Time to Love
One Love
Sweet Mystery
Night Magic
Good Woman Blues
Gotta Get Next To You
Soulful Strut
Tell Me Something Good
Tender Touch
Louisiana Love Box Set

Watch for more at www.lynnemery.com.

# About the Author

Mix knowledge of voodoo, Louisiana politics and forensic social work, and you get a snapshot of author Lynn Emery. Lynn has written over twenty novels so far, one of which inspired the BET made-for-television movie AFTER ALL based on her romantic suspense novel of the same name. Holly Robinson Peete and DB Woodside starred as the lead characters.

Her romantic suspense titles have won and been nominated for several awards, including Best Multicultural Mainstream Novel by Romantic Times Magazine.

Get exclusive offers each month in Lynn's newsletter and a free short story when you sign up! Go to:

https://www.subscribepage.com/s1y8j8

Visit www.lynnemery.com to see a full list of Lynn Emery novels.

Read more at www.lynnemery.com.

www.ingramcontent.com/pod-product-compliance
Lightning Source LLC
Chambersburg PA
CBHW031931110726
47902CB00001B/131